D0773282

COMMONWEALTH

A NOVEL BY JOEY GOEBEL

ALSO BY JOEY GOEBEL

The Anomalies

Torture the Artist

COMMONWEALTH

A NOVEL BY JOEY GOEBEL

MACADAM CAGE

MacAdam/Cage
155 Sansome Street, Suite 550
San Francisco, CA 94104
www.MacAdamCage.com

Copyright © 2008 by Joey Goebel
ALL RIGHTS RESERVED

LIBRARY OF CONGRESS CATALOGING-IN-PUBLICATION DATA

GOEBEL, JOEY, 1980-
COMMONWEALTH / BY JOEY GOEBEL.
P. CM.
ISBN 978-1-59692-279-2
1. BROTHERS—FICTION. 2. POLITICAL CAMPAIGNS—FICTION. 3. POLITICAL
FICTION. 4. SATIRE. I. TITLE.
PS3607.O33C66 2008
813'.6—DC22
2007050789

PAPERBACK EDITION: ISBN 978-1-59692-296-9

Printed in the United States of America.
Designed by Dorothy Carico Smith

Publisher's Note: This is a work of fiction. Names, characters, places, and
incidents either are the product of the author's imagination or are used
fictitiously. Any resemblance to actual events, locales, or persons, living or dead,
is entirely coincidental.

For my love, Micah, whose dimples I just saw as we passed each other, me driving from work, her driving to work. Someone at work had upset me, but Micah's smile erased it. I only wish everyone could find that one person who can make up for everyone else.

—WEDNESDAY, FEBRUARY 6, 2008

Somewhere in the middle of America…

For as long as he could remember, Blue Gene Mapother had not felt well. If anyone ever asked him what was wrong, he couldn't say because he didn't know himself. All he knew was that he always felt a deep kind of tired, and no amount of sleep seemed to fill the hole that tiredness scraped out in his brain.

Through all his days he carried a vapor of disappointment, similar to how you feel when you come out of the darkness of a movie theater and step into the letdown of daylight, with everything the same as you had left it. Only for Blue Gene Mapother, this feeling never left his side. And though he had accepted his poor health long ago, he still became quietly frustrated when he noticed that everyone around him seemed to feel perfectly fine. Everyone always wanted to do something or go somewhere. Blue Gene wanted only to sit.

His friends eventually stopped calling. They grew tired of his rejecting their invitations to watch wrestling or to go bowling, things they knew he loved to do. Over the years, telephone rings had become a less and less common noise in Blue Gene's trailer, until finally they stopped altogether. This pleased him because he had never been much for talking on the phone—he considered it an effeminate way to pass the time—but every once in a while, on those Saturday nights when nothing good was on TV, he felt forgotten. He consoled himself by saying that he and his friends were getting to that age where everyone starts getting so busy, when you go from loving mail to hating it.

And while it was true that his old friends had become overwhelmed with low-paying jobs and expensive babies, no one had forgotten Blue Gene.

At the wrestling matches in the National Guard Armory, at the checkout lines in Wal-Mart, and at the occasional keg party out in the county, seldom did a congregation of young, be-denimed wage-earners materialize without his name popping up.

"Talked to Blue Gene lately?"

"Nah. Wouldn't return my calls. Gave up on 'im."

"Where's Mapother been hidin'?"

"Still in Bashford, far as I know. Last I heard, he was sellin' stuff at the flea market, but that was a while back."

"We oughta call him up."

"Don't bother. He'll say he ain't feelin' up to it."

For the folks asking about Blue Gene's whereabouts, their question could be answered in one of two ways: Either he was holed up in his trailer, shirtlessly loafing among his guns and sweatpants, watching the TV seasons pass by as takeout Chinese food and Mountain Dew mingled in his belly, or he was waiting out the workday, licking droplets of coffee off his mustache, craving a cigarette, looking for the correct combination of thoughts that might unlock some momentary happiness. One of the two, invariably.

Until one particular day arrived, the first Friday of June in his twenty-seventh year, an election year...

PART ONE

I.

In the flea market parking lot, amid the pickups, Thunderbirds, Camaros, and El Caminos, sat a brand new Lexus LS. An elegant lady who bore a strong resemblance to the romance novelist Danielle Steele emerged from the gray SUV, closed its door, and pressed a button that made it chirp attentively. She looked around to make sure no one was planning to attack her, since, after all, Story Boulevard, where all the drug dealers and prostitutes did business, was just a scream away.

Her high heels clicked with conviction toward the building, and as she got closer she recognized the aroma of barbecue in the humid June air. She considered the smell delicious until she saw who stood over the barbecue pit, poking the meat with a fork.

It was a squat, androgynous person with a Pomeranian tattooed on a flabby arm, who bounced in rhythm to a song that kept saying something about "getting you some." Observing the portly cook's sweaty face and obscenely short cotton shorts that rode up into the body cavity, the well-dressed lady imagined the barbecue smell to be the cook's natural body odor. For a fraction of a second, through her Cartier sunglasses, she could visualize the crimson face of Satan grinning over the grill.

The woman, a sixty-one-year-old named Elizabeth, strode through the automatic doors and surveyed the length of the enormous room, its fifteen rows of booths, each with long rectangular tables covered in what she considered rubbish. Some booths had more elaborate displays than others, such as the ones with tall partitions covered with T-shirts that said things like WANTED: REDNECKS WITH LONGNECKS AND MUD TRUCKS. Others had only tables where flea marketers sat, attempting to sell Rebel flags, Camel cigarette products, and sports memorabilia.

Elizabeth looked to her left, hoping to see the equivalent of a front desk. Instead she saw a mind-boggling amount of flip-flops, each brightly colored and covered in frilly, feathery material. A sign read: FANTASY FLIP-FLOPS: $8 AND UP. She was startled by the sight of a little boy trying on the feminine footwear.

Rows of long-tubed lights brightly lit the entire scene. The walls were a bland shade of beige, heavily smudged and unadorned. Chains hung from the high ceiling, some with signs attached, most just dangling. The huge room was plain and forgettable, yet something felt familiar about it.

After scanning the room once more, Elizabeth resigned herself to searching the building by foot. She began walking around the right edge of the room, past a snaggletoothed man who shamelessly looked all the women up and down and offered free samples of his peanuts, past a woodwork-selling Nigerian saying to someone, "Let me give you my card." She made sure she showed not a hint of interest in anything, for fear that the dealers would lure her into their booths. She kept her eyes on the filthy off-white floor and its square tiles, glancing up periodically to see dimpled cellulite and bird's-nest ponytails.

Soon she was in the thick of flea land, rubbing elbows with interracial couples and forty-year-old grandmothers, with long-haired men and people who wore T-shirts and caps showing the names of college sports teams—though she knew full well that few of them had actually been to college. She also saw some hyper Mexican men playing with a remote-control car, a voluptuous black woman with a tube top that appeared to be melded to her surplus flesh, and the spitting image of Santa Claus.

By the time she got to the end of the first aisle, she realized why the place seemed familiar. She'd forgotten only because she had been there just once before. In another era, this building—just around the corner from the once wholesome Story Boulevard—had thrived as Bashford's very first

Wal-Mart. It had closed more than twenty years ago because a second, bigger Wal-Mart had been built, the one that had been vacated last winter when the brand new Wal-Mart Supercenter had its grand opening.

$ $ $

Blue Gene's booth was toward the far corner, between a baby boomer selling samurai swords and an elderly couple selling bald-eagle statues and fiber-optic religious paraphernalia. Day after day, he sat in his booth on a metal folding chair—the kind pro wrestlers hit one another with—often massaging his Fu Manchu mustache, occasionally trying to feel if his pills were helping, deciding they probably weren't, since every antidepressant he'd ever tried had *depression* listed as a side effect.

After extended trials of Prozac, Celexa, and Paxil, Blue Gene had settled on Zoloft, which he had been on for the past two years. No one knew this except for his doctor and the girls at Ralph's Pharmacy. He carefully guarded this secret because the last thing in the world he wanted was for another man to call him a certain obscene word, one that held power over him, for he at once avoided it and craved it. He had a similar relationship with the word *chicken*.

Blue Gene thought he was weak for taking medication, but when he tried to wean himself off it, he felt so on edge that he snapped at the flea market customers for no reason. Whether the pills truly helped, he couldn't say. He still felt tired, still felt down, but on the other hand, he wondered what kind of shape he would be in without them.

Jackie Stepchild would later offer Blue Gene the theory that he and everyone else like him experienced such general malaise because they were infected with brucellosis, a manufactured virus that caused its human hosts to lose interest in living and therefore not care what happened to them. She even went so far as to claim that laboratory-hatched mosquitoes spread the virus, and that in the darkest hours of the morning, the government dispatched hundreds of millions of them all over the country like an armada of blood-sucking soldiers. Blue Gene dismissed Jackie's theory, preferring to summarize his tiredness with a phrase he had often heard a coworker say in his Wal-Mart days: "My get-up-and-go has got up and gone." This coworker was in his mid-seventies.

But Blue Gene figured that's one thing life does to you, especially when you spend your best years working: it'll turn a young man old.

This particular day at work had begun like all the others: he drank coffee from a Styrofoam cup and watched the other dealers trickle in and yank the bedsheets off their merchandise. At two minutes till nine, the owner of the Commonwealth County Flea Market made his morning announcements over the PA system, hoisting his voice over the Apollo 13 glasses and Happy Meal toys, the imitation jewelry and *NSYNC dolls, the *Gone with the Wind* plates and Beanie Babies, the bobbleheads and Lincoln Logs, the knives. His smooth baritone sounded like Johnny Cash, but with optimism.

"Good morning, dealers. As always, if you have anything illegal, put it under your table. We'll try to get the air conditioner working better for you in the next month or so, and we *will* be here for the next month or so. I don't care what Curran Boggs says. We'll be here next month and the one after that and the one after that and forever to kingdom come. I know it's been slow, but this summer'll be better. So let's have a good flea market. Oh—I almost forgot. Did you know that when you start vacuuming your bed, it's time to change the sheets? All right, then. Open those doors and let 'em in."

Every morning Blue Gene listened closely to the owner's announcements, mainly because he liked the jokes. They were always snappy, folksy jokes, such as "Did you hear the one about the farmer who couldn't keep his hands off his wife? He divorced his wife and fired his hands!" More than the comedy itself, Blue Gene appreciated how the owner had new material prepared every day.

As always, after the morning announcements, Blue Gene spent the next several hours watching customers saunter by, sometimes giving them a quick upward nod but nothing more. It was his policy not to speak to customers unless they spoke to him, because he was determined

not to be mistaken for a salesman. This was one of several strict policies
he had made for himself at the flea market. For instance, he insisted on
keeping regular hours, even though he didn't have to punch a time clock
or even bother showing up if he didn't feel like it. He felt guilty that sitting in a booth was so much easier than his last job, working stock at
Wal-Mart, so to compensate, he sat at his booth without fail from nine
to five, Wednesday through Sunday; he had not missed a day in the nine
months he had been there.

To the flea market dealers who had taken the time to meet Blue Gene
in those nine months, he was a sullen man's man who could make you
crack up with no visible effort on his part, and he was the type of guy
"who tells it like it is," who could call you "buddy" without sounding
condescending, because it sounded like he meant it. As for the dealers
who hadn't met him, Blue Gene was that long-haired guy with the mustache who never smiled and who walked with a slight limp, which must
have been why he sat there for hours on end.

For some dealers, the closest thing to communication they'd had
with this rough-looking fellow were the loud sinus snorts coming from
his booth, which caused them to turn and look at the dark, sunken, unhealthy eyes with deep gray and purple lines underneath, staring out
from under the shadow of his baseball cap. Because of his incredible
work ethic—they noticed he always seemed to be the first dealer there
and the last to leave, and because of the hardened, hangdog way he carried himself, Blue Gene became a curiosity to the people who had booths
close to his. They gossiped about his past, from the strange ways he had
chosen to pass his time on Earth (it was said that once, for six months
straight, he watched nothing but *Cannonball Run*) to improbable tales
of his upbringing.

$$$

While so many others at the flea market looked as if they were molded from
dough, Elizabeth's facial structure was like well-sculpted ivory. She had

made for a strikingly beautiful young lady, and most of that beauty had remained, marred only by the sagging flesh at her throat and the pronounced
veins on her hands. Hers was the kind of high-cheekboned, pristine-teethed
beauty that made people who had never met her assume she was stuck up.
Her prim manner didn't help endear her to such judgmental strangers.

She wore a conservative amount of makeup and had dark-brown
hair that was tied back perfectly with a ribbon. She dyed her hair often
and brushed it religiously, believing that one could tell a lot about people from their hair, because people's hair suggested their thoughts. Elizabeth had gotten this idea from the modern-day prophet Edgar Cayce,
who believed that in our dreams, hair symbolizes thoughts because, like
thoughts, hair comes forth from the head. She had read about Cayce
when she was researching dreams and prophecies—topics on which she
had read more than two hundred books.

She was stalled in the second aisle behind a small glob of patrons
headed by an ancient woman with tennis balls on the legs of her walker.
Sick of looking at the obscene T-shirt worn by the man in front of her—
it said, ENJOY THE VIEW, and featured a bulldog's posterior, a bold asterisk beneath its tail—Elizabeth turned to one of the booths and allowed
herself quick eye contact with one of the flea market people. She was relieved when the old woman didn't say anything. She then looked down
at what the woman was selling, and within ten minutes found herself
making a purchase completely of her own volition.

"These are so neat," said Elizabeth as she paid the little old woman
with a rouge-plastered face and shorts pulled up to her bosom. "Do any
other booths have them?"

"Yeah, but mine are the cheapest." Like many of the dealers, this
woman specialized in only one item, hers being illuminated religious
pictures. Elizabeth picked the least gaudy rendition of *The Last Supper*,
every inch of it aglow and vibrant. She thought it was a bit tacky, but it
would make a great prize for her church's bingo nights.

"I've never seen pictures like these," Elizabeth remarked. "Are they
new?"

"You mean that glow like that?"

"Yes."

"Nah. I been selling 'em a couple of years. I been sellin' 'em longer than anyone else here."

"I guess I've been missing out."

With the framed picture safely in a cardboard box, the woman slid it into a big plastic Wal-Mart sack and handed it to Elizabeth.

"Thank you," said Elizabeth.

"Thank *you*," said the woman. "God bless you."

"Oh. God bless *you*." Elizabeth smiled at the woman for a moment before another customer entered the booth.

Elizabeth hadn't considered the possibility that religious items would be for sale at the flea market. Actually, she had no idea what to expect from the flea market in the first place, since this was her first visit to one in all her life. The heiress to the fortune of a high-profile financier named James Hurstbourne, Elizabeth was the only person in the building who could say she knew what it was like to fly in a private jet.

Since her first encounter with a flea marketer had been so pleasant, she allowed herself to look for more items to purchase and donate to her church raffles. She soon found some T-shirts that showed bloody stripes crossing Jesus' scourged back and that said, TO UNDERSTAND JESUS' LOVE, READ BETWEEN THE LINES. She bought ten.

As Elizabeth proceeded, she noticed for the first time that she was conspicuously overdressed in her black-and-white-print silk wrap dress. Current fashion trends apparently held no sway here. The other people's outdated wardrobes made her feel as if she had entered a time warp to the previous decade, or maybe the one before that. At the flea market, it was as if the eighties and nineties had never happened.

She also noticed that she seemed to be the only person buying anything. The other flea market shoppers suspiciously picked up items and turned them upside down and sideways, searching for the flaws that surely had to be there, and even if no flaws were found, the little yellow price tag was still asking too much. She knew the type: those who believed that they couldn't be too careful, who went through life unable to shake a vague sense of having been cheated. Without realizing it, they clutched their rhinestone-laden purses and hot-pink fanny packs desperately.

While a few dealers at the Commonwealth County Flea Market probably did prey upon their patrons, the venue was not sinister by design. At worst, it was an organized attempt to gain profit from things no longer wanted. The flea market was an opportunity for vendors to wring one last buck out of an article that had finished making its rounds in the economy. With unfixed prices and no need for bar codes, it was commerce at its crudest, like an old-world bazaar but with the likeness of Elvis consistently appearing on its goods. Ultimately, it was a place where the country's excesses ended up for one last chance at claiming value.

$$\$\,\$\,\$$

Because this was one of the largest flea markets in all of Middle America, even a slower day like today provided enough customers for steady pedestrian traffic in front of Blue Gene's booth. But most of the customers moseyed by, uninterested in anything Blue Gene or the other 152 vendors had to offer. It wasn't until around eleven-thirty that Blue Gene got his first serious customers of the day, when his merchandise snagged the attention of a little boy whose face was laced with scratches. The boy attempted to run up to one of Blue Gene's tables but was held back by his grandmother, who kept him close with a leash connected to a harness strapped around his torso.

"Hold on," said the grandmother. "I'm a-comin.'" A mechanical buzz preceded her. She slowly rolled up in a red automated scooter wheelchair. She was obese and braless—her breasts drooped to her waist, and burn marks coiled around her massive legs.

"Wow," said the boy, now that he could see Blue Gene's items more closely. Blue Gene nodded upward at the grandmother, who smiled back.

"Hi," she said.

"Hidey."

"Look at all he's got, Mamaw," said the awestruck child.

"Yeah, he's got a world of 'em, don't he?"

"Wow," the boy repeated.

Blue Gene couldn't help but feel a twinge of pride when a customer reacted like this to his display. He had to admit, his toys *did* look so pretty all clustered across the table, all those colors mixed like a kaleidoscope, except he'd never use the word *pretty* aloud when referring to anything having to do with himself.

His three tables were among the most colorful in the building, but then, most of Blue Gene's items had been produced in a particularly colorful decade. When Blue Gene thought of the eighties, his mind saw jellybean colors: neon green, neon pink, purple, orange, and yellow. The entire spectrum of colors was present on his tables, with a slight emphasis on green. There lay Moss Man and Battle Cat, Golobulus and Lady Jaye, Cosmos and Scavenger alongside Teela, Dr. Mindbender, Captain America, Bumblebee, Lion-O, Buddy Bell, Bib Fortuna, and all their allies and enemies.

Blue Gene mostly sold action figures, all of them taken out of their packages long ago. He had Star Wars, Masters of the Universe, Thundercats, Battle Beasts, Marvel Secret Wars, Captain Powers, Starting Line-Ups, C.O.P.S., and Teenage Mutant Ninja Turtles. They were jumbled, with all their little appendages reaching up and overlapping. Similarly, as a child he had enjoyed mixing Fritos, Cheetos, Doritos, and Lay's in one big bowl. If he ever got married, he planned to offer a giant bowl of mixed chips at the reception, which would likely be held at the local Moose lodge.

Also for sale at Blue Gene's booth were Transformers, Go-Bots, Nintendo games, Weebles, Hot Wheels, Micro Machines, and figurines such as the Get-Along Gang, Smurfs, and California Raisins. But more than any other item, he had G.I. Joes. He had accumulated every G.I. Joe that had been made between the years 1982 and 1989. These sold particularly well at the flea market.

"Mamaw, I *want* this." The boy had selected one of the larger toys, a

Transformer named Galvatron that could change from a robot into a futuristic gun.

"Give it here," said the woman, taking the plastic robot and looking at the price sticker with her bifocals. "Nuh-uh."

"Pleeease?"

"Says three. Will you take less?"

"I'll take two," said Blue Gene without hesitation. The boy eagerly watched his grandma as she made up her mind.

"Nope. We still gotta get Papaw his buckle."

She set the toy back on the table. The little boy frowned and moved on to the other two tables. Blue Gene sat in the middle of the horseshoe shape his three tables made, which had proven to be the most effective setup. A helpful dealer who had four booths on the other end of the building had told him he should arrange his tables so that the patrons didn't have to walk into the booth. He had learned that most preferred to observe from outside.

"Let's go," said the old woman, yanking at the leash with one hand and steering her wheelchair with the other. Blue Gene noticed that the boy looked longingly at the toy one last time before turning away.

"You can have it," blurted Blue Gene.

The boy spun around and the woman hit her automated wheelchair's brake, causing a screech.

"Do what?" she asked.

"He can just have that one." Blue Gene picked up the robot and handed it to the little boy. "Go on and take it."

The boy looked scared and didn't take it.

"Are you *sure*?" asked the woman, puzzled.

"It's been a slow morning," he said in his deep, muffled drawl, "and I just wanna get rid of the stuff."

"Well, let me give you something for it," said the woman, reaching for her purse.

"No, ma'am. Just take it." He looked at the boy. "My gift to you."

"Well, what do you say, Cody?"

"Thank you!"

"You're welcome."

"Thank you," repeated the woman. "That's mighty kind of you."

"It ain't no thang."

The boy walked away smiling, the red lights on his shoes blinking merrily with each step. Seeing this made Blue Gene happy for a little while, for about as long as the song playing over the flea market racket lasted: Faith Hill's "This Kiss." It wasn't the first time he had given an item away. Usually the initial reaction was confusion. Several times, the recipients of Blue Gene's generous offers assumed that he was somehow scamming them, and they refused to accept a gift from a stranger. After all, why would anyone give away something bearing a price tag? Sometimes customers even appeared to be offended by such an unheard-of offer. But then there were people who would smile and graciously thank him three, four, sometimes five times, and he would thank them for taking the item off his hands.

Not long after the little boy and his grandma left, Bob, a tan seventy-something holding a can of RC Cola, stopped in front of Blue Gene's booth. Bob and his wife sold patriotic statues and Christian items in the booth to Blue Gene's right. In his Wranglers and black boots, Bob had the vibe of a wise and work-weary cowboy, though it was the violent East, not the Wild West, that had given him such a hard crust of experience. Like many of the older men at the flea market, Bob was a veteran, a fact proclaimed by the cap he always wore that read, ONCE A MARINE, ALWAYS A MARINE. He had fought in the Korean War, where he had been left with two distinguishing features: a faded U.S. flag tattoo on one forearm, and a gnarled brown stump for the other. He liked to say that he hadn't had a right arm for fifty-two years.

"How you doin' there, Blue Gene?"

"Can't complain."

"Been a slow morning, hasn't it?"

"Yep. Was thinkin' maybe there'd start bein' more customers, what with it gettin' into summer."

"Yeah, you'd think so, but it's got so it's slow even in the summer anymore."

"It don't matter," said Blue Gene.

"Nope. Hey, I's supposed to tell you that Connie said somebody was calling for you yesterday afternoon."

"Why they just now gettin' the message to me?"

"Oh, you know how they are in the back."

"Who was callin' me?"

"That's what I said. Who'd be calling *that* pecker?"

"Ah, come on now. Who'd she say it was?"

"She said it was some woman. Wouldn't leave her name."

Blue Gene's gray eyelids lifted. "Thanks for letting me know."

"You're just as welcome as the day is long. See you later."

"A'ight. Take her easy, big nuts."

Bob's weathered face came alive with laughter. "I'll never get tired of that one."

Because of Bob's message, Blue Gene's day had suddenly taken on an atmosphere of hope and excitement. All he could think about was the possibility of a woman trying to track him down. He had no idea who it could be. Maybe it was one of his customers. There was a bleach-blond with a stripper build who had come to his booth several times with her kid, and she seemed to really enjoy talking about toys. Or maybe it was one of those girls whose crowd he used to run with, back when he still felt like running. There were a number of them he had felt attracted to, like that one dancer who called herself Missus Sizzle. His on-again, off-again relationship with his first and last love, Cheyenne Staggs, kept him from getting to know any of these women well. When he and Cheyenne broke up the third time—the only time they were able to make their breakup stick—all that stopped him from pursuing a new girl was his lack of energy.

But now here was some girl who had taken the lead, who was obviously interested in him. All he would have to do was make a date.

Blue Gene then realized that the perfect event to take a new love interest to was coming up the very next day. The ThunderNationals monster-truck rally would be at the Bashford Civic Center tomorrow night. He had seen ads for it on TV. He hadn't been in years, since back when he and Cheyenne used to go. Surely anyone calling him would want to go to that sort of thing.

Restless, Blue Gene suddenly craved one of the Parliament cigarettes resting in his front shorts pocket, but because of a smoking ban enacted about a year earlier, no smoking was allowed inside *any* public place in Bashford, including bars, which was another reason Blue Gene spent all his time at home, where he could smoke his tonsils off.

While it would be a nice little breather to go outside and smoke, Blue Gene didn't want to leave his booth unattended that long. Giving away toys was one thing, but having them stolen was another. This had happened once before when he took a smoke break, to his infuriation. He couldn't stand the idea of someone getting the best of him.

$ $ $

By quarter to twelve, Elizabeth was sweating under her makeup as she struggled to carry three sacks full of merchandise through the stuffy building. Among her purchases were a dozen coffee mugs that said, GOT JESUS? and some colorful Mary tapestries bought from some affable Latinos. Shopping was Elizabeth's only vice, though most of these items were for her church. For herself she had bought only a small statue of Saint Columbanus, the patron saint of motorcyclists, a fact she had gleaned from her obsessive studies of saints.

As she walked along, she said hello to each of the vendors, who always smiled and replied. So far, everyone had been so sweet and seemed grateful that she was buying something, and the women were good about complimenting her outfit. Only once had she felt out of place: a man gave her a funny look when she asked if he took Visa. But he went on to accept a personal check.

Elizabeth was charmed not only by the plain folks' unabashed piety, but also by their infectious patriotism. Everywhere she looked she saw red, white, blue, and camouflage. She saw a people who were proud of their beliefs, and what they lacked in grammar, physical fitness, and dental care, they made up for in values. She was clearly among the fabled salt of the earth, and she expected she would one day be spending a lot of time with them.

Elizabeth kept seeing more she wanted to buy, but she reminded herself she had been sent here on a mission and resolved to stop shopping. She was stuck behind a hunched old man in denim overalls and couldn't pass him because a trio of palsied teenagers blocked her path. As the old man slowly rounded the corner and entered the next aisle, Elizabeth was able to see down the edge of the room. Toward the far corner, she saw the reason she had come here, rubbing his mustache and eating a burger. The good spirits the flea marketers had put her in dissipated instantly. He looked scruffy, scraggly, dirty, and druggy—worse than ever before. It was amazing how much damage could be done in four years.

The closer she got, the better she could see bluish-green ink-works, displayed on a pale canvas prone to sunburn and mosquito bites, pulled tightly over a tall frame just starting to pack on flab. His spindly arms and legs suggested a hunger that was not so, as his beer belly proudly attested. As he was otherwise skinny, his bowling-ball abdomen made him look pregnant, and he patted his stomach as if it held a prized possession.

His ratty hair was longer than ever and hung unevenly on the sides. His mustache had grown thicker and more obscene, looking like a fuzzy brown St. Louis Arch that doubled his frown. The poor thing looked awful.

But she reminded herself that this poor thing was not poor in the least. There he sat—this cat-dragged beast-child who besmirched the family name with his mug-shot face and criminal eyes, obviously trying to look as tacky as was humanly possible, posing as hill stock, exuding the air of a truck driver, this trashy thing.

But this trashy thing was hers. He was a splotch on the family

Mapother—one of several splotches that had surfaced through the years—but a Mapother nonetheless.

She prepared a smile for him.

$ $ $

Instead of having a smoke, Blue Gene had his usual workday meal of two plain cheeseburgers, Grippo's barbecue potato chips, and a can of Ski. He was unable to enjoy his lunch, however, because he noticed a couple of dealers down the aisle laughing at him. He gave them a stare as cold as a doctor's stethoscope until they turned away.

Incidents like this happened every once in a while, and because Blue Gene had come to expect them, he was always on guard. As a result, the offenses he caught people making were sometimes only in his imagination. He always assumed they were laughing because he was a grown man selling toys.

Usually, though, if someone was looking at Blue Gene in what he saw as the wrong way, it was actually because of his general appearance, which was something he thought little about.

He thought nothing of wearing the same generic black flip-flops every day, with white footies if it was cold outside. He thought nothing of his denim shorts—formerly Faded Glory jeans—with white threads hanging over his knees due to a sloppy cutting job. Nor did he think anything of wearing stained T-shirts with slogans, such as the one that said, OPERATION DESERT STORM, with pictures of both American and Iraqi flags and Spider-Man swinging in between, or the one he was wearing today that said, AUSTIN 3:16.

Some thought did go into cutting the sleeves off all his T-shirts, though. Firstly, it was comfortable, and secondly, it allowed him to exhibit his tattoos: "Cheyenne" in rope cursive above an Indian headdress on his left bicep, and an angry eagle head on the right.

If Blue Gene gave significant thought to any aspect of his appearance, it was his hair. His stringy, dark-brown mullet draped to the middle of his shoulder blades, while the front and sides were trimmed short. Rarely did anyone see the front and sides, however, since Blue Gene never appeared in public without a baseball cap, usually a green camouflaged one.

As Alan Jackson and then Tim McGraw sang on the radio, Blue Gene scarfed his lunch while fuming over the dealers who had laughed at him. He continued staring at the men—one older, with slicked-back hair, the other young and porky—even though they were no longer paying attention to him. Then he noticed that, directly across the aisle, the young man who sat with his mom at her silk-flower booth had fallen asleep. In addition to his mother's flowers, the man attempted to sell computer printouts of his poems for fifty cents a page. Blue Gene disliked how this man wore skimpy shorts that showed off his muscular legs, and he was peeved about how the man always bowed his head to passing customers.

Blue Gene looked for the man's mother to see if anyone was watching the booth while he slept, but she wasn't around.

"Hey, Chris," he said to the weapons salesman to his left, who set down the sword he was handling and walked over to Blue Gene. In addition to his vast collection of samurai swords, the man sold knives, crossbows, blowguns, and "defense items."

"Look at him over there," said Blue Gene. The flower-man's eyes were closed, and his mouth was open. "That there's what you call a bad business move." Chris laughed. "We should throw somethin' at him."

"If you got a penny, I'll throw it," said Chris.

Blue Gene stood and dug the pocket change out of his denim shorts. "Here you go."

Chris threw the penny like a fastball. It hit the man in the chest and landed on his lap. He awoke to see two hairy men staring at him.

"Why'd you throw a penny at me?"

"Because you're a fag," said Chris. Blue Gene held back a laugh. The man stood. "I was just kiddin', dude," continued Chris. "Just thought you should wake up in case you had customers."

The man started to say something, but Chris turned to help a customer interested in a katana. Blue Gene sat and pretended to be organizing his toys. Then the flower-man was distracted by a customer asking if he'd take less for one of his poems.

"That's what I thought, woman," said Blue Gene under his breath.

Blue Gene was visualizing power-punching the flower-man in the solar plexus—an image that regularly occurred to him—when he reminded himself that a woman had called. Then he drifted into a daydream of making love in a gazebo.

His daydream burst when Elizabeth stepped into his field of vision. At first it didn't register that he knew this woman, since it seemed impossible for her to exist inside these four walls. He didn't think that she could even be aware of the flea market, let alone walk in and find him.

"Hello, Gene," Elizabeth said calmly.

"Hey, Mom."

"Let's hug."

Blue Gene set his cheeseburger aside and stood, but his merchandise table separated him from Elizabeth. Elizabeth leaned over the table and reached her arms around him. He hugged back feebly.

"Your skin smells like smoke. How have you been?"

"Can't complain. How you?"

"Fine, thank you. We've missed you."

"Huh." Blue Gene folded his arms. "How is everybody?"

"Fine. You wouldn't even recognize Arthur. He's getting so big. Here—" she reached over the table at his face. "You have flakes of dry skin on your face." Blue Gene stepped back.

"I got 'em there on purpose."

"Oh, Gene," she said with a weak laugh.

"What are you doin' at the flea market?"

"I just wanted to see you. It's been too long. Did you know I had never been to one of these before? I'm glad I came. Look at all I've found." She rummaged through her sacks, pulling out the religious items for Blue Gene to see. He hardly responded, as he was busy trying to figure out how he should feel about her popping in like this, and, more important, if she would get in the way of his seeing whoever it was who had called earlier. "So, actually, I'm here because we were wondering if you'd like to come over for dinner tonight."

"What for?"

"Because, Gene, I've been dwelling on it a lot lately, and the way we've become so—how can I say it? So *separate*. It isn't very Christian of us. We can't let ourselves go on like we have been. There are so many horrible things going on, as if the Lord has left for good, and I don't want us to become a part of that climate. Do you? I swear, we're on the verge. Why, just this morning I read the most horrible thing in the paper. Did you read about that mother who—I hate to even say it—there was a mother who *cut off her own child's arms*."

"I don't take the paper."

"You should. Why don't you?"

"Don't care to read it."

"You should. Have you been going to church?"

"Last time I went was for a funeral, I guess. Over a year ago."

"Do you still pray?"

"Yeah. When I remember to. I pray every time I hear ambulance or fire engine sirens."

"Well, that's a nice gesture." Elizabeth smiled apologetically. "I sent flowers, by the way. Did you see them?"

"What are you talkin' about?"

"To the funeral I assume you were referring to. I sent flowers. Did you see them?"

"Yeah."

"Were they pretty?"

"I can't remember. I'm sure they were."

"That was awful. I'm sorry that happened."

"Thank ya." Blue Gene hated the seriousness. A ring of heat started to constrict his head. "What's this about John runnin' for office?" he asked, adjusting his ball cap.

"Oh. You heard? Well, he won the primary. I'm so proud of him. And now we have to wait for November. He'll be there tonight. I know he'd love to see you. Won't you come?"

"I don't know."

"Please?"

"Who else is gonna be there?"

"Your father and I, of course. And John, Abby, and Arthur. That's all."

"I don't know."

Elizabeth perused the toys. "What do you mean, you don't know?—Gene, do you need some money?"

"No."

"Because I've just noticed that you seem to be selling all of your childhood possessions."

"So?"

"You used to cherish these. Remember when you saw—well, you probably *don't* remember. You were only four. But anyway, you saw how I kept my dishes in antique china cabinets, and you said you wanted one of your own to keep your toys in. So we got you one. And now here you are, *selling* all of them?" Elizabeth picked up random toys. "You're not asking much, either."

"They was just collectin' dust."

"They *were* just collecting dust. You know better."

Blue Gene sighed and sat back down. He looked up the aisle to see if any young women were headed his way.

"Have you checked any price guides for these? My Lord, isn't this one of the *Star Wars*? I read that these are worth *a lot* of money. You're asking only two dollars?"

"I'd be asking a quarter for 'em, but I found that if you make something *too* cheap, people'll think something's wrong with it."

Elizabeth shook her head and continued looking over the toys, checking the prices. "You know, I *do* have to point out that you didn't even *buy* any of these. Your father and I spent a fortune on them, and here you are, practically *giving* them away."

"I'm the one who's gone to the trouble of settin' up this booth to get rid of 'em. But if they're that important to you, you're welcome to take 'em."

"What would I do with them?"

Blue Gene sighed again.

"Oh, well. They are *your* toys, I suppose. You can do whatever you want with them." She added a smile.

"If it's any consolation to you, I'm keepin' all my wrestlin' figures."

"You could've thrown *those* away."

Blue Gene sighed yet again.

"Are you okay?"

"Why you ask?"

"You keep huffing and puffing like something is troubling you."

"I always do that. I always take long breaths."

"Do you have trouble breathing?"

"No. Maybe. I don't know. I feel short of breath sometimes."

"Then you should go to the doctor. You still smoke, don't you? You reek of it."

"Yeah."

"Well, that's why. You need to go see Dr. Wharton. Do you still go to him?"

"No."

"I'll make you an appointment."

"No, don't. I don't think I breathe heavy 'cause of health problems. I just do it when I feel frustrated."

"You feel frustrated?"

"Yeah."

"Over what?"

"I don't know. Everything—Jesus, Mom, you haven't been here five minutes, and you're already gettin' me all riled up."

"Sorry." Blue Gene sighed. "Is this what you do for a living now?"

"Yeah."

"They said at Wal-Mart you had quit a while back. Why'd you quit?"

"What do you mean *they said* I quit at Wal-Mart?"

"I couldn't reach you at your house—sorry, your trailer, rather—so I tried calling you at Wal-Mart yesterday, but they told me you'd probably be at the flea market."

"Wait a minute." His face tensed. "Was that *you* that was calling for me here yesterday?"

"Yes. I *did* call here yesterday, but the woman who answered the phone wasn't very cooperative. I was able to determine that you were here, at least, so I decided to come on over today."

Fast as a spasm, Blue Gene pounded the table, causing a few toys to fall to the floor. Elizabeth looked around. No one was watching. Most of the dealers in that vicinity had their eyes on a young black man with cornrows and silver teeth.

Blue Gene immediately started picking up his toys.

"What is *wrong* with you?" asked Elizabeth.

"Nothin'."

"You're on drugs right now, aren't you?"

"Don't start in on me, man."

"You're high as a kite as we speak, aren't you?"

"I haven't done drugs since I was a teenager."

"You really expect me to believe that when you sit there with a tattoo of your live-in girlfriend who *I know* died of a drug overdose?"

"Hold on, now. Me and her were broken up a year when that happened. We didn't have nothin' to do with each other by the time she died. That there's guilt by association."

"Well, let's say you're *not* on psychochemicals. Then why are you banging on tables?"

"Because! Look, Mom, I'm real busy here."

"But you're not busy at all." No one had stopped at Blue Gene's booth for the last ten minutes. The owner's voice came on over the PA system, interrupting Alabama's "Cheap Seats."

"Dealers, if any of you are selling decorative Bic lighter covers, please come back to the back."

"Why are you banging on tables?" she repeated. "Are you that mad that I called?"

"No. It's just I'm wantin' a cigarette and feelin' the jitters, and I was expectin' an important phone call, and I just got mad when I found out it was you and someone else didn't call after all. Got my hopes up."

"Oh. The phone call you're expecting, is it about you getting a better job?"

"Yeah, Mom. It's about me getting a better job."

$$\$ \, \$ \, \$$$

After brushing off his tantrum, Blue Gene switched subjects by pointing out a few notable folks who were at the flea market that day. There was the oldest man in all of Commonwealth County, so thin that he looked like he was wearing a corset, yet still healthy enough to be out and about; some intimidating bikers with tattoos of insects on their necks, who Blue Gene explained were members of the 'Nam Vets biker gang; and a man with a long white beard who had one of the world's largest stamp collections. Elizabeth had to admit that the building contained an impressive miscellany of humanity.

"So anyway," she said, "we'll be expecting you at around six. I'll be serving your favorite. Fried pork chops."

"Now hold on, now. I haven't said I'm goin'. You come in here out of the blue after goin' four years without seein' me, and you expect—"

"You've made no effort to come and see your father or me, either. It's a two-way road. And you *chose* to lead this life. You know we were always good to you. We always provided for you. But you got so all you seemed to care about was finding the girl with the largest mammary glands possible."

"Well, hell yeah, she had some mammals on her."

"Oh, Gene. You're so—oh, never mind."

"What?"

"Nothing. Never mind."

"What were you going to say?"

"Nothing. So tell me, with whom are you shacking up now?"

"Nobody. Tell me what you were going to say! See now, whatever it was you was gonna say's been built up and'll come out even worse than if you'd gone on and said it in the first place."

"Fine, but if I tell you, you can't pound on the table."

"Okay."

"If you must know, I was going to say that you're so *trashy*. But we have to remember that you're not *really* trashy. You're trashy-*acting* and trashy-*looking*, but you're not truly trashy."

Blue Gene looked over at the swords.

"See," said Elizabeth, "now I've made you mad. I didn't want to say that. I thought better of it, but you *made* me say it. I know you're not trash. You just look like it. That shirt, your tattoos—they're all affectations."

"Leave me alone, man."

"Well, it's the truth! You look like everybody else here, except you're *trying* to look your worst, and they're probably trying to look their best. You're better than this. Now, don't get me wrong. They seem like good people, and I admire some of their values that I've seen today, but you know what I mean. It wouldn't take much for you to look better than they. And you're not *ever* going to attract a decent woman, dressing like that."

"Why you keep pushin' me?"

"I'm not."

"I don't talk about the way you look."

"There's nothing to talk about. I take pride in my appearance."

"I bet you've had that Botox done."

"I haven't."

"It makes people look like cats."

"Do I look like a *cat*?"

"No, but you don't look like you've aged much since I seen you last."

"Thank you. Why don't you go to my salon and get your hair styled?"

"I ain't goin' to no salon!"

"Lots of men go there."

"I ain't gettin' my hair cut. You know, on the History Channel the other night, they was sayin' that in olden times, poets and artists were *expected* to wear their hair long."

"It's not the length that's so bad, really. I know you love your long hair. It just needs to be *styled*. It looks awful like that, like you cut it yourself."

"Why we always gotta talk about hair?"

The length of Blue Gene's hair had been an ongoing source of contention between the two of them for years. Elizabeth always said he shouldn't grow his hair long, because it curled up on the ends once it grew to a certain length, which wasn't a flattering look for a man. This didn't stop him from threatening to grow it straight down to the small of his back. She told him that certain people just couldn't grow long hair correctly, and he was one of them.

After a few beats of silence, Blue Gene blurted: "Hair ain't real!"

"*What?*"

"Hair's got no feeling. It ain't alive. It ain't real. What difference does it make?"

"I just don't know why you'd want to go around looking like that."

"Hey now—I don't question *you*, you know? I never said *you* was kooky all those times you talked about seein' an angel. I *thought* you was kooky, but I never *said* it."

Elizabeth's petite form went rigid. She leaned forward over the table. Her eyebrows became immovable warning symbols. "You know that is a sacred topic for us," she whispered.

"Don't get all mad. You was sayin' I's a piece a trash. I had to defend myself."

"You have been *behaving* like trash. You've had the *morals* of trash. But I know you are *not* trash. As hard as you try, you never will be. Not all the way."

"If I've had the morals of trash, why you even talkin' to me? That'd make me a sinner just like all the rest of the little people, and that means I'm in trouble, according to your dream. Ain't that right?"

"Not in public, Gene."

"What'd y'all call it that's gonna happen to everybody who hasn't been saved or whatever?"

"*Gene.* This isn't—"

"What'd y'all call it? *Nervous* death?"

"You *hush!*"

Blue Gene hushed as Elizabeth nodded sharply at a customer who was approaching, a heavily tattooed pregnant woman who resembled Jon Bon Jovi. She eventually held up a little red soldier. "Is he a G.I. Joe?" she asked.

"Yeah. He's a Crimson Guard."

"My boyfriend *loves* G.I. Joes and I don't think he has this one. Will you take a dollar for him?"

"Sure."

Elizabeth cleared her throat. The woman looked over at her, and Elizabeth looked down.

"You want a sack?" asked Blue Gene.

"No, thanks."

"A'ight. Thank you."

"Gene, why did you do that?"

"Do what?"

"You went so cheap. You accepted her first offer."

"I always accept the first offer."

"That's not good business, son."

"I got like twenty of that particular figure. I had y'all buy me like twenty Crimson Guards 'cause on the cartoon there was a whole army of 'em, not just the one. So I think I can spare one."

"You could've at least asked a dollar fifty. Have you even turned a profit here?"

"Three of the months I did, but I don't care."

"How many months have you been here?"

"I ain't sayin'."

"How much is your rent?"

"Seventy-five a month."

"Oh, Lord. And what's your most expensive toy?" Elizabeth shuffled through his items. "Five dollars? And why don't you just sell things on eBay? You'd do a lot better."

"You don't get it. I like to take all this in." Blue Gene went on to point out a pair of black-clad teenage boys with long, wet hair and pantyhose on their arms, and a buck-toothed blond with scrawny legs and ridiculously big breasts. "I like to listen to the people talk. Like, you ever noticed how old men always ask each other if so-and-so can still drive? Besides, I can't eBay 'cause I don't got a computer."

"Fine, but really, you shouldn't accept the first offer. You could've said a dollar fifty."

"For the life of me, Mom, you're the richest woman in the whole damn state, and you fall to pieces over a dollar. Here, you can have this."

Blue Gene stood and attempted to hand Elizabeth the dollar, but she pushed it away.

"Go on, now. Take it."

"I don't want it," said Elizabeth firmly.

"Take it."

"No. You sit down."

Blue Gene ripped the dollar bill in half.

"Oh, that was *so* mature, Gene."

"*I* gladly would have taken it," said the one-armed man standing in the next booth. Elizabeth and Blue Gene turned to him. Elizabeth laughed quietly.

"I know *you'd* take it, biggun," said Blue Gene.

"Ooh—I love that statue," said Elizabeth, pointing to a fiber-optic Mary statue changing colors. He was also selling statues of firemen waving the American flag, bald eagles, and unhappy-looking Indians.

"We'll make you a deal."

"How much?" asked Elizabeth.

"I was askin' thirty, but since you seem to know Blue Gene, I'll take twenty-five."

"I'll take it."

$$$

As Bob wrapped the statue, and his wife with the oversize glasses traded pleasantries with Elizabeth, Blue Gene felt furious and silly for deluding himself into thinking a girl had called. He had let breasts put his mind in decline, but it worked out because he didn't want to fool with that monster-truck rally anyway. It would've been a hassle, what with the civic center parking as hectic as it was. Everything was a hassle. He was better off staying in his trailer.

Blue Gene couldn't finish his second cheeseburger. His craving for a cigarette was stronger than ever. He pinned his hopes of easing the disappointment of this day on having a smoke break. He decided he would have to ask his mom to watch his booth.

"May the good Lord take a liking to ya," said Bob, as Elizabeth returned.

"Thank you," said Elizabeth, carrying another sack. "Gene, your neighbors are so *nice*."

"I know it. Hey, you wanna sit back here with me? I can get a extra chair."

"Oh. No, thank you. I have to be going."

"I'm sorry 'bout earlier, talkin' like that. I'll buy you a Ski—or no, you like iced tea, don't you?"

"No, really. I must be going. It's time for my prayer walk, and then I have to run by the annex. Will we see you tonight?"

"I don't know. Let me see how I feel after work."

"Please, Gene. The Lord wouldn't approve of the way we've been."

"Well, if you're askin' me over to get in better with the Lord, you don't have to, 'cause like you say, it ain't like *I* been keepin' in touch with *you*. You don't have to be feelin' all guilty."

"But it's more than guilt. We *want* you back in our lives."

"That's *you* talkin', though. Not Dad. Does he even know you're askin' me over?"

"Yes. In fact, it was his idea."

"Yeah, right."

"It *was*. He agreed with me that it wasn't right, the way we've been, and he proposed that we have you over."

"Then why isn't *he* here?"

"He's at work. You know how your father is about work. Please come over. What if I die soon? You'll feel awful if you don't grant me this one request and then I die."

"Why you gotta play that card? That's no fair."

"I read in the paper that one thousand baby boomers are dying each day now. So it *is* possible."

Blue Gene rubbed his mustache. "And you say John'll be there? With his boy?"

"Yes. They'd love to see you."

Blue Gene let out one final, surrendering sigh.

"Well, I guess I could come over, long as you don't try to start something."

"Oh, good! Be there at six."

"A'ight."

"Great. Well, we'll see you then!"

"A'ight.

He had given in to Elizabeth for two reasons: because he didn't feel like arguing anymore, and because all he could think about was smoking a cigarette. Plus, he wouldn't mind seeing John at least, and John's kid.

After Elizabeth was out of sight, he looked at the toys his parents had bought him, and used them as points of reference for different periods of his life. He knew it must have been 1985 when his family moved into their current home because that was the year he started collecting He-Men. That was the year his father completed a merger that combined his tobacco corporation with its biggest competitor. The Mapothers had a mansion built outside the city limits, and Blue Gene had a separate room just for his toys.

He saw that his mother was right. He wasn't *earning* his money here;

it wasn't his money that had been invested in the toys. She had already gotten to him. His day had gone to hell. And to think—for a little while there, his old heart had been raring to thump out a tune he could slow-dance to.

A moment later, the owner of the flea market walked past Blue Gene's booth, talking to a fellow white-haired gentleman. Blue Gene heard the owner say to the man, "Did you know that when you start vacuuming your bed, it's time to change the sheets?"

It occurred to Blue Gene that the only instance when the owner had even spoken to him was the time he'd misplaced Blue Gene's monthly rent check. Come to think of it, maybe the owner was charging the dealers too much for rent in the first place, and maybe he was the only one even making a profit.

Blue Gene was mad at everything—the flea market owner, the ripped dollar bill on the floor, the Wal-Mart employee who had told Elizabeth of his whereabouts, the weak country-pop strains of Kenny Chesney that were currently being played over the PA. A motorcade of violent images paraded through Blue Gene's mind: itching the roof of his mouth with a gun, yanking out toenails with pliers, closing a revolving door on the flower-man's muscular calf.

He crawled out from under his front table and limped off toward the back exit, deciding that if anyone stole from him during his smoke break, he'd hunt them down and whip them. As he walked out, he had to go past the men who had been talking about him. He gave them one last hard look as he exited.

$ $ $

"I told you, I told you! Like the 'leventh or twelfth biggest family fortune in all the United States, I read. Time to pay the piper!"

"I wouldn't have believed you till she come in here."

"What happened to *him*, though?"

"Don't know, but I'd 'magine it's 'cause of his dad. His dad is a real son of a bitch. His brother is too."

"He's that one that's runnin' for something, isn't he?"

"Yeah."

"Well, I guess I owe you twenty bucks, then."

"Ah, you don't have to pay me."

"Good, 'cause I didn't have but five."

II.

There was New York and L.A. Then there was Chicago, Houston, Philadelphia, and so forth. Then came Nashville, Omaha, and St. Paul; then Greensboro, Dayton, and Flint; and a day or two down the list, you'd find Bashford. By the time of Blue Gene Mapother and Jackie Stepchild, Bashford had firmly settled itself into the status of a small city of about fifty thousand inhabitants, or three McDonald's. It was large enough to have a shopping mall, but too small to have a minor league baseball team. There were enough people there to justify a community college, but not a public airport. It wasn't so big that the destitute begged openly downtown; there were homeless people in Bashford, but they weren't as visible as in bigger cities. If you were to beg for money on the streets of Bashford, there would be a good chance you'd run into someone from high school.

Bashford contained all the necessities of modern living: ATMs were always but a burp away, the Office Depot sold even the rarest variety of printer ink, and in the past year a Starbucks had opened. But it was not a destination. There were no universities, museums, or beaches. The bands you loved would never play a show there, and a president had never visited, except the time Harry Truman had waved at the city from the back of a train. Because of Bashford's cultural shortcomings and general sense of stagnation, for many young people, living the Bashford dream was *leaving it*. The closest thing the city had to a skyline (and the opportunities that a skyline represent) was a row of smokestacks on the south end of town. As for the buildings downtown that comprised the economic center of the city, they appeared to be products of ambition-less architects, nothing fancier than four-story, red-bricked cubes. The buildings would never be marveled at, but they were strong and sturdy and good enough.

Some famous people were from around there, some of them truly gifted and others known mainly for being wild, but all of them left and never returned. The area's gray and green terrain proved fertile for breeding dreams, but once the dreams matured enough, they migrated toward larger cities, leaving the young people to decide whether or not to chase after them.

Blue Gene saw no point in relocating, since his goals of being a flea marketer and settling down with the right woman could be attained without leaving his birthplace. Furthermore, he actually *loved* his old hometown, which was a unique view for a twentysomething living in Bashford. He considered Bashford as good a place as any, and a fine place to raise children. But then, Blue Gene had seen more of the world than most people his age, since his parents had taken him and his brother to both U.S. coasts and all over Europe. He had seen the kind of architec-ture that could make you feel like an idiot, and he had been to cities so beautiful they had made him want to litter. With each trip he came to ap-preciate his hometown more.

Listening to a slow, brooding song that he didn't particularly like by a band called Staind, Blue Gene drove his red 1988 Chevy S-10 pickup into a dreary trailer court on the south end of town, close to the ceme-tery. He drove past the long row of identical gray mailboxes, past the BE-WARE OF DOG signs, past plastic toys strewn upside down, past run-down 1980s sedans and mud-covered 1990s pickups with SUPPORT OUR TROOPS magnets on their rears and sides. The heat had turned the court into a ghost town with the trailers tightly shut and the window blinds down. He pulled up to the curb next to his trailer, which was similar to the other trailers: white with streaks of rust, an air conditioner sticking out of the side and propped up by a wooden plank, and an American flag out front. On the small square driveway sat a seldom used four-wheeler and Blue Gene's other car, a non-functioning 1984 Trans Am with slabs of concrete wedged behind its back wheels.

Blue Gene got out of his truck and limped toward the front door, all the while looking up the road at a set of concrete stairs leading to nothing. The trailer these five steps had once led to was long gone, gobbled up and chundered out by a tornado twenty-five years ago, a neighbor said. Blue Gene found the pointless stairs funny and depressing, and he looked at them every chance he got.

$ $ $

As John Hurstbourne Mapother came out of his corner office, he felt like he was forgetting something, but he usually felt that way. He checked his pants pockets for his wallet, cell phone, and car keys. They were all there, so he closed his office door and moved on.

As was his daily custom, he had waited until five-thirty to leave, since most everyone would be gone by then and he could get to his car without having to talk.

But sure enough, the next minute he was on an elevator with one of his employees.

"How are you doing, Mr. Mapother?"

John took a moment to consider whether the man had asked *how* he was doing or *what* he was doing. As was so often the case with these greetings, the words had not been spoken clearly.

"I'm fine. I'm going home."

"Tell me about it," said the man with a laugh. When the elevator door opened, John motioned for the man to exit first.

"Thank you, Mr. Mapother."

"You're welcome. Have a good evening."

After allowing the man a good head start, John followed him out of the building, still wondering whether he had said "how" or "what." Regardless, his response serendipitously worked, since the man apparently thought John was making a little joke, that he was fine only because he was going home. Sometimes things like that worked out when talking to people, but usually not.

John climbed into his black Escalade with the Jesus fish emblem on the back, and as soon as he turned the key in the ignition, "Sleepers, Awake!" by Johann Sebastian Bach came on. He didn't even like classical music, preferring the eighties pop and rock he had listened to as a teenager, but he found the song had a soothing effect. In recent years, since becoming sober, he had played it more and more often to calm himself, until finally it became the only song he listened to. After it was decided that this would be his year to run for Congress, John had burned himself a CD with nothing but "Sleepers, Awake!" over and over. But this past week, since he had known he was days away from seeing Blue Gene, the song's hypnotic, half-triumphant/half-sad melody couldn't pacify him. He worried without end.

John banged on the steering wheel upon realizing he had left something in his office. It was a photograph of himself with Blue Gene, when he was twenty and Blue Gene was seven, which Elizabeth had asked him to have enlarged so that she could have it hanging when Blue Gene arrived tonight. John gave his secretary instructions to blow up the photo from wallet-size to eight-by-ten, to get rid of the red eyes, and to do what she could to alter that look on her boss's face, the same sort of look that the paparazzi were always able to capture when a celebrity was on a binge, like he was coming up for air at the precise moment the picture was being taken.

$ $ $

After showering, shaving, and smoking a few cigarettes, Blue Gene stood in front of his bathroom mirror. He placed a sleek pair of sunglasses on the bill of his camouflage cap and tossed back his head in hopes of making every strand of hair fall into place. When he saw this wasn't going to happen, he left his hot, smoky-smelling trailer, with the twelve-gauge shotguns propped up in the corner and the motorcycle posters on the wall, and got into his truck. He lowered the windows, refusing to use the air conditioner since fuel was expensive these days.

He hung his left arm out the window as he maneuvered his truck around the cul-de-sac and headed out of the trailer court, turning up the radio when ZZ Top's "Tush" came on. The truck had a tape deck, but Blue Gene preferred listening to his favorite rock station, 105 ROQ, no matter what its DJs played. He pulled out onto Elliot Street, a colorful, desolate road clustered with desecrated churches. There was an old church on nearly every block in this part of town. Altogether, there were ninety-four churches in Bashford. One of them, St. Francis of Assisi—where Elizabeth went—was the tallest building in town.

In addition to the churches, Blue Gene passed one white shack after another and noticed one surrounded by sunflowers, which he thought was nice because at least they were trying. Next to the sunflower house was an abandoned home with graffiti on the front that said, "FILTH AVENUE" in impish handwriting.

Many of these shacks' inhabitants shared similar ancestry. Their papaws' papaws had found the land desirable because it was cradled by the river, which was crucial for trading up and down the frontier, and because it was good farmland. The rich soil provided corn, soybeans, and, most important, tobacco. Blue Gene's ancestors on his father's side reigned as tobacco kings.

He lit a cigarette as he took a side street to get to River Town Road, which ran from one end of Bashford to the other. Toward this end of the road was Bashford's main industrial zone. With its numerous factories and their thousands of employees—many of whom were employed by Westway International, which Blue Gene's paternal grandfather had founded—Bashford could be regarded as a working-class town, though Blue Gene was headed for the end of River Town Road that might contradict this idea.

Besides Highway 81, which was the easiest way out of Bashford, River Town Road was Bashford's busiest thoroughfare. Its four lanes were lined with used-car lots, fast-food restaurants, gas station/ convenience stores, and banks. Most of these were chains that could be found in any American city. As in most cities of this size, two or three roads had kept up with the times, steadily developing and expanding, constantly erecting new neon signs with corporate logos: BP, Kroger, Blockbuster, Papa John's. But aside from River Town Road and Highway 81, Bashford went unmolested by the hands of change.

So Blue Gene headed down River Town Road toward his former home, his mullet flapping in the wind as he appreciated flashes of the bustling street whenever he could: the billboards advertising fried chicken and catfish, the packed Golden Corral parking lot, the group of baggy-clothed black boys hanging out at the car wash, the Goodwill store where he found many of his T-shirts, the long-haired Latinos exiting the pawn shop, and the cars starting to file into the old drive-in theater to see the latest Will Ferrell movie. He couldn't take everything in the way he wanted, though, because he knew the police regularly patrolled River Town Road, and he was driving without a license. He had to keep his eyes on the rearview mirror almost as much as on the road.

$ $ $

John hated driving. He considered it incredibly dangerous because of all the dumb people who were allowed to drive cars. It never ceased to amaze him that there weren't more car accidents than there were, considering all the natural idiots who were allowed to have driver's licenses. All that kept the roads from being murderous pits, John figured, was that the dumbest of the dumb couldn't afford to buy cars—that, and the fact that people like him were twice as careful to compensate for everyone else's carelessness. Of course, he hadn't always been so careful, but that was before he had come to see his own body as something that must be protected. Nowadays, without waver he obeyed the speed limit, used his turn signals, and checked his blind spots. He obsessively checked his rearview mirrors so that he would be completely aware of everything that was going on around him. He constantly anticipated all the other drivers' moves, using the sort of caution that most motorists reserved for a street full of trick-or-treaters on Halloween.

With such intense concentration on the act of driving, John hardly noticed the scenery of River Town Road, save for glimpses of derelicts outside the Family Dollar, the flashing lights of the drive-through liquor store sign, and a billboard here and there, like the one that said, DON'T METH AROUND.

As "Sleepers, Awake!" ended and started again, John couldn't stop thinking about how this would be the first time that Blue Gene and Arthur would be in the same room together since Arthur had been a baby. He kept glancing at the framed picture of himself with little Blue Gene, which was now resting on his passenger seat, until he was distracted by a funeral procession coming down the other side of the road. He knew to slowly come to a stop and wait until the procession had passed. A car in the left lane followed suit, pausing alongside John. For all the frustration this town inspired in him at times, John felt proud that he lived in a place that would still pause somberly for an old tradition like this, one that implied a healthy respect for death.

Then he heard a honk, a rare sound in Bashford. He looked in his rearview and was not surprised to see a goateed man in a pickup truck behind him, angrily motioning for him to drive on. John's face turned red hot. He shook his head and waved a dismissive hand at the impatient man. Once the funeral procession had completely passed, John advanced. A minute later, the man in the pickup was riding alongside him, shouting obscenities. John replied by pressing his foot hard on the accelerator, leaving the old pickup far behind. In his rearview he saw the man turning into Lee's Famous Recipe Fried Chicken. When he returned his eyes to the road, he saw that the light ahead was yellow. He slammed on his brakes, causing an embarrassing screech.

Then he felt as if someone was staring at him, even though he usually felt that way in his car. Men in cars always had to look over at you. In the BMW next to him sat a doctor friend of his father's, staring with a concerned look on his face. John concluded that his dad's friend had seen the whole incident. He didn't know whether he should wave or not. He decided not to, but then he second-guessed himself, and the longer he went without waving, the more uneasy he felt. He cursed his luck at having his father's friend witness what a fool he could be, and he damned this small town that smothered him so, where he couldn't go anywhere without running into someone he knew.

Sweat popped out all over his brow. He went to turn the air to full blast, but it was already turned as far as it would go. Then he turned up his song and loosened his tie and unbuttoned his dress shirt. But nothing could stop the sweat from slithering down his spine. He would have to stop by his house and take a Xanax. He tried to remember to take deep, cleansing breaths, and at first it worked, until he pictured that trashy man eating a chicken breast with his bare hands, not a care in the world, not giving a second thought to the trouble he had caused. He seethed.

This was another thing he hated about driving: to put a person in a car was to give him power, because it surrounded him with mass and steel and force, and it put him on equal footing with every other person who was in a car. Outside of his car, the person might be the lowest of the low, but once he was protected by the four-wheeled body armor of an automobile, he could throw around his weight the same as anyone. If only they could all be pedestrians.

$ $ $

The area where Bashford lay had come to be known as the heartland of the nation, that land which was originally considered America's frontier, the former outskirts of the New World where the less fortunate went to settle since all the desirable coastal property had been taken. Before whites called the eternal dibs of God on this fringe land, Native Americans cherished the area as an invaluable source for hunting and fishing (as did Blue Gene much later). It was so cherished that opposing tribes battled over who had the rights to hunt and fish there. The Mapother mansion occupied a clearing that had once been a disputed forest, over ground with long-dried blood in its crust.

A quarter of a mile behind a black iron gate, the mansion stood alone on a hill in white-bricked, white-columned majesty. Six miles outside the city limit, the house's inhabitants had no neighbors to contend with; the closest residencies were those in Vandalia Hills, the upscale neighborhood where John lived, next to the Bashford Country Club. The gate was left open. Blue Gene pulled his pickup into the long driveway at 5:50 p.m. At the end of the driveway stood a little boy wearing khaki shorts and a light-yellow polo shirt. He was pretending to be a crossing guard, waving imaginary traffic past him while making the halt signal with his other hand. When he saw Blue Gene's pickup coming toward him, he gave it the halt signal. Blue Gene played along and waited until the boy allowed him to proceed down the drive and park in front of the four-car garage. He got out of his truck, and the chubby-cheeked, sandy-haired little boy stood in front of him.

"Hey," said Blue Gene.

"Hello."

"How's the traffic today?"

"There's been nine wrecks."

"Dang. You're Arthur, I bet, ain't ya?"

"Yeah."

"I'm Blue Gene. I'm your uncle."

"I know. My mom and dad talked about you."

"What'd they say about me?"

"They said you had long hair."

"It's only long in the back. Does my name come up very often at your house?"

"No."

Blue Gene nodded. Because he didn't want to be inside the house any longer than he had to, he lit a cigarette and paced around the front lawn, with its immaculate grass and shrubbery. He considered leaving but decided not to, since his dad and John would think he was a coward if he didn't show.

Arthur watched Blue Gene smoke for a while.

"What's wrong with you?" Arthur finally asked.

"What do you mean?" Blue Gene prepared to explain his long hair or big mustache.

"Why don't you smile any?"

"Oh. Huh. I don't know."

"I found a dead snake once on the tennis court here, but it wasn't really dead."

"Yeah. I seen a few snakes around here myself. I used to live here, you know."

"No you didn't."

"Yes I did, too. Lived here from the time I was—what are you, five?"

"Yeah."

"Lived here from the time I was your age till I was twenty-one."

"You *did*?"

"Yes. I'm your dad's little brother. You do get that, don't you?"

"Yeah."

"Well, him and me lived here together, 'cept when he was off at school. See that tree over yonder?"

"Uh-huh."

"We had a little dog. It was your daddy's dog. He named him Troubles. Our dad taught him to never beg for food. Anyway, one day your dad tied Troubles' leash to the bottom branch of that there tree, and long-story-short, your daddy was playin' with me and not payin' attention to what the dog was doin', and the leash got wrapped around a tree branch somehow, and the dog hung himself. We found him just a-swingin' with his tongue hangin' out."

Arthur looked hurt.

"Hey, now. I'm sorry. I don't know why I told you that—well, I told you 'cause I wanted to prove to you I lived here, 'cause you were actin' like I was makin' it up. Anyways, I'm just sayin', don't tie your doggie to a tree."

"Dad won't let me have a dog."

"Figures."

"But what's wrong?"

"What do you mean?"

"You won't smile."

"I don't know, man. I just don't feel well and I'm tired and nothing's good. That's the best answer I can come up with. Nothing is good. At least for the time being."

"Yeah huh."

"What's good, then?"

"Um, well, for one thing, sometimes there are toys."

"I sell toys. I'll give you a bunch of 'em if I see you again. But not all of 'em, 'cause they're my livelihood at the moment."

"Okay."

Blue Gene flicked his cigarette butt at the lawn. "Well, Arthur, I reckon I better go on in. You go by Arthur or Art?"

"Arthur."

"I go by Blue Gene. You can call me Uncle Blue Gene, I guess."

"My nanny calls me Art sometimes, but I like to be called Arthur better."

"Oh, so John got you a nanny. Who's raised you? Your nanny or your parents?"

"My parents. My nanny is Faye."

"Mine's name was Bernice. She pretty much raised me. I liked her a lot. You like your nanny?"

"Yeah. She is nice. She is *so* nice."

Blue Gene remembered that for a little kid, people were either nice or mean, with no in-between. He looked at Arthur looking at him, with his tattoos and his face that didn't smile.

"I reckon I got a few minutes. Would you want to show me how to be a crossing guard? You seem to have a pretty good handle on it."

$ $ $

After playing crossing guard with Arthur for ten minutes, Blue Gene rang the doorbell. A round little Mexican woman, the latest in a long line of ever-changing housekeepers, opened the door. His parents never seemed to keep their help long. Bernice Munly had been kept the longest by far, but she was many years gone.

"Hello. You are Mr. Mapother?"

"You can call me Blue Gene." Blue Gene stepped into the inviting whiteness of the massive foyer, and Arthur ran in past him and down the hall. "What's your name?"

"Roberta."

Elizabeth entered from a wide, arched doorway underneath the curved double staircases.

"Hello, Gene!" Her greeting echoed.

"Hey."

"So glad you could make it. Roberta, did you offer Blue Gene something to drink?"

"No, ma'am. I—"

"She didn't have a chance to. I just come in two seconds ago."

"I made sure we had your favorite," said Elizabeth. "Isn't Pabst Blue Ribbon your favorite?"

"Uh, yeah."

"Would you like one?"

"Okay. Thank you."

"Roberta, they're in the back of the refrigerator. And do you know what pilsner glasses are?"

"Yes, ma'am."

"Serve it in one of those, please."

Roberta nodded and hurried off. Pabst Blue Ribbon was actually Blue Gene's third-favorite beer, behind Miller High Life and Milwaukee's Best. He didn't correct his mother, not out of politeness, but because he was trying to figure out why she was being so hospitable toward him, especially in the way of alcoholic beverages. When he had lived at home, Elizabeth had nearly disowned him because of his two DUIs, both of which were made her problem by phone calls from jail at three in the morning. She had gone through similar ordeals with John.

"I'm sorry, but would you mind taking off your shoes?"

"Oh, yeah. Been so long, I forgot." Blue Gene slipped off his flops.

The Mapothers lived in a spacious, high-ceilinged house—about three trailers high—where the windows were never opened and the furniture never changed. So far, Blue Gene hadn't noticed anything different. He followed Elizabeth, who walked hurriedly under the arched doorway and through a corridor. He scanned the many framed photos on the walls, searching for one of himself, but found only one or two because he was normally the one taking the pictures of his parents and John. Elizabeth led him to the parlor, one of the few rooms in the house with no TV. The Mapother house had eighteen televisions in all, plus a few more on the grounds, since there were two guest cottages.

On the parlor floor, next to an antique gun cabinet, Arthur sat Indian-style with a pile of toys in front of him. His mother, an attractive woman with long blond hair, sat cross-legged in her high heels by the fireplace.

"Hey, Abby."

"Hi, Gene." She got up and met Blue Gene halfway across the room. They hugged, Abby with her head turned away. "Your mustache sure has grown."

That she had to mention something about the way he looked annoyed Blue Gene, but he didn't know Abby well enough to argue with her. "Yeah, well, it's something interesting to touch."

Abby laughed politely and sat back down. "John sure has missed you."

"Is he here?"

"He called and said he'll be running a little late."

Blue Gene looked around the room, which was the same as he remembered it. He stared at a mounted deer head above the mantel, thinking about what it would be like to see John, wondering why he hadn't called if he had missed him so.

Arthur banged a couple of trucks together, and Blue Gene got down on the floor with him.

"Hey, you got Transformers. I used to play with them. Course, these are remakes of the old ones."

"I believe your father is in the den, if you want to go say hi," said Elizabeth.

"I'm gonna hang out with my nephew for a little bit."

"Would you like some wine, Abby?" asked Elizabeth as she took a seat.

"Oh, no thank you."

"You sure? It's okay. You said John will still be a little while, right?"

"No, thanks."

"Okay, Arthur. Let's play," said Blue Gene. "You want to be the good guys or the bad guys?"

"Bad guys," said Arthur. Everyone laughed.

"I'm like you. I've always been partial to the bad-guy wrestlers. Hey—you like wrestling?"

"No," said Arthur.

Blue Gene frowned and then shrugged his shoulders. "Okay. Round up all the Decepticons."

"I'll go see what's taking her so long with your beer," said Elizabeth.

"It's okay. It don't matter."

But she was already up and out the door. Blue Gene proceeded to set up battles between the toys, flipping a penny to see which character would win each duel, which was how he used to play. Roberta brought Blue Gene a pilsner glass full of Pabst Blue Ribbon, but Elizabeth didn't return.

Blue Gene soon saw he could get a laugh out of Arthur by making up voices for the toys.

"Officer," he said in a squeaky girl's voice, holding up one of the Transformers. "I didn't mean for you to *arrest* him. I just wanted you to *talk* to him."

He held up another character. "Now you gonna have to bail me out," he replied in a deep, monstrous voice.

Arthur giggled, and before long Abby was laughing too. It pleased Blue Gene to have a woman laughing at him. He had no feelings for Abby—she was all nostrils and teeth to him—but she had that Barbie-queen-blond look that most men went for. And her kid was cool because he could have so much fun without the slightest buzz. Arthur struck Blue Gene as really having his stuff together.

With the beer and the company of his nephew, he passed through the next few moments feeling at peace on the plush white carpet.

"Hey, Arthur. Do you like monster trucks?"

"I don't know," said Arthur.

"I bet you would. There's gonna be a monster-truck rally tomorrow night. Would you wanna go with me?"

"Yeah!"

"Would that be okay, Abby?"

"Actually, he's visiting his grandma tomorrow night—my mom. Sorry, but she's expecting us."

"Oh. That's a'ight."

Blue Gene tinkered absent-mindedly with one of the toys as he pictured himself sitting alone at the monster-truck rally. He decided once again not to go.

$$\$\ \$\ \$$

Elizabeth eventually returned to the parlor and announced that they could at least be seated for dinner. She led everyone into the dimly lit dining room, where Henry Mapother sat up straight at the head of the table.

"Eugene." He stood.

"Hey, Dad," said Blue Gene, seeing no emotion in his father's eyes or lips, both of them small and scrunched, which, along with his sharp nose, made him look hawklike.

"How are you?" He and Blue Gene shook hands firmly.

"Can't complain. How 'bout yourself?"

"Outstanding."

Blue Gene took a slurp from his pilsner glass and looked down at his father's tan socks, then at his light khakis with neat creases in the middle.

"Thanks for having me over."

"Glad you could make it." He spoke deeply, with absolutely no accent. "Good to see you."

"Good to see *you*." He noticed that his dad's hair was almost white now, but it still had that sporty, preppy look because of the way it swayed and swooped across his brow, which had a few fresh liver spots. He was as trim and tan as ever, though, which was especially impressive since he was pushing seventy.

"Have a seat." Henry motioned for Blue Gene to sit to his left, between him and Elizabeth. On the opposite side sat Abby and Arthur, with a chair to Henry's right reserved for John. "Would you like another beer?" he asked after everyone was seated, himself included.

"Sure. Thank you."

Henry got up and left the room.

"So, how did the rest of the day at the flea market go?" asked Elizabeth.

"Fine."

"Blue Gene sells toys at that flea market off of Story Boulevard," Elizabeth explained to Abby, who smiled and nodded. "You wouldn't believe how much I found there—mostly for church. It's a really neat place, in a kitschy sort of way."

"Is it really kitschy, though," asked Abby, "if it's not *meant* to be kitschy?"

Elizabeth laughed. "That's a very good point, Abby. Gene, I was wondering, how does one get involved in the flea market business?"

"You just go in there and tell 'em you want to have a booth, and they charge you rent. That's all there is to it."

"So what inspired you to do that?"

"I don't know. Just something I always wanted to do. Bernice used to take me to flea markets and yard sales when I was little. I don't guess you've heard from her, have ya?"

"No. Abby, did John tell you what time he'd be here?"

"No. He just said he had to run by home."

"We're all so excited for John," said Elizabeth. "We've already started renting out his campaign headquarters. It's the old JCPenney building downtown on Main Street. Of course, you're too young to remember that. The JCPenney *you* know is in the mall, isn't it? But used to, it was downtown. It was better then."

Henry returned with a fresh can of Pabst Blue Ribbon and poured it into Blue Gene's pilsner glass.

"Thank you."

"You're welcome." Henry sat down and sipped his wine. Everyone sipped their drinks as silence overtook the room. "Did you see that basketball game last night?" Henry finally asked.

"No. I pretty much stopped watching sports altogether."

"Why is that?" Henry's arched eyebrows lowered.

"My teams never seemed to win. So I just quit watchin' 'em."

"Even basketball?"

"Yeah. I swear, whatever team I'm rootin' for is gonna lose. And that gets old after a while. I still watch wrestling, though. Course, you probably don't consider that a sport."

"That's true. I don't." Elizabeth cleared her throat. Henry checked his silver watch. "So, is John going to make it or not?"

"He should be here any minute," said Abby.

"I'm going to have Roberta go ahead and serve the salads, then," he said, leaving the room again.

And that's how Blue Gene remembered his father, as a man who was always on his way to another room, always in a state of departure. It didn't bother Blue Gene, though, since anytime they were in the same room together, he had a strange feeling that he was doing something wrong just by being there.

$ $ $

As Roberta brought out salads and little silver containers of Roquefort dressing, Abby placed Arthur's cloth napkin on his lap, which reminded Blue Gene to do the same. He hadn't had a napkin in his lap in years, although the younger version of himself would've felt naked at the table without one.

"Is everyone okay on drinks?" asked Elizabeth. Everyone nodded. "Okay. Oh—before we begin, would you like to give the blessing, Gene?"

"That's a'ight. Go'r't ahead."

"But we always let the *guests* say grace here."

"You think of me as a guest?"

"Well, yes. What did you *think* you were? You don't live here anymore, so you're a guest. The guest of honor."

"Guess that means I don't have a room here no more."

"Actually, in a sense, you *do* still have a room here because we made your room into a guest room, and you're a guest."

"Oh." Blue Gene stared at his salad, thinking about the comforting messiness of his old bedroom.

"I'm sorry, Gene, but it's been four years. Did you expect us to keep your room the way it was?"

"Well, no, but you already got, like, five guest rooms. How many you need?"

"Would somebody give the damn blessing?" asked Henry.

"Gene, would you, please?"

"In the name of the Father, Son, Holy Spirit, amen," he said as he made the sign of the cross. Then he folded his hands and bowed his head. "Bless us oh Lord and these I give which are about to receive from the bounty through Christ our Lord, Amen."

"Amen," said Elizabeth. "Did you say *these I give*?"

"I told you I didn't want to say it."

"I'm sorry. No—you did just fine. Thank you."

For the next few moments, the only noise came from Blue Gene chomping his croutons. He looked around the room, which was also just how he remembered it. The room was almost somber with its dark wood floors, a dimmed chandelier, two imposing antique china cabinets, and a skinny Christ hanging on the wall.

"So, what have you been doing with your life?" asked Henry.

"Workin'."

"At Wal-Mart?"

"Yeah. Well, up till this past year. Now I'm at the flea market."

"You had been at that Wal-Mart for so long. I would imagine you had some rank by the time you left."

"You'd think so. How bout y'all? What've y'all been up to?"

"We work, too," said Henry without looking up from his salad.

"I still volunteer at church," said Elizabeth. "That keeps me pretty busy."

"Just out of curiosity, where do you see yourself in five years?" asked Henry.

"I hear Daddy!" said Arthur, springing out of his seat.

$ $ $

Maybe it was because he was carrying his five-year-old son, but John looked older to Blue Gene, like a genuine, full-fledged adult. He was forty now, and just as his father's hair was gray on top and turning white at the sideburns, Blue Gene noticed that John's dark-brown hair had turned gray at the sideburns. He was still so good-looking, like someone out of a black-and-white movie. Blue Gene had always wondered why he had turned out the way he did when John looked like some kind of glamour god. Blue Gene wasn't especially ugly, nor was he particularly handsome. Underneath the mustache, he was plain. He once asked Elizabeth if he had been adopted, and she swore that he shared the same Mapother blood that they all had. At least John's face wasn't completely flawless; he had thick lines under his eyes that made him look tired.

Tonight, he looked like he could hardly keep his eyes open.

"Blue Gene."

"Hey, John." He pushed his chair out and got up.

"Gotta set you down, Snigglefritz, so I can give my little brother a hug." John carefully placed Arthur on his feet and hugged Blue Gene briefly, patting his back. "How are you?"

"Can't complain."

"Hey, everybody. Sorry I was late. Got held up at work."

"It's all right," said Elizabeth. "Sorry we started without you. I'll have Roberta bring your salad."

Elizabeth left. Blue Gene and John took their seats next to Henry.

"So how are you? Oh, I already asked that, didn't I? What have you been up to?"

"Got a flea market booth."

"That's great."

"You makin' fun?"

"No. I know you always wanted to do that. Remember how we used to play flea market when you were little?"

"Not really."

"We did."

"Blue Gene and I played crossing guard," said Arthur.

"You *did*? How did he do?"

"Umm...he did pretty good."

Elizabeth returned, followed by Roberta with John's salad.

"Hey, honey," said John, just then noticing Abby.

"Hey. Are you feeling any better?"

"Feeling just fine." He turned away from Abby.

"Are you not well?" asked Henry.

"No, I'm fine. So, Blue Gene, you got a funeral to go to or something?"

"Huh?"

"You're wearing all black." He had selected black jeans and a black muscle shirt for the occasion, the closest things to dress clothes he owned.

"I *knew* one of y'all would criticize my outfit."

"Hey, hold on. I was just kidding. You look fine."

"I thought this would please y'all. Should've known."

"You are so *sensitive*. I didn't mean anything."

"I ain't sensitive, man. Don't say I'm sensitive."

"Did you watch the game last night?" Henry interjected.

"Yes," said John. As John and Henry talked about an NBA playoff game, Blue Gene considered screaming that basketball was for gays because of all the butt patting. He studied John, looking for something to make fun of in case he made another comment about his appearance. But there was nothing. Like his father, John was so clean-cut that a meal could be eaten off his face. His hair looked freshly cut, so short and ordinary that it hardly had a style at all. He wore a short-sleeved white dress shirt with a white undershirt. He seemed cool and calm and strong, but also sleepy.

"What about you?" said John, turning to Blue Gene. "Did you watch the game last night?"

"He quit watching sports," said Henry.

"Even basketball?" asked John.

"Y'all burnt me out on 'em."

"Oh. So whatcha been up to, Blue Gene?" asked John. "Did I already ask you that?"

"Yeah. Workin'."

"I see you got a new tattoo there since I saw you last."

"Why you keep pushin' me?"

"I'm not pushing you."

"He's not pushing you," said Elizabeth.

"Yes he is. He knows exactly what buttons to push, and he always pushes 'em. I know none of y'all like my tattoos, and he had to call attention to 'em."

"I like them," said Arthur, who hadn't touched his salad.

"Thanks, Arthur man," said Blue Gene with sincerity. "But I know you don't approve of my tattoos, John, so why you gotta bring 'em up?"

"God, you're touchy," said John. "Are you PMS-ing or something?"

"You look like your wife dresses you."

"You shut up, Blue Gene," said John, suddenly alert. "You're just as hotheaded as ever, aren't you? You shut up."

"John, tell me to shut up again, and see what happens."

"All right, boys," said Elizabeth.

"You don't talk to *me* like that," said John.

"Not in front of Arthur," said Elizabeth.

"Sorry, Mom," said John.

"He was startin' stuff, makin' fun of my clothes."

"You look fine," said Elizabeth. "Is everyone ready for the main course?"

"It wouldn't have hurt him to put on a shirt with sleeves."

"*Henry*," said Elizabeth.

"I'm only observing," said Henry, "that he constantly seems to be trying to test the boundaries of informality. If anything, he is pushing us by exposing those tattoos."

"Sleeves make me uncomfortable!" Arthur laughed at Blue Gene, causing him to realize what he must've sounded like.

Blue Gene decided that as long as Arthur was in the room, he would let any comments from his family roll off him. He remembered being a little kid at a fancy restaurant downtown (which had since gone out of business), and accidentally knocking over his orange juice. A waiter rushed over and began wiping up the juice, and Elizabeth made a point of telling him, "He did it," pointing at Blue Gene, causing him more shame than his little body could withstand. He started bawling, and Elizabeth asked John to take Blue Gene outside, but John refused to do it, and then Henry told him he needed to show some responsibility. They fought the rest of the meal, and no one ended up having to take Blue Gene out because he cried out all the tears he had.

$ $ $

As everyone dined on the main course, Blue Gene directed most of his attention toward Arthur, who was eating chicken tenders since he didn't like pork chops. Blue Gene tried to remember things that little kids like, and so he and Arthur had in-depth discussions about Kool-Aid and boogers. Meanwhile, Henry and John had a separate conversation about tennis and then baseball. Elizabeth and Abby listened silently to both conversations.

"You know, I've always wondered something about athletes," said Elizabeth once everyone stopped talking. "With all that traveling they do, isn't it hard for them to play the away games?"

"Why would that be hard?" asked Henry.

"I know that when I fly somewhere, by the time I get out of the airport and then settle into the hotel room, I hardly feel like doing anything. I need a day or two to acclimate myself to my new surroundings. But when professional athletes travel, they're expected to fly somewhere and *immediately* be ready to play, aren't they? So doesn't that give the home team a distinct advantage?"

"That right there's a straight-up *girl* question," said Blue Gene. John laughed.

"I think it was a valid question," said Elizabeth.

"I'll have to agree with Eugene," said Henry. "I don't think a man would ever ask a question like that, because we know that the body of a man—especially an athlete—can handle things like traveling with relative ease."

"It was a reasonable question, Mom," said John, speaking as he yawned, "but women look at sports from a completely different angle than we do. It's like when we go to the track, you two always pick your horses based on their names or the jockey's outfit."

"And we win more than you men do," said Abby.

"No, you don't. Well, more than I, maybe, but not Dad."

"Bloodlines are everything in horses," said Henry. "That's how you pick a winner."

"Y'all been goin' to the track?" asked Blue Gene.

"Yeah," said John.

"Since when?"

"Since a year or two ago. A friend of Dad's gave him season passes."

"Surprised I haven't seen you there. Couple summers ago I got in the habit of goin' quite a bit."

"We stay up in the Sky Room," said Elizabeth.

"Oh, that explains it. I was always in the grandstands."

"It's so hot down there," said Elizabeth. "How can you stand it?"

"I like it."

"And did you do well at the racetrack?" asked Henry.

"Usually not. I usually bet on the longshots, and one time one come in forty to one, and I had two on it to win. After I cashed my ticket, I went over to the paddock and asked if I could talk to the horse, to kind of thank him, and so I kind of befriended him."

Everyone laughed, except for Henry.

"The little Mexican jockeys thought I was ate up. I said, screw y'all little wetbacks. Your horse got my ass paid."

Everyone laughed again, even Henry this time. Roberta returned.

"Would you get Eugene another beer, Roberta?" asked Henry.

"Yes, sir."

"Roberta, Abby and I will help you with dessert. Come on, Abby."

Any need for conversation seemed to leave the room with the women. The only sound was Arthur, who was bouncing in his seat.

"His chair might scuff the floor, John," said Henry. Blue Gene realized that it was the first time that his father had even acknowledged the child's presence.

"He's getting restless," said John. "Come here, Arthur." Arthur came over and sat in his dad's lap. "What do you think about your Uncle Blue Gene?"

"I want to *hug* him, and *squeeze* him, and love him *aaaall* night."

John laughed and yawned again.

"I think he likes you," said John. Blue Gene just nodded. "You okay? You seem tired."

"So do you," said Blue Gene.

"It was a hard day."

"Mine too. But I'm always tired."

"Neither of you exercise enough," said Henry, who jogged daily and worked out in his gym upstairs. John and Blue Gene shared a look. Then, for no apparent reason, Arthur started making faces at Blue Gene, and Blue Gene returned the favor until John cleared his throat and spoke.

"So, did you know that I'm running for Congress?"

"Yeah. I seen something about it on the TV a while back."

"What do you think?"

"You *look* the part."

"Is that all you have to say for me?"

"I mean, what do you know about politics?"

"I know enough."

"He knows more than enough," said Henry, "and he'll have my team behind him. And he knows what's right and wrong, which is more than I can say for that whoremonger he's running against."

"Who you runnin' against?"

"Grant Frick. He's the incumbent. He's been in there forever, but when his sex scandal broke, we knew it was time for us to make a move."

"Our charismatic leaders have led us astray," said Henry. "It's time for, as your mother says, a good Christian man to steer us back on the right course."

The women returned with drinks and dessert.

$$\$\,\$\,\$$

After the chocolate mousse had been reduced to brown swirls, Roberta collected the plates. She offered coffee, and everyone but Blue Gene and Arthur took some. John told her to leave the pot on the table, since he felt so sleepy. Blue Gene excused himself to have a smoke out on the deck. He returned to a still and quiet room.

"Honey, why don't you take Arthur to the family room to watch TV?" John said to Abby.

"I don't wanna watch TV," Arthur whined.

"Can't he stay?" asked Blue Gene.

"We should let you all talk," said Abby. "Come on, Arthur." Abby and Arthur left the table.

"See you later, nutball," said Blue Gene.

"See you later," said Arthur, pouting.

Blue Gene looked at the grandfather clock in the corner.

"Is that comin' up on seven-thirty?" he asked. "I'm missin' *Smackdown*."

"Hold your horses," said John. "We haven't seen you in forever."

"Gene, it's so good to see you," said Elizabeth, squeezing Blue Gene's wrist.

"You too. Thanks for the meal."

"You're welcome."

"So, what are you doing on the Fourth of July?" asked John.

"Probably workin'."

"What about that night?"

"I don't know," he replied, though he knew he'd most likely be sitting in front of the TV, or maybe watching the trailer-court kids shoot off fireworks.

"I'm having my first campaign rally over at the Ambassador Inn."

"Already? Election ain't till November, right?"

"Yeah, but we really want my rally to be on the Fourth. It's meant to be a launching pad for my campaign, to introduce myself to the voters of the district and show them who I am. We're going to have food and fireworks, and I'm going to speak. Would you want to come?"

"I guess. If I feel like it when the time comes. I never know how I'm gonna feel."

"We'd really like for you to be there, and we were thinking maybe you could introduce me before I speak."

"Uh-uh. Hell nah. Why would you even *want* me to?"

"Well, could you at least make an appearance with me onstage? We could do it on your terms."

"I don't wanna be up in front of people. What do you want *me* for, anyway?"

"Here's the deal. I've already won the primary. Of course, I ran unopposed, so that was the easy part. Now I gotta beat Frick in November. The good news is that our polls said that 65 percent of the voters plan to vote against Frick."

"That's righteous."

John poured himself another cup of coffee as he went on. "But there was one figure in our polls that we found alarming. If *I* were the person running against Frick, 53 percent would vote against *me*."

"They just haven't recognized your greatness yet," said Elizabeth. "They will."

"They don't know any better," said Henry.

"What it is," said John, "is that according to our polls, I have a bit of an image problem. It's not that I have a *bad* image; it's just that, well, Westway is the biggest employer in the district, and therefore a good number of the voters in this district are employees of ours. So they see Dad and me as these boss figures. And who likes their boss, right?"

"I do. I liked my bosses at Wal-Mart."

"Yeah, but it's different with Dad and me. They see us as these rich, corporate bosses in our ivory towers. They don't consider us one of them. They've come to associate the name Mapother itself with being rich, so naturally, there's some resentment there. That's why we were thinking that *you* might want to get involved in our campaign."

"So that's what all *this* is about?" Blue Gene waved his hand at the dinner table.

"Absolutely not," said Elizabeth. "We *wanted* to see you. My viewpoint is that if it takes a congressional campaign to bring us together again, then so be it."

"Right," agreed John. "If you don't want to have anything to do with my campaign, that's perfectly fine. At least it's given us a chance to reunite. But with that said, if you're willing to help out on the Fourth, we'd love to have you."

"Are you bein' *serious* right now?"

"Yes. I know you're in touch with a lot of the people who will be there."

"Not really. I never go anywhere no more."

"Look, I understand if you don't want to speak. But could you at least stand there and smile with me, maybe do a little meet and greet on my behalf?"

"So, you're really gonna *sit there* and ask me to do that for you after going four years without talking to me?"

"You didn't talk to him, either, though," said Elizabeth. "Remember that."

"Wait, Blue Gene. I'm going to be completely honest with you." John took a deep swallow of coffee. "The reason I haven't talked to you in so long is because a lot of people told me that if I wanted to stay off drugs and alcohol, I needed to stay away from anybody who might get me back into those things."

"What the hell!? I ain't on drugs! Y'all think just 'cause of the way I look and dress that I'm on drugs, but let me tell you somethin' I learned in high school. If you wanna see who's the biggest into drugs, if you wanna see who's dealin' 'em in the first place, you just look for the best-dressed, cleanest-cut kids, and that's where you'll find 'em. Looks got nothin' to do with it. I mean, look at you, John. Goin' to Harvard, wearin' all those nice clothes. I bet there was enough drugs in your dorm to make your head spin, and you was doin' all kinds of drugs with the best of 'em."

"But that's in the past. I've got my act together now. I've been completely clean for over six years. I have a family. I've found God again."

"I never lost 'im."

"You said earlier that you don't go to church," said Elizabeth.

"It don't matter."

"It *doesn't* matter."

"There you go." Elizabeth rolled her eyes. "That really pisses me off, you sayin' you didn't come around me 'cause I was on drugs."

"I know how Cheyenne died," said John.

"Yeah, but you're just like Mom, wantin' to lump everybody together.

Cheyenne and me are separate people. I stopped smokin' pot three years ago. Last time I ever did was at my friend's house out on Second Street, and a cop come in lookin' for somebody or another, and there was a whole room full of people, but of course he looks down at me, and he sniffs the air and says, 'Sir, have you been smoking marijuana?' And I was freakin' out, and I come out and said yes 'cause I didn't know what to do. And he asked me if I had any marijuana in my pants, and I said no, 'cause I *did* have it in my pants, but I had just bought it and it was an eighty-five-dollar bag of pot and I wasn't about to give that up. Anyways, they said that since that was my first offense, they let me off at court with just a fine. But that was enough right there that I got so I didn't even want to fool with pot no more. Haven't touched it since."

"We know all about that incident," said Henry. "I'm the reason they gave you such a light sentence."

"Do *what* now?"

"I have some friends at the courthouse, and I made sure they realized who you were. I assumed you would know that there was a reason you got off scot-free."

"I had no idea."

"You should have. That wasn't even your first offense, Eugene. You already had two DUIs."

"Yeah, but what I *meant* was that was the first time they got me on *possession*. You seriously got me off the hook?"

"He did," said Elizabeth.

"Well, you sure didn't have to do that."

"I wasn't going to let my last name be dragged through the Court Beat section of the newspaper any more than it had to be."

Blue Gene imagined his dad had probably been studying the *Bashford Register* every day for the last four years, waiting for his lowlife son to screw up. Blue Gene thought about telling him off for fiddling with his personal matters, but how could he fuss at someone for keeping him out of prison? So he remained quiet as he listened to his parents talk about how great John was, how John could find the light only by first exploring the darkness, how John was born again into a stronger form, and how he was now ready to lead all the others stuck in their own darkness, though he would need Blue Gene's help to get the votes that would allow all this to transpire.

"All that's fine," said Blue Gene. "Good for you, John. All I'm sayin' is don't be actin' like I'm on drugs, 'cause I'm not."

"You still drink, though?" asked Elizabeth.

"What the hell? You been offerin' me beers all night!"

"You're right. I was just asking if you still drink regularly."

"When I can afford it, I might get a six-pack of High Life on the weekends. And I only drink beer. Nothin' hard. I stopped drinkin' whiskey, 'cause last time I got drunk on whiskey, I got into it with my friend and got underneath his car and cut his brake line. But I felt bad about it afterward and told him about it. I was so out of it I—"

"You don't have to confess every transgression you've committed in the last four years," said Henry. Blue Gene realized that he was talking more than he should. He blamed it on the beers.

"Blue Gene, I'm truly sorry I haven't kept in better contact with you," said John. "But I had a wife and a kid, and I just did what I thought was right for us. I'm sorry I neglected you."

"Stop apologizing," said Henry. "He made no attempt to contact you. Don't let him lay the guilt trip on you. He's the one who defected."

"Well, you know how it is," said Blue Gene with a mucous snort. "You go so long without talkin' to someone, and the longer it goes, the bigger a deal it becomes to reach out and talk to 'em, 'til finally it gets so big you give up on it altogether."

"That's the way I felt, too," said John. "But we're together now. That's what counts. So will you come to my rally?"

"Surprised you'd want to be seen with a dude you thought was on drugs. Why would you wanna be seen with me?"

"Honestly, I want to be seen with you because I think you're authentic."

"What's that supposed to mean?"

"It means that if my constituents see that I'm related to someone like you, they'll be more likely to vote for me. They'll think, 'Why, he can't be all that bad.'"

"What do you mean, *someone like me*?"

"Well...come on. It's no secret that you've chosen a particular *station* in life."

"Compared with John," said Elizabeth, "you're more of a *working* man."

"Right, and if they saw me with you, it might help counterbalance the whole corporate executive image I was talking about."

"Sorry, but I ain't interested."

"Okay," said John. "But can I ask you why?"

"Ain't my style, smilin' and wavin' at people. I ain't gonna be some bitch tryin' to get votes."

"But he's family," said Elizabeth. "Can't you do it for your *family*?"

"Sorry."

"You realize we're just asking you to be there the one night," said Henry. "Just the Fourth of July." Blue Gene nodded. "We would never ask for your help again. We're only asking for your help in this particular case because this is a regional election. The fifth district is made up of twenty-one counties, and Commonwealth County is by far the largest. So a lot of the voters will have some affiliation with our company, and even though we pay their bills, they might take out their frustration with work by voting against the president of the company."

"I get it."

"Unlike the statewide elections or national election that John will have in the future, this is the only election in which local reputation will play a role. Therefore, you could swing a lot of votes John's way just by showing your blue-collar brethren that you support him, which could be easily accomplished with a photo opportunity on the Fourth of July."

"Our motto is 'Go hard or go home,'" said John. "And you could be our secret weapon in this election. You could be a decisive factor in getting the votes I need to push me over the top."

"We cannot let John lose," said Henry. "You have a chance to help him in this one election, and being in the House will be an important step before he makes a name for himself on the national scene."

"Get real," said Blue Gene. "You haven't even been elected on the *city* level yet. And you're talking about makin' a name on the *national* scene?"

"But he already has a name," said Henry. "The business community the world over knows the name Mapother. I've worked all my life to make sure of that."

"You *know* we've always planned on this," said Elizabeth. "It's his destiny."

Blue Gene drew his head back and squooshed his lips at Elizabeth.

"You also have to take into consideration," said Henry, "that there will be greater scrutiny of our family during this election, and there is the possibility that Grant Frick's campaign team might make a spectacle of you because of the different lifestyle you've chosen for yourself. They could even use you against John. So if you don't come out for your brother early on, you might, in effect, hurt his chances of winning."

"I hear what you're sayin', but I'm tellin' y'all once and for all, I ain't interested. Y'all 'bout disowned me over my *different lifestyle*, and I ain't gonna pretend like everything's hunky-dory all of a sudden."

"You disowned *us*," said Elizabeth.

"I offered to get you into any college in the country," said Henry. "Is that what you call disowning you? Do you not realize how fortunate you were?"

"I didn't go off to college 'cause I wanted to keep livin' here for Mom's sake, 'cause her other son was in and out of rehab. Don't make me into the bad guy. Y'all did me ever' bit as wrong as you think I did you."

"You didn't go to college because you didn't want to," said Henry.

"I'm sorry you feel that we did you wrong, but regardless, don't you believe in forgiveness?" asked John.

"Yeah, but let me ease into it. You said even if I don't get involved in the campaign that we could still be friendly, right?"

"Yes," said John. "Yes, I said that."

"Well, I'm okay with that, then. I ain't ready to be up on a stage with you or anything like that, though."

"Fine," said John.

"It is *not* fine," said Elizabeth. "This is your *destiny*. First the House, then the Senate, then the presidency. I will not allow a member of your own *family* to hurt your chances of realizing your destiny."

"Mom," said John. "Stop it. It's okay. We'll figure out something else."

"No. Our time has come. The battle for the Holy Land is being waged as we speak." Blue Gene shook his head. "Don't you shake your head at me. With John's help, God and Allah will hold hands. Our savior could be out there already. Now *you* have an opportunity to make sure He arrives, but you won't let go of your grudges."

"Would you *listen* to yourself?"

"You used to believe in my dream."

"Yeah, when I was a little kid and didn't know any better."

"Eugene, I understand your skepticism, but look at this way," said Henry. "Do you believe in the Bible?"

"Course I do."

"The Bible is filled with prophecies. Do you believe that the prophecies in the Bible took place?"

"I guess so."

"No. You don't guess so. You said you believed in the Bible. Therefore, you have to believe the events within it are true. So yes, the prophecies did take place, did they not?"

"Yeah."

"Then if we truly believe in the Bible, we have to admit that it is possible for a legitimate prophecy to occur, even in modern times. If you believe in the Bible, then you have to believe in prophecy."

"Fine. But if it's a prophecy, it'll happen whether you have my help or not, won't it?"

"It is our moral duty to fulfill our own destinies," said Elizabeth. "We need you at this rally."

Blue Gene found himself weighing his options more carefully now that his decision suddenly seemed so monumental.

"Forget it, y'all. I ain't goin'! Y'all been so ashamed of me. Like your shit don't stink!"

"Oh, God," said Elizabeth. "That is just *crude*."

Henry arose and looked down at Blue Gene. "Show some couth," he said before leaving.

Blue Gene also got up. "Thanks again for the pork chops. Or I guess I should be thankin' Roberta."

"You're welcome," Elizabeth said, before laying her head down on the table.

"See you 'round, John."

"Here, let me walk you out."

John followed Blue Gene down the main corridor where all the family pictures hung. Blue Gene wanted to say goodbye to Arthur before he left, but he decided against it.

"Hey, you remember this?" John asked. He pointed to a picture hanging near the front of the hall. It was a picture of John with Blue Gene when he was little. Blue Gene didn't remember seeing it before. "Look how happy we were."

"I look happy. You look drunk."

John laughed it off. Blue Gene stared at the smiling seven-year-old he once had been, long before his eyes turned dark and circled, back when snow days brought heaven to Earth and he knew only a jolly God.

"You see that?" said John, pointing to the photo in which he and little Blue Gene had their arms around each other. Little Blue Gene was looking up admiringly at John. "That's what all those people sitting on bar stools all night are looking for. They just don't know it. They're looking for love. They might think they're looking for the love of a one-night stand, but they're really looking for the love of their families. I know because I used to be one of those people on a bar stool."

"Why you gettin' all emotional on me?"

"Because I can tell you're not well. You said so yourself. And maybe you're not well because your family has been missing."

As Blue Gene looked at the picture, which seemed to have a soft, happy 1980s glow to it, the reflex to back-sass his brother for telling him what was good for him did not come.

"Maybe I'd feel better, too, if you were back in my life," continued John. Blue Gene shook his head and walked toward the front door. "Hey, forget all that Mom said. Won't you do it just to help *me*? I'm your brother, for Christ's sake."

"Sorry, man."

"I'll pay you."

"You know I don't want your money."

"Then what *do* you want? Isn't there anything *you* want, something that *I* could do for *you* in return?"

"Nope." But he paused at the door and rubbed his mustache before stepping out. John stood at the threshold.

"Okay, but I meant what I said. Even though you said no, we can still keep in touch. If you ever need anything—"

"I reckon there is one thing you can do for me."

"What? You name it."

Blue Gene kept rubbing his mustache as John looked on, biting his lip.

"Will you take me to the monster-truck rally tomorrow night?"

III.

"Just so you know, when the trucks come out, we're for the Chevys," said Blue Gene as he, John, and Arthur took their seats in the fifteenth row of the Bashford Civic Center. Here was one man in a sleeveless camouflage T-shirt and denim shorts, another in a nice blazer and black slacks; one in flip-flops and the other in dress shoes; one shaggy and the other perfectly kempt— perhaps a criminal and his parole officer. "I wouldn't be caught dead sittin' with somebody rootin' for Fords. A'ight?"

"Whatever you say," said John. "You got that, Arthur? We're for the Chevys."

"Okay." Arthur's little hands barely reached around a giant blue Pepsi cup. He appeared to be using all the concentration his little form could muster to drink through the straw. He eventually stopped drinking in order to say "I wanna sit next to Uncle Blue Gene."

"You can sit in my lap later," said John. John had made sure to sit between Blue Gene and Arthur so he wouldn't have to be next to a stranger.

"But I wanna sit next to him now."

"Come on," said Blue Gene. "Can't he sit next to me, man?"

"Okay. Here. Get on my lap." After he got situated on John's lap, Arthur and Blue Gene didn't even talk. John laughed to himself. It was just like a couple of little kids. "I've always wondered," he said after a while. "What's the deal with Ford versus Chevy for some people?"

"What do you mean, *what's the deal*?"

"I mean, why do you all make it into such a rivalry? They're similar brands. They're both American-made trucks."

"Well..." As Blue Gene let his sentence hang, John stared at the brown, white, and gray junk cars lined up perfectly in two rows on the arena floor, all tacky, seedy-looking seventies models now driven mostly by ex-cons or the elderly, all presumably waiting to be flattened by the gargantuan wheels of a monster truck. "You know what Ford stands for?" Blue Gene finally replied.

"What?"

"Found On Road Dead."

John laughed and shook his head. "That's good. But still, why do you love Chevy and hate Ford so much?"

"Why does the sun rise? Why do people climb mountains? I don't know. I been hatin' on Fords long as I can remember. I reckon it's 'cause most of my friends favored Chevy, and I think they did 'cause their dads did. And they're just a good-made truck, John. You'll just have to take my word for it."

"Good enough." John was surprised to see there was no dirt on the arena floor, only smooth concrete. Of course, he had only caught glimpses of this sort of thing on TV.

Arthur suddenly started having a coughing fit.

"Goodness," said John, taking the Pepsi from his son. "Did you swallow the wrong way?"

Arthur nodded between coughs. His eyebrows frowned as he tried to breathe normally. John told him to raise his arms as he patted him on the back. Several people turned around and looked, which doubled John's heart rate. He wished someone would turn off the lights so no one could watch him and his coughing son. He patted Arthur faster, hoping it would hasten the end of his coughing, which it did. Arthur went right back to drinking his Pepsi. John wiped fresh sweat from his brow.

"You're going to have to sit in your own seat, Snigglefritz," said John.

"You're making me hot."

Arthur obeyed. John stood and removed his blazer and rolled up the sleeves of his black dress shirt. He always wore either solid black or solid white shirts because they showed underarm perspiration the least.

"You okay now?" John asked Arthur.

"I'm okay," said Arthur. Arthur was one of Blue Gene's conditions. He said that if both John *and* Arthur came to the monster-truck rally, he would attend the Fourth of July rally and do whatever John asked him to do there, as long as he didn't have to give a speech. "How come nobody sits in those rows?" Arthur pointed to the first three rows, which were roped off.

"That's in case the monster trucks go airborne and into the seats," answered Blue Gene.

"Does that *happen*?" asked John.

"Nah. Not that I know of. The trucks have mechanisms in 'em where they can be shut off automatically by remote control if something goes wrong. Don't be scared."

"I'm not scared," said John.

"I was talkin' to Arthur."

John played off his mistake with a little laugh. It was true that he wasn't scared of the monster trucks soaring into the audience. The audience itself, though, was another story. He imagined them all turning on him, surrounding him, swarming him, suffocating him.

"One hundred fifty-one days," he said, trying to think of something positive.

"Do what?" asked Blue Gene.

"Just thinking aloud. One hundred fifty-one days until Election Day."

"Hmm."

"You know, I *am* going to win. I feel an electricity in the air. This is what we've been waiting for all my life." Blue Gene rolled his eyes, which tempted John to tell Blue Gene that his breath stank from smoking cigarettes. "Don't you roll your eyes at me. This election is the beginning of my destiny. I can feel with every fiber of my being that I'm doing exactly what I'm supposed to be doing. It's God's plan. It took me a while to get here, but I'm ready for my destiny. It feels *right*."

"I don't care, man. Whatever pumps your 'nads."

"*God.*"

"What?"

"You have no respect for what Mom and Dad and I are trying to accomplish with my political career, do you?"

"Exactly what is it that y'all are trying to accomplish?"

"Lots of things, but if everything goes as planned, and if everyone cooperates with me, our ultimate goal has always been peace. We want the final peace, the one that will hold. Nothing new, really. It's what every leader wants, I suppose."

"Well, yeah. I knew you wanted peace and all, but with Mom's dream, it wasn't that peaceful. I's tryin' to think yesterday, what was that one phrase? *Nervous death*? I never can remember what y'all called it, but I remember it used to give me the heebie-jeebies."

"What you're referring to is only a possible scientific explanation for the thing that happens in her dream." John looked to see if Arthur was paying attention. He was playing with his nose. John turned to Blue Gene and said quietly, "We can talk about this some other time, but I'd prefer not to in front of Arthur."

Blue Gene nodded.

"I should've never told you about any of that stuff she saw."

"You were drunk."

The three of them sat between a family of five on one side and two men on the other. John was relieved that at least he wasn't completely enclosed, because the seats in front of him were empty. But by the time Guns N' Roses' "Sweet Child o' Mine" ended, a ponytailed man and a woman in a T-shirt that said LEGALIZE IT over a marijuana leaf were sitting in front of him. He took deep breaths and tried not to think about being in the middle of such a large crowd.

It was a small arena that had been built three years earlier to provide a better place for high-school basketball games. The construction of the civic center had infuriated some because it was built with money that was originally earmarked for a fine-arts center. John hadn't been to the civic center but once, when a tennis exhibition between John McEnroe and Jimmy Connors was held there for charity, an event set up by Henry Mapother. Compared with the tennis match, easily twice as many people attended the monster-truck rally.

Beyond the first three rows, nearly every dark-blue seat held eager families and boisterous roughnecks. As "The Stroke" by Billy Squier blasted over the PA, it looked like the civic center was filling to capacity. John looked out at the noisy expanse of people, most of them restless and having trouble getting situated. This was the crowd that would get him into office, upon which his future depended: rugged men with arms stiffly out to their sides and hard-looking women with sun-punished skin, a nebulous mass of earth tones, some, like Blue Gene, even disguising themselves as the earth with camouflage. It was a far cry from the country club. These were the type of people whose phones were disconnected, who looked ten years past their age, whose homely faces had a defeated look, as if they were resigned to a life of whatever—the indigent, the unemployable, the unreliable. Yet they could vote.

John knew that conjuring a vote out of a man would require him to actually talk to one, to press his clammy palm against another's. He would have to look each one in the eye and ask for his vote, which would be difficult for him. He had the handsomest eyes, but they never knew where to look.

$ $ $

Blue Gene spotted a lot of folks he hadn't seen for a long time. He hoped they wouldn't think he had been blowing them off to hang out with the highfalutin' fellow sitting next to him.

He leaned across John to tell Arthur what he could expect tonight. Blue Gene had wanted to sit in the middle, too, but John snuck his way between him and Arthur, which probably meant that John didn't want him getting too close to his son.

John's cell phone vibrated, and he took the call, the third since he had picked up Blue Gene earlier that night. As John talked, Blue Gene gave him dirty looks. He had been the same way growing up. He was fun to play with, but it was rare for him to finish a game of Battleship or Operation because he always had to take a phone call or go somewhere more important.

"Why are you looking at me like that?" John asked after hanging up.

"I guess you're going to be talking on the phone all night."

"No."

"That kills me how people will take their cell phone calls right in the middle of a conversation with you."

"You and I weren't conversing."

"We were on the way here and you took a call in the middle of it. I wasn't gonna say anything, but this is gettin' ridiculous."

"I'm sorry, but sometimes I have to take calls. That was about the campaign."

"The campaign. That's all you wanna talk about."

"When you're running for the United States House of Representatives, sometimes you have to take calls, no matter what you're doing at the time."

"You don't have to *like* being here. I know you don't wanna be here. But at least stay off the damn cell phone for the rest of the night. That's just common courtesy."

"I *do* want to be here."

"Then turn your cell phone off."

"I'm not going to do that. And don't tell me what to do."

"Man, someday you're gonna look back on your life and all you'll see is yourself talking on a cell phone. I bet you hate him talkin' on that phone, too, don't you, Arthur?"

"Yes."

"Arthur has no place in this argument."

"I'm just sayin', you need to think of other people sometimes."

"Do you not have a cell phone?"

"No."

"You should. What if there's an emergency?"

"Don't talk to me like I'm a little kid."

"I'm going to get you one."

"No."

"Why not?"

"It interferes. Didn't you just hear your son? He don't want you on the phone all the time."

"Don't *you* lecture *me* about how to raise a family. My marriage and family are at the center of my life."

"Not with all this campaign business goin' on."

"This campaign business is *for* my family. It's for a better life for them and all the other good families of America. But first I have to get elected, and that requires talking on the phone."

"Just turn your cella-phone off, Daddy."

"No. I'm sorry, but that's not how it works. A father doesn't take orders from his son."

"He's just scared of missin' a call, Arthur. I swear, John, you're just like you always were. All you think about is you. But I guess I can't blame you, since you can get away with it."

"What's that mean?"

"Mom and Dad still give you all the credit in the world."

"Don't be such a baby. Yeah, maybe Mom and Dad aren't as hard on me as they are on you. I'll give you that. But you were the one who ruined your relationship with them."

"No, now, I ain't talkin' about recent stuff. It's been like that as long as I can remember. When I was, like, seven or eight—and I'll never forget this—I had saved up all my coins, all the change I had accumulated, and I wrapped 'em up and had Bernice take me to the bank to cash 'em, and I had even saved up some money from my birthday, and I used the money to get you and Mom and Dad something for Christmas, 'cause I wanted to be able to say I paid for the gifts myself. So I got Mom and Dad a plate I thought was fancy at an antique mall, and on Christmas Eve when they opened it, you sat there on the parlor room floor and said, 'I chipped in on that.'"

"I don't remember that."

"Take my word for it, man. It happened. I'll never forget it. You said it with a straight face, and I threw a fit and told 'em you had nothin' to do with my gift, that I had saved up and picked it out myself, but you kept sayin' you paid half, and I started cryin' till finally you admitted you hadn't chipped in on it, but then you said that you would pay me back for your half. But what hurt most was that Mom and Dad thanked you for the gift anyway, and then they scolded me for actin' up."

"Did I ever pay you for my half?" asked John, reaching for his wallet.

"No! I wouldn't let you, but that don't matter. That's beside the point."

"You say you were seven or eight?"

"Yeah."

"Let's see...I would have been around twenty-one then. I was all mixed up. That's when I was up in Massachusetts. I remember when I'd come home for break, I was always having to pretend like I was doing fine around Mom and Dad. But I was really—" John looked to see if Arthur was paying attention. He had found a way to sit backward in his seat, one of several contortions he had discovered in the last few minutes. "I was just the biggest mess, with my lifestyle being what it was. I didn't know if I was coming or going. I apologize. I was awful back then."

"I accept your apology. Now if you could only get Mom and Dad to apologize—that'd be something."

"When's this thing going to start?" asked John, checking his Rolex.

"Yeah. That's right. Switch the subject."

"Well, what do you want *them* to apologize for?"

"For thanking you. For letting you get away with that and then scoldin' me. It burns me up just thinkin' about it."

"That's something you'd need to take up with them."

The house lights were turned off, instantly firing up the crowd, which hooted with anticipation as spotlights flew around the arena.

"Dad'll hardly even look at me," Blue Gene shouted over the hoopla. "He's always had it in for me."

"All I'm hearing is a bunch of whining from you," John shouted into Blue Gene's ear. "You need to stop whining about how Mom and Dad treated you and be a man."

The crowd roared even louder when a camouflaged military Humvee crept onto the arena floor. The oversize armored jeep stopped in front of the two rows of junk cars. The spotlights were turned off, except for one focused on the Humvee's top.

"Don't be tellin' me to be a man!" screamed Blue Gene into John's ear. "You've never even held a real job."

"I'm the president of a Fortune 500 company. Does that not qualify as a real job?"

"Yeah, but your daddy hired you."

"God! You could've had a job, too. Quit your whining."

"Please rise for the National Anthem," a deep, chipper voice said over the PA system. Blue Gene and John stood in unison with everyone else.

"I ain't whinin'. Just don't be acting like you're all—"

"Be quiet!" shouted John. "It's the National Anthem."

Blue Gene gave John a narrow-eyed glare before taking off his cap and looking down at the Humvee. Its top slid open and a young woman emerged. With only the top half of her body coming up out of the vehicle, she began, "Oh-oh, say can you see..."

With their right hands pressed against their hearts, John and Blue Gene gazed respectfully at the gigantic American flag hanging from the rafters next to all of the high-school basketball championship banners. John lifted Arthur's hand to his heart when he saw that Arthur wasn't paying any attention and was trying to climb over the back of his seat. When the song ended, they applauded, and Blue Gene let out a heartfelt "Woo!" before sitting.

"She sounded good, didn't she?" asked Blue Gene.

"She sure did," said John, smiling.

"Woo!" yelled Blue Gene once more. Blue Gene loved those couple of minutes during the National Anthem when every person in the room was together on something. He would have liked to jump in the Hummer, run off with the singer, and take her with him wherever he went. "Those Hummers are some mean machines," he said as the vocalist ducked back into the mammoth military vehicle.

"Tell me about it," said John, smirking. "I had one."

"Nuh-uh."

"Yeah. Had a black one a while back."

"You know, GM makes those."

"Yeah."

"I can't see you in one of those."

"Yeah, they're pretty conspicuous. I mostly kept it in the garage. They're the safest car possible, though."

"Why don't you have it no more?"

"It's a long story."

"I wanna hear it."

The MC came out onto the floor, wearing black jeans and cowboy boots.

"The show's starting," said John.

"I don't care what that fool has to say," said Blue Gene. "Go on."

"Well, remember a few years back when we had that blizzard?" John asked while the MC welcomed everyone.

"Yeah."

"One of the nights of the blizzard, the cops called me. One of them happened to know that I owned a Hummer, and he asked if they could use it since the roads were so bad and their cars were having trouble. He said no one else in town had one. So I thought it over and said no. I just didn't think it was right for them to be asking that. I mean, I don't go calling up strangers and asking them if they'll loan me their car. But then I felt kind of bad about it afterward, and I got to thinking, 'If this is what's going to happen every time there's a snowstorm, I'd just as soon not have the thing.' So I traded it in for a Saab. And of course we haven't even had a big snow ever since."

"That is exactly what I was talkin' about, man. You could be helping others, but—"

A monstrous roar came from beyond the arena-floor entrance. One at a time, four monster trucks entered the arena. Blue Gene was spellbound. He screamed, "Woo!"

"Arthur, man, look at those wheels. They're five-and-a-half-foot-tall wheels."

Like many of the men in the arena, Blue Gene fantasized about owning a monster truck. He pictured himself rolling over idle cars while they waited for the light to turn green.

John made Arthur put in some earplugs. As the monster trucks circled the arena floor, Blue Gene saw only one Chevy among them, one with the frame of a '55 Chevy sedan. Blue Gene was disappointed, since this sedan was painted bright red with yellow flames. But still, it was a Chevy.

"We're for the War Wagon," shouted Blue Gene. John nodded.

After a donut contest, two of the trucks, Full Boar and Extreme Overkill, returned to where they had come from, leaving the War Wagon to face off in a match race against Deep Fear, a Ford. Both trucks backed up side by side and revved their thunderous engines, each poised to demolish a row of junk cars. At the green light, they charged ahead, producing a staggering roar that caused women and children to recoil. Arthur looked shocked that anything could be so loud. He reached for his father, who put his arm around him and screamed, "It's okay!"

Meanwhile, Blue Gene kept his eyes on the War Wagon. The momentum of running into the first car pointed the War Wagon's hood toward the ceiling, sending it soaring for two seconds before it pounced mercilessly on top of the second car. The truck bounced recklessly over the next three cars, sending shards of glass into the air, forcefully denting their frames before landing on the concrete floor and finishing before Deep Fear. Occurring within the space of five seconds, this explosive display of industrial power sent the crowd into a frenzy.

"I don't know what it is, but I get off on that," said Blue Gene.

"I see what you mean," said John, petting his son and telling him not to be afraid.

The monster trucks took turns racing one another, flattening forsaken Oldsmobiles and Chevelles beyond repair, though none could match the unbridled might of the War Wagon. Through three more rounds of competition, the War Wagon shamelessly exhibited its powers of devastation, throwing around its ten thousand pounds like an abusively drunk giant, ravaging the junk cars to the point of obscenity.

As he watched, Blue Gene fought the urge to kick the hard plastic seat in front of him, to stomp it with the sole of his flip-flop and send a painful jolt through the spine of the man sitting there. He used to have the same wicked urge every time he went to a movie theater. But he didn't give in to the urge, and instead watched Arthur's reaction to the monster trucks. Arthur had gone limp, his back in the seat where his behind should've been.

After the hulking Chevy's convincing victory, the other three trucks retreated into the recesses of the civic center, now seeming docile compared with the intensity of the almighty War Wagon.

"Let's see if we can get a few words out of the War Wagon's driver, T.J. Durbin," said the MC, walking toward the triumphant monstrosity of an automobile. A pair of gloved hands poked out of the driver's side window and hoisted out a body in a black jumpsuit. The driver looked tiny next to his colossal vehicle. He jumped down to the arena floor, still wearing his helmet. Blue Gene was curious to see what kind of man was behind this machine.

"Congratulations on your victory tonight, T.J.," said the MC. The driver took off his helmet to speak, revealing neither a chiseled juggernaut with brutality in his eyes nor a fair-haired youth with a confident smile. It was a bony-faced old man with male-pattern baldness and white strands of hair behind his elongated ears.

$ $ $

By intermission, the civic center reeked of hot rubber and smoke. After the carnage of the monster-truck competition had come a much tamer round of four-wheeler "quad races" that interested the audience only when someone wrecked or fell off. Now, as the raucous Mötley Crüe anthem "Girls, Girls, Girls" played, people filed up the stairs to use the bathroom, buy overpriced refreshments, and have a smoke outside.

"What do you think, Arthur man?" asked Blue Gene.

Arthur shrugged his shoulders and rubbed his forearm across his nose. Then he inserted a finger in each nostril.

"You ain't scared of those trucks, are ya?"

"No!"

"How would you like to drive one of those big ol' trucks when you grow up?"

"I want one. I want to be friends with one. We could drive over bushes and signs."

"Hey, man, maybe Arthur's found his calling."

"No," said John. "I don't think he has."

Though he wasn't about to show it, the more John thought of Blue Gene's comment concerning his never having had a real job, the more it stung. It was true, his father had always been his boss, but that didn't mean his work was easy; Henry Mapother was a tyrant of an employer even to his own son. Furthermore, he actually did have a so-called "real job" once. As a teenager, he worked as a busboy at the Commonwealth County Country Club, but he was fired because he couldn't serve coffee or tea without spilling it, since his hands shook. Not long after that, John discovered that drugs and alcohol could keep his hands still, no matter how many people were around.

"I need to smoke a smoke," said Blue Gene. "Y'all wanna come outside with me?"

"No, but I have to use the restroom."

"A'ight."

Just as the three of them started walking toward the stairs, they heard a deep-voiced man yell, "Blue Gene." They looked up a few rows to see a burly biker in a black and orange Harley-Davidson T-shirt already leaving his seat and heading down to see Blue Gene. Blue Gene met the middle-aged man at the end of the row and shook his hand. To John, the man had the face of a stereotype. He was bearded and bandannaed, the same tough-guy biker-man whom he had seen speed past on a motorcycle a thousand times before, the one who was too cool to wear a helmet, too cool for car doors. John couldn't help but be proud of Blue Gene, though, for having a big biker-man go out of his way to talk to him.

"What's goin' on, big nuts? Anything good?"

The man laughed. "Same old, same old. Where you been?"

"Flea marketin'. D'you see my Chevy molestin' on your Fords down there?"

The biker's rotund stomach shook with laughter. "No, that's not what I saw. We must've been watching different programs." He started to scoot backward to let the well-dressed man behind Blue Gene pass through to the stairway. When John managed to make eye contact with the man and smiled, the man's face flared with surprise.

"Oh, yeah," said Blue Gene. "This here's my brother, John, and my nephew, Arthur."

John stepped around Blue Gene and took the biker's hand, making sure he gave it several firm pumps. "Nice to meet you. What's your name?"

"Jeff Stone. I actually think I work for you."

"You work at Westway?"

"Yes, sir."

"I thought you looked familiar. What department?"

"Shipping."

"Shipping. That's what I thought. You all sure are doing a fine job."

"Thank you."

"No, thank *you*." John tried to be as friendly as humanly possible, because he knew what his workers thought of him. From the go-getters in accounting to the dull-eyed guardians of the conveyor belts, everyone thought of him as the snob who never left his office, misinterpreting his aloofness as arrogance, never considering that the boss could be as anxiety-ridden as anyone.

"Me and Jeff are ol' wrestlin' buddies," said Blue Gene. "He was always down at the armory when they had wrestlin' there."

"Still am. We've been missing you."

"I've missed y'all. What's your son been up to?"

"Oh. Guess you haven't heard. He got sent overseas."

"Really?"

"Yeah. Got an email from him earlier today. Said those guys whose chopper went down last week were in his regiment."

John reared his head back in surprise. Several of his employees at Westway had gone off to war, but he hadn't spoken to them directly, since there were so many managers between him and his factory workers. To hear someone talk about his own son being in the war intrigued him.

"Dang," said Blue Gene. "How's he doin'?"

"He's all right. Homesick. Misses his wife. She's been staying with us."

"Is Matt back yet?"

"Actually, since I saw you last, Matt's come back and left again for a second tour."

"Damn," said Blue Gene. "Well, I'd be right there with 'em if it wasn't for this bum leg of mine."

"Yeah. Well, I better be getting back to my kids, but it was nice seeing you."

"You too, Jeff."

"Come down to the armory sometime."

"I will."

"Nice to meet you, Jeff," said John.

"You, too," he said. "So long, Blue Gene."

"So long you couldn't handle it," Blue Gene said with his usual deadpan delivery. Jeff walked away laughing.

"Nice guy," said John as he followed Blue Gene up the steps.

"Yep." Ted Nugent's "Cat Scratch Fever" came on over the PA.

"You should always introduce people if they don't know one another."

"I *know* that. Don't be talkin' down to me. I just couldn't remember his name."

"He sure remembered yours."

They reached the top of the steps and walked through a short corridor.

"So you got friends in the war?" asked John.

"Yeah. Two or three, and then some acquaintances. One of my acquaintances got killed. Man, I hate to hear that. Somebody goin' over there twice, and here I am, haven't even fought once. But at least I tried. Went down to the National Guard and told 'em they could give me a physical or whatever, and they did, but they said with my leg the way it is, there's no way they could take me."

"You mean you tried to enlist?" asked John.

"Yeah."

"You feel that strongly?"

"Well, hell yeah, I feel that strong. I wanna defend my country. I've always wanted to defend my country. Here—bathroom's that way. I'll meet you back at our seats."

"You know, I think we'll join you."

So the three of them walked outside, where it was still hot even with the sun going down. John could see why Blue Gene wore shorts and T-shirts with the sleeves cut off, and though he'd never be caught wearing such an outfit in public, he recognized the appeal in Blue Gene's apparel: it was exactly what Blue Gene wanted to be wearing.

Despite the heat, John liked it better outside. There was more space, and he could get away easily if he had to. He made sure Blue Gene's cigarette smoke went nowhere near Arthur, who was walking the curb like a tightrope.

"I know those folks pretty well," said Blue Gene, nodding toward a couple who was waving at him with cigarettes in their mouths. "I reckon I better say hi to 'em."

John and Arthur followed as Blue Gene walked over to a mustached, goateed man in cowboy boots with a tobacco canister in the back pocket of his skintight Wranglers. He was around Blue Gene's age, and accompanied by a little girl and a big-boned tan woman with a rose tattoo on her calf. Blue Gene introduced them as Steve and his woman and their daughter.

John wasn't a smoker, but he stood in the smokers' circle, holding Arthur's hand. Arthur and the little girl both hid behind their parents' legs, peeking at each other. John wished adults could do that sort of thing instead of having to talk. He hung back without talking, but then felt self-conscious for being so quiet. He tried to come up with a topic, but all he could think of was how hot it was, and it was such a cliché to talk about the weather, and in this postmodern age it was even a cliché to point out how clichéd talking about the weather was, but to bring up that point might be over their heads. So he remained silent and observed how Blue Gene interacted with the commoners. He envied how talking to these people came so easily to Blue Gene, who clearly knew how to smoothly navigate their folkways. Blue Gene was by no means convivial, looking as gloomy as ever among the group, but he had a talent for offering pithy, entertaining commentary on any topic from the best Laundromats in town to snakebites to rifled slugs.

Once the talk turned to war, John was pleased to hear that he already spoke the same language as these people. Now, if only he could look natural in a pair of jeans and learn what terms like *off-road suspension* meant and use a double negative without hurting his tongue.

The political slant of the conversation soon tilted back to wildlife.

"Haven't seen you down at the goose pit in years, Blue Gene," said Steve, who had a short, curly mullet. That Blue Gene had continued hunting through the years came as a surprise to John. He figured Blue Gene would've rejected it, since he rejected everything else that John and his dad liked.

"Yeah. I been busy flea marketin'," said Blue Gene, pride in his voice.

"That's cool. What you selling?"

"Ah, just various stuff."

"Hey—you selling any your guns?"

"Dream on, dreamer. You ain't gettin' any my girls." Among Blue

Gene's guns were some valuable vintage rifles that his father had bought him. As Steve and his lady friend laughed, Blue Gene started digging in one of his pockets. "That reminds me. Hey, Arthur and—what's your name?" he asked the little girl. She wouldn't answer.

"That's Charla," said her mom.

"Hey, Charla and Arthur. Y'all check this out. If anybody makes me mad, you know what I do? You know what I show 'em?"

"What?" asked Arthur with a grin.

Blue Gene pulled his hand out of his pocket and held up a bullet. He picked a piece of pocket lint off it and continued holding it up, staring at Arthur and the girl as if he were waiting for a response.

"It's a bullet," said Arthur.

"That's right," said Blue Gene, putting the bullet back in his pocket. "Show 'em I mean business."

"So if someone makes you mad, you hold a bullet up to them?" asked Steve.

"Yep. Just hold it up to 'em and don't say a word. They know what I mean."

"Blue Gene's a straight-up trip," said the woman with a laugh. She wore an oversize T-shirt that read: DANGER: HIGH-VOLTAGE BITCH.

"You don't carry a piece on you?" asked Steve.

"Nah. My luck, it's liable to go off in my shorts," said Blue Gene. "Blow my scrote to hell."

"Not if you have your safety on," John chimed in. "Of course, you know that." Blue Gene shot a quick, annoyed look at John. "Say," he said, wanting to avoid an argument in front of the people. "If you all aren't doing anything on the Fourth of July, we'd love to have you at the Ambassador Inn. We're going to have a huge fireworks display."

"That's cool," said Steve.

"The whole town's invited," said Blue Gene. "He's runnin' for Congress."

This got everyone's attention.

"I lost my driver's license," said the woman. "You think you can do something about that?"

"Do you mean in terms of getting you your license back, or changing the laws, or...?"

"I's just kiddin'," said the woman with a big laugh.

"Oh. Me too."

"No, but don't get me wrong. If you could help me, that'd be awesome. But I's just kiddin'."

"Can you do anything about that smoking ban?" asked Steve.

"Possibly. Obviously, there's no doubt about my being against it, since my family owns Westway."

"That's right. Hey—Blue Gene, how come in all the years I known you, you never once let on that your family owned the tobacco company?"

"Never come up, I guess. And didn't want you askin' if I could get your cheap ass some free cigarettes."

Everyone laughed.

"*Could* you?" asked Steve.

As more laughter came and went, Arthur and the little girl started to warm up to each other. Arthur broke the ice by making a flatulent noise with his mouth, but then the angry roar of a motor caused everyone to turn. It came from a black Dodge Ram pickup truck speeding past them. The truck had extra-large wheels and half a dozen SUPPORT OUR TROOPS magnets.

"There goes Balsam," said Steve, "showin' off his new truck. He spent ever dime he got from his dad dying on that truck. His last truck—this is funny—he was wanting to piss off the gay people he was in school with, so on his tailgate he had a big picture of the Incredible Hulk, and he had the Hulk saying, HULK SMASH QUEERS! and off to the side it said, NO FAMILY VALUES."

"Can you *do* that?" asked Blue Gene.

"Well, nobody stopped him that I know of."

"Freedom of speech," said John.

"That's hilarious," said Blue Gene. "Who is this guy?"

"Name's Josh Balsam. He's just a kid, seventeen or eighteen, but you wouldn't know it 'cause he's a big ol' boy."

"Dad?" said Arthur.

"Yes?"

"How come he parks like that?" Arthur pointed to the black pickup backing into a space.

"I guess he thinks it'll make it easier to pull out when he leaves," said John.

"That there's the way a *man* parks," said Blue Gene.

The driver smoothly backed his truck between the lines, revealing the vanity plate on its front: a Confederate flag over which the initials J.A.B. appeared.

"That boy's ornery as hell," said Steve. "I used to work with him at Alliance. He was ornery then, and that was *before* his dad got killed."

The figure lingered in the truck, smoking.

"How'd his dad get killed?" asked Blue Gene.

"In the war. One of them IEDs or whatever they call 'em blew up underneath him."

This was what John had assumed. A Balsam had been on the front page of the *Register* a month or so ago for posthumously receiving a Purple Heart for saving several other people.

"One time I seen Balsam get in a fight with a boy at a party," said Steve. "And he took the boy's head and rammed his temple into the corner of a table. I seen it firsthand. Boy never talked right since."

"Dang," said Blue Gene.

From the truck emerged well over six feet of white meat, held tightly together with muscle and rigid posture. He strode across the parking lot with a gait so aggressive that each step seemed to attack the pavement.

"Hey, Balsam!" yelled Steve. "Like your truck! Bet you got some pipes on her." Balsam headed over to the smoking circle while lighting a cigarette. "Y'all, this is Josh Balsam."

John offered his hand to Balsam and made a point of making eye contact, though it seemed not to matter, since Balsam's eyes had such a blank expression, like grapes with vision.

"John Mapother," he said. "Nice to meet you."

"W'sup," Balsam replied, shaking John's hand. It was quite possibly the firmest handshake John had ever felt.

"You're Lucas Pritchett's cousin, ain't ya?" asked Blue Gene.

"Yeah."

"Yeah, we met before out at Lucas's. What's Lucas been up to?"

"Nothin'."

Balsam took a forceful drag from his cigarette. He wore slightly baggy blue jeans, white Nike basketball shoes, and a wife-beater tank top that revealed fierce, jagged tattoos on both arms. His buzz cut was so short that it was impossible to determine his hair color.

Steve complimented Balsam's newest tattoo, a portrait of his father on his right bicep, with the date of his death underneath.

"I was thinkin about gettin' a teardrop done on my face for him, too." When Balsam spoke at length, his voice took on a mellow slur. "But I'm gonna wait till after my next court date, 'cause the judge would judge me if he saw a tattoo on my face. My dad said never get a tattoo that couldn't be covered up in front of a judge."

"Why you going to court?" asked Steve.

"So maybe they'll let me see my daughter. Her mom's family won't let me go near her 'cause they think I'm crazy. But I just wanna see my kid. I already got one daughter I can't fuckin' see."

"You still with Amber?" asked Steve.

"She's the one that won't let me see my baby. Shit. That stupid bitch been knocked up twice. One ain't mine. How fuckin' hard is it to not get pregnant? All she had to do in life is not get pregnant, and she couldn't even do that."

Blue Gene nodded, as if to say, "Ain't that the truth." John wished there was a subtle way to put the earplugs back in Arthur's ears.

"Man, you gotta be careful with those teardrop tattoos, though," said Blue Gene. "I worked with a guy, said his brother got two tattoos, one for each of the guys he killed in prison, but the guy who done the tattoos in prison wasn't too good an artist. So it ended up lookin' like he had a couple a little turds on his face."

Everybody laughed. John was amazed to see that even Balsam, in his stern detachment, cracked a smile.

"After I get a teardrop on my face," said Balsam, looking at Blue Gene, "I'm gonna get me a tattoo of a woman's leg going down my arm." He pointed to the inside of his impressive bicep. "And then I'd like her other leg to be tattooed down my side," he said, pointing up and down his rib cage, "and then when I lift my arm up, it'd cause her to spread and you'd see my armpit hair in the middle."

Though he found the seriousness with which Balsam presented his tattoo idea to be disconcerting, John laughed along with everyone else. Seeing that Arthur and the little girl were both staring at Balsam with looks of fear on their little faces, John picked Arthur up. Arthur put his arm around his father's neck.

"Yeah, well, I's thinking about gettin' me a tattoo of a naked lady on the insides of my eyelids," countered Blue Gene. "That way, every time I close my eyes, I'd have something nice to look at."

Balsam retorted immediately. "My friend had a tattoo of a naked woman all laid out on his forearm, and he was always shootin' up meth, so he had it so his vein was right in between the naked woman's titties so he could always find his vein easy."

"I better take Arthur to the restroom," interjected John. "Nice to meet you all. Oh, and before I go, Josh, I just want to tell you how much I appreciate the sacrifice your father made for all of us." John shook Balsam's hand again. "On the Fourth of July—"

Arthur shifted his position in John's arms, getting a tighter grip on his father.

"Ooh, Daddy! You're all wet. Grody!"

John set Arthur down as everyone snickered. He could feel redness creeping around the edges of his ears, a sign that he was about to have what he knew only to call a hot flash. "Well, nice to meet you all. I better get him to the restroom." And he took Arthur by the hand and headed toward the civic center.

"Now, Arthur, what did I tell you about embarrassing me in public?"

"You said don't do it. But Daddy, why are you so wet?"

"Because I'm sweating! It's hot out here. Don't embarrass me like that again! Don't ever make any comments about how I'm sweaty."

"I'm sorry."

"That's okay. Just don't do it again. Nobody likes to be embarrassed."

"But you're always embarrassed."

"Not always. Just in public."

$ $ $

The show had already resumed by the time Blue Gene joined John and Arthur back at their seats. Hot Rod the Clown was entertaining the children by riding a tiny motorcycle, and amusing the adults by telling Viagra jokes. He then introduced the freestyle BMX team. On a ramp that had been set up during intermission, the bicyclists performed stunts with dangerous names like "cliffhanger" and "kiss of death," none of which could hold Blue Gene's or John's attention.

"So how well do you know that Balsam boy?" John asked, holding a bottle of water. He put his other hand on Arthur's leg because he was fidgeting.

"Not well. I just met him once before. Used to be friends with his cousin." Blue Gene vaguely remembered meeting Balsam out at his friend's barn in the country years ago, probably when Balsam was barely even a teenager, but both he and Balsam were messed up at the time on pot and hooch.

"Oh."

Blue Gene gobbled some nachos, occasionally licking salt and cheese off his fingers. He offered John some. John declined. Then he changed his mind and ate a single nacho.

"I was thinking," John said. "His dad is a hometown hero, don't you think?"

"Of course he is. If it weren't for men like him fighting over there, they'd all be comin' over here, wantin' to fight us here on our turf."

"I think we should have some kind of special tribute for him at my rally. Maybe I could present something to his son. What do you think?"

"That's righteous." With a chip, Blue Gene shoveled a clump of cheese into his mouth.

"I thought maybe if you knew his son well enough, you could call him for me and ask him if he'd like to participate. I figured he'd be more likely to do it if *you* asked him."

"I don't know him well enough to call him. And I don't know if I'd *want* that dude to participate."

"Well, I certainly wouldn't have him *speak*. But it's for his dad. Don't you think his dad deserves more recognition than just a feature in the *Register*? He died for our freedom."

"Don't even act like I don't support our troops, John."

"I support our troops, too. That's why I want to do this. The man deserves some respect. And I bet his son has never received any sort of praise or recognition in all his life. His father was good to his country, and now it's time for his country to be good to him."

"A'ight. But what are you thinkin'? Would you give his son like a scholarship or something?"

Arthur was looking up at the rafters and kicking at the air.

"Sit still," said John. "Maybe that, or maybe an American flag folded into a triangle. Maybe some sort of plaque or medal."

Blue Gene nodded. He always got goosebumps when he saw servicemen folding the flag so perfectly while taps played.

Arthur suddenly climbed into his father's lap and held his arm up to Blue Gene's face. "Smell my muscle!" he said, pretending to be tough.

"*Smell* your muscle?" asked Blue Gene.

"It's just something he likes to say," said John. "When he first started talking, I tried to teach him to say, '*Feel* my muscle' because I thought it would be funny. But it kept coming out as '*Smell* my muscle,' and he found he's always able to get a laugh out of it, so he still does it."

"Smell my muscle!" Arthur repeated. Blue Gene took Arthur's pudgy arm and smelled it.

"Smells strong."

"Can we go now?" asked Arthur.

"Yeah, how much longer is this thing?" asked John, checking his Rolex.

"I don't know, but we gotta stay for Truckasaurus or whatever he's called. The deal was y'all had to stay for the whole thing."

John took a big swallow of bottled water. "That's fine. Arthur, watch the bike riders, okay?" Arthur pouted and then started swinging his head all around, making the shape of an infinity sign. "I think Balsam will be much more likely to do it if you're the one asking. Won't you do it for me?"

"Yeah." Ever since the war had started, Blue Gene had wanted to contribute somehow. Even though calling Balsam was a minor task, he saw that he finally had a chance to help out with the cause. "I reckon I can track down his number."

"Great!"

The cyclists continued to soar through the air. Hundreds of cameras flashed each time one of them was in flight, and Blue Gene held up his middle finger.

"Stop that," said John. But he was laughing.

"So if I get Balsam to come to your rally, does that mean you won't need *me* at the rally no more?"

"Oh, no. I still need you there. You're not getting off that easily. Without you, I'd have no street cred."

"What you talkin' 'bout? I don't got no street cred."

"Oh, come on. I saw tonight what a popular guy you are. People love you. Hey, let me ask you something. If you have so many friends, then why did you ask Arthur and me to come?"

Blue Gene considered the question as he licked cheese off his mustache.

"I guess 'cause with y'all, I knew I could be myself. When you hang out with your friends, you have to put on a show, act like you're happy even when you're not."

"You're not happy?"

"I'm a'ight. Just tired."

"Well, I'm glad you asked us to come."

"You only came 'cause I made you."

"Yes, but I mean it. It's been nice to spend some time with you. I've missed you, Blue Gene." John cleared his throat as if to erase the emotion stuck to his vocal chords. "Arthur, you're making me hot again." Arthur got back in his seat.

"Hey, if you win the election—"

"*When* I win the election," John corrected.

"Whatever. *When* you win the election—you know how Steve's wife was askin' you about her driver's license?"

"Yes."

"Well, do you think you could get me *my* driver's license back?"

John laughed. "Are you serious?"

"Yeah."

"I'm not sure, but I'll see what I can do. In the meantime, let me get you a driver to take you around."

"Ah, hell nah. I don't need no chauffeur. Lots of people drive without licenses. But I'd still prefer to have one, though, so I wouldn't have to worry 'bout the pigs so much. I just figured that since Dad got your DUI expunged—he did do that, didn't he?"

"Yes."

"I figured if Dad could do that and he wasn't even holdin' office, then surely a congressman could do it."

"Not necessarily. Dad has way more clout than most congressmen. A lot of the politicians work for *him*."

It was true. As Jackie Stepchild would later explain to Blue Gene, in all the elections, both state and national, the most powerful men, like Henry Mapother, often made generous contributions to both candidates so that they could have access to the winner regardless of the outcome.

"Why don't you just ask Dad for help?"

"No way. Dad hates me."

"He does not."

"Yeah huh."

The bicyclists were now performing their gravity-defying finales as some fast, punky song that Blue Gene had never heard played in the background.

Arthur yawned and leaned his head against John's arm. "Can we go?" he asked.

"We gotta wait for Truckasaurus, little man," said Blue Gene. "He's a dinosaur. You like dinosaurs, don't you?"

"He had a dinosaur phase," said John. "Lately he's really into the planets."

"We went to the planetarium and saw explosions," said Arthur.

"Yeah. We took him to the planetarium at the Museum of Natural History in New York."

"I remember they had some really cool dinosaurs there," said Blue Gene.

"Yes, and I remember we went there just for you because you wanted to see the dinosaurs. Don't be so down on Dad. He was good about including you—including *all* of us—on his trips. He and Mom never took a vacation by themselves. They always brought you and me. That's rare for parents. So don't go around saying that he hates you. Don't be an ingrate."

"I'm just sayin' I don't wanna ask him for a favor pertainin' to me gettin' another DUI, 'cause that'd be one more thing he'd use to lord over me. And I don't care what you say. He's had it in for me ever since I could remember. I don't wanna give him any more fuel, you know what I mean?"

John nodded.

"Hey, man. Did he ever spank your friends?"

"*What?*"

"When you were little and you had friends over, did he ever spank your friends when they did something wrong?"

John laughed. "No. He did that to *your* friends?"

"Yes," said Blue Gene, emphatically. "Just once, but still. You remember my best friend growin' up, Mitchell Gibson?"

"Yeah."

"One time Mitchell and me was playin', and we were doin' something Dad didn't like, and first he gave us a warning, and I don't remember what it was we did, but whatever it was, we must have done it again, 'cause he took me aside and spanked me real good. That right there was embarrassing enough to happen with my friend watchin', but then, I'll be damned if he didn't pull Mitchell aside and spank him just like he done me."

"Really?" John laughed.

"It ain't funny! Rest of the day, Mitchell was all quiet and wanted to go home. He never wanted to come back to my house again. Stopped inviting me over, too. I hated Dad for that."

"I had never heard anything about that."

"That's 'cause you was always runnin' around. Did he ever spank you?"

"Yeah, but spanking you and me was one thing. I think that was okay."

"Yeah."

"But he definitely overstepped a boundary when he did that to your friend."

"I hear that. He wasn't thinkin' 'bout boundaries, that's for sure."

"I shouldn't have let that go on. If I'd have known, I'd have said something."

"Wasn't your place to do anything about it."

"Do you need any money?" asked John hurriedly. "Is there anything I can do for you?"

"No. I wouldn't take money from you."

"It wouldn't be from me. You have your own coming to you, don't forget."

"Don't want it. Why you askin'?"

"I hate to see you living in that dinky little trailer."

"I don't expect you to understand, but I like it there just fine."

"I understand."

$ $ $

After another lackluster four-wheeler race and one more quick monster-truck exhibition, the house lights were turned off for the grand finale, Truckasaurus, which entered the arena in the form of a tank with no turret. Arthur had finally settled down and was resting his head on John's shoulder. John had become sleepy once he and Blue Gene had stopped conversing. There was something about the constant, steady murmur of a stadium audience that always made John drowsy. But his drowsiness was spiked with worry, because he could feel anger coming from the next seat.

"Are you mad?" John finally asked.

"No. Just don't be talkin' 'bout how I live."

"Okay. I won't. You know, you and I aren't that different, really."

"I *said* don't worry about it. It's all good."

"Just hear me out. I want us to get along."

As eerie music played, a recorded voice explained the robot's fictional origin: a juvenile yarn about how scientists built him to destroy mutants on a remote island, and how his mechanical heart pumped fifty gallons of gasoline per minute.

"Sure," John went on, "we have different lifestyles, different looks, but being here with you tonight, hearing you talk to your friends, I've realized that we're actually a lot alike."

A spotlight shined on the top of the tank, from which a metallic *Tyrannosaurus rex* slowly unfolded itself.

"Are you seein' this, Arthur?" asked Blue Gene.

"Yeah," he said, half-asleep.

"Our values are the same," John continued. "And that's what matters. We're different on the outside. I wear a suit and you wear what you wear, but on the inside, our values are the same."

Blue Gene said nothing, watching Truckasaurus breathe fire from its nostrils, leaning over and trapping a junk car in its gigantic clamp hands.

"Are you even listening to me?" asked John.

"Yeah. Our values are the same, and that's what matters, right?"

"Right."

"I'm with you. I agree."

Truckasaurus lifted the junk car up to its sharp steel teeth and closed its jaws, tearing into the car, to the audience's delight.

"Are you just saying that, or do you really believe it?"

"Uh-huh."

The mechanical dinosaur was having trouble slicing completely through the car's frame.

"Damnit, Blue Gene! You're like a little kid. I'm trying to talk to you here."

"Jesus, John, I'm trying to watch this dinosaur eat a car!"

John waited for the dinosaur to finish. Both halves of the car plummeted to the concrete floor, and Truckasaurus started to back away from his kill.

"It's just important that you see that even though we have our differences, we believe in the same things."

"I know. I hear you, man," said Blue Gene, now giving John his full attention. "Just the fact that you're willin' to have that Balsam dude at your rally, that tells me something. You got some good ideas. You got my vote."

"*Really*?"

"Really."

The house lights came back on, and Truckasaurus now appeared to be smiling. At a snail's pace, he left the arena floor in reverse. Inexplicably, "Don't You Forget About Me" served as the soundtrack for this moment.

"Is that the song from *The Breakfast Club*?!" asked Blue Gene.

"Yeah. That's really inappropriate for that thing's exit," said John. "Not the right tone at all."

"That's the gayest thing I've ever seen."

"It *is* awfully gay."

The MC thanked everyone for coming and invited them to come back next year. The people had already begun to file out of the arena.

"See, that wasn't so bad, was it?" asked Blue Gene as he and John stood. John carried Arthur, who was drifting in and out of consciousness.

"They put on a good show," said John, taking one last look at the crowd.

The three of them joined everyone else in a sluggish exodus to the congested parking lot. Neither John nor Blue Gene spoke on the way out. Once they were in John's Escalade, with Arthur sound asleep in the backseat, John remembered a loose end from earlier. He considered explaining to Blue Gene that the phrase he was trying to come up with earlier was "universal central nervous system death," which wasn't nearly as ghastly as it sounded because it was the quickest, most painless way to end the war that was to end all wars and fulfill his mother's prophecy of the eternal peace. But he knew that since Blue Gene didn't seem to believe Elizabeth's dream was anything more than a dream, bringing up the topic would likely start another argument. So John kept quiet and let Blue Gene pick a radio station, rather than having him listen to "Sleepers, Awake!"

IV.

Outside, it felt like the date: July fourth. Sticky heat enveloped Blue Gene as he started the long walk to the hotel. Tired as usual, and not eager to put on a happy campaign act, he had waited until the last possible minute to arrive at John's rally. He had to park way down Main Street—coincidentally, in front of the building Elizabeth had said would be used for the Mapother campaign headquarters. He preferred not to walk long distances because he didn't like calling attention to his limp, and he had briefly considered using the valet service that was being offered tonight at the Ambassador Inn, but he could just see the clean-cut teenage valet boys exchanging looks once they saw they were going to park such an unfashionable piece of junk as a 1988 S-10 with numerous decals, including 110% BAD-ASS in fierce white letters on the front windshield and SIZE DOES MATTER between the sprawling antlers of a deer on the back windshield. They'd have no idea that the man in the cruddy old truck had helped orchestrate tonight's rally, which in the last four weeks had been transformed into "Westway International Presents: An American Soldier—A Tribute to Tim Balsam."

Blue Gene ended up enjoying the chance to walk, though, because downtown Bashford had a certain feeling. It was like you became a part of the past when you were there. He wished he had a reason to go downtown more often. He liked exchanging a quick nod or a gruff hello with folks on the sidewalks. Unlike in bigger cities, it wouldn't be an inconvenience to greet each passerby here, since there were so few. Other than the post office and three banks, there were no places of business down-town that encouraged a continual flow of customers. Despite the mea-ger amount of traffic and the vacant buildings, city officials said the area was in the process of revitalization. They had been saying this for more than thirty years.

As in any other downtown in America, every place in downtown Bashford had once been some other establishment, which in most cases had at least ten previous incarnations, none even one-quarter as suc-cessful as the original. The building currently known as the Ambassador Inn, for instance, had emptied twice and changed its name and man-agement four times since the 1960s. In its heyday, its showroom had at-tracted some big-name talent, like Lou Rawls and Loretta Lynn. Nowadays, the shows there were few and far between, and the perform-ers who did come were either on their way up or on their way down.

As he continued down Main Street, Blue Gene noticed how every building was connected to the next and imagined them as one immense building with no walls in between, a superstructure that took up a whole block where the entire town could gather at once. Currently occupying these buildings were a few law offices, a couple of shoe stores, an antique mall, a pawn shop, a musical instrument store, and various gift shops, all family owned, all closed at five and on the weekends. Blue Gene had al-ways wanted to live in one of the apartments above these stores so that he could watch all the happenings during the Nut-Fest, a street festival he used to faithfully attend every October to eat funnel cakes and bar-becue sandwiches, drink lemon shake-ups, and ride the rides, which had been known to lose parts while careening through the air. He had al-ways thought it would be funny to propose to Cheyenne inside their fa-vorite ride at the Nut-Fest, the Gravitron, but their living arrangement suited him fine the way it was.

Tonight, the sidewalks were more active than usual, and all of the diagonal parking spaces up and down Main Street were taken. "A Trib-ute to Tim Balsam" had been advertised in the *Register* and all the other major papers of the district every day the past week. John's campaign staff canvassed the entire district by phone, and while they had potential voters on the line, they invited them to the tribute. Meanwhile, many of Henry's and John's associates and friends had received personal invitations in the mail.

Blue Gene walked as slowly as possible. The Mapothers had hosted dozens of social events through the years, but he hadn't been to one since he was seventeen. Before he turned the corner that would lead him to the hotel, he decided to stop in front of the musical instrument store and smoke a cigarette. He puffed and blew and relieved himself of sputum before some words on the store window caught his eye:

"UNCLE SAM'S FINGER"

It was a flyer a madman must have made, its letters assembled in the style of ransom notes from the movies, its border made of decapitated heads from celebrity magazines—Justin Timberlake, Pamela Anderson, R. Kelly, Ashlee Simpson—all with X's over their eyes. "UNCLE SAM'S FINGER, Corpsegas, and Huey Newton and the Lose," the flyer read. "Live, 4th of July, Basement at 884 S. Elm, 9:00 p.m. FREE!"

This sounded like a lot more fun than the event he was headed to, but Blue Gene reminded himself that the tribute to Tim Balsam actually meant something. It was his chance to show appreciation for a man who had died for his country, and he was proud that he had helped make this night possible. So he flicked his cigarette to the sidewalk and checked his reflection in the music store window before making adjustments to his hair. For once, he wasn't wearing a cap.

$ $ $

Red, white, and blue dominated the showroom, from the centerpieces on the tables to the banners streaming across the ceiling. The luxurious venue was crammed with smiling, sociable people, some sitting at round tables covered in white tablecloths, some congregating in dense huddles on the room's margins, pressed toward the glass walls that provided a scenic view of the sun descending over the river. People were starting to line up for the buffet, which featured catfish and prime rib, cornbread and croissants.

The long, sprawling Vegas-style showroom, with three levels of seating, contained a mixture of people rarely found within any single place in Commonwealth County. At one table sat a group of factory workers who had never tipped a bellboy in their lives, and who could be heard comparing their motorboats. At the next table sat some VIPs with master's degrees who had never participated in a tailgate party, and who could be heard discussing the waterfront properties where they summered. Not far from a six-pack of long-bearded, God-fearing Vietnam vets was a highborn assortment of old friends whose Mercedes logos preceded them wherever they drove, often on streets that bore their surnames.

Henry Mapother had made this fusion of societal species possible; it was his idea and his money that had provided for this evening in the first place. He made sure certain tables were reserved for his friends and business associates: gray or graying colleagues, like the man who once lured Elvis Presley to one of his extravagant soirées, only to refuse to shake his hand; a famed college basketball coach who had raised more money for dying children than anyone else in the country; a local anchorwoman who had once had an affair with the mayor; the mayor and a scattering of former congressmen; and a self-made millionaire whose mother and wife had died within the same week. As bowing waiters served them aperitifs, some of these upper-echelon citizens of Bashford sat back and observed the meaner, wilder element that increased by the truckload with each passing minute.

$ $ $

"Not a college degree among them, I bet."

"Be nice. It isn't easy living check to check, you know."

"Sure. It just goes to show how badly Mapother wants this."

"Oh, does he ever. He's wanted it since before his boy was even born."

"I actually think I see his younger boy over there."

"Where?"

"On his way in. In the American flag shirt."

"You must be joking."

"I'm not. I had heard he let himself go after that accident. See, that has to be him. He's got a little limp, poor thing."

"He's so…he's not so well-groomed, is he?"

"Elizabeth had him thirteen years after John was born. Maybe by the time this one came along, all the grooming had been used up on John."

"Oh, yes. That's one thing that can be said for John. No one's ever been so well-groomed."

$ $ $

As he walked further into the showroom, Blue Gene was overcome by the garble of a few hundred people combined with the country song "Have You Forgotten?" His father was standing at the bar in the corner, surrounded by several familiar faces Blue Gene hadn't seen since he was a teenager, except on the local news.

Underneath fluorescent but dimmed lighting that gave the scene a soft, surreal glow, he saw other aged faces from his childhood, but more than anything, he saw people he recognized from the flea market, Wal-Mart, and other frill-free Bashford hot spots such as the bowling alley. Blue Gene wondered what he should do with himself. He had never been around his family and their kind of people and *his* kind of people at the same time. He imagined how a conversation with an old buddy of his and Cheyenne's might lead to talk of how the Mapothers were a bunch of two-faced bastards. He stood near the entrance and squirmed until he saw Elizabeth leaning over one of the tables of better-dressed diners. He looked at her helplessly until she saw him and walked over.

"Hi, Gene!"

"Hey, Mom."

Before he knew it, she was picking stray hairs off his shirt. "You have razor burn on your throat. You should be more careful."

"Shouldn't have even bothered shavin'. Just tryin' to look nice."

"Oh, you do, you do. You look fine. Your shirt is so appropriate for the occasion. How have things been going at the flea market?"

"Slow as usual. I'm finally gonna have to give it up pretty soon."

"I'm sorry to hear that."

"It don't matter. I reckon I can get my old job back at Wal-Mart."

"What about the job John offered you?"

In the last several weeks, John had twice offered Blue Gene a full-time job on his campaign staff: once when he invited Blue Gene over for pizza, and once when he called his trailer just to talk. He told Blue Gene that he had been thinking about it, and after seeing him interact with the people at the truck rally, and after seeing how similar their priorities were, it only made sense to make Blue Gene a major part of the campaign staff. He said he could see Blue Gene becoming his right-hand man, and not just for this first campaign, either.

"I ain't interested in that."

"Why not?" asked Elizabeth.

"It ain't a real job. I don't wanna be workin' for my brother."

"Why hello, Elizabeth!" said a loud voice from behind.

"Ellen! Look at you. You look darling." Elizabeth and the woman hugged. They were both wearing pantsuits.

"Oh, my," said the woman. "This is quite a crowd."

"I haven't seen you for so long," said Elizabeth. "Do you still live in that beautiful home on Water Street?"

"Why, *yes*. Did someone tell you I didn't live there anymore? Who told you that?"

"No. No one told me that. That's not what I meant, dear."

"We would never move out of that house."

"I wouldn't either. It's a lovely home. Ellen, this is Gene."

"Hello. Oh—why, is this *your* Gene?" Blue Gene's sunken eyes dropped down to the frumpy, generic white tennis shoes he had picked tonight over flip-flops.

"It sure is," said Elizabeth, patting Blue Gene's hair into place. "All grown up, isn't he? Gene, this is Ellen Fitzsimmons, Dr. Fitzsimmons' wife."

"How are ya, Mrs. Fitzsimmons?"

"I haven't seen you since you were a little boy. Where have you been hiding yourself?"

"He stays awfully busy," said Elizabeth.

"Was he a Harvard man like John?"

"No. He decided he wanted to stay close to home."

"There's nothing wrong with that. Where'd you go?"

"Actually, I ended up not goin' to college."

"Oh. Well, college isn't for everybody."

"No, ma'am."

"Ellen, we've saved you and Allen a seat up front. Just have that hostess there seat you."

"Thank you. Great to see both of you. And you let me know if you remember who it was that told you we had moved."

Elizabeth turned back to Blue Gene and smiled. "Don't feel bad, Gene. You know, I didn't finish college. I married Henry instead. Of course, it was different back then, but anyway, don't feel bad."

"I don't. So here I am. What am I supposed to do?"

"I'm not certain. Let's see. Where's John?" They looked all over the showroom but couldn't find him. "He must be backstage. I'll go find him."

"Hold up. Where am I supposed to sit?"

"I don't know. Wherever you want, I suppose. Let me go find John."

"Is that a cash bar?" asked Blue Gene, seeing a second, smaller bar set up across the room.

"Yes, but here." Elizabeth reached inside her little black handbag and pulled out some perforated tickets. "You can get free drinks with these. I've been giving them out to friends."

Blue Gene hesitated before thanking her for a few tickets. Elizabeth went to look for John, and Blue Gene headed over to the cash bar and asked the white-jacketed server if any draft beer was available. It wasn't, and the server showed Blue Gene a row of beer bottles, both domestic and imported, as well as some wines. He chose a Bud Light, which would have set him back $3.50 without the ticket. Feeling guilty that others had to pay for their drinks, Blue Gene left two dollars in the tip glass.

After throwing away the napkin the server gave him, Blue Gene was again faced with not knowing his place in the room.

He felt a rush of relief when he saw his nephew sitting with Abby at a table in front of the stage, which was draped in bunting. Careful not to bump into anyone, he snuck his way to the front.

"What do you say, Fraggle Rock?"

"Hey, Blue Gene," replied Arthur, who was wearing a suit and tie.

"Hey, Abby Road."

"Hello." Her cheerless tone clued Blue Gene not to pursue a conversation. But Arthur kept grinning. Blue Gene shook the little boy's hand as if he were just another adult with a wife, kids, and a 401(k). Then he squatted down so he could see Arthur better, and Arthur soon had a strand of Blue Gene's mullet between his fingers. Arthur placed it underneath his nose to make it look like he had a mustache.

"Let go of his hair, sweetheart," said Abby.

"It's okay," said Blue Gene. "You look nice in your suit, Arthur."

"Dad made me wear it. My throat hurts." Arthur tugged at his collar. "Watch this." Arthur took a drink from his glass of water, tilted his head back slightly, and gurgled a familiar melody.

"That's good," said Blue Gene, holding back a laugh since his nephew had put so much effort into his performance. "Was that that song off *Dirty Dancing*?"

Arthur swallowed his water. "Yes. It's 'I Had the Time of My Life.'"

Blue Gene gave Arthur and Abby a funny look.

"I let him watch it. I fast-forwarded through the dirty parts."

"He *wanted* to watch it?"

"Yeah," answered Abby.

"Huh. Oh well. Hey, Abby, do you know if I'm supposed to sit with y'all or what?"

"No."

Blue Gene sighed. A tall, thin man with a red-white-and-blue bow tie led Josh Balsam to Abby's table, along with a ponytailed woman who could have been Balsam's mother or sister, and a little girl in a sundress and jelly sandals. As Blue Gene looked on, the tall man introduced Balsam and his family as the guests of honor to Abby, who stood for them until they took their seats.

"Hey, Josh," said Blue Gene.

"What up?" Balsam had grown a thin blond mustache. With a pair of baggy jeans, he wore a red Tommy Hilfiger shirt that was unbuttoned enough to show his gold necklace and wife-beater tank top underneath. Blue Gene was also wearing a gold necklace, one with a crucifix his mom had given him when he was a teenager. The crucifix was nestled in a telling patch of chest hair, which was visible since Blue Gene wore no undershirt.

"Where'd you get that beer?" asked Balsam, with watery eyes.

"Over there, but I seen some waiters runnin' around, too."

"I'll go get you one," said Abby, already getting out of her chair. "What kind would you like?"

"Just whatever." After taking the woman's and little girl's orders of a beer and a Coke, Abby made a point of taking Arthur with her to get the drinks.

The day after the monster-truck rally, Blue Gene had tracked down Balsam's phone number and called him. Balsam had been hesitant at first to accept the invitation for his family to be the guests of honor. For starters, he didn't talk much to his stepmom or half sister and didn't like the idea of having to be around them. He also questioned why Blue Gene's brother was so interested in his father. It wasn't like they had even known each other. In his own words, Blue Gene explained to Balsam that the tribute to his father was all about respect. It was a chance to show how much his father's sacrifice meant to the country. Blue Gene went on to say how Balsam's father had done something Blue Gene could only dream of doing, since the military wouldn't take him because of his bum leg. After hearing this, Balsam suddenly had a change of heart. He said he would call his stepmom and they'd be there. He made it clear, though, that he would not be talking in front of people. Blue Gene explained that John said this would not be expected of him.

$$$

John tried as hard as he could to be the finest man anyone had ever met. But he soon learned that there was such a thing as trying too hard, as he irreparably flubbed a conversation with only the third person he attempted talking to. Things had been going fine until the man mentioned that his son had just gotten back from Korea, and John, so busy trying to sound interested, said, "Wow. Korea? Was he there for business or pleasure?" The man gave him a funny look and said, "He's in the military. Yeah. Going to Korea for pleasure. Some vacation." John laughed and tried changing subjects, but became tongue-tied and soon found himself turning what felt to be hot pink. He excused himself and hurried backstage to his dressing room, where he locked the door.

He paced and gritted his teeth. He should've waited for Blue Gene before he tried talking to the people, but it was something he was going to have to do on his own sooner or later, and he had sworn to himself he would take on the challenge starting tonight. He had to go back out there. Why should he even care what these people thought of him? He had already put so much work into this campaign. Who else would keep organized notes on everyone he spoke to so that when he saw them, he could ask how their wife's heart condition was or how their son was enjoying Princeton? Who else would keep facts and statistics and vocabulary words on the back of his bedroom and bathroom doors so he could study every chance he got?

But nothing had prepared him for actually standing face to face with someone, trying to make each one feel like he was the only person alive, when the truth was, John felt like he himself was the only person alive and that the whole world was watching his every move, seeing every little nervous tic, swallow, and mistake.

When John played tennis growing up, his father told him that every fraction of movement within a tennis stroke should be so textbook flawless that in any particular millisecond, a photographer could snap a picture and the resulting photograph would show the player having picture-perfect form, from the position of his feet to the angle of his wrist. Last fall, when it was decided that John would be running for office, Henry had sat John down and told him that politicking was like playing tennis: every smile, gesture, and motion had to be perfect, frame by frame by frame, especially in this case, since the photographers wouldn't be hypothetical.

He hunched over his dresser and studied himself in the mirror. He told himself that, if nothing else, he definitely had the face of a leader. His chin looked strong and authoritative, the bridge of his nose was slender and intelligent, and his head was a good, lean, long size. He recalled reading that movie stars normally have heads that are slightly larger than average, which would confirm that he was born for the role of political star. If only his eyes didn't look so worried. They were shifty even looking at his own reflection. He was an exceptionally handsome man who had enjoyed the life of an exceptionally handsome man, but he saw that his darting eyes were those of a scared child.

Then came a knock on the door, to which he made no reply.

"John? Are you in there?"

"Yeah, Mom." He opened the door.

"Gene's here. He's wanting to know what he's supposed to do."

"Okay. I guess I need him to meet and greet with me. I'll be out in a minute."

"Are you okay? You look upset."

"No. I'm fine. I'm *perfectly* fine."

"You sure?"

"Yes. Sometimes it's hard talking to people, that's all. But I'm fine."

Elizabeth looked John up and down. She rubbed her thumb across his full, expressive eyebrows, which punctuated his dashing looks. "You look great, and you'll do great. Just remember, you have to make the most of each encounter you have out there. Think of it like this." Elizabeth paused and looked up with her enthusiastic brown eyes. Then she smiled beatifically. "Imagine that at some point in your life there will be one person that you meet who will be God Himself. But the *catch* is that you'll never know which person that is. So, just in case, you have to treat each and every person you meet in this campaign like he or she might be the Lord our God."

John sighed and turned his back on Elizabeth.

"What? What is it?"

"That's too much pressure, Mom, telling me I have to act like each person is God."

"It's not literal. It's just something I picked up in one of my books. I was just making a point."

"Well, I've already been out there once, and I'm pretty sure that none of those people are God."

"Then pretend like each person you meet might one day be famous."

$$\$ \$ \$$$

After Abby returned with the Balsams' drinks, Arthur wanted to get in Blue Gene's lap. Blue Gene bounced him up and down and made motorcycle noises, and Arthur turned around and grabbed both sides of Blue Gene's mullet as if they were handlebars. As he was doing so, Blue Gene spotted Mitchell Gibson, his best friend from childhood, standing across the room. Blue Gene had heard that Mitchell was gay, and seeing a frosted-haired man right next to him confirmed it. Blue Gene snarled his lip and tried to remember if Mitchell had shown any signs of homosexuality when they were little. He did remember that Mitchell had always cried over little things.

After all these years, Blue Gene could still remember Mitchell's phone number. They became best friends in first grade, and for the first time in his life, Blue Gene had someone to talk to on the phone, not counting Bernice, whom he called until his parents said he was no longer allowed to. Blue Gene and Mitchell would call each other and talk for hours at a time, sometimes watching the same TV shows, like *Family Ties* or *Salute Your Shorts*, while they were on the phone, just so they could hear each other's comments. Now that Blue Gene thought about it, talking so much like that was actually pretty gay. He shook off the thought and set Arthur on his mom's lap.

Elizabeth approached the table. "You must be the Balsams! Hi. I'm Elizabeth Mapother." After the Balsams offered lazy hellos, Elizabeth turned to Blue Gene. "Gene, John would like you to go backstage. I'll take you to his dressing room."

As Elizabeth led Blue Gene toward a side exit, the elegant *ding-ding-ding* of a utensil on glass quieted the crowd. "Excuse me," said a voice over the PA. "May I have everyone's attention?" It was Reverend Smith, the area's oldest and most beloved minister. Elizabeth paused at the edge of the room to listen. "I've been asked by my dear friend Henry Mapother to bless this meal tonight." The white-haired reverend bowed, as did his audience. "Almighty God, we gather before you tonight with humble hearts, on this night of nights commemorating when our liberty was won, in this land where freedom rings so loud and so proud. We thank you for our kind and caring community, and for those who make this community what it is, so many of them gathered here tonight. And we especially thank you for brave men like Timothy Balsam, whose sacrifices have allowed us to come out and gather in public like this. Amen." The crowd echoed, "Amen," and continued their talking and eating.

Without a word, Elizabeth took Blue Gene through a back corridor to John's dressing room.

"Wow," said John. "You dressed up. I was wondering what was underneath that old baseball cap."

"Are you makin' fun?"

"No. Not at all."

"I'm so hot-natured. I can't stand wearin' a uniform like you're wearin'."

"I wouldn't want you to dress like me," said John, in his black suit and red tie. "You look fine."

Blue Gene's button-up American flag shirt was tucked into a pair of tight white jeans with no belt. John's suggestion that he wear whatever he wanted tonight had seemed suspicious to Blue Gene, and he had imagined a dining room full of dapper Dans pointing and laughing at him in his usual flip-flops, shorts, and muscle shirt.

"Hey, man, where am I supposed to sit out there?"

"Wherever you want."

"By God, I can't get a straight answer outta anyone I know."

"Mom and Dad don't have a place to sit, either. They're just kind of mingling. Isn't that right, Mom?"

"Yes," said Elizabeth. "John, was it you or your father who asked Reverend Smith to give an invocation?"

"Dad."

"I could've done a much better job. I even had a little something prepared. I don't know why he didn't ask me. He knows I love giving the opening prayers."

"Dad thought it would make us look good to have Reverend Smith up there."

"I think I'll go find your father." And with that, Elizabeth was gone, her high heels clicking aggressively down the hall.

"So are you ready to do this?" asked John, as he looked at himself in the mirror and adjusted his tie.

"Do what?"

"Talk to the people."

"Yeah."

"So if it's someone who knows you, make sure you introduce me as your brother. Or just always introduce me as your brother, no matter what, okay?"

"Okay."

"And don't forget to tell them to vote for me. That's the most important part."

"Hey—I seen the lady from the 'Don't you buy no ugly truck' commercial out there."

"Yeah. She's going to sing the National Anthem. Blue Gene, if you see that I'm—well, if you notice me having any sort of problem at all communicating with the people, you'll need to step in, okay?"

"What are you *talking* about?"

"Nothing. Come on. Let's get this over with."

As they walked down the corridor back to the showroom, the tall, thin man with the red-white-and-blue bow tie rushed up to John without noticing Blue Gene. He was middle-aged and wore glasses with frames so thin, they were hardly visible.

"Your dad just got done talking with the head of Hartag-Lewis. He got him to agree to have a fifty-dollar-a-plate dinner for you in the fall."

"That's great. Hey, Mark, I want to introduce you to my brother."

"Oh. You're Blue Gene." He shook Blue Gene's hand vigorously. "I've heard a lot about you."

Blue Gene didn't know how to reply.

"Mark is my campaign manager," said John. "He's Dad's friend Hugh Howard's son." Blue Gene nodded.

"Your dad was asking where you were," said Mark. "He says you need to be out there shaking hands."

"Yeah, we're on our way to do that."

"Good. Nice to meet you, Blue Gene," said Mark, already heading off.

"You too, big nuts."

Mark paused. He turned around, eyes widening in his bean-shaped face, and he let out an uproarious laugh. He looked at John, who also laughed.

"You were right about him," said Mark. "You're the real deal, Blue Gene."

Blue Gene turned to John with a question on his face. John said, "Come on," and headed toward the showroom. Blue Gene felt the bizarre urge to chop the campaign manager in the Adam's apple.

"Your campaign manager is a fag," he found himself saying as they entered the showroom.

$$\$ \ \$ \ \$$

With "Proud to Be an American" and then "Wind Beneath My Wings" and then "American Soldier" playing in the background, John and Blue Gene worked their way around the edge of the vast room, meeting, greeting, and telling everyone to vote for Mapother in November. Sometimes John quietly told Blue Gene to skip some people, usually the sons and daughters of the area's favorite patricians, whose votes he already had locked. These people annoyed Blue Gene with their talk of the Hamptons and prenups. The cackling women wore bright, optimistically colored dresses, and the men wore polo shirts, and even when they had the buttons undone and their chests showing, the men still maintained an air of preppy cleanliness. Some of these highborn studs could even grow their hair long in a way that looked chic because they had it tousled just so.

Blue Gene knew quite a few of the attendees of a lesser pedigree, and he introduced the gentleman next to him as his brother. John met some people often referred to as "characters" that night: guys named Tony and Ricky who worked legal terms like *intent* and *possession* into conversation; a jovial old man with probably the most well-known face in town, for he was a greeter at Wal-Mart; a woman who, for some reason, asked John if the Ambassador Inn was hiring and if he could "get her on there"; and a young married couple who were known for taking their seven dogs to local nursing homes to cheer up the patients.

At first Blue Gene did most of the talking for John, telling people his brother was a good guy, and that they should vote for him because he was for the same things they were for: God, America, family, and freedom. It was pretty easy, saying the same things over and over and making small talk with the ones he knew personally. After a while, John loosened up and even got so he asked people to pray for him after telling them to consider him to represent the interests of this district.

And they did consider him, some because they knew Blue Gene, and some because they just plain liked John now that they had actually met the man behind his title, president of Westway International. Of course, people had always been apt to confuse John's handsomeness with charisma. With his perfect posture, ceaseless smile, and Californian good looks, he didn't have to say much, as it turned out, to impress the people. They forgot the stories they had heard about how he wouldn't attend meetings that he himself had called, because here he was now, with this magazine-gloss air and even a good ol' boy to vouch for him.

At about eight-thirty, a few reporters showed up with tape recorders and notepads in hand. News crews were also beginning to arrive, as were some photographers, who stood around looking bored. People were finishing up their desserts and waiting for it to get dark so the fireworks could begin, which, along with the free food, were the main reason a lot of them had attended.

$ $ $

John Henry Mapother the Fourth had all the charisma of a paperweight. He was well aware of this; it was why he lost his own bid for the U.S. House of Representatives in 1968. He was told he just wasn't as huggable as his opponent, some slang-tongued upstart named Lawrence Pendergraft, whom he considered nothing more than a hippie in businessman's clothing. Though it had been more than thirty years, Henry still felt uncontrollable contempt toward the voters for picking such a lowlife heathen over him.

What Henry lacked in charisma, he more than made up for in wealth. Just as the Fourteenth Amendment rendered corporations legal though intangible persons, Henry considered his own corporate wealth to be a sort of imaginary being, like a bodyguard who always stood nearby. And wealth, which made for a big fellow, could be a bully at times, so with a guy like that backing him up day and night, naturally,

Henry was going to have a cocky slant of a smile, and his words might automatically come out condescending. His wealth might come at the expense of his charisma. But because that imaginary bodyguard looking over his shoulder actually had more personality than he did, when Henry was at a social function like this one, it was his *wealth* that worked the room. And when wealth was working the room for him, he didn't have to.

Henry's wealth had been doing the talking for him since he had arrived at the Ambassador Inn, and it continued to do so as he strode from the bar toward John. People noticed him from across the showroom and talked about how much he was worth, how he had invested in all the right companies, how he belonged to so many boards and was even a partner in a private-equity firm, and how he had turned his father's regional company into the global tobacco superpower that it now was. They talked about how strong and healthy he looked for his age. When he walked past, they saw how tightly his skin was pulled over his skull, and how the sharpness of his features gave his face mean angles. Overall, there was something savage about his looks. Savage but dignified—and, above all, classy.

Heading toward John, Henry stared at Blue Gene's long hair because he hated it. He cringed at the thought of his own blood occupying a form that could be attached to such a vulgar coif. Hair was the first thing he noticed about a person. He made sure his own was always well managed, especially at the neck.

He waited for John and Blue Gene to shake one last couple's hands, and then he pulled John aside. "It's time."

"I have five minutes," said John, looking at his watch.

"No. It's time." Henry had recently come up with the idea of keeping his watch set five minutes early so that he would feel ahead of the rest of the world. "Hello, Eugene."

"Hey, Dad."

"John needs to be backstage now. Come on, John."

"What am I supposed to do?" asked Blue Gene.

"I don't know, but make yourself useful," said Henry.

"You can relax for now, Blue Gene," said John. "Just enjoy my speech."

Blue Gene gave him a look that said, "Whatever you say." Henry and John headed backstage.

"How has he done?" asked Henry.

"He's done great. He's so good with people."

"The populist appeal."

"I think that by the end of the night, he'll agree to be on our staff."

"I will not have him on our staff. I told you to forget that. Tonight is enough. Don't get too close to him."

"But you haven't seen him in action. He's one of them. It's effortless for him."

"Do not get too close to him. I mean it. It's already gone too far."

"I was thinking, though, maybe he fits into our plan after all. Maybe Blue Gene happened for a reason. Because we needed him."

"Get in there," said Henry, pointing to John's dressing room. He slammed the door behind them. "Don't you see he's already getting in the way? He's coming between us. You shouldn't even be thinking about him right now. Your mother and I have been with you from day one. You should be thinking of us, not him. I don't want to be fussing about this right now. You need to be ready for your speech. This is what we've been waiting for all our lives. So make me proud. I believe in you. I know that you will be the one who will bring back the good old days."

Henry was referring to the 1950s, the decade that he associated with happiness. To Henry, everything was better then. It was when America was America. It was what he thought the country should aspire to be. He had been a teenager in the fifties, too young to be drafted for the Korean War. "You'll make everything good again," he continued. "Are you ready?"

"Yes," John said quietly.

"Of course you are. I'll have them begin." At the door, Henry turned. "This is your chance to make up for everything."

$ $ $

After his father left, John turned out all the lights but a small lamp in the corner. He sat in front of his mirror, but immediately decided he was too anxious to sit. He stood and walked ovals around the small room, picturing himself in front of the crowd, which was larger than he had anticipated. He thought about how he hated the sound of his own voice. His undershirt was drenched in armpit sweat. Even his back felt moist. He wished Arthur were back here with him; just seeing him gave John a sense of peace. But he heard the MC asking everyone to direct their attention to the raising of the American flag, which meant he would soon be onstage. He heard applause and cheers for the raised flag.

John's campaign manager knocked and popped his head in the door and told him it was almost time. John told him he'd be out in a moment. He felt so jittery, and he wanted to try to calm himself. He then heard the MC asking everyone to stand for the National Anthem, and when the local celebrity started belting out the song a cappella, John felt his heart race like it was speeding toward some horrendous conclusion. If there were ever a time to return to the chemicals that he had once let himself marinate in, it was now. He thought about how when he used to get drunk or high, he could actually speak more articulately and confidently. He pictured himself pointing the bottom of a Johnnie Walker bottle straight toward the ceiling and allowing the alcohol to cascade down his gullet. He wished there was some way he could immediately procure a bottle from the bar, but felt a prick of self-hatred for even allowing himself to entertain this line of thought. He kicked the chair at his dresser clear across the room. He knelt before his dresser and watched himself pray in the mirror while the National Anthem continued.

He prayed to the Lord that he would be granted strength, endless strength, so that he would be able to carry out the destiny that had been placed upon his shoulders so many years ago by way of the prophecy implanted in the mind of his dear mother. He asked that his body and mind support him as he stood upon the stage tonight. He asked that his speech go perfectly and be well received, and that this night be a triumphant beginning to a glorious rise to leadership.

He heard the crowd whoop exuberantly when the lady from the truck commercials hit the high note on "for the la-and of the *freeeeee*." It was time to end his prayer and leave the dressing room.

He concluded by promising he would carry out God's will and do his part in preparing the path for the Messiah to reclaim His earthly throne. He vowed to the Lord that he would show them all the way—he just needed strength. He asked that he be granted strength not only for tonight, but also for the remainder of this campaign and all his future campaigns. And he prayed that he would always be doing the right thing.

He checked himself in the mirror one last time and then rushed to his position backstage. Upon John's arrival, a man with a headset cued the lights to be lowered. John felt sweat droplets forming at his temples. He wiped them with a handkerchief and looked around to see if anyone was watching him sweat. Sure enough, most of the campaign team gathered backstage had their eyes on him. As he watched a man putting a CD into a stereo that was hooked up to the PA system, he felt sweat trickle down his back. A solitary trumpet played a majestic melody as John thought he could feel sweat entering the crack of his butt. He saw Arthur and Abby sitting in front of the stage and wished he were at home with them on the couch, watching a Disney movie. Meanwhile, a jumbo-size screen slowly descended center stage behind the podium. The screen showed a gigantic American flag waving.

The words *honor, liberty, pride, faith,* and *freedom* soared across the screen, and a full orchestra joined the trumpet while stage lights flashed red, white, and blue. John couldn't stop thinking about his wet butt and how it must have looked to all the people backstage. They were probably all back there thinking he was incontinent, which made him sweat even more. He wiped his damp palms on his slacks and then checked to make sure he hadn't left any stains. As the announcer said, "Ladies and gentlemen," John knew he was about to be announced and took a deep breath. He checked to see if his teleprompter was on, wiped his brow one last time, and prayed to God someone had remembered to put a bottle of water inside the podium, because his mouth was so dry and the saliva just wasn't coming.

"...Please welcome John Hurstbourne Mapother!"

He was aware of every step he took while the spotlight followed him to the podium. He prayed he wouldn't die.

$$$

To see the name John Hurstbourne Mapother appear on the screen gave Blue Gene an inward chuckle. John never called himself by his full name, nor had Blue Gene ever heard anyone call his brother this, except maybe when his mom scolded him when he was a drunk-driving teenager. Someone on his campaign team must have thought "John Hurstbourne Mapother" was more important-sounding, and that was fine, but they sure better not call him Eugene Dewitt Mapother.

After a long awkward pause, John opened his mouth and a strange combination of "hello" and "hi" came out. He cleared his throat. "I thank you all for attending this tribute to an American soldier." His voice was noticeably shaky. "I am honored to deliver the keynote address on this birthday of liberty, right here in the heart of the heartland, in the greatest sovereign nation in the world." His voice trembled so badly that he hardly made it through the sentence. He took a bottle of water from inside the podium and drank with an unsteady hand.

Blue Gene thought that maybe this was what John had been referring to earlier when he said he might need help. He must have had a bad case of stage fright. Whatever it was, Blue Gene had never seen John look so weak, and he couldn't stand it.

As John ran the back of his hand across his brow, Blue Gene started chanting, "USA! USA!" His favorite wrestler at the National Guard Armory often did this to get the crowd fired up. The audience turned around and looked at Blue Gene, who had ended up in the back of the room, leaning against the wall. Their stares made him feel like a fool, but within seconds the chant was several hundred voices strong.

As they chanted, John drank some more water and looked over the room. The chant sent away the tension, and a less formal feeling replaced the stuffy, official one. John smiled and spoke with more force as the chant died down.

"USA indeed. That is why we are here tonight. But I am also here tonight because I want to tell you a story. It's the story of a man, an *American* man through and through. This man's favorite colors were red, white, and blue." John motioned at the patriotic banners above him. His voice no longer shook. "Coca-Cola ran through his American veins, and the milk of the heartland cow made his bones strong. The Ten Commandments were imprinted on his mind's eye, and the melodies of Garth Brooks and Bob Seger were often stuck in his head. As a teenager, two things happened that transformed him into a man. One, he became a young father. Instead of running the other way, he boldly faced the challenge of parenthood. Two, he heard an adventure calling him, an adventure that would show him the world while at the same time satisfying his love for country. Again, instead of running the other way, he faced the challenge that this adventure presented. This adventure went by the name of the United States Army."

Blue Gene had gone from feeling sorry for John to being surprised by his speaking skills. He spoke slowly and with such earnest emotion that each syllable seemed to carry weight.

"The Army showed him places he had never dreamed of seeing. He was stationed in remote, beautiful regions full of palm trees and orchards. But more important, the Army showed him firsthand an all-important truth that he had always suspected. That truth is this...freedom isn't free.

"When he returned home, he took a job at the aluminum factory, and when he drove his pickup truck home after work, he felt tired, tired but proud that his manpower would materialize into bread for his family. He endured fifty-hour workweeks just to make ends meet, yet he somehow found the time to instill in his son and daughter the values that mark us as a people: honor, integrity, faith, and a profound respect for God and country.

"Then came that fateful day when this man saw freedom being challenged in a way it had never been challenged before. He knew there had been a reason why he had felt compelled to remain a part of his military's reserve force. When the call to duty later came, he knew what he had to do. He answered it.

"Through two tours of duty, he fought his way through sandstorms of orange, liberating the oppressed all along the way as part of a vanguard platoon. But sadly, just eight weeks ago, this man would end up making the ultimate sacrifice, putting that American body in harm's way for the sake of his brigade commander. His wife and children had to hear those five dreaded words from the stern lips of a military officer: 'We regret to inform you...' But his family took comfort in the fact that their man left this world and entered the next knowing that he had done more than his part in ensuring the enemy didn't destroy the American way of life. For his efforts he was awarded a Purple Heart, which is appropriate, because I suspect his own heart was purple. After all, what's the color you get when you mix red, white, and blue?"

Tepid laughter came and went in a beat. Blue Gene didn't laugh, but he gave the people around him a dirty look when he saw that they weren't laughing.

"He was an American soldier, and he fought for his country, for you and for me. He was a friend of freedom, and therefore a friend to us all.

"Now, when I was trying to figure out what to say about this heroic man tonight, something occurred to me, something that struck me as tragic, and that tragic truth is this: The best of men this world has seen have names we'll never know. For every George Washington, there were twenty Unknown Soldiers. For every Dwight D. Eisenhower, there were twenty G.I. Joes. That is why tonight, I wanted one of the very best of men to have his name known by all. He was the American soldier whose story I've told you, and his name was Tim Balsam."

John stopped and applause burst forth from the audience. He smiled at Josh Balsam and his family. Blue Gene hooted not once but twice.

"At this time," John continued when the applause died down, "I'd like to address our guests of honor, the family that Tim Balsam had to leave behind. With us tonight are Tim's son, Josh, his daughter, Tara, and his wife, Cindy." A spotlight shone on the Balsams, and everyone applauded. "Josh, Tara, and Cindy are living tributes to Tim Balsam, honoring him through their pride and strength in the face of sacrifice.

"And now, I would like Josh Balsam, Tim's only son, to accept a token of our deep appreciation for his father's service to nation. Come on up, Josh."

The spotlight shone on the back of Balsam's fuzzy skull. He turned to his stepmother, who motioned for him to go on. With the lazy strut of an eighteen-year-old, he went up onstage.

"Josh, on behalf of Westway International, we would like you to accept this symbol of our national gratitude." He reached inside the podium. "It wasn't easy, but we acquired a modern-day relic, one sacred to our nation." John held up a flag that had been neatly folded into a triangle and placed in a triangular glass case. The flag was dirty and had a red stain. "This is an American flag that was found deep within the ruins of our fallen World Trade Center. It carries stains of blood, honor, and democracy. It is what your father so proudly fought for, and we want you and your family to have it. Without men like your father, we have nothing."

Blue Gene felt an electric chill pass through his body. He swelled with pride as Balsam took the flag from John and stared at it intensely. John shook Balsam's hand as the applause and flash photography came. Then John whispered something in Balsam's ear. With both hands, Balsam lifted the triangular flag high above his head, like a wrestler who had just won a championship belt.

This image was immediately bombarded by camera flashes, and the applause grew louder than ever. A few men wearing black silk jackets with Marine Corps insignias were the first to stand. Soon everyone in the showroom joined them, and the photographers took pictures of the standing ovation. Then they took more pictures of the slain soldier's son and the politician, who again shook hands and directly saluted the cameras.

$$$

No one at the Ambassador Inn could hear it, but across town an irate voice was coming from under the ground. The voice was half screamed, half sung, and hurled forth from the raw throat of a young woman holding an electric guitar. Foreboding bass and drums accompanied her words, which she read urgently from a spiral notebook as though the place would be shut down any minute:

"A reading from the book of Genocide. Once there was nothing here but pure verdure and dandelions, no exploits to speak of but the wind gently blowing itself. Big-game hunters were the first interruption, chasing hairy elephants across the Bering Strait, trailing the mastodons whose broad legs and bright tusks paved the original interstate highways. Hunting and gathering made way for Agraria. Skin toughened and reddened. They were plain folk, relatively peaceful and respectful toward women. But united they weren't. Then came the occidental germ to a mistaken Asia, opening the New World with a flick of a sword. A con's quest. Sin is so Old World, they said. No more sins here. Nobody here but us saints. Your scalp sure would look nice on my vanity. What are you doing for dinner? The Bible made me do it. Yes, it's okay. I double-checked the pertinent verse. They had it coming. I've decided it's gonna work out over here after all. So come on over. Send the kids along. And send some comedians. We'll need some comedians. No taxation without representation! Battle cry or slogan? The rich can pay for a substitute, I hear. But what if I can't afford a substitute? Then you have to fight. I guess I'll be fighting, then. Can't afford not to. I'm not so sure I want to fight. I'd just as soon fight them. They're the ones who hold me down and don't pay me enough. Can't feed my mouths and got pumpkins for furniture. But this isn't about you and me. It's about US. One nation, spangled and festooned. They can't tell US what to do. We hate their accents, those sippy-tea-tongued accents that drive our women wild. No more rich or poor. No more masters or servants. Just Americans. Peasants and immigrants with gurgling stomachs. The Redcoats can't believe how ferocious their opponents are. They act like they're mad at something. But if the substitute dies, does his ghost haunt you, whispering into your ear, it shoulda been you, your highness? The thing about revolutions is that they're like designated drivers that end up getting drunk. King George. No, please, call me President George. The richest man in America."

$ $ $

John knew it was Blue Gene who had started the impromptu "USA" chant. He was touched that Blue Gene would do something like that for him. This sweet gesture from the normally tough Blue Gene had opened something inside John, some deep interior compartment that contained thoughts like "Everything is going to be okay," rather than his usual standbys: "People kill me" and "Just leaving the house is setting yourself up for a fall."

Eschewing a close call with what could've been his most catastrophic attack to date, John was now halfway through the most important speech of his life. The presentation of the blood flag, maudlin as it may have seemed to some, had gone over better than he had expected. As Balsam took his seat and everyone settled down after their ovation, John blurred his vision ever so slightly, a trick his father had taught him. Henry had told him it was easier to speak in front of people if you can't see their faces, and blurring your own eyes by squinting or crossing them just a tad turned any audience into a mass of shapes. John spoke confidently to the predominantly white shapes:

"Now, when we first called Tim Balsam's family and asked if they would be our guests of honor tonight, they reluctantly accepted, but on only one condition: only if they didn't have to talk in front of everybody."

A whimper of laughter wafted through the room.

"I said, that's fine. I'll just do the talking for you. So the Balsams agreed, and while at first I was proud that I would be the one to give a speech honoring Tim Balsam, I then realized I had agreed to a rather difficult task, for I had agreed to speak for a hero. I thought, am I up to this challenge? Do I even have the *right* to speak for this brave desert warrior? I then thought, who *would* have the right to speak for Tim, if not Tim or his family? Well, it would have to be someone who believed in his country and everything it stood for. It would have to be someone who respected those who fought and gave their lives for their country. And it would have to be someone who believed in the traditional American values that Tim believed were worth fighting for, the values of faith and freedom, the very values our enemies want to do away with. I decided that if these were the qualifications for someone to speak for Tim Balsam, then that someone might as well be me. After all, Coca-Cola runs through my veins, too, which might explain my high cholesterol."

The audience laughed more freely. Blue Gene shook his head, though he too snorted out a laugh.

"So why *not* me? I do love this country that has been so good to my family and me, and I especially love it right here in Bashford. I have always called Bashford my home. I've run up and down its many basketball courts, I've partaken in many of its barbecues, I've hunted its game, I've caught its fish, and I've enjoyed its quiet Sunday afternoons as much as anyone. I know this part of the country, and I'm confident that I know what it would say if it were given access to a microphone. And so I've decided that I *am* up to the task of speaking for Tim Balsam. But I cannot, in good conscience, stop there."

John paused dramatically and slowly scanned the room. Josh Balsam awaited the next sentence with his mouth slightly ajar, exposing a front tooth that grew diagonally.

"I cannot stop there, for something deep in my soul tells me that I should speak for you, too. I want to speak for you, the old couple who sits on their front porch wondering where things like faith and moral values have been hiding in this day and age. I want to speak for you, the disenchanted farmer who winces as he reads the newspaper and wonders what happened to his leaders' honor and integrity. And I want to speak for you, the frightened child who wonders if her daddy is fighting over-seas for the right reasons. I want to speak for all of you. That is why I am asking you to place me in the United States House of Representatives this fall."

On the big screen behind John, white letters pronounced on a dark blue background: JOHN HURSTBOURNE MAPOTHER: *ALWAYS*. Underneath, small red letters recommended him for Congress, District Five.

"Tonight is a celebration of the values that form the core of my can-didacy."

"Bring on the fireworks!" a man yelled. Some of the audience laughed, and so did John, who had prepared himself for something like this.

"I *will* bring on the fireworks," he said. "Just hear me out for another couple of minutes. Consider this the price of your free meal. You have to hear me talk for just a little bit."

The audience laughed again.

"I realize what I'm getting into won't be easy. Because of the constant lying of leaders like the one I'm running against, it's gotten to the point where the people *automatically* think a politician is a liar and a scoundrel. So let me be the very first to tell you that in my case, there *is* some truth to that line of thinking. In my life, I *have* been a liar, and I *have* been a bad person. I am telling you right now that in my younger days, I was completely seduced by drugs and alcohol. My mind became so warped that I felt like only half a man until the drugs or alcohol filled me and made me whole. I completely lost my way. I mean, I was such a mess that I went from not knowing what day of the *month* it was to not knowing what day of the *week* it was."

The audience liked this one, and John had their full attention. He could see their heads leaning forward like gossips. He was relieved to see that Arthur, just in front of the podium, was paying more attention to his own nose than to his father's speech.

"I'm telling you this to let you know that my dark days are behind me. You will not see me cheating and lying my life away in office, be-cause I've already gone down that road, to its very end, and I found there was nothing at the end but emptiness and sorrow. Thankfully, a while back I did manage to figure out what *year* it was. I saw that the new millennium was approaching, and I figured it was a good time to start over, and that's exactly what I did. I allowed God back into my heart, where He has remained ever since, guiding my every move. I rediscovered my family, who took me back with open arms, and I even started a family of my own. Today, my days of sinning are a thing of the past. I promise you I will not lie, and I will obey the laws of the land, so help me God."

This received a robust round of applause.

"Thank you. Now is a time of great division in our country, but I believe we can be united with our thirst for freedom and our hunger for values, and our conviction that we are truly right in the eyes of an all-knowing God. I want to represent this unity, this unity that I see right here in this room, for this very room *is* America. America isn't a metropolis of pagans or a coastline of deviants. America is closer to the center of this great hunk of land than New York or California. America is right here in this room, and I am confident that I can represent every person in here."

His nervousness was gone.

"I believe in my country. I believe in embracing the ideology that made our nation great in the first place. I believe in one nation under God. I believe in traditional morality. I believe that if a leader can't abide by the laws of morality, then he should be held responsible for his immoral actions. I believe in our moral obligation to lesser nations who need our help in rebuilding. I believe that your tax money should *not* go toward *helping* those who attack the American way of life. I believe in the institution of the family. I believe in the Bible. I believe that marriage is a biblical term that should always hold sanctity. With that said, I will go on record right now to tell you that I once fell in love with a man...He was a tall, dark, and handsome fellow, and his name was Jesus Christ."

This one received the biggest laugh yet. As John went on, he could feel his words groping the audience. For once, he was completely in control, becoming the kind of man his son could be proud of.

$ $ $

Blue Gene looked for Mitchell and his man-friend, curious to see their reaction to John's gay comment. They were whispering in each other's ears and not smiling. Then the man-friend left the showroom. Blue Gene gave him a dirty look as he exited. Everyone else seemed to be behind John 100 percent. He was kicking ass up there. Maybe Blue Gene would have a good opening line with the chicks later: "Hi. I'm John Hurst-bourne Mapother's brother." There were definitely some fine women here tonight, but they were all with some hair-gelled guy. Scattered across the showroom, there was enough hair gel to fill a condominium.

"Once elected this November," continued John, "I will not be enforcing policies. I will be enforcing *values*. I will not advocate any agenda that in theory promotes fairness but in practice would legitimize immoral lifestyles. In doing so, I will ensure that the kingdom of God, the new promised land, is built right here in the United States of America.

"But I won't be alone in my quest to represent you. As I said, family is a key value for me, and my family will be with me every step of the way. I will be joined by Abby Mapother, the strong, loyal woman I've been proud to call my wife for six years, and my five-year-old son, Arthur. Please stand, you two."

Abby had trouble getting Arthur to stand. Once the spotlight was on them, Abby pulled Arthur's hands away from his snug collar.

"They are living proof that the American family is not dead, and I am blessed that they belong to me. I will also be joined by my mother, Elizabeth Mapother, the woman who taught me the importance of faith."

Elizabeth stood from the table of diners where she had settled. Her hair was perfectly pulled back and wrapped in a red-white-and-blue bow, and her head glistened in the spotlight.

Seeing that John was singling out each member of his immediate family, Blue Gene became nervous, not because he was afraid of everyone looking at him, but because he feared the possibility that John would not mention him at all. Sure, he was good enough to be shown to all the working stiffs, but would his brother publicly acknowledge him in front of the Bashford elite?

"This is a woman who is so religious, she measures distances with rosaries. For instance, if you ask her how to get to the grocery, she'll say, 'Oh, it's sixty-five rosaries up the road and fourteen rosaries over to the left.'"

By now, John's jokes hit their marks every time.

"And I know that most of you know my father, the man who made me realize my responsibility to the public, Henry Mapother."

Everyone turned and followed the spotlight toward the back of the room.

"As CEO of Westway International, my father took my grandfather's already thriving company and made it thrive even more, providing hundreds of more jobs for the citizens of Commonwealth and surrounding counties. His generosity and leadership in the area through the years make him a local institution, and I'm lucky to get to call him Dad."

The audience clapped. Blue Gene's heart pounded. He was angry at himself, thinking he shouldn't care whether or not John included him. This time last month, he hadn't had a thing to do with his family.

"And last but definitely not least, I'll be joined on this journey by my little brother, Blue Gene." Blue Gene squinted in the spotlight. "Blue Gene is truly a man of the people, and he has taught me so much that you'd think *he* was thirteen years older than *me*."

Blue Gene felt a hand patting him on the back. He turned and was shocked to find that the hand belonged to his father.

"I am nothing without my family, and I look forward to becoming a part of your families once I am elected. Again, I thank you for coming out tonight to pay tribute to Tim Balsam and his family, and thank you for listening to me as I begin my own adventure. To the Balsam family: it has been an honor to speak for you, just as it will be an honor to speak for the people of this district, from Commonwealth to Braden County, from Wells County to Alexander and all the counties in between.

"With all that said, I assure you I *will* get the job done. I want nothing more than to be the voice for the voiceless, the sight for the sightless, and the power for the powerless, not to mention a true friend of business. Thank you, and may God bless the United States of America, now and forever, amen."

Six hundred palms slapped out approval, Blue Gene's included, and were soon joined by an instrumental version of "My Country 'Tis of Thee."

"You started that 'USA' chant, didn't you?" asked Henry, still standing next to Blue Gene. As usual, Blue Gene couldn't tell whether his father was pleased or angered.

"Yeah. He was dyin' up there."

Henry patted Blue Gene on the back, hard enough to move him forward an inch. "Good job, Eugene. That was quick thinking. I'm glad you came."

"Thank you." And with a stiff nod, Henry left. John lingered onstage, smiling and waving at no one in particular, while expensive-looking fireworks started going off in the background, bursting picturesquely over the river, to the audience's excitement. Blue Gene was a full-fledged participant in this moment and yelled, "Woo!" For once, he didn't feel that tired.

$ $ $

"Is that you, Blue Gene?"

Blue Gene, now standing at one of the panoramic windows that ran the length of the room, turned away from the fireworks to see his best friend from childhood standing before him. "Yeah."

"I thought that was you. I'm Mitchell Gibson."

"I know who you are." Mitchell shook Blue Gene's hand. As Blue Gene had predicted, his grip was flimsy.

"It's so good to *see* you."

"You too."

"Wow, so your brother sure has come a long way."

"Yep." John was in front of the stage, giving statements to some reporters.

"I remember back when I used to come over to your house—that was the first time I had ever been around a drunk person. And remember how he used to give us rides? I was so afraid of his driving. He drove so *fast*."

"Yeah. He don't drive like that these days."

They proceeded to get caught up with each other. Blue Gene acted cordial but kept looking around to see if anyone was watching him talk to the slight man with the weird habit of sucking his cheeks in like a fish. As it turned out, Mitchell had moved from New York back to Bashford after his father died, so that he could live closer to his mom. Blue Gene was about to ask Mitchell if he remembered when they used to push two beds together and pretend they were wrestlers when he spotted Josh Balsam heading their way. He hoped that Mitchell had enough sense not to use the phrase "my partner" in front of Balsam.

"Hey, Mapother," said Balsam. "You think your brother'll need help cleaning up here?"

"Nah. I reckon the hotel staff'll do it."

"'Cause I'll help clean up for him."

"He probably wouldn't let you."

"That's mighty white of y'all, doin' all this for us."

"Don't mention it," said Blue Gene. "Least we can do."

"I was wantin' to talk to him."

"Looks like he's talking to those people over there." John was now receiving well-wishers who had been wowed by his speech.

"I'll wait it out."

Blue Gene considered introducing Balsam and Mitchell but thought better of it. He wished one of them would leave. He tried to ease his own tension by telling a joke.

"I wanted to talk to John, too, but it looks like we're both in for a long wait, 'cause see that line waitin' to talk to him? It's about seven Shaquille O'Neal wieners long."

Mitchell laughed, but Balsam didn't. For a laugh to come out of Balsam's solid face, it would have to break through a die-cast mold of a scowl, which was fixed with narrowed eyes that made it look like he saw the entire world as a target, as if bull's-eyes were painted on everything in his sight. The three of them silently watched the fireworks for a minute. Then a friend of Mitchell's saw him and called for him. Blue Gene was relieved when Mitchell told him goodbye.

After a while, John finally made his way over, carrying some folded T-shirts.

"What'd you think?!" he asked. He put his hand on Blue Gene's shoulder and smiled like a seventh-grader on the last day of school.

"That was great, man," said Blue Gene.

"Thank you. Josh, thanks so much for letting us do this."

"I wanted to thank you, Mr. Mapother. For the flag."

"Yeah, where'd you get that flag, John man? On eBay?"

"No. Dad got it at an auction in New York."

"I liked the things you said," Balsam went on. "I ain't ever even been to a speech like that or nothin', but you was sayin' things that I had been thinkin' a long time. I wasn't plannin' on votin', but I'm goin' to after that."

"Thank you, Josh. That means a lot, coming from you."

"I'd like to help you out on your campaign. Anything you want, I'll do it, and for free. Like if you need help cleanin' up tonight or whatever, 'cause I really 'preciate all this."

"Wow. Thanks, Josh. I can't let you work tonight because you're my guest of honor, but I may have to take you up on that in the future."

"I'm fuckin' serious. I'm gonna help you."

John nodded and straightened his smile when he saw Balsam's grave demeanor.

"I was like him," continued Balsam, nodding at Blue Gene. "They wouldn't take me in the Army. I gotta do something to serve my country, so I wanna help you."

"I appreciate that, Josh. We have your phone number, so we'll be in touch with you. Hey, guys, check this out." John gave a T-shirt to

Blue Gene and Balsam. They held the white shirts up to see JOHN HURSTBOURNE MAPOTHER: *ALWAYS* printed in red and blue.

"Aw, yeah," said Blue Gene.

"Keep it. It's yours."

"For real?"

"Yeah."

"Thanks. That'll look real good with the sleeves cut off."

John smiled and shook his head. "I have to go talk to some more people. Thanks again, Josh, and I'll let you know next time I need you. But for tonight, you're my guest. I'm working for *you*. Can I get you anything?"

"I don't know. 'Preciate a beer."

"Of course. Let me see." John looked around for a waiter.

"I'll get him one," said Blue Gene.

"Thanks, Blue Gene. I'll see you all later."

Blue Gene led Balsam over to the cash bar. As they silently waited in line, they could overhear some people talking nearby.

"Freedom, freedom, freedom! All he ever talks about is freedom!" Both Blue Gene and Balsam turned to see who was talking. It was Mitchell Gibson, talking to a teenage boy and girl with artsy, jet-black haircuts. "His whole speech was freedom this and freedom that, and *freedom* sounds great as a word, but then when it's time to actually *give out* the freedom, he won't do it. You heard what he said. He's clearly against gay rights. Jeremy got so offended he left. And John Mapother's *obviously* for the war."

"Motherfucker," said Balsam, already heading over to Mitchell.

"Hold on, man. Let me get you that beer."

"You gonna let him talk about your brother like that?"

Blue Gene didn't know how to respond, and during his hesitation, Balsam interrupted Mitchell's conversation by staring him down at close range.

"My dad fighting let you have that opinion."

"Excuse me?" said Mitchell, taking turns looking at Balsam and Blue Gene.

"I heard you puttin' down America, but it's people like my dad that died so motherfuckers like you can run your mouth."

"Maybe so," said Mitchell with a laugh, "but I wasn't talking about your dad. I was just saying *John Hurstbourne Mapother* didn't fight for *anybody's* freedom."

"You gettin' smart with me?"

"No. I'm just saying—wait. His brother is right there. I don't want to offend Blue Gene."

"Blue Gene's a big boy. He can take it. Can't you, Blue Gene?"

"Yeah," said Blue Gene.

"Fine. I'm sorry, but I think this whole night is a PR gimmick for John Mapother."

"What do you mean by that?" asked Balsam.

"I mean, I think the fireworks, the flags, all the talk about freedom and democracy—it's just for show. Just to get votes."

"Mapother, you gonna let your friend talk about your family like that?"

"He ain't *my* friend." Blue Gene looked away as he said it.

"So you sayin' the tribute for my father wasn't real? You sayin' it was just for show?"

"I'm saying that if John Mapother really believed in freedom, he'd allow *everyone* to have the same rights. My partner and I—"

"Somebody needs to shut the fuck up."

"What is *wrong* with you?"

"Ain't nothin' wrong with me. You're the motherfucker puttin' down your own motherfuckin' country at a tribute to my dad. My dad would-n't even want you here, so I ain't havin' it. Let's go."

Mitchell looked speechlessly at Blue Gene and the couple he had been talking to, as if to say, "Is this really happening?"

"Eugene, come," Henry said as he walked past. "Quickly. We need to have a family portrait taken in front of the fireworks before they end."

"Y'all want *me* in a family portrait?" asked Blue Gene.

"You heard me. Come on." Henry was already headed toward the exit.

"Go ahead, Mapother," said Balsam. "I'll take care of this one." Balsam grabbed hold of Mitchell's arm. "I'd normally beat his ass right here and now, but out of respect for your brother I'll take it outside."

"Uh—" said Blue Gene.

"Oh my God. You actually think that we're going to *fight*?" asked Mitchell, pulling his arm free.

"Hell yeah, we're gonna fight. You were talkin' shit to the wrong guy."

"I'm not going to fight you."

"That don't surprise me, seeing as how you're a faggot. Come on." Balsam grabbed Mitchell's arm again and pulled him away.

"Blue Gene, do something!" cried Mitchell, looking back at Blue Gene. "You know him. Do something. I'm not going to fight. He's crazy!"

"Blue Gene!" hollered John from across the room. "You have to come. Now! The fireworks are ending." The photographer had Henry and Elizabeth in place for the picture.

As Blue Gene hurried outside for the picture, he imagined the brutality with which Mitchell would be beaten, and how, if the legends of Josh Balsam's fury were true, his childhood best friend might never be the same again. But with each flash of the camera, he forgot a little more about the violent scene that was about to take place in the parking lot. These photos had been a long time coming. He wasn't about to give up this opportunity for somebody who had put down his own blood.

$$$

Inside, as they drank champagne with one arm draped over the back of their chairs, some of the guests watched the Mapothers.

"He won't even smile when his picture's being taken."

"Oh, he's not quite right."

"That's putting it mildly. He's sick. He's literally worth millions but lives like a pauper. He got his grandfather's inheritance, the same as John did. Hasn't spent a dime of it."

"You don't mean it."

"You'd think they would at least put him in a pair of slacks or something."

"I'm sure they tried. They can't do anything with him."

PART TWO

V.

Jackie Stepchild and Blue Gene Mapother first met at the Bashford National Guard Armory, of all places. It was early August, a Wednesday night, which for generations had been the traditional night of the week for local pro wrestling.

The Mapother team's latest canvassing had shown that after the success of his Fourth of July extravaganza, John led Grant Frick by eight percentage points. He could not have had a more spectacular arrival on the regional political scene. True, there were still those who could not divorce the image of a golf club-wielding corporate executive from the word *Mapother*, but in the eyes of many voters—not to mention the local media—the grandiose tribute to Tim Balsam made John look like an unstoppable force of public service, overflowing with goodness and radiating might. Meanwhile, the only time Frick's name seemed to be mentioned in public was in connection with his extramarital affair with a Hooters waitress, a story that had originally broken more than a year earlier.

Luckily for Frick, he made his living as a hedge fund manager and could afford to compete. Once his own staff's poll numbers came back in late July, Frick shifted his campaign into a higher gear. He printed multiple campaign pamphlets, each tailored to a specific audience. For instance, some pamphlets explained how Frick would be the right choice for local farmers, and he had them sent to every rural mailbox, even in the most remote counties of the district. He also increased his staff and had them show up outside factories at five-thirty in the morning to dis-tribute leaflets as late-shift workers came out. To top it all off, by the first of August, his television commercials had started popping up regularly during primetime network slots.

Back in the Mapother camp, the bow-tied campaign manager and his strategists were securing media time for the fall and brainstorming new ways for their white-collared candidate to blend with the largely blue-collared voters. They considered purchasing a pickup so John could ride through all the towns, waving at people from the back, but decided buying a new truck would not be necessary, because once the time came, the newest campaign staff member could drive John around in his rus-tic Chevy S-10.

After his Fourth of July speech, John asked Blue Gene once again to join his staff. This time, Blue Gene accepted. Everything in his life sug-gested that he should stop being so hardheaded and allow his family to employ him. First and foremost, his savings—which he kept in a Pringles can—had dwindled to thirty dollars. No one was buying his toys at the flea market, and the longer he stayed there, the more foolish he felt for even attempting to follow such a childish dream. And while he could have reapplied for his old job at Wal-Mart, after John's rally, he saw that working for his brother would be much more worthwhile—much more important—than unloading trucks. Besides, his old job would proba-bly be waiting for him once the election was over. From now until No-vember, he could serve God and country by helping out with his family's cause.

So Blue Gene agreed to take the job, but on three conditions: First, he wanted to be treated the same as all of John's other staff members. Second, he wanted to keep regular hours. His time working on John's behalf had to equal a minimum of forty hours a week. And third, he wanted minimum wage. After these demands were easily met, Blue Gene packed all his wares at the flea market and told his neighboring vendors goodbye. He now stored his childhood toys in the walk-in closet of the Mapothers' poolhouse.

This was another major life change for Blue Gene. In late July he moved out of the trailer he had lived in for six years and into the poolhouse. Elizabeth had invited him to return home and sleep in his old room, at least until he was earning enough money to support himself again. Blue Gene refused, and Elizabeth offered him the poolhouse as a compromise. He decided that staying there wouldn't be surrendering his independence.

The first week of living on the Mapother estate had gone smoothly. Living there allowed him to spend more time with Arthur, since John was always dropping him off before going to dinner meetings with precinct captains and ward leaders. Blue Gene gave Arthur one of his old toys every time they saw each other.

The fact that he lived in the fully furnished little house behind his parents' mansion reminded Blue Gene of a show he had once seen about some deeply troubled California types. He had liked the show. It centered on a guy from the wrong side of the tracks who had to coexist with a bunch of rich people. He decided not to watch it again, though, because it was too much like a soap opera, and the music was fruity.

$ $ $

Until tonight, Blue Gene had mostly done physical work for John, helping a crew get the old JCPenney building cleaned up and converted into a campaign headquarters. But now that Frick was starting to make some threatening lunges toward keeping his seat, what with his TV spots airing, Henry said it was time to put Blue Gene to better use. While the rest of the Mapother team was busy preparing some commercials of their own, Blue Gene could be out among the voters. And when John told Blue Gene to go wherever a lot of working folks gathered, Blue Gene knew to be at Bashford's National Guard Armory on Wednesday night.

John told Blue Gene to think of what he was doing tonight not as campaigning, but as "spreading the good word." For the next ninety-one days leading to November 2, Blue Gene was supposed to make the most of every encounter he had with his old friends, because they were more than just people now. They were voters. Still, Blue Gene wasn't that comfortable "spreading the good word." He *did* mean every word he said to the voters, but it still felt phony just to be asking someone for a vote. At least it got him out of the house.

After smoking a Parliament and admiring the canopied war trucks outside, Blue Gene passed under an eagle statue spreading its wings above the armory entrance. He wore a new pair of light blue denim shorts, one of several pairs Elizabeth had bought him when she noticed he was going around wearing his older shorts unbuttoned to accommodate his maturing stomach. With his new shorts he wore his MAPOTHER FOR CONGRESS T-shirt with the sleeves cut off and his usual black flip-flops. After paying seven dollars—it had been six when he used to attend—he went upstairs to the white-walled, white-floored armory gymnasium, where several old acquaintances came his way, glad to see him since he had once been such a loyal supporter of Heartland Championship Wrestling.

"Hey, y'all," said Blue Gene. "What's the word, Thunderbird?" he specifically asked a rat-tailed little boy.

"What do you say, Blue Gene?" said the boy's father, a tubby gerbil of a man wearing a T-shirt supporting the wrestler Triple H. "Where the hell *you* been?"

"Ah, workin' mostly. Same ol' shit. Different days."

"Haven't seen you here in forever. We thought you was dead."

Blue Gene pictured himself decomposing on the couch in front of *American Chopper* in his stuffy trailer. "Yeah, well...time flies when you're killin' flies."

Everyone laughed. With easy country courtesy, he invited his old wrestling cronies to get him all caught up on their lives. One explained how he had won back his ex-wife with a shrimp dinner and a carton of cigarettes. Another one had gotten arrested at Ralph's Pharmacy because she had forged a prescription for Vicodin, adding a zero to change the quantity from 30 to 300. As Blue Gene listened, he was pleased to see that nothing had changed at the old armory, which had been built in the 1940s. Basketball goals hung at both ends. There were no bleachers, only metal folding chairs set up around the four sides of a rickety wrestling ring. A couple of wrestlers set up merchandise tables in the corners of the gym, but their pitiful selection was mostly just personal photographs of themselves. Blue Gene did spot one new sight: a drum kit and some guitar amplifiers sitting in the back, unattended.

The conversation stalled when a gigantic, clinch-jawed young fellow joined the group. Blue Gene introduced him as Josh Balsam, the late Private Tim Balsam's son, which was exactly how John wanted him to word it. Balsam looked preppy around the edges with his Hollister shirt, khaki shorts, and Nike basketball shoes, but a thick black cross tattooed on his calf muscle publicized his ruggedness.

"They got a band playin' here now?" Blue Gene asked to restart the conversation.

"Yeah," said Jeff, the bearded and bandannaed biker from the monster-truck rally. "That started about a month ago. They play before the show gets started and in between the matches, I guess because people were getting restless during those long lulls."

"Can they rock it out?"

"Hell no," said a frizzy-haired woman in sweatpants and a T-shirt showing a grotesque wrestler named Mankind. "They just play that real fast, noisy stuff. You can't understand a word they sayin'. And their singer's always bitchin' about something."

"Who is he?"

"It's a girl," said the gerbilish man, "and I don't know who she is, but me and her 'bout got into it one time over her puttin' down guns."

"Hmm," Blue Gene said, rubbing his 'stache as he looked at the deserted instruments.

Then they talked wrestling. They all agreed that they missed Stone Cold Steve Austin, that the Rock was a son of a bitch for quitting wrestling to become a movie star, and that at least they could always rely on the Undertaker. But they were split over the latest World Wrestling

Entertainment champion, John Cena. Blue Gene dismissed him as a pretty boy and got a laugh by saying Cena probably popped a boner every time he touched another wrestler.

"Anyway, y'all, while I's here, I's gonna help out my brother. We'd 'preciate it if you could go out and vote for him on November 2."

"Who's your brother?" asked the frizzy-haired woman.

Blue Gene opened a plastic Wal-Mart sack he had been holding and took out some leaflets. "Him," he said, pointing to John's leading-man face.

"*Really?*"

"Yeah. If y'all'd vote for him, that'd be awesome." He passed out leaflets as he talked. "I know it ain't like me doing something like this, askin' for a vote and all, but I wouldn't be doing it 'less I believed in my brother."

"Ain't he in charge over at Westway?" asked the gerbilish man.

"He's second in charge behind my dad, actually. But that ain't what he's about in terms of his politics."

"What's he about, then?"

"Values. The traditional ones. And he's all about freedom. Like, for instance, I'm big on my right to bear arms, and he's all about people bein' free to do that."

"That sounds good."

"Yeah. He believes in defense. Supports our troops. And he cares about the simple folk. Obviously. He's got me as a brother. That there's all you need to know."

"Me and Doug don't normally vote in nothin' 'cept for the presidential elections," said the woman. "But normally our friends don't got their brothers runnin'."

"There it is," said Blue Gene. "That's what I'm sayin'. Well, it was good to see all y'all. I'll leave y'all alone now."

Blue Gene shook everyone's hands, thanked them kindly, and even said, "God bless y'all" before he and Balsam moved on.

"How long you been here?" Balsam asked sleepily.

"Not long. They were the first ones I talked to."

"Fuckin' foreman kept me after."

"That's a'ight. Let's hit them next." Blue Gene nodded at a family waiting in line at the concession stand set up in the armory's kitchen. "Hold on," said Blue Gene, stopping short of the family. "I feel like I'm talkin' too much. You just jump right in anytime you want to say something, a'ight?"

"I ain't much on talkin'. Gimme those and I'll be in charge of handin' them out." Blue Gene handed Balsam the Wal-Mart sack full of leaflets.

"Well, we sure do 'preciate you helpin' us out like this."

"Way I see it, I'm a grown-ass man. 'Bout time to be showin' some responsibility. My dad would fuckin' kill me if he seen the Army wouldn't take me."

Blue Gene wondered why the Army wouldn't take such a big, strong man who was so passionate about defending his country. There appeared to be nothing physically wrong with him, except for his slanted teeth and the little scars on his scalp where his buzz cut didn't grow. But Blue Gene wasn't comfortable asking Balsam a personal question and probably never would be.

"You and me both are doing our duty right now," he replied. "We're gonna get my brother in office, and he'll use his power to defend the country. That one that's in there now, he ain't gonna be supportin' the troops or anything. He's too busy bonin' people. This here's patriotism." Blue Gene pointed to the leaflets, covered in photos and promises.

For the rest of the night, Blue Gene and Balsam approached people who looked to be of voting age, and Blue Gene did the talking, except for when someone hesitated in taking a leaflet. "Take it," Balsam would say. "It won't rot your hand off."

Balsam told Blue Gene that back on the Fourth of July, he had managed to give Mitchell Gibson only one good punch to the back of the head before he got away. After Blue Gene relayed this incident to John, John became hesitant to accept Balsam's offer to be a volunteer. That sort of thing, he told Blue Gene, that sort of unnecessary violence, was not something he would want to be associated with during campaign time.

But Balsam kept calling Blue Gene every few days, asking what he could do to help, until finally John decided that having someone like Josh Balsam at his disposal was a bonus he could not pass up. Besides his war-hero name recognition, there was the young man's zeal. Balsam hardly knew John, yet he had already gone to the trouble of defending him against a dissenter. John said it was kind of creepy that Balsam had taken to him so quickly and so adamantly, especially since he didn't even want pay. Blue Gene said he could understand, though, because none of this had anything to do with money. Balsam's father hadn't defended his country for money. He had defended it for all the reasons John talked about in his speech. Money didn't matter. Blue Gene said he understood this better than anyone.

$$\$\,\$\,\$$

At six fifty-one, the armory echoed with the sporadic pop of a snare drum, the four individual hums of bass strings, and the stunted blasts of electric-guitar power chords. Then a woman's voice came out of two PA speakers and into the ears of the eighty-five wrestling fans sitting in the metal chairs, not to mention the six fans of Uncle Sam's Finger who stood in the back, facing the music.

"Hi. I'm Jackie, and we're Uncle Sam's Finger from right here in Bashford. This first song's called 'Don't Be a Man' because I think that no three words in the English language have caused more pain and suffering than *be a man*." The singer nodded to the slender, spiky-haired drummer, who rapidly clicked his drumsticks to start the song.

Blue Gene had never seen or heard anything in Bashford quite like her. First of all, it was a *girl* making such a big, badass noise, and a petite little thing at that. Sure, he had bought a Lita Ford tape at the flea market, and he didn't complain when Janis Joplin came on the radio, but Blue Gene had never seen a female play electric guitar in person. The few female musicians he had ever seen on stage played bass and were like breasted props mixed in with the background of some bar bands playing at Shooter's Pool Hall. And he had definitely never seen a band *fronted* by a female and backed by two males. He concluded the guys in this band must have been hardcore gaywads.

Her guitar, which looked about as long as she was tall, was covered with bold yellow and red headlines cut from tabloid magazines. The guitar screamed BRITNEY'S DRUG NIGHTMARE and PARIS HILTON CAN'T READ. Blue Gene remembered sitting in Bernice's lap when he was little as she read him the *National Enquirer* and *Star*. To this day, sometimes at the checkout line at Wal-Mart he was tempted to buy a copy for old time's sake.

The singer was really getting into it, her pale arms leading out of a red T-shirt that said, "The more I learn about women, the more I like my truck." She attacked her gaudy guitar with buzzsaw downstrokes, her wide, possessed-looking eyes staring fearlessly at the audience. As for Blue Gene's own eyes, he became conscious of blinking. He was trying not to.

She wasn't that good-looking, really, so skinny and convulsive and elfin in the face. But there was something about her that Blue Gene found attractive. Maybe it was her energy. The noise she and her band produced had enough energy to knock someone conscious.

Her brunette bangs swung like Christmas ornament tassels as she strummed away and spouted lyrics from an unruly mouth. Blue Gene's eyes settled on her wild, bony knees poking out at him like possibilities from gaping holes in her jeans.

As for the sound of her band, Blue Gene didn't quite know what to make of it, except that it was fast, angry, sloppy, and even a little sad. Some of the notes she played sounded like they were crying, and the melodies frowned, too, but the overall noise coming out of the speakers still sounded like a teenage keg party. Whatever it was, it didn't belong in the National Guard Armory. The wide-open gymnasium space made for murky, echoed acoustics, and Blue Gene could make out only a few random phrases she sang in her not-so-lovely voice, like "War breeds war breeds war breeds war" and "I've never seen a purple mountain. Have you?" That last phrase sounded familiar, but before he could figure out where he had heard it, Balsam was yelling in his ear.

"Come on Mapother! Let's get some fuckin' votes."

Blue Gene nodded. As he turned, he saw that most of the audience had their backs to the band and looked annoyed. Blue Gene and Balsam approached an older man in a wheelchair but quickly saw they couldn't compete with the loudness of the band. Balsam cussed. He handed the man a leaflet and screamed, "Vote for him!"

The song was over in two minutes, and its abrupt ending was met with the silence of a pursed-lipped audience. Blue Gene raised his hands to clap but lowered them when he saw he was alone, except for the six punky teenagers who were there to see the band, not the wrestling.

"Sorry we don't sound more like Kenny Chesney," said the singer to the wrestling crowd, her voice oozing with sarcasm.

"Sorry you sound like shit," said Balsam to Blue Gene, who laughed at both comments.

$ $ $

As was the custom at Heartland Championship Wrestling, before the first match a recording of the National Anthem was played. Everyone stood, many with baseball caps over their hearts as they stared at Old Glory hanging from the rafters—everyone except Jackie Stepchild, who sat on her guitar amp through the entire song.

As soon as the song ended, Balsam asked Blue Gene, "You see that little bitch over there sittin' during the National Anthem?"

"No," said Blue Gene, though he'd had his eyes on her the whole time.

"Well she did. Sat there the whole fuckin' time."

Blue Gene shook his head. "Bitch. I mean, I reckon that's her right, but she oughtta show some respect."

"Yeah, it's her right, and it's my right to smack her in the fuckin' head."

A wrestler's theme music came on. It was Black Sabbath's "Iron Man," whose opening riff excited several members of the audience. Blue Gene and Balsam had decided ahead of time to sit during the matches. Blue Gene didn't want to bother anyone during the action; plus, he wanted to watch it himself.

A haggard, fisherman-looking fellow in the front corner announced the wrestlers, but the music drowned out most of what he said. First, he announced Turbulence, whom Blue Gene remembered from when he used to drag Cheyenne to the armory. Turbulence, an average-size fiftysomething, strutted down the aisle and snarled at the audience. A toothless seventy-year-old woman screeched, "Kiss my ass!" She had been coming to the matches for years, always sitting on the aisle. Everyone got a kick out of her. She seemed to unload all her worldly frustrations that had built up over the past week on the bad-guy wrestlers. The only thing that separated her from the wrestlers was a thin rope. Sometimes the villains acted like they were going to step over the rope to shut her up, but everyone knew this could never happen.

The haggard announcer/soundman faded out "Iron Man" and replaced it with "Save a Horse, Ride a Cowboy," by the country duo Big and Rich. This one really got the crowd going. A young wrestler named Charley Horse came out wearing tasseled brown boots and a black horsetail attached to his rear. He neighed as he trotted down the aisle, which the children seemed to like. As soon as he slid under the bottom rope, Turbulence grabbed him by the tail and pummeled him, stomping his foot on the mat with each blow.

Pro wrestling was a childhood obsession that Blue Gene had never outgrown. He and Mitchell Gibson had started watching it together on Saturday mornings, back in the glory days of Hulk Hogan and "Macho Man" Randy Savage. He was fascinated by the idea of two men acting as if they wanted to kill each other but then laughing about it in the locker room, complimenting each other on how well they had done and going out for beers afterward.

That night at the armory, Blue Gene soon found he couldn't gather the small amount of concentration necessary to watch Turbulence hip-toss and clothesline his way to victory over his goofy opponent. He couldn't stop staring at the singing girl, who still sat on her amp, occasionally sharing a laugh with the drummer and the rockabilly bass player with big muttonchop sideburns. He bet she slept with both of them.

He couldn't stop dwelling on how she had ruined everything by not standing for the National Anthem. He had never seen anyone do that in all his life. Nothing short of paralysis could justify this.

He knew the type: too cool to show respect for her own country, putting down the government that kept her safe every chance she got. Even if the current system were replaced by a completely new kind, she'd put it down too, bitching just to be bitching. It could never work, having his world and hers mix their oceans. She'd take one look at him and laugh. Screw her. If she was so cool and unique, then why was she wearing those black Chuck Taylors, just like all the other rock 'n' roll people?

After his finishing move, an inverted piledriver, Turbulence pinned Charley Horse, and a fragile referee slapped the mat, one-two-three. After the ref raised Turbulence's arm in victory, the band sped through another couple songs, one called "Lavender Quagmire," the other called "False Alarm." Blue Gene was able to catch a few lyrics here and there: something about "Jeffrey Dahmer and the Unabomber," something about "scraped skies and compromise," something about people being "walking depositories for Starbucks coffee," and something about "tyrants with ties on." Then there were some words in the second song she kept repeating, so much so that Blue Gene found it obnoxious. Blue Gene assumed the words were foreign. They sounded like *emmo anywhy*.

$$$

Most of the HCW wrestlers fell into one of two categories: they were either large, middle-aged men like Biggun' McGraw, whose weight was distributed in fat, not muscle, or they were sixteen- to twenty-five-year-olds, like the Stranger, who had completely ordinary physiques. None were the ultramuscular, thick-necked type as seen on TV. Also unlike the big-time wrestlers, these men did not shave their body hair. They were not ready for that kind of commitment.

Biggun' McGraw joyfully assaulted the Stranger, whom Blue Gene didn't recall from the old days. Blue Gene didn't like the Stranger because instead of boots and spandex trunks he simply wore shorts and an undershirt. But then, the Stranger was clearly determined to be disliked: insulting the audience, telling them their lives were meaningless, and periodically yelling, "None of this matters!" as Biggun' gorilla-pressed him up and down the squared circle. After Biggun' pinned him with a fisherman's suplex, the Stranger shrugged his shoulders and said, "What difference does it make?" When he ambled back down the aisle, the loudmouth seventy-year-old yelled, "You didn't even try, you little shit!"

"This song's for all you sports fans," the spunky singer said drily after both wrestlers had returned to the locker room. "It's called 'When Jocks Cry.'" The band started another fast, indecipherable number. Blue Gene had to admit that the title was pretty funny. When he played on Commonwealth County High's basketball team, he used to think his teammates were ridiculous for crying when they lost a big game. These were guys who probably hadn't let loose a tear since childhood, yet that's what it took to make them cry: losing a ballgame.

Blue Gene never could understand why people took sports so seriously. He first noticed it when he was eleven, when Henry forced him to play Junior Pro basketball. Before his first practice, young Blue Gene had assumed that since everybody seemed to like sports so much, and since sports were basically just games, the practices would be fun. He soon saw that the atmosphere of a basketball practice was serious to the point of graveness. At least the games had music and popcorn and people cheering. But the practices had no light moments—just these taskmaster coaches who seemed to try their hardest to make the boys feel bad about themselves. On through high school, he attempted to joke at practices, such as when he'd suggest the team practice signaling for timeouts in midair right before they fell out of bounds. The coaches scolded him every time. Nobody laughed anyway. All the players acted afraid to do anything at all. The practices felt like punishment to Blue Gene, and when the maiming of his legs ended his sports career, he was secretly happy that he'd never have to frown and sweat through another one again.

The downside of no longer playing a sport was that he and Henry had absolutely nothing to talk about. What made Blue Gene's stunted basketball career even harder for Henry was the fact that John had also been a disappointment in the way of sports; he had failed a drug test his freshman year.

"When Jocks Cry" came to an abrupt end, and silence again prevailed, except for the underwhelming applause of the six punk rock kids. Jackie didn't bother saying the title of the next song, and she wasn't showing the manic effort she had been earlier. After this song was over, a wrestler named Satan suddenly marched out and grabbed the microphone from the ring announcer. Satan accused another wrestler, B.J. "Wild Oats" Dufrane, of cutting him off on River Town Road on the way to the armory. Wild Oats came out and denied this, but Satan wouldn't let it go, until finally he challenged Wild Oats to put the soul of his mother (who was also his manager) on the line in a falls-count-anywhere match.

This sort of thing was exactly why Blue Gene loved wrestling. Unlike the more respectable sports, pro wrestling was a show first and foremost. Satan went on to beat Wild Oats Dufrane with a finishing maneuver he called Eternal Slamnation. Wild Oats's mother fled to the locker room before her soul could be sacrificed, and Satan scurried after her.

That's one thing Blue Gene could say for himself: he liked what he liked. He bet the singing girl didn't let herself like what *she* liked. She probably thought everyone here was a moron for liking wrestling, without ever giving it a chance herself. He wished her band would've stayed down in whatever basement it had crawled out of. Probably all she cared about was being hip, just like some of the metal kids he used to party with in a shed out in the county. They wouldn't admit to liking any Metallica albums recorded after the band's original bass player, Cliff Burton, was killed, which was the fashionable opinion for die-hard metalheads. No one could ever accuse Blue Gene of being fashionable.

$ $ $

After the announcer called for an intermission, Uncle Sam's Finger began another song. Jackie's vocals turned cross as she watched the nicotine-deprived crowd herd itself toward the back door. Blue Gene was one of them. He turned his back to the band as he passed. Only forty-five people remained in the armory, half of them children.

Now that they were outside and audible over the music, Blue Gene resumed the campaigning while Balsam mostly repeated, "That singin' bitch didn't stand for the National Anthem." When the band finished its song, this time, in place of silence, Balsam led a chorus of "boos."

"You know," Jackie said firmly into her microphone, "you can show some *class* even when you don't have any." Everyone looked into the armory through the propped-open double doors. "You are exactly the people who I want to hear these songs, and you won't even listen. All you want to do is smoke your cigarettes. Even when it's a hundred degrees out."

"You got no room to talk!" yelled a burly man in an Orange County Choppers T-shirt. "We're supposed to listen to *your* ass when you wouldn't even show enough respect to stand for the National Anthem?"

The smokers reinforced the man's statement with "yeahs" and "for reals."

"Wait," she replied. "Hold on. There is a very specific reason I don't stand for the National Anthem. I don't do it to offend people."

"Too late, bitch!" someone yelled.

"Wait. Hear me out. I'm not against standing for the National Anthem. I actually think it's a nice gesture. I'm just against standing for the National Anthem *at sporting events.*"

The smokers grumbled. "What the hell?" Balsam said to Blue Gene. Blue Gene took a squint-eyed drag from his cigarette and kept listening.

"Think about it. The *only* time we actually sing our National Anthem is before sporting events. Congress doesn't sing it before they're in session. No one sings it before the president comes in for his State of the Union. Just sporting events." Outside they yelled, "Shut up," but Jackie overpowered them with the mic. "Why don't we ever sing the National Anthem before movies, or plays, or concerts? It's because those things are products of the *mind*, products of the *intellect*, and we don't value the intellect in this country. That's why Paris Hilton is the most famous woman in America. And look at the morons we elect to be our leaders." She kept going, talking quickly, as if she had been waiting years for the chance to say all this and was afraid she wouldn't get it all out. "In this country, we only celebrate the physical, not the intellectual. Our national motto should be 'Anything but Thinking.' That's what should be on our quarters. We've been conditioned to think that anything that's smart or brainy is negative. Our artists are marginalized, and our athletes are worshipped. The reason we stand for the National Anthem at sporting events is so we'll associate the feeling of patriotism with competition and with men engaged in physical conflict. We're taught at an early age to stand up and show pride in these things. We're brainwashed to be obsessed with *winning.* It's just one more subversive thing that makes the public more likely to support wars, because after all, war is a physical conflict, too. It's a competition."

"Shut the fuck up, bitch!" shouted Balsam from outside. His comment received a favorable response from the crowd, but it only made her laugh and roll her big brown eyes.

"If we start singing the National Anthem before things that celebrate the mind and not just the body, *that's* when I'll join all of you, because *that's* what we should truly be proud of about America. This is the country that has given the world rock 'n' roll and jazz and *Star Wars* and Frank Sinatra and Bob Dylan and David Letterman and Louis Armstrong and *To Kill a Mockingbird* and the *Godfather* movies. Our creativity, our talent—that's what we should be proud of. Not our ability to win wars."

"You need to remember," yelled a man with a high-and-tight haircut, "there were men that fought in wars so you could have that opinion. That's who we're standing up for."

"You all *always say that*. Like if our military doesn't invade these poverty-stricken third world countries, our entire democracy will just cease to exist. The reason we fight wars is for imperialism. For the richest people to get more money. I don't want anyone to die for the sake of money. Why do *you* all?"

"I don't care if she is a woman," Balsam told Blue Gene. "I'll beat her head off and walk away from it and not even think about it."

"Love it or leave it!" someone yelled.

"I *do* love America! But it's not *perfect*. You all act like America is *infallible*. Horrible things happen here, just like anywhere. Women get raped at our rest stops. There were *slaves* for most of our history. We're like the only modernized country without universal healthcare. And the low class is so—"

Suddenly, her voice was no longer amplified. She turned around. Frowning at her next to the PA was Turbulence, who had changed out of his trunks and into Zubaz pants and a fanny pack.

"You're done," he said. "Get out."

"*Chuck*," she said. "Did you hear what all they were saying to me?"

"They're my customers. They can say whatever the hell they want. I told you to stop that preaching, but you didn't, and I want you to pack up your stuff. I don't want y'all playing here anymore."

Turbulence walked to the opposite side of the gymnasium and ordered the ring announcer to play a radio station over the PA. A song by Justin Timberlake called "SexyBack" came on, and order was restored.

$$$

Outside in the humid August heat, everyone was calling the outspoken girl a crazy bitch. Blue Gene agreed. "She talks like somebody who gets everything she knows out of books," he said, "but nothin' from talkin' to actual people. Pro'ly never even *met* a soldier."

But that rigmarole about celebrating the physical—bits of it made sense to Blue Gene, though he wouldn't dare say so to the others. He found one glaring mistake in her argument, though: pro wrestling was not a true sport. Yes, it contained plenty of physical conflict, but it was all scripted. So, according to what she said, she *should* stand for the anthem before a pro wrestling event, because wrestling had writers. But for people like her who were so full of talk, saying and doing were two entirely different affairs.

Within five minutes, Jackie exited where everyone, even her bandmates, was smoking. She rolled out her rectangular Crate amp with its two twelve-inch speakers. Once she reached the back steps, she had to lift it. Blue Gene briefly considered helping her, but he figured she was the type that would be insulted by his even offering, and it also might look bad to the voters. The amp looked like it weighed more than she did, and in no time, it was tumbling to the pavement. She nearly fell with it but was able to hold herself up on the rail. Everyone was looking at her. She blushed.

Her bandmates came over to the bottom of the steps. One turned the amp right side up, while the other picked up all the cords and spare guitar strings that had fallen out.

"You all *saw* I needed help," she said to her bandmates in a shaky voice.

"Damnit, Jackie," said the bass player. "Every time we offer to help you, you tell us you can do it yourself."

"I *clearly* needed help this time, but all you could do was just stand there and smoke. All you all ever *do* is smoke. Neither of you ever have a dime, but you always have enough money for your cigarettes, don't you?"

"Would you stop it?" said the drummer. Of the three musicians, he seemed to be the one most devoted to rock 'n' roll, with his cement-spiked hair and arms plastered in tattoos.

"I'm sorry. I know it's not your fault. That's the genius of the to-bacco companies. They know that people will buy cigarettes even when they're poor. Of course, you don't have to allow that to happen, but I guess it's none of my business." The bass player told Jackie to shut up and walked back inside. She started to push her amp away.

"You just can't stop runnin' that fuckin' mouth, can you?" asked Balsam before taking a drag from his cigarette. He approached Jackie, tow-ering over her.

"I wasn't *talking* to you."

"You're standin' there puttin' down smokers right here in the mid-dle of a bunch of smokers. I think somebody needs to teach your ass some respect."

"Come on, Jackie," said the drummer. "Let's go."

"That's right, little boy," said Balsam, now facing the drummer. "Run away."

The drummer laughed. "Are you in third grade?"

"No, but I'm gonna fuck you up."

Blue Gene walked over and stood next to Balsam. He didn't appre-ciate the girl's smoking comments, either, and the drummer had this with-it, rockstar way about him that he hated, but he had told John that he would keep himself and Balsam out of trouble. This was his job now, and Blue Gene always took his job seriously.

"Come on, Balsam. Let's go smoke another smoke."

"I'm sorry I said anything," said Jackie. "What's stupid about this is that I'm on *your* side. These big tobacco corporations have got it so we have a biological need to poison ourselves. They even get us to *pay* to poison ourselves! We spend our money on cigarettes, we get poorer and sicker and die, and the rich, old, white businessmen just get richer and richer and live and never even thank us."

Now that he was close to her, Blue Gene saw a slight gap between

Jackie's front teeth. Her mouth looked gawky, like it didn't know how to situate itself.

"Is she your woman?" Balsam asked the drummer.

"So what if she is?"

"'Cause if she was my woman, I'd be keepin' her ass in line." The drummer gave Balsam a hard look that implied, "Keep talking." At this point, everyone outside seemed to forget about their cigarettes. They all stretched their necks with expectation.

"Stop it, you all," said Jackie. "I fall for their schemes, too. I love buying scratch-off lottery tickets. But if you go in a convenience store, who do you see buying lottery tickets? It's never some guy in a nice suit, paying for gas for his Lexus, is it? No. It's us. *We're* the ones that buy lottery tickets, the ones who can only afford five dollars of gas at a time for our shitty old cars. We're the ones who buy lottery tickets because we *need* to win the lottery the most, or we at least need that hope. Yet we're the ones who lose our money because of it. We're being preyed upon. It's just like with fireworks. Take a good look at who buys the most fireworks for the Fourth of July. It's not the rich. Take a good look above Vandalia Hills on the Fourth, and you won't see a thing. They're probably sitting in their backyards by their pools, watching *us* shoot off *our* fireworks for free. We buy all the Roman candles that'll fit in our carts, yet we have the *least* to celebrate. We have the *least* reason to be patriotic."

"All I know is you can love it or leave it," said Balsam.

Blue Gene had almost said it himself. He joined the others in saying, "Yeah" and "'At's right." He took a defiant drag from his cigarette.

"You speak in clichés," Jackie replied.

"Listen here, bitch. If you're puttin' down patriots, you're talkin' to the wrong guy. Now I'm tellin' you right now, shut your motherfuckin' mouth!"

"Would you *cool* it?" asked the drummer.

Balsam glared at him. "We didn't pay to listen to her bitch," he said. The smokers grunted their agreement.

"No," said the drummer. "But you did pay to watch a bunch of half-naked men have fake fights."

Balsam's entire being clinched. He started toward the drummer, but stopped when he heard a deep voice speak up.

"Don't call it fake." After he said it, Blue Gene coolly blew smoke out of the side of his mouth and ran a finger across his mustache. Jackie looked at him and covered her mouth.

"*What*?" asked the drummer. Blue Gene slowly moved between him and Balsam.

"*Fake* ain't the right word for wrestling. It's *staged* and it's *scripted*, just like a movie. But you wouldn't call a *movie* fake, would ya?"

The drummer wouldn't answer. Balsam continued glaring at him.

"And so what if it *is* fake?" asked Blue Gene. "Isn't that better than if it was *real* and these guys really *were* trying to kill each other? That's what they did back in olden times, in ancient Rome, so aren't you at least glad that the violent stuff we watch *is* fake and not real?"

"Yeah," agreed the smokers.

"Hey," said Jackie. "Don't be treating us like we don't know anything about wrestling. Believe it or not, I'm one of the *bookers* for HCW. I even made up the match for tonight's main event, and all of you should pay close attention to it. You might learn something."

Blue Gene looked off across the parking lot.

"I don't care *what* you say, dude," said the drummer, taking advantage of Blue Gene's silence. "There *are* a lot of idiots out there who believe what they're watching is real."

"No, now, they *want* to believe it's real," said Blue Gene, making a conscious effort not to look at Jackie. "There's a big difference there. We *want* to believe it's real, 'cause believin' that lets us escape just a little bit on Monday nights when it comes on TV. And if we want to escape for a couple hours, why don't you just let us enjoy it, man?"

"Whatever, man," sighed the drummer. "Come on, Jackie. I'll put that in your car."

Jackie sighed and mumbled something before rolling her amp across the parking lot. Balsam stared at them, waiting for them to say something, but they didn't. The smokers gathered around Blue Gene and complimented him on how well he had defended their beloved pastime. He brushed off their praise, saying he'd had the same argument with his parents a hundred times before.

$ $ $

Besides running his own flea market booth, the one other job that Blue Gene always dreamed of having was being a writer for World Wrestling Entertainment. With a new thrill belching through him, he waited for a chance to talk to the singer. The smokers went inside when they heard the next match being introduced, but Blue Gene lingered, saying he wanted to smoke one more Parlie. He watched Jackie as she sat in her car, a mid-nineties Pontiac Grand Am with stickers on the back for bands he had never heard of. Her drummer had already gone inside, and when she walked back toward the building alone, Blue Gene went down the steps and met her halfway across the parking lot.

"So you really make up stuff for wrestling?"

"Yeah." She looked at Blue Gene suspiciously and kept walking. He followed her.

"That's really cool. Are they hirin' anybody else?"

"No—well, I don't know. I'm pretty sure I'm fired now, so maybe they are. You'd have to ask Chuck Thurby."

She started up the stairs. "When's your band gonna play again?" Blue Gene asked the back of her head. She stopped and turned around.

"Why do you ask?"

"I liked y'all."

"No you didn't."

"Don't tell me what I like. I know what I like."

"Sorry."

"That's okay. Y'all kicked it. Ass."

"Thanks." She turned and went up the stairs.

"Wait. When's your band gonna play again?"

She turned. "Oh. No telling. This was the only place we had to play at in this stupid town."

"What about the bars?"

"They only let you play if you're a cover band, and I refuse to play covers." Blue Gene nodded. "We have a MySpace page. If we ever get some more shows, I'll post them on there. Just look up Uncle Sam's Finger."

"Right on." Again, she turned the first chance she got. Blue Gene watched as she headed toward the door, mad at her for clearly not wanting to talk to him, and mad at himself for looking like something a tomcat coughed up. Feeling uneasy, he craved another cigarette, a craving that mercifully allowed a joke to occur to him.

"Hey, can I just ask you one more thing?" She turned at the doorway. "You got a cigarette on ya?"

"Did you not just *hear* what I said about—"

"I'm jokin', man."

"Oh." She smiled. "You got me." Blue Gene noticed that she was actually more attractive when she wasn't smiling, and she must have known it, because she hastily hid her smile with her hand. "I know I shouldn't have said all that to you all about cigarettes. I shouldn't have said any of that stuff. I get so carried away when I'm in front of an audience, and then the promoter kicked me out, and then I dropped my amp, and—well, I'm sorry."

"That's a'ight. Most of us would quit smokin' if we could. I tried those patches, but the damn things wouldn't stay lit."

Thankfully, she laughed. "Hey—I agreed with what you were saying before," she said, coming down a couple of steps. "I hate it when people call wrestling fake, too."

"So you do *like* wrestling, then, right?"

"I *love* wrestling." Before she completed the sentence, as if by reflex, Blue Gene's arm shot out for a handshake.

"What'd you say your name was?" She eyeballed his hand before giving it a quick shake.

"Jackie."

"Good to know you. May I ask your last name?"

"Stepchild."

Blue Gene laughed but stopped when he saw her face wriggle.

"It's my stage name."

Blue Gene stared at her face in the streetlight. She had a severe sort of attractiveness, all of her features shouting out at you so that you really noticed them. Because of this, her profile didn't do her justice.

"How'd you get a gig writing for wrestling?"

"I shouldn't have said anything about that. The promoter made me swear I wouldn't talk to any of the fans about anything because he's so secretive about—oh, who cares? He kicked me out, so what difference does it make? Hey—yeah, I know what I'll do. I'll tell you all I know about HCW, and then you should tell all your friends everything I've told *you* so everyone will be in on it. Yeah. That'll stick it to him."

"That's righteous." Blue Gene pulled out a cigarette but couldn't find his lighter. Jackie raised her index finger and reached inside her jean pocket. She pulled out a gold lighter, flipped it open, and produced a flame like a seasoned tobacco addict.

"Well, I'll be. All that big talk, and look at you. Pro'ly smoke with the best of 'em."

"No. I really don't smoke. I always keep a lighter on me in case someone needs a light." She lit his cigarette, casting a glow on his mustache and gray-ringed eyes. "So anyway, Chuck Thurby, he's the promoter. He's also one of the wrestlers."

"Which one?"

"Turbulence."

"*Really?*"

"Yeah."

"Huh. You wouldn't think that."

"Yeah. He's a boring wrestler. He doesn't even *have* a gimmick."

"A *gimmick?*"

"That's wrestling terminology for a wrestler's character or their shtick. You know, like Val Venis's gimmick is that he's a porn star. So let everyone know that Turbulence runs the whole show so that it ruins people's illusions."

"That reminds me of Vince McMahon. When I was little, they portrayed Vince as bein' just one of the commentators callin' the matches. Then, during that big steroid trial, I come to find out he's the head of the entire World Wrestling Federation. Blew my mind."

"Yeah. I was the same way. But later on I became a smart fan. I started reading books on wrestling, and then the internet came along, and really, it's the second, deeper layer of wrestling—all these things going on beneath the surface of the actual matches—that I like about it. I don't really even like the wrestling itself. I hate the violence. Anyway, Chuck's day job is being a contractor, and so he was doing some work on my house—well, my *mom's* house—and we kind of got to know him. I liked talking to him since I was so into wrestling, and then he found out I had a band and offered me this gig playing at his matches." Jackie and Blue Gene moved out of the way for her bandmates, who were coming down the steps with their equipment. "And you know, this is actually a pretty good-sized crowd compared to what we're used to, because we normally played in garages and basements and crappy little clubs in Donato Falls. And also I thought it would be cool to sing these political, antiwar songs in a National Guard Armory. So we started playing here, but I noticed the setups for his matches were just *awful*, just so stupid and unoriginal, and I offered to come up with some ideas, and he started using some of them, and then he told me I could be co-booker with him. A booker is the person who comes up with the angles—which is another word for storylines—for the matches."

"So some of that in there tonight was your ideas?"

"Yeah. The Stranger was my idea. I don't know if anybody really gets that gimmick, but he's supposed to be a heel, and people seem to hate him, so I guess it works. You know what a heel is?"

"Uh-uh."

"A heel is wrestling jargon for a bad-guy wrestler. The good guys are called faces. That's short for *babyface*."

"Cool. Who else d'you come up with?"

"Oh, let's see. I'm ashamed to say I came up with Charley Horse. There's a story behind the Charley Horse gimmick, actually. He's a newer guy here, and he was wrestling under his real name, but one night before one of his matches, Chuck found him in the locker room smoking a joint, and Chuck's really against that. So as punishment, Chuck wanted me to come up with the dumbest gimmick possible for this guy. So that's why he has to be Charley Horse. He specializes in submission holds that induce leg cramps that last about a minute."

Blue Gene found himself nodding at nearly every word that came from her bodacious mouth. A woman talking wrestling was a sound he could get used to.

"But what I'm really proud of is this new tag team I came up with. Chuck trained a couple of these Mexican guys to be wrestlers, but they couldn't come up with a gimmick. So I found a way to tie them into an angle with the politician wrestler and the priest—but you'll see that at the main event. Let's see, what else? Oh, the guy that plays Satan is a disc jockey for one of the local radio stations."

The drummer and bass player of her band came up to her. "That's everything," said the drummer, hardly noticing Blue Gene. "We're heading out."

"Okay. I'm gonna stay for the main event to see if the new guys get over with the crowd."

"Did Chuck pay you yet?" asked the bass player.

"No," she said sheepishly.

"You didn't ask him, did you?" asked the drummer.

"*Yes*, I asked him. He said the only reason he was even letting us play here was because we were doing it for free, and I said, well, we want to be paid now, and he said he'd pay us if we started playing only covers, and I told him no way."

"*God*, Jackie," said the bass player.

"Hey, if you want to get paid for playing, like, 'Sister Christian,' then maybe you should join another band."

"I got a kid to feed! I need all the pay I can get."

"And you know Shelley and me are gonna get married soon," said the drummer, relieving Blue Gene. "You need to grow up. All you ever talk about is money, saying everything in the whole world goes back to money, and here you are, not even getting your bandmates paid."

"I say all the *problems* of the world go back to money. And it's the truth. We wouldn't even be arguing right now if it weren't for money."

"I'm sick of your bullshit," said the bass player. He stormed off, and the drummer followed.

Jackie turned to Blue Gene. "I gotta go talk to them. Nice meeting you."

"You too." But he hadn't even told her his name.

"Tell all the other marks in there everything I told you."

"The other *what*?"

"Oh. Sorry. The other *fans*."

$ $ $

The next couple of matches featured especially lame bottom-of-the-card wrestlers, and neither Blue Gene nor Balsam spoke as the haphazard exhibitions of Irish whips, sunset flips, and atomic drops unfolded in the ring. Occasionally Blue Gene would offer a high-pitched "woooo!" after one of the wrestlers got chopped across his bare chest. But he mostly spent the next hour keeping an eye on Jackie's guitar, waiting for her to come back inside for it.

He still knew it couldn't work. She had said some awful things about his country, but maybe he could change her, make her see things his way. Sure he could. He was the man, and she was a woman. But at least they had wrestling. They could build on that. Not even Cheyenne had been a wrestling fan; if she watched it with him, it was only because he made her.

He looked at *Cheyenne* tattooed in cursive across his pasty bicep. He had always known he would have to do something about that tattoo if he ever got serious with another woman. After all, it was only fair. He wouldn't want his woman having a tattoo of an ex on *her* arm. He had thought of a possible solution, though: if things got serious with a new woman, he could go into one of Bashford's four tattoo parlors and have the abbreviation *WY* added underneath *Cheyenne*, which would be a lot cheaper than having it removed or spelling out *Wyoming*.

He pictured himself standing with his arm around Cheyenne, God rest her soul, as they bent over the jukebox at the bowling alley, taking turns making song selections: first an Aerosmith, then a Foreigner, maybe some "Chattahoochee" action for good measure. He imagined Jackie in Cheyenne's place and wondered what she would think of the songs he picked. Screw her if she was going to judge him for liking Poison. Like she was too cool for toilets.

But there was no shaking it. He had a raw, exposed feeling, the worst it had been since that first time he had seen Heaven twirling around a pole. It then occurred to Blue Gene that he hadn't even gotten a good look at this new girl's breasts.

$ $ $

After "Wildlife" Jones submitted to a scorpion deathlock, Blue Gene and Balsam looked around the armory and saw that they had solicited all the votes they could. At half past nine, as they waited for the last match to begin, Balsam finally started talking, building a conversation on the solid foundation of silence he and Blue Gene had established over the course of the evening.

"I got some night-vision goggles," Balsam said.

"Cool. Where'd you get 'em?"

"They were my dad's."

"What you gonna do with 'em?"

"I got this idea," he leaned in closer to Blue Gene. "Like, if I put night-vision goggles on while I'm drivin', then that means I don't need to have my headlights on—you know, 'cause I'll be able to see without 'em."

"Yeah, but the other cars wouldn't be able to see you."

"I know. But say it's like two in the morning, and I'm goin' home after I've been gettin' fucked up. If I'm out on the bypass, I could be goin' a hunderd miles an hour, but the cops wouldn't even see me 'cause my lights wouldn't be on. They'd just see like a hunderd miles an hour pop up on their speed guns just out of the blue, but they wouldn't see me. They'd be like, 'What the fuck was that?' Nobody would see me, and I could drive however the fuck I wanted."

"That's a cool idea, man."

As they talked, Blue Gene felt twinges of guilt because he was getting paid to be here tonight and Balsam wasn't. Balsam was donating his time and energy purely for the cause, the Mapother cause of God and country.

"Ladies and gentlemen, this is tonight's main event!" The announcer blasted Madonna's "Like a Prayer" over the PA speakers, which returned Blue Gene to good spirits, since it reminded him of his childhood. "The following tag-team contest is scheduled for one fall. Weighing in at one-hundred and seventy-six pounds, accompanied to the ring by Sister Hoolihan, from Bethlehem, Pennsylvania...Father Flanagan!"

The crowd jeered at Father Flanagan, a two-faced priest who rebuked them weekly for their immorality, even though he himself cheated in the ring, usually with the help of Sister Hoolihan. Neither performer was convincing in his or her role—the priest was a sporty twenty-year-old, and the nun was a sluttish teen.

"That nun's got some fuckin' titties," said Balsam.

"I hear that," said Blue Gene, still watching for Jackie to return.

Then "Hail to the Chief" started playing. "And introducing his tag-team partner, weighing in at two hundred and twenty-five pounds, from Washington, D.C....Clark Charismo!" Charismo, a portly fortysomething, was a deceitful politician who was perpetually running for office. On his way to the ring he offered a handshake to the loudmouthed old woman at the aisle, but she rejected it and screamed, "Suck a dick."

Blue Gene saw Jackie enter. She put her guitar in its case and then watched the show, leaning against the back wall.

"And their opponents..." AC/DC's "You Shook Me All Night Long" electrified the audience. "Weighing in at one hundred and fifty pounds, accompanied to the ring by the Latch-Key Kid, from right here in Bashford...Gary 'the Orphan' Dorphin."

Gary "the Orphan" Dorphin was a longtime HCW fan favorite. He was a skinny but scrappy tough guy who wore costumes of tattered flannel and camouflage. An HCW veteran even though he was only twenty-four, Dorphin often complained of being poor and said he was wrestling to make ends meet for his son, the Latch-Key Kid, who was seven.

"And his tag-team partner..."

John Mellancamp's "Small Town" came on, causing the crowd to stand.

"Weighing in at two hundred and two pounds, hailing from parts unknown, he is your HCW champion...Mr. America!"

An out of shape thirty-nine-year-old, Mr. America was Heartland Championship Wrestling's most popular performer. He wore American flag trunks and often made speeches about his love of country and how he hadn't been seeing eye to eye with his boss. He had only one known weakness that his opponents occasionally stumbled across: he was extremely ticklish.

The announcer rang the bell, and Charismo and Dorphin locked up. Mr. America started a "USA" chant to encourage his partner. Soon the audience was so enthralled with the match that Blue Gene was able to break away. Balsam was busy staring toward the ring with his mouth open, not at the wrestlers but at Sister Hoolihan's comely fanny.

"I'm gonna go get a Coke," said Blue Gene. Balsam paid no attention. Self-consciously, Blue Gene walked unevenly toward Jackie.

"Hey," he said.

"Hey," said Jackie, a worried look on her elfish face. She would hardly look at Blue Gene, so he stood next to her and joined her in watching the match.

"I was meanin' to ask you." He coughed and cleared his throat. "How old are you?"

"Why are you asking?"

"To see if you're of voting age. That's why. Why else would I be asking?"

"I'm twenty-five."

"That's righteous." He rubbed his mustache. "'Cause I'm not sup-posed to bother askin' for somebody's vote if they're too young."

A typical match developed. The momentum went back and forth at first, with plenty of heads bouncing off turnbuckles and tags between partners.

"So you're asking for votes for Mapother, I guess?" She nodded at Blue Gene's sleeveless MAPOTHER FOR CONGRESS shirt.

"Oh, yeah. Here," he handed her a leaflet. "I'd 'preciate it if you'd vote for him on November 2."

"I'd never vote for Mapother," said Jackie, immediately handing back the leaflet.

"Why not?"

"A number of reasons."

"You votin' for *Frick*?"

"No. I wouldn't vote for him, either. It's not even a *choice* with those two."

"Yeah it is."

"Come *on*. They both went to the same college."

"Can't be complaining later if you don't vote."

"I'd vote if there were a third candidate, if he didn't represent big business."

"Mapother doesn't do that. Here, read the leaflet."

Father Flanagan decisively turned the match his way when Charismo distracted the ref and Sister Hoolihan racked up Gary Dor-phin's testicles from behind.

Jackie laughed as she read the front of the leaflet.

"*What?*" asked Blue Gene.

"Reasons to vote for John Hurstbourne Mapother," she read. "He obeys the laws of the land. He's respected. He *never backs down?*"

"Yeah. That's all true."

"It's so *vague*. You could say this crap about anybody. Are these things actually working?" she asked, holding up the leaflet. "Well, I'm sure they are, knowing this crowd."

"Give it here if you're gonna make fun of it." Blue Gene swiped the leaflet from her bony little fingers with their chipped green polish.

"Why would *you* help *that guy* campaign?"

"I don't have to explain myself to you. It's a free country."

"What he *ought* to print on those pamphlets in big, bold letters is:

IF ELECTED, I WILL HELP REDUCE THE
TAX BURDEN ON CORPORATIONS AND THE
WEALTHY. NOTHING LESS, NOTHING MORE."

The Orphan was suffering a merciless beating at the hands of Father Flanagan, but just before the evil priest could execute his finishing move, the Taberknuckle, the Orphan managed to crawl to his corner and tag Mr. America in the nick of time. The crowd went wild as Mr. America abused the priest all over the mat.

"You don't even know John Mapother. He might be a great guy, for all you know."

"But where is *he* right now? And what do the Mapothers care about me or you?" Blue Gene's mustache flared. "What do they care about anybody in this room?"

"Then don't vote for 'im. Sorry I come over here." He started to storm off.

"Wait, wait. Watch this. Here it comes." She nodded at the ring.

As Mr. America signaled for his own finishing maneuver, a powerbomb, he was distracted by a song that suddenly came on over the speakers. It was Neil Diamond's "America." Two dark-skinned men entered the armory, their faces and body language teeming with malevolence. One of them had a turban wrapped around his head, a Hitler mustache, and a T-shirt that said "McDonald's Sucks." The other had a long, unkempt beard, a dashiki, and no shoes. Mr. America and Charismo stopped wrestling and watched the exotic men as they marched over to the announcer table and snatched the microphone.

"I am Chico Yamaguchi," said the one in the turban. He handed the microphone to the other.

"And I am Ali LeJong. Together we are Ethnics in Effigy. Eee I Eee!"

"Eee I Eee! Eee I Eee!" they both shrieked. Mr. America and Charismo looked at each other incredulously.

"Hey, fatsos. We here for one reason and one reason only," said Chico in a strange Mexican/French accent. "To destroy America and Americans' way of living. We hate you and your backward baseball caps and your chewing gum like cows."

The crowd released a current of "boos" and profanity.

"Ooh," said Ali. "Look at the Americans with they pretty haircuts. We hate your hip-hop. Lance Armstrong, he a woman. You men so obvious about looking at women's butts. Apple pie is gross."

"Hey!" screamed the loudmouthed Clark Charismo from inside the ring. "You can't talk about America like that! This is the greatest country in the world!"

Mr. America nodded. "That's one thing we can agree on, Charismo! Your asses are mine! Come getcha some!"

The Ethnics in Effigy raced across the armory and slid into the ring. The referee lost control and signaled for the announcer to ring the bell to end the match, but the repeated ringing of a bell could not bring an end to the mayhem. Though they had been enemies just moments before, Mr. America, the Orphan, Charismo, and Flanagan all joined forces and took on the blood-crazed foreigners.

"That's a nice twist, havin' everybody come together like that," said Blue Gene. "You come up with that?" Jackie nodded.

Though they were small men, the Ethnics in Effigy were holding their own against the four Americans. They easily drop-kicked Charismo and Father Flanagan out of the ring. Mr. America and the Orphan continued to battle the wildmen.

Ethnics in Effigy overcame Gary Dorphin, and they were now ganging up on Mr. America. Luckily, the Latch-Key Kid had the presence of mind to hand Mr. America the great equalizer of professional wrestling: a folding steel chair. Mr. America raised the chair, but before he could bring it down upon the brown bodies of his rivals, they fled the ring. Blue Gene could hear Balsam screaming obscenities at Ethnics in Effigy as they backed up the aisle.

Both tag teams stood in the ring together, all of them raising one another's arms in a show of solidarity, all facing Ethnics in Effigy, who taunted them at the end of the aisle. Then Father Flanagan shook hands with Mr. America and the Orphan, while Charismo picked up the steel chair that Mr. America had just wielded. He smashed the Orphan's back, making a sick smacking noise.

"Damn," said Blue Gene.

Father Flanagan then restrained Mr. America while Charismo walloped his head with the chair. The crowd booed as Charismo and Flanagan celebrated and waved at Ethnics in Effigy, who smiled and saluted and continued insulting America and screaming, "Eeee I Eeee!" Blue Gene noticed that Balsam had left his seat. Balsam was now at the aisle, cussing his heart out at the wrestlers, who retaliated by saying, "America sucks one."

"See. Why would you want to help people like that?" asked Jackie, pointing to Charismo and Father Flanagan.

"Because," Blue Gene said defiantly. He then opened the leaflet and pointed to the picture of himself with his family that had been taken outside the Ambassador Inn with fireworks in the background. He shoved it into Jackie's hands. She looked at it and a smile slowly formed, which she immediately covered.

"Wait a minute. *Blue Gene*?" She looked at the photo and then at Blue Gene and then at the photo again. "I think I've heard of you."

Meanwhile, Blue Gene was shocked to see Balsam spitting at the wrestlers. One wrestler had to hold the other back as he screamed in a foreign tongue at this overzealous fan.

"They're your *family*?" she asked.

"Yep."

Balsam was climbing over the thin rope that separated the audience from the wrestlers.

"Shit," said Blue Gene. "I gotta go." He ran toward Balsam.

"Please, do not touch the wrestlers!" shouted the announcer over the PA. "Please, do not touch the wrestlers!" Ethnics in Effigy backed away from Balsam, toward the locker room. He was bigger than the two of them put together, and he looked crazed out of the eyes. Blue Gene jumped over the rope and stood between the wrestlers and Balsam.

"What the hell you doing?!" Blue Gene asked.

"I ain't gonna sit there and take that. I fought for my country. I sacrificed for my country!"

"Goddamn, Balsam! What are you even talkin' about?"

"I've been through so much more than they have. I could kill 'em."

"It's part of the show!"

The men portraying Ethnics in Effigy retreated.

"Come on, man," said Blue Gene, putting his hand on Balsam's solid back. Balsam was breathing heavily as Blue Gene walked with him back over the rope. "It's just a show. It's what you call an angle."

"That's what that dyke must have been talkin' 'bout. She said to watch for the main event. She put them up to this. Look at her over there with her shit-eatin' grin."

Blue Gene saw that Jackie was indeed smiling at them.

"I swear I'll blow her half in two!" Everyone in the armory was watching, and Blue Gene decided they should leave before something else happened.

"Come on, Balsam man. Let's get out of here." Reluctantly, Balsam followed Blue Gene to the exit. At the doorway, Blue Gene looked back at Jackie one last time. She waved at him, smiling awkwardly. He waved back. His mustache formed right angles at the corners, like a bracket placed snugly over his chapped lips, which were suddenly situated in an unusual position.

It was a smile.

$ $ $

Back in the ring, Mr. America struggled to get on his feet as the crowd chanted, "USA! USA!" Meanwhile, the Latch-Key Kid was leaning over his fallen father, who lay motionless on his stomach. He shook his dad's shoulder and got no response. Mr. America and the referee stood nearby.

"Look at all that snot coming out of Gary's nose. That's a nice touch."

"Yeah."

"Dad wasn't supposed to take any chair shots! Y'all knew he had a bad back!"

"Relax, Toby. We talked about it in the locker room. He volunteered for it."

"Yeah. He's just selling it extra well. He told me he was going to. Hey—who was that trying to fight with the new guys?"

"He's just a kid, but he looks like a grown man. That soldier that got killed, it's his son. He's got a few screws loose. So does that other guy that was with him."

"Wasn't that long-haired one the one who used to go around town with his shopping cart like some ol' bag lady, even though he was really rich?"

"No. That's one of those urban legends."

"Shut up! Something's wrong with Dad! Dad! Come on, Dad, answer me!"

"Gary? Move your foot if you're okay...Gary?!"

"What's wrong, y'all?"

"What are you doing out here, Clark? Stay in character. They're still watching."

"Did I hurt him? Is that mucus?"

"Either that or it could be spinal fluid."

"Are you *serious*?"

"I've seriously heard of it coming out of people's noses."

"Oh God. Gary! Gary, if you can hear me, it's Clark. I'm sorry, brother. I didn't mean to hit you that hard. Please wake up, brother."

VI.

Jackie Stepchild averaged fifty-seven nightmares a month. She blamed this on her nerves. The terrifying scenes her mind made her watch during her sleep—the madmen chasing her with paper-cutter claws, the minotaurs shoving remote controls into her every orifice—were only nightly extensions of her daily anxiety. And being nervous made sense to her. She said that when you look around at the world, really, the only appropriate response you can have is to be nervous.

When Jackie looked at the world, she saw everything, from contemporary pop music to the earth itself, in a state of progressively rapid deterioration. This included herself, since her life had been deteriorating since childhood. Her teenage years were but a series of heartaches and embarrassing moments. Early adulthood showed her a succession of episodes that all seemed to teach the same lesson: the older you get, the more life will sink its meathooks into you and pull you in a hundred different directions, and if you want to keep yourself from being splayed into a sleepless, worried mess, you're going to need money, and lots of it.

Money, she said, was like some elemental force that not only binds the individual together, but also connects one human to all the rest as it flows endlessly from wallet to wallet, bank account to bank account. And to think this force was just rectangular pieces of cotton. She had seen firsthand the damages that a deficiency in this precious cotton can cause:

the constant strain on her parents, which hastened their divorce when she was eleven—not to mention the constant strain on her mother's current marriage; her mother's financial struggles after she was fired by a sexist boss; the repeated mortgaging of her childhood home just so her family could survive; the end of vacations; the lack of funds to put her alcoholic older brother in rehab; and her own frugal situation, brought on by her difficulty in finding a slot as a self-sustaining member of what her know-it-all teachers had loved to call the "real world."

She had grown up following the rules so that someday she could make money and live the fabled good life, but all the hard work—all the straight As, the full scholarship to a small university forty miles away, the consistent appearances on the dean's list, the bachelor's in business (which in Bashford allowed her a chain of jobs in retail), and the master's in political science (which she knew wasn't practical, but she had seen where a practial degree got her)—all that had only secured her a job as a high-school substitute teacher.

Jackie slept in the same bedroom where she had spent her teenage years studying for math tests. She liked living with her mom and tolerated her stepdad, but she always felt like she wasn't getting anywhere, and she yearned to live in a big city where she could open her window and hear bus farts and baritone-voiced men cussing at themselves. She planned to leave Bashford someday, but for right now, she couldn't even afford the gasoline to leave town.

There was one place where all this nervousness and frustration left her alone: the stage. Uncle Sam's Finger was her third band, after the Stepchildren and Tabloid. She had taught herself to play guitar, thinking that being in a band might provide her a way to enjoy her boring small-town life more. She was seventeen when she took up guitar, and ever since, her opinions had been shaped for the most part by punk rock and her hero, Kurt Vonnegut.

$ $ $

The night he got home from the armory, Blue Gene lay in bed for three hours, excited about meeting Jackie but doubting he could have a future with her. When he saw that he wasn't going to fall asleep, he let himself into his parents' house and got on the computer in Henry's den. He looked up the MySpace page for Uncle Sam's Finger, which led him to Jackie Stepchild's own MySpace. There, he could read her many blogs, which divulged all sorts of personal information. For instance, her greatest fear was that there was a rock band in existence that could profoundly affect her but that she would never discover. Her second-greatest fear was that somewhere, someone was making a serious attempt to adapt *The Catcher in the Rye* into a movie. Her hobbies were reading, playing music, and going for walks. She loved Al Pacino, Thursday nights, and getting a good head cold that let her feel like she could lie in bed all day without feeling guilty. She hated *Two and a Half Men*, muscles, and the ageist way that young people were treated. Her favorite sound was the world-wise slur of Shane MacGowan's vocals; her least favorite sound was the mowing of lawns. Her favorite book was *Winesburg, Ohio*. Her favorite wrestlers were Kurt Angle and the Bushwhackers. She had no tattoos. And most important, she was single.

Most of her blogs consisted of random complaints, like how she thought children using cell phones was a perversity, or how blogging on MySpace was lame. Blue Gene scrolled through all of it until his eyes went bloodshot, but nowhere in her rants could he find the one thing he needed to know the most: her last name, so he could look her up in the phone book. She at least made a passing reference to the name of the street she lived on, a street that sounded familiar, but he couldn't place it.

After learning all he could about Jackie Stepchild, Blue Gene was futilely searching for himself on the internet when the door swung open violently. He saw a speeding blur of pajamas and a pistol.

"Don't!" Blue Gene sprung out of the chair, adrenaline surging through what felt like every organelle. "It's me!"

"Eugene!" said Henry, lowering his gun. "What are you doing here?"

"I'm lookin' on the internet. What are *you* doing?"

"I was getting Elizabeth some milk. I saw that the door to this room was closed."

"Goddamn! You coulda *knocked*! You coulda hollered and asked who it was!"

Henry pushed a swaying strand of gray hair from his forehead. He set the revolver on his desk. "Because we own all that we do, I had to assume you were a burglar." Blue Gene sat back down, snorted, and sighed. He knew better than to expect an apology. "What is so important that you had to get on the internet at three a.m.?"

"Nothin'. I didn't get home till, like, ten, and then I couldn't sleep, and Mom gave me a key, so I thought I'd come over here and hop on the 'puter."

"Since when do you even use the computer?"

"I wanted to look something up."

"What?"

"It don't matter."

"It's obviously something important."

"No. Geez—all it is was that they had a band playing at the armory, and I liked 'em and wanted to look 'em up."

"Oh," Henry sat down in front of the desk. He wore tan slippers and burgundy silk pajamas. "How did it go tonight?"

"Went real good. Probably fifty or so people said they'd vote for John."

Henry nodded and straightened his posture. "Are you comfortable in the poolhouse?"

"Yeah, thank ya."

"We'll get you a computer in there soon."

"Nah, don't bother. Seldom as I get on one, it ain't worth havin'."

"We'll get you one. In the meantime, if you need to get on the internet, use the computer in one of our offices upstairs."

"A'ight."

"I have so much work saved on my computer."

"Okay."

"Henry?" asked a voice from the hallway.

"In here, dear," said Henry. Elizabeth entered the den, wearing a flowery robe. Even this late, her hair still looked perfect. "Eugene came in to use the internet."

"Dad pulled a gun on me."

"My *Lord. Henry*—"

"I thought we were being burgled. I was playing it safe."

"Thank God no one was killed. Are you both all right?"

Blue Gene and Henry mumbled "yes."

"What are you doing up so late?" asked Elizabeth.

"Couldn't sleep it."

"Sometimes I read the Bible when I can't sleep. It gives me a sense of calm. Do you have a Bible? I'm pretty sure I furnished the poolhouse with one. Do you have one?"

"Where's Oxmore Drive?" Blue Gene blurted.

"That's in Aberdeen Acres," said Elizabeth.

"*Really?*" Aberdeen Acres was one of the nicer subdivisions of Bashford.

"Yes. Why?"

"I just met somebody that lives on Oxmore Drive. That's all."

"Was it a girl?" asked Elizabeth, her eyebrows lifted. It was no secret that her highest hope for Blue Gene was for him to find a nice girl and "marry up."

"No. Sure wasn't."

"You wouldn't tell me if it were."

Henry let out a toothy yawn. "While we're all in here," he said, "Eugene, you know we don't mind you being back at our house, but would you mind wearing more clothes while you're here?"

"What are you *talkin'* about?"

"Look at you." Henry pointed to Blue Gene's bare chest. He was wearing only a pair of gray cotton shorts and his gold crucifix necklace.

"I'm hot-natured."

"Sometimes friends stop by," said Elizabeth, "and also people from

Henry's work. It's just setting the wrong tone."

Blue Gene sighed, almost growled. "Fine. I'll just keep myself locked up over in the poolhouse. I'll stay over there and get naked and let my balls flap all over the place."

"*Ooh*," said Elizabeth with a wince.

"Don't act like that," said Henry. "We're only asking you to put a shirt on, at least."

"I think everybody else should take their shirts *off*. How 'bout that?"

Henry gave a sigh of his own. "I'm going to bed." He picked up his gun and stood.

"Don't worry, y'all. Pretty soon I'll have enough money to live on my own again. You won't have to put up with me much longer."

Henry laughed. "You talk as if you were a common bum. You have enough money to build a neighborhood all your own from the ground up."

"Oh. So you're sayin' I should take out some of that money so I can move out as soon as possible?"

"No, no. You misinterpreted me. I'm saying that if you need some money, you have it."

"Didn't earn it. Don't want it."

"Whatever you say." Henry spoke over his shoulder as he left. "You can stay here as long as you like, but please, respect the rules of my house. Throw on a shirt before you come over. I'm going back to bed. I'll let you get your milk."

"Okay," said Elizabeth. "I'll be up in a minute." Henry left. "Gene, I wanted to tell you something." Now Elizabeth took a seat in front of the desk. She bundled her arms together as if she were cold. "We're up because I just had my dream again."

"As much as he works out, you'd think *he'd* like to take *his* shirt off," said Blue Gene.

"Forget about that for a minute. *Listen* to me. This is important. I've been having my dream the last five nights. The exact same dream I had all those years ago. Except *this time*, the feeling in my head at the end isn't happiness. This time it feels like terror." Elizabeth tilted her head back and closed her eyes. "Oh, heavenly Father, give me strength. Oh Lord, let this be the right path."

"I always thought that dream sounded creepy."

"I know the vision was unsettling, but before, the feeling it gave me was always blissful. The Lord was speaking to me again tonight, but I feel as though he was giving me some kind of warning." She closed her eyes again. "Oh Lord, allow me the knowledge to determine what this new feeling means for us."

She was praying with all her might. "You're probably all nervous over the campaign," said Blue Gene. "I read that nerves and stress can cause you to have nightmares." Blue Gene was only saying this to comfort her; Elizabeth's role in the campaign had been stress-free so far. When she asked Henry what she could do to help, he gave her a job at the campaign headquarters downtown, a job that required little more than taking phone calls and waiting for anyone who might stop by.

"Until this week, I hadn't had that dream for over twenty years. The Lord is trying to tell me something."

"I know it's important to you and all, but have you ever thought that maybe it wasn't a vision or a prophecy or whatever at all? I mean, John's lookin' good right now, but he ain't no Messiah."

"No, he's not. You've got it wrong. I never said that John was the Messiah. That would be sacrilege. The dream shows us that John will *prepare* the world for the Second Coming. He's a sort of precursor to the Messiah, an usher, but not *the* Messiah. And that's a *good* thing. Why have I been given this *bad* feeling?"

"I don't know. I'm sorry you had it. What can I do for ya?"

"Just be careful. Be safe. And make sure John stays safe, too. Make sure everyone around you is careful and safe."

"Why do you say that?"

"The dream...I don't know. It's so hard to explain because it makes sense only when I'm in it. But the whole dream, it reeked of *death*. Gene, has anything out of the ordinary happened to you lately?"

"No. Why?"

"I read that recurring precognitive dreams can alter themselves if something major happens in reality that throws off the chain of events. So there were no surprises or anything out of the ordinary that happened to you lately? I'll have to ask everybody that."

"Nah. Same ol', same ol'. Campaigned for the first time, but it went pretty well."

"Nothing significant happened, though?"

"Well, I was constipated earlier in the day. That's pretty rare for me."

$$\$\,\$\,\$$

Into the suburbs where brick mailboxes matched brick houses and basketball goals stood next to light-gray driveways, John drove his black Escalade with Blue Gene as his passenger. Campaign signs were starting to sprout up like dandelions all over the city, advertising candidates in every race from constable to Congress.

It was a Saturday in the middle of August, half past three. John and Blue Gene had been putting up signs since ten, taking a quick lunch break at Arby's for some beef-and-cheddar sandwiches. They had already gone to the three nicest subdivisions in Bashford, the ones on the outskirts of town, including Vandalia Hills, where John lived. Next week, they and the other staffers would spread their signs across the other counties of the district.

So far, John was satisfied with his performance today. He commanded the conversations, made unshakable eye contact, and hadn't said or done anything wrong yet. He had begun to think of himself not as John, but as John Hurstbourne Mapother, which he now considered worth the time it took to say. That Blue Gene was back in his life added to his red-carpet confidence, because embracing Blue Gene helped make him feel less the sinful hog. Whatever the cause, he felt his mind becoming as clean-cut as his face. In fact, since the rally, he had been feeling so strong and able that he had begun weaning himself off his anxiety medication. He planned to be completely chemical-free by the time he walked into the Capitol.

He slowly drove past the lawns, which had been turned yellow-brown by the two-week-long heat wave. Despite the dying grass, Aberdeen Acres had some lovely homes, most of them ranch-style with a tree in the yard, sometimes an evergreen. The flower gardens were well tended, and the shrubs were fastidiously shaved.

"Lot of drug money bought these homes, I bet," deadpanned Blue Gene.

"You say that about all the neighborhoods. There are some people who can do well for themselves by making an honest living. Hey—put on your seat belt, would you, please?"

"You're only going thirty miles per hour."

"*Always* wear your seat belt. You know what Mom said about being safe."

"*Okay.* Geez." Blue Gene sighed and strapped on his seat belt.

"Thank you," said John. "I know *I'm* a good driver. It's the *other* drivers you have to watch out for. You never know what they're going to do."

John obeyed all the four-way stops as he cautiously proceeded. For the door-to-doors, he liked to go deep inside the subdivisions and work his way outward.

"I've been meanin' to ask you," said Blue Gene, "if you win, will—"

"*When* I win," interjected John, dead serious.

"When you win, you lookin' forward to learnin' the secrets the government's been hidin'?"

"What do you mean?"

"Like UFOs, JFKs, Swamp Thing. All that kind of stuff."

"I don't think those sorts of things are disclosed to the House."

"Yeah, but you're planning on taking this all the way to the top, aren't you?"

"Yes."

"And if you become president—"

"*When.*"

"My bad. *When* you become president, have you thought about how awesome it'll be to know all those secrets?"

"Yes. I have, actually."

"Will you tell me some of 'em?"

"No."

"Aw, come on, now. Maybe just about the UFOs?"

"No way."

"How come?"

"I just can't. The people aren't meant to know what the government knows. They couldn't handle that kind of knowledge. It's for your own good. From the moment my hand is on that Bible, my lips will be forever sealed. But I tell you what. When I'm president, I'll definitely be able to get you your driver's license back."

"Well, that's something. But man, if I got to be president, and I got in on all those secrets, I'd get 'em to break in all the TV shows with one of those special reports, and I'd get on there and tell everybody watchin' at home all the secrets." John laughed. "I'd just tell all of 'em at once. Every secret they've been keepin' from us all these years."

"You'd be stopped. Someone would cut the cameras off on you."

"I thought about that. I'd just have to talk real fast. I'd be like, here's where we been hiding the aliens, this is who shot JFK, this is what Elvis has been up to. Just bam, bam, bam, one secret after another."

"You would make a horrible leader."

"One minute all the people at home would be watchin' *Everybody Loves Raymond*; the next minute they'd know everything they had ever wondered about."

John shook his head. He knew that the stability of most people's lives was made possible only because the most important events of their lives were kept hidden. Why should the government be any different? Everyone had secrets, even the Mapothers, but they all went on like nothing had ever happened.

Twisting around and craning his neck, looking out the windows like an excitable mutt, Blue Gene was clearly hoping to see someone or something. But when John asked him what he was looking for, he said, "Nothin'," and because of John's respect for secrets, he didn't pry.

His cell phone rang. He took the call with one hand and steered with the other.

"You're so big on using seat belts," said Blue Gene after John hung up, "but you'll talk on the cell phone while you're driving."

"I thought I told you to stop questioning me."

"You question *me*."

"I'm your elder. Would you please not start in on me today, Blue Gene?"

"Fine. What's new with Arthur?"

"Oh, Abby and I are dreading him starting school next week."

"How come?"

"He's so sensitive. I've tried to protect him from the world, but it's been easy so far since he hasn't actually been out in it. I wish we could keep him home forever. Kindergarten was one thing, but now he'll be gone all day."

"He'll be a'ight."

"I hope so."

"He won't have to win over the other kids 'cause they'll recognize him from the commercials. He'll be a star."

"Yeah." John's commercials had started airing earlier in the week. At the end of the commercial, John smiled with Abby and Arthur at the downtown riverfront.

"When he gets older, you gonna make Arthur play ball?"

"Probably. Why?"

"I think it's too much pressure for a kid."

"But look." John pointed up the street. "Look at all those basketball goals. It's a religion here. Of course, by the time he's in high school, we'll be living in D.C., according to our plans."

"Well, if he does play ball, don't make a spectacle of yourself like you did with me."

When Blue Gene was eleven and went to his first Junior Pro practice, he was the only boy there who didn't know to bring a pair of shorts to change into. John happened to answer the phone when Blue Gene called that day, saying his coach wouldn't let him play until he got some shorts. When John got to the gymnasium, he saw all the kids dribbling around, except for Blue Gene, who sat Indian-style in his khaki pants at the far end of the gym. After John gave Blue Gene the shorts, he asked if the coach had been mean to him. Blue Gene said yes, the coach had treated him like he was stupid. John nodded calmly. Then he scuffed his dress shoes across the basketball court, walking through all the boys doing their drills. All the little boys watched as John told the coach that if he ever said another unkind word to that child over there on the sideline, he would have him fired.

"That embarrassed the hell out of me. Why'd you do that?"

"You looked so pitiful sitting on the sideline all alone. You'll understand someday when you have a son. I was thirteen years older than you. You were always like a son. Anyhow, I was trying to help you. Was he nice to you from then on?"

"No. He was a dick to me and to everybody else."

"Why didn't you tell me?"

"You weren't even around to tell."

John pulled over and put the car in park. He turned and talked to the frowning mustache. "You always know how to make me feel awful, you know it?"

"I don't mean to."

"Tell me how I can make it up to you, and I'll do it."

"It's done too late now. Just be good to Arthur."

"I *am* good to Arthur. Are you saying I'm not?"

"Nah, I know you're good to Arthur. Just make sure that if you say you're going to do something with him, you do it. Don't just show up every once in a while in his room and act like you're his best friend if you ain't gonna follow through with the things you say."

"I spend time with Arthur every day."

"What's this about you not takin' him to Chuck E. Cheese? I told him I'd take him, but he says you'd get mad."

"That place is a scam. You spend ten dollars' worth of quarters there, and then they'll give the dinkiest prizes in exchange for those little tickets. So, in effect, you end up paying ten or twenty dollars for a plastic snake and some Chinese finger cuffs. That place is absurd."

"*You're* absurd. Like *you* can't afford ten dollars' worth of quarters."

"It's a waste."

"No it ain't. Chuck E. Cheese is part of being a kid."

"Mom and Dad didn't take either of us."

"Bernice took me."

"Good for Bernice. God bless good ol' Bernice. I get sick of you holding her in such high esteem, like she's some kind of angel, and then you put down Mom and Dad."

"Well, no, I ain't sayin' she's an angel. She upped and left me like it was nothin'. I'd write her letters and call her. Never would hear back from her. She blew my ass off. She's no angel."

John grabbed a stack of leaflets from the dashboard and got out of the car.

$$\$ \$ \$$$

With purpose and a smile, John Hurstbourne Mapother walked from house to house. Meanwhile, Blue Gene sat in the driver's seat, listening to 105 ROQ, scooting John's SUV along as John progressed down the street. If any of the homeowners expressed interest in having a Mapother sign, Blue Gene was supposed to get one from the trunk and hammer it into their lawn because, unlike John, he didn't mind getting sweaty. Underneath his Harley-Davidson cap, he wore a red, white, and blue bandanna folded into a headband.

Once they reached Oxmore Drive, Blue Gene watched for a maroon Grand Am with stickers on the back. Eventually, at around four-thirty, John got to a house whose mailbox read, RIPPLEMEYER. It was a nice, one-story, brown-brick affair, its front walk lined with shrubs and lights—a typical abode for this neighborhood—except loud music came from within. John rang the doorbell, and the screen door opened to let the music out of the house and into the blue suburban sky, loud enough for Blue Gene to hear. In an instant, he was out of the car.

"Hello," John said, raising his voice over the music. "Is your mom or dad home?"

"No, but I'm an adult," said Jackie.

"Oh. Hi, I'm John Hurstbourne Mapother. I'm running for Congress." He handed her a leaflet. "I'd appreciate your vote on November 2."

"Hey," said Blue Gene, now at John's side. Jackie had her shoulder-length hair in a little ponytail.

"Hi."

"Oh. You two know each other?"

"Yeah," said Blue Gene.

"Then maybe you could ask your friend if you could put a sign up in her yard."

"Don't even bother with this one," said Blue Gene. "She'd pro'ly just as soon have us take a dump on her lawn than have one of those signs up."

John laughed. "Really? Is it something I said?"

"It's nothing against you," said Jackie. "I hate Congress in general."

John was taken aback. "I beg your pardon?"

"They ruin everything. Any good that someone tries to do, they either reject it or compromise it until it hardly even resembles the original idea. Like, for instance, there was the Indian New Deal. It was a *great* idea, but then Congress got ahold of the proposal and just watered it down. They've kept us from getting universal healthcare, too."

"I agree with you—may I ask your name?"

"Jackie."

"I agree with you, Jackie. Congress has made its mistakes in the past, but that's why we need to breathe new life into it. And I will do that. I will do my part to make sure Congress makes the big changes, because I believe in change. If you keep walking across our great land in a straight line without ever changing your course, you will eventually end up walking into the ocean. You'll drown."

Jackie nodded. "Yep," she said. She and John stared at each other for a moment.

"Okay," he said. "Good to meet you, and thanks for your time."

"You go on ahead," said Blue Gene. "I'll catch up with you later." John's mouth opened as he looked at Blue Gene. "You don't care, do you?"

"No, no. Not at all. I'll just meet you back at the car when I'm done. Is this where you'll leave it?"

"Yeah. Here," Blue Gene reached into the pocket of his denim shorts and pulled out a cell phone. "I'll turn this thing on, and when you need me, just give me a buzz. I'll come pick you up."

"All right," said John. "See you later." He headed to his Escalade and pulled out some signs.

"How ya been, Little Miss Thing?" asked Blue Gene.

"Okay," she said shyly.

"Wanna shoot the shit?"

"Um, I guess."

They stood silently at the door while the song played. It was up-tempo with a sad melody, and the singer was complaining about being lost in a supermarket. Blue Gene found it pretty catchy.

"We could go for a walk," he said. "If you like to walk."

"Okay. It's hot, but that sounds okay. A short walk. Let me get my shoes."

Blue Gene figured she was going inside to get some pepper spray. John started to trudge to the next house with a stack of signs underneath his arm.

"You ain't sore over this, are ya?" Blue Gene hollered. He met John at the end of Jackie's walk.

"Not at all. Who is that girl?"

"Just some burger I met at the armory."

"I don't think she's right for you."

"What are you talkin' 'bout? She's just a friend."

John smiled. "Okay. I'll call you when I'm done." He started walking to the next house.

"She's into wrestling," Blue Gene shouted.

"Sounds like a keeper."

$$$

Walking with Jackie on the smooth blacktop along the suburban gutter, Blue Gene felt a tight pinch of guilt when he looked back and saw John in his nice slacks, putting up a sign in the distance. But being with Jackie was the thought he had gone to sleep with and woken up to for the last two weeks.

"Anything happen after I left the armory?" he asked as he tried to hide his limp, with little success.

"Let's see...When'd you leave?"

"I left after I kept that one dude from stompin' on those Mexicans."

"Oh, yeah. What was that guy's *problem*?"

"I don't know. I hardly know him."

"Actually, something *did* happen after that. The paramedics had to come and take Gary 'the Orphan' Dorphin off on a stretcher, which I hated to see, because out of all the guys at the armory, he was one of the few that was nice to me. He's the sweetest guy."

"What happened to him?"

"I don't know. I tried to find out, but the promoter won't return my calls. I totally lost that gig."

"Dang."

"I'm kind of relieved, actually. Nobody at the wrestling matches liked my band. And as for being a booker, it was really hard to write for those guys. You get all those guys together that think they're so tough, and they all have these *humongous* egos. They would get mad if I had them lose a match. But it was a good experience. I'm gonna write a screenplay about wrestling someday, so this experience will help with that, I guess."

"You write screenplays?" asked Blue Gene, though he already knew this from her blog.

"Yeah. I know they'll never sell, but still, it's nice to dream."

"You never know."

"No. They'll never sell. I don't know why I even bother. I could never please the film industry. Everybody thinks that *Chinatown* is just the most well-written screenplay ever. I *hated* that movie. I mean, I *love* Jack Nicholson—*Cuckoo's Nest* is one of my favorites of all time— but *Chinatown* was mediocre *at best* to me. It's the same way with *Tootsie*. One of those lists called it the number-one comedy ever made. I just don't get it. *Tootsie* is *not funny*, and yet all the screenwriting experts say that it is, like, *the* exemplary comedy. It's like, if enough people say something, it automatically becomes true. Or maybe I just have weird taste."

Stealing glances at her, Blue Gene enjoyed her weird taste. She was petite but packed with interesting details: worn-out Chuck Taylors with black shoelaces, pink argyle socks, slim-fitting blue jeans rolled up in big cuffs high enough to expose an inch of her calves, a T-shirt that said, DON'T TALK TO ME. I'M DANCING, more bracelets than were necessary, and brunette bangs that gave her an old-fashioned look.

Jackie Stepchild looked like the type of person who would stay up late. But she was more worried than wild, with an energetic awkwardness about her. She playfully raised the little red plastic flag on someone's mailbox, then lowered it.

"This sure is a nice neighborhood," Blue Gene said.

"If you say so."

"You don't like it here?"

"It's just so dull. There's no scenery. One of my favorite things to do is to read a book outside, but it'd be nice if I could look up and *see* something every once in a while, you know? All there is here are fences and lawns. Everybody here is *obsessed* with their lawn. That's how they choose to spend their free time—caring for their lawn. They're probably all in hysterics since their grass is dying."

"I know what you mean, but some people'd give anything to live here."

Everyone here had a two-car garage crammed with not only cars but also tools, trash cans, refrigerators, and furniture. Everyone's garden hose was neatly wrapped in a plastic spool.

"I know. But there's no character here. There's nothing inspiring."

"Look up yonder." Blue Gene pointed at two little boys on their bicycles. "Right up there in front of you. That's inspirin'."

"Kids riding bikes?"

"Yeah. That's America right there. In the neighborhood I lived in when I was little, 'fore we moved out past the city limits, the kids didn't even ride bikes. They drove golf carts instead."

"Really?" She looked at him closely, closing one eye because of the sun.

"Yeah. I always thought that was weak."

"It's so easy to forget that you grew up rich. Were you adopted?" she asked with an elfin grin. Blue Gene looked down and shook his head. "I'm sorry. I didn't mean anything by that. You just—well, for someone with your background, you don't put on any airs. None at all."

"It's a'ight. It was a reasonable question."

As the boys on their bikes came closer, they regarded Blue Gene and Jackie curiously, watching them instead of the road. One showed off, riding without hands.

"All right, boys," said Blue Gene in a deep voice. "Need to see your licenses and registrations." The boys looked at each other bewilderedly. Jackie giggled. She covered her mouth as she laughed, and Blue Gene wanted to yank her hands away and kiss her. He looked back to see if John was still in sight. He was, but smaller. He pulled out his cell phone to make sure it was on and that no buttons had been pressed accidentally.

"So were you born in Bashford?" he asked.

"Yep. Were you?"

"Yeah." He was already getting so hot and sweaty that he considered taking off his shirt, but he wasn't quite ready for Jackie to see his beer belly. "D'you go to County?"

"No. St. Anthony's." It was the Catholic high school in Donato Falls, forty minutes away. Blue Gene carefully rolled his T-shirt sleeves past his shoulders. He was wearing a B.U.M. Equipment T-shirt, one that he had just bought, and he hadn't had time to amputate the sleeves. Now that his tattoos were showing, he felt a bit more confident. Displaying his tattoos made Blue Gene feel like he had a slight edge over those without them.

"Who's Cheyenne?" asked Jackie, pointing to the name written in cursive underneath an Indian headdress.

"That's Cheyenne, Wyoming."

"Why do you have a tattoo of Cheyenne, Wyoming?"

"It's where I was conceived."

"I was conceived on the WEDway PeopleMover at Disney World."

"No, you weren't."

Jackie laughed at herself. An elderly woman in a nylon sweatsuit passed them, walking aggressively. Blue Gene waved, and she waved back.

"Why is the place where you were conceived so significant to you?"

"Because. That's where it all began. You gotta show respect for where you come from." Blue Gene suddenly wished he actually knew something about the city of Cheyenne. He sighed and spat. "You—oh, you know what? I suck at lyin', man. Cheyenne's actually my ex."

"Why didn't you say so?"

"I don't know," he said with a shrug.

"See, that's why I'll never get a tattoo, because you never know what your life is going to be like down the road. You have to think long-term. I mean, fifteen years ago my favorite band was, like, Spin Doctors. If I had a Spin Doctors tattoo today, I'd probably kill myself."

"I hear that. I used to be real into rap. I was all about the Wu-Tang Clan and Master P and all those guys. Can't stand the stuff now."

"What do you listen to now?"

"Rock."

"What kind of rock?"

"Ain't none that you like, pro'ly."

"I might. What do you like?"

"105 ROQ stuff. Disturbed. Van Halen. Led Zeppelin. Godsmack."

"Yeah, you were right. I don't like any of those." She laughed.

"There goes a rabbit," said Blue Gene as a brown rabbit scampered off. He and Jackie walked around a curve. "I see where you're comin' from about the tattoos, but I don't regret any of 'em. Not even the Cheyenne one. 'Cause she's dead."

"Oh. I'm sorry to hear that."

"I mean, we broke up well before she died, but that's one thing I like about that tat. It's kind of a tribute to her. She OD'd on meth."

"*Really?*"

"Yeah." He saw he had piqued her interest. "Had a stroke at twenty-five. That's actually why it didn't work with us, 'cause she wouldn't stop using. She got so she was impossible."

"Did she have sores all over her?"

"Oh, yeah. Big ol' welps the size of quarters."

"That burns me up to hear things like that. She never would've had that particular problem if it weren't for the government."

"She did it to herself. She came from a real messed-up family, though."

"Yeah, but did you know why meth was created in the first place?"

Blue Gene shook his head.

"In World War II, both sides, the Allies and the Axis—they manu-factured meth to give to their soldiers so they could go for days on end without sleep, so they could just fight, fight, fight without end, like zom-bies. And now they wonder why people are abusing it."

"Sounds like a conspiracy theory to me."

"It's a *fact.*"

"I never heard it before."

"Yeah, well, it's not something that gets advertised. It's not some-thing you can fly a flag over. It's just one more way the masters have ruined the lives of the servants. It'll never end, either, because the servants support the very wars that keep them in their place as servants." A sour expression appeared on Blue Gene's face, like the one he got when the Double Dragon didn't get the General Tso chicken right. "All that wealth going to military spending when it could go to feeding people, helping them. But then, all of the wealth in this country goes to the wrong things. Look at how much actors and athletes are paid. Yet the servants are the first to defend it all."

"Hey, now. Get real. You don't fight wars, you don't have freedom. That's just the way it is."

"*Amazing.*"

"What?"

"It never ceases to amaze me that as soon as one person points out how horrible and senseless war is, there will always, *always* be another person who rushes to defend it. If I live to be a thousand, I will never understand it. Maybe *you* could explain it to me."

"I ain't explainin' shit," said Blue Gene, lifting his cap up and down to get some air to his suddenly hot scalp. "For the life of me, *I* don't understand how someone can't see that if we don't stand up for ourselves and fight, some crazy foreigners will come over and bomb our asses. Isn't that plain as day?"

"Crazy foreigners? *We're* the craziest foreigners of them all! Why do we need to invade other countries when we're already by far the richest, most powerful country in the world? Isn't enough *enough?*"

Blue Gene had been afraid their conversation would go bad like this. "I don't wanna argue with ya, man." Taking a cue from her bloggings, he turned the dialogue toward common ground. "Say, you ever have those dreams where you wake up with a jerk and your heart feels like she's gonna blow?"

"Every night."

"Me too. Nightmares suck it big-time."

"I'm always getting killed in mine. Either by a car wreck or by strange men shooting me. Or stabbing me."

"I had this wild one the other night. Don't ask me why, but I was tryin' to cut my wiener off."

"Interesting."

"I'll tell ya, it was a pretty tough piece of gristle."

"*Gross*. I have this recurring one. You know that black-and-white fuzz on the TV when you don't have the cable hooked up right?"

"Yeah. I know how to get free cable."

"Cool, but I have this dream where I get stuck in the middle of the fuzz. The static becomes like a substitute for the air, and I'm inside it and can't get out and it suffocates me."

"Maybe you watch too much TV."

"Probably."

"What do you watch 'sides wrestling?"

"I love *Cops*."

"Me too. D'you ever see the one where the guy kept porno magazines inside the front of his pants?"

"I don't think so."

"I partied with that guy. He was from Fort Worth, but he lived here for a while."

Jackie smiled. "So he had to sign a release for them to air that, right?"

"I reckon. I never thought to ask him. Hey, there's another rabbit."

"Yeah. There are tons of rabbits in this neighborhood. When they started building the Super Wal-Mart, it scared off all the rabbits that lived in that field over there. They started showing up in people's lawns. One time I saw one that a lawnmower had torn in half. What really sucks is that because they just *had* to build the Super Wal-Mart next to this subdivision, it's lowered all the property values around here. You can't tell any difference yet, but fifty years from now this will be a slum."

"I tell you, though, man, a lot of poor people *depend* on Wal-Mart 'cause it's so cheap."

"Yeah, but it's only cheap because they don't take care of their employees. Like, I heard they won't give women promotions."

"Everybody says that crap, but it ain't that bad. I worked at Wal-

Mart for seven years, and I *liked* it. I think they're more than fair."

"Why?"

"For one thing, they won't fire you over anything. I mean, you'd have to murder somebody or maybe steal to lose your job there. But everybody's gotta be all down on Wal-Mart."

"It's the biggest retailer in the world, but their average wage is well below the poverty level."

"Yeah, but you never hear about the good stuff they do 'cause it doesn't make for a good news story. I seen 'em do all sorts of things for the community."

As they passed the residence of the neighborhood's one black family, Jackie switched to the topic of racism, saying how it was at the root of all wars, especially America's wars, all the while kicking the curb with her Chucks. Blue Gene changed the topic to wrestling.

$ $ $

John had officially become involved in politics in January, when he filed for the primaries. Since then, it had taken eight months to hear a word of dissent—and to think it came out of such a tranquil and harmless streetscape. He wished he had a leathery façade that no words could penetrate. At least the words were coming from a naïve girl with no social standing. He knew her act just by seeing her outfit: a disillusioned college kid who thought she could bypass categorization by dressing "differently." He knew the type from high school and college, the ones who dismissively filed him under "filthy rich," who assumed someone with such a rich daddy couldn't know what problems were, though the truth was, the darkness of John's home life could engulf theirs as an oil spill would an inkblot.

Careful as always, John committed that name to memory: Ripplemeyer. He resented the fact that Blue Gene had used the door-to-door campaigning as an excuse to see her. He now felt foolish for thinking that Little Brother had actually wanted to spend the day with him. But he knew better than to say anything against her to Blue Gene, or it would be a repeat of his parents nudging him toward the black-hole hickey-suck of an exotic-dancer enchantress.

John kept walking from house to house and had something extra in his step—not a spring, but a firmness. He was surprised to see so many pickups in this neighborhood. One of them passed him at a reckless speed, even with some little boys riding their bikes down the road. The boys soon passed John, reminding him that he needed to take the time to teach Arthur how to ride a bike. Then again, maybe it would be best if Arthur never learned. John's life would have been so much simpler if he had never learned to ride the bicycle that allowed him the freedom to leave his own neighborhood and navigate the other part of town that contained such sin for him. If it were socially acceptable, John would keep Arthur from learning to ride a bike or even drive a car. If the campaign weren't going on, John would've found a way to homeschool him. John remembered the very first day he'd started grade school, how he'd thought, "I have to go through twelve more years of *this*?" He'd go in Arthur's place if he could.

When John thought of Arthur and his chubby little face and the innocent, amazing things he did—like the way he sat inside the refrigerator and ate slices of cheese, or like the other night, when he fell asleep in his underwear with a bowl of Fritos in his lap—he never wanted to spend a day apart from him. Yet so many of these people felt just the opposite about their children: that they were back-sassing inconveniences who would mercifully go away once they were eighteen. How quickly it had crept in, the death of the family. And it was the ones like that Ripplemeyer girl that let it happen, the ones who shook their fists at every injustice while letting their own homes fall apart. That's what happened when the world loosened so without the structure of values; the first to fall were the walls of homes.

John's dad had always warned him that the greatest adversary between the Mapothers and the realization of their dream would never be the other name on the ballot. It would be this self-righteous culture of

people with a distorted sense of freedom, who confused legitimizing immoral lifestyles with liberation, who would swear irrationally that their
lives were controlled by microscopically fine print on the very documents that allowed them to cavort as they did. These people were impossible to reason with, Henry told John, because even if you told them
exactly what you were truly after—untainted *good*—they would still turn
it into something foul. You could tell them that you were devoting your
entire lifetime to bringing the Promised Land down to Earth, like putting a warm security blanket on a shivering war orphan; they would still
give it their pet names of "greed" and "corruption." John accepted that
his syllables would never glimmer for these turncoat heathens the way
they would for the other sleepers, but they too would love their country
once they saw it burning. John smiled at the sky.

$ $ $

When Blue Gene and Jackie turned the corner that would lead them
back to her house, he figured it was time to make a move.

"I actually own *WrestleMania VI*," he said. "Since you and me both
like it so much, would you wanna get together and watch it sometime?
Watch Hogan pass the torch to the Ultimate Warrior?"

"That was only so Hogan could take off from wrestling and be in
Suburban Commando."

"You ruin everything. Would you wanna get together and watch it
sometime?"

"Okay." But her eyes showed something less than enthusiasm.

"Like, when would you want to do that?"

"I don't know."

"A'ight, then. Never mind."

"I mean, I don't know if I know you well enough."

"It ain't like a date, if that's what you mean."

"No, I didn't mean that. It's just, you're still kind of a stranger to
me."

Blue Gene rubbed sweat off his mustache. "Well, you could ask me some questions to get to know me better. Or maybe you just plain don't want to know me. I don't care."

"No, I have some questions for you."

"Shoot."

"Okay. One thing I've always wondered—and I might never get the chance to ask someone this again—is this: Do people with mullets know that their haircuts are called *mullets*?"

"Yeah."

"But is that something that's unique to *you*? Because you're clearly not a typical mullet-head. Do other guys you know with mullets use the word *mullet*?"

"I don't know. I don't sit around talkin' to other guys about their hairdos."

"Then how did *you* find out that *yours* was called a mullet?"

"Some faggot called me a mullet-head at the skating rink long time ago. I told him to shut up or I'd push his face into the back of his head." Jackie laughed, which Blue Gene took as encouragement. "I told him, if you back down, you're a bitch, and of course he backed down."

"Do you fight often?"

"Nah. I always, you know, *defend* my nuts, but it usually don't go past a lot of talking. My last real fight was in high school, but ask me somethin' else."

"What do you do for a living?"

"Right now I'm on John's campaign staff, which, on one hand—I love helpin' out my brother and all, but I'm just better suited to manual labor than all this networkin'. Hey—you heard of kickin' ass and takin' names?"

"Yeah."

"Well, I call politics a bunch of *kissin'* ass and *droppin'* names." Again, she covered her mouth and laughed. "'Fore that, up till recently, I was a flea marketer, but that didn't go too good. 'Fore that I was at Wal-Mart."

"What time do you get up for work?"

"'Round six."

"What do you do in your free time?"

"Watch TV. Car shows mostly, but also wrestling, of course. And I like huntin', fishin', trappin', four-wheelin', muddin', outdoor stuff, even though I haven't been doin' much of it lately 'cause I reckon I've lost interest, and also it's so hot out. Here lately I've been hangin' out with my little nephew."

"How many guns do you own?"

"Thirteen. No—twelve, 'cause I pawned one here recently."

"What's your favorite movie?"

"Anything with John Wayne in it."

"Did you know his real name is Marion Morrison?"

"Shut the hell up."

Jackie laughed. "It *is*."

Blue Gene shook his head. "You're so full of it, your hair's gone turned brown."

"*Gross.* Have you ever been arrested?"

"Four times."

"Ever been in prison?"

"Nah. Probably should've gone, but my dad's lawyer kept me out."

"What were you arrested for?"

"Twice for DUIs, once for possession of a controlled substance, and once for aggravated assault."

"Who'd you assault?"

"Somebody from high school. I ain't gettin' into that, though."

"Do you do meth or crack?"

"Did meth just a time or two. I ain't proud of it, but you asked."

"Just a couple of times?"

"Yeah. I stopped 'cause Cheyenne had a kid from a previous relationship livin' in her trailer with me and her, and that just ain't right to be doing that stuff around kids, you know? I don't care even if her kid was ornery as all get-out—that wasn't right. So one of us had to straighten up."

"Do *you* have any kids?"

"I'll come up and say it—me and Cheyenne were *supposed to* have one once, but it didn't happen. She stopped usin' and everything once she found out she was pregnant, but there was no way it was gonna happen. That was actually the beginning of the end for us, once she had her miscarriage, 'cause I blamed her and she blamed me."

"How old were you when that happened?"

"Twenty-one, twenty-two. It was best she didn't have the kid. I definitely wasn't father material. I mean, at that point in my life, I pro'ly still had possums comin' 'round, sniffin' out my reefer."

Jackie cracked up so that she had to put both hands over her mouth. "What?"

"*Possums sniffed out your reefer?*"

"Oh, yeah. Someone was always comin' and goin' at our trailer, and oftentimes they'd forget to close up the screen door, and by God, one time a possum snuck in our trailer, sniffed out the reefer I kept under the couch in a sock, and he took off with it."

"*Wow.*"

"I'd like to get ahold of that possum."

"You're fascinating."

"I am?"

"Yes. What is your *story*?"

"What do you mean?"

"I mean, I've heard of people coming from well-to-do homes *dropping out*, or whatever you want to call it, but you've taken it to a whole new level. You've made it into an *art form*. Have you *always* been like this?"

"Like a ham-and-egger?"

"I mean like—" she motioned a hand up and down Blue Gene's body "—like *you*."

"No. I ain't *always* been this way."

"How long *have* you been this way?"

"I don't know. Ten years or so."

"So all of your adult life?"

"Oh, yeah. Hope you don't mind this," he said, taking out his cigarettes and lighter.

"I don't mind. Am I getting too nosy?"

"Nah. But now let me ask you some questions."

"Okay."

"Why you into playing that kind of music you play?"

"You mean punk rock?"

"Is that what it is?"

She laughed. "I guess so. For lack of a better term. Well, for one thing, punk rock is the only kind of music I *can* play. But what attracted me to it is that I saw that you were allowed to *mess up* when you played it. And that idea appealed to me, because all my life I was so *shy*, and when you're shy, you're usually nervous and always worrying about embarrassing yourself in front of people."

"I wouldn't've thought you was shy."

"But I was. I still am. When I'm onstage, that's like a mask I'm wearing. I never would've dreamed I'd end up talking and singing the way I do onstage. I still shock myself, like that night at the armory. Anyway, I had always wanted to be in a band, but I was afraid of making a mistake onstage and humiliating myself in front of everyone. But then I learned with punk rock that making mistakes is not only *allowed*, it's *encouraged*. Even with people watching you in the audience, it can be sloppy and reckless and imperfect and even *incorrect*. I totally needed something like that when I was like a nineteen-year-old trying to do well in school so I could make something of myself, taking life so seriously."

"Shit. That's a good answer."

"I've given it a lot of thought."

In one wordy regurgitation of nouns and verbs, she had found the words that described precisely why he had settled into this lowly lifestyle. Blue Gene didn't have to worry about what he looked like. He didn't have to worry about saying the wrong thing. He didn't have to worry about making mistakes, because at the trailer park or the Wal-Mart stockroom or the flea market or the monster-truck rally, everything was messy and dirty and expected to be wrong to begin with.

Jackie laughed.

"What?"

"It's just funny," said Jackie, grinning and covering her mouth. "We're walking, and walking is good exercise, yet you're smoking while exercising."

"Smoke 'em if you got 'em," said Blue Gene firmly, hoping to end the topic.

"Do you smoke the brands that Westway makes?"

"No. Always been partial to Parliaments."

"Why?"

"They're cheaper."

"So I guess this whole sea change with smoking becoming outlawed indoors, I guess that has your family freaking out, huh?"

"I don't talk to them about business. But I doubt it. Tobacco ain't but part of where their money comes from."

"Where *does* it come from?"

"Nothin' illegal, if that's what you're getting at. Both my mom and dad inherited a lot from their parents, and Dad's got investments all over the place. All over the world."

"It's getting harder and harder for the cigarette companies to find new customers in America, so isn't it true that now they're trying to find less educated people in developing countries to smoke?"

"I don't know what they're doing, but don't start in with bad-mouthin' smoking again. Smoking ain't the *devil*. It's helped a lot of people make a living. I know it ain't as important as it once was, but this whole country was built on tobacco. In fact, that's what the country *started* as. It was a real good place to grow tobacco."

"Yes! I'm so glad to hear you say that, Blue Gene."

He couldn't help but notice it was the first time she had called him by name.

"Why?"

"Because you admitted that America started for the sake of *commerce*. It wasn't about just ideals and freedom."

"Hey, now, don't be puttin' words in my mouth. I only said that 'cause my ancestors were some of the ones who were part of the first tobacco companies here, the ones that turned the land into colonies in the first place. My dad always said that the history of our country is in the tobacco leaf."

"I believe that. Did you know that at one time, Bashford was the second-richest city per capita in America because of all the tobacco barons that lived here?"

"What went wrong?"

"Well, sorry, but your family is what went wrong. Used to be, the wealth was spread out among all the tobacco companies, but then your grandfather overpowered them all. So instead of being a wealthy town per capita, there was just one extremely rich family—the Mapothers."

"How you know all this?"

"I'll admit it. The night I met you, I looked you and your family up on the internet."

A subtle smile appeared underneath Blue Gene's mustache. "What else d'you find out?"

"That's it. Basically, what your family did was like what Vince McMahon did with the wrestling industry. Originally, the business was divided into territories all over the country, each with its own independent wrestling promotion. Then Vince came along and invaded everyone's turf and bought out their talent. Vince hogged the whole business for himself."

"Yeah, but my grandpa worked hard all his life to be that successful. Died in his forties. And my dad's worked hard, too. Don't act like they didn't earn it."

"I'm sure that's true, but I bet their workers worked just as hard for only a fraction of the profits. From all you've told me about yourself, it seems like you'd be on the workers' side. That's what I don't get about you."

"I *am* on the workers' side."

"If that's true, then how come you and your family aren't at each other's throats?"

"We are sometimes. Lately we've been okay, but there were four years there where we weren't even on speakin' terms."

"I guess they started speaking again when they needed your help with the campaign?"

"Yeah," he said. Jackie nodded knowingly. "What are you sayin'? That they're just usin' me?"

"Do *you* think they are?"

"No, I don't think they are. But I sure don't 'preciate you suggestin' that."

"Sorry."

Blue Gene noticed a wooden fence half-covered in mold. "And even if they *are* using me, you know, maybe I don't mind. 'Cause maybe it's nice to not be ignored. Course, I ignored them, too. But maybe it's nice to get some attention for once."

"Okay."

Blue Gene clammed up. A man with a pink-nosed Labrador walked past, and Blue Gene didn't bother waving. He was still brooding when they got to Jackie's house, which he noticed had ashen streaks of pollution on its gray roof. They stopped at her mailbox.

"So I guess you're mad at me?" Jackie asked.

"I ain't mad at you, but who wants to be told they're being used?"

"You were the one who said it."

"You were gettin' at it."

"I'm sorry that I offended you. And I know what it feels like to be ignored, by the way. So I'm glad you told me that."

"A'ight then."

"Do you want to come in for some water?"

Covered in sweat and short of breath, Blue Gene nodded. He stubbed out his cigarette in the gutter and looked up and down the road for John, but he was nowhere in sight.

$ $ $

Standing in a small foyer, Blue Gene looked into a perfectly clean, feminine room with snow-white carpet and a marble-top table covered in antique glassware. There was no TV in this room.

"That's the room that no one ever goes in. Except for company sometimes."

"Yeah. We got a bunch of rooms like that," said Blue Gene.

"It's kind of wasteful, but it's nice, I guess." Blue Gene nodded and followed Jackie into a living room that was so cluttered that the furniture could hardly be seen. This room did contain a TV, not to mention a DVD player, VCR, and stereo. She told him to have a seat on a couch that was half-covered with mail, magazines, and ads from the newspaper. While Jackie went to the kitchen to get both of them some ice water, Blue Gene looked around. This was the type of house where any flat surface would soon collect a pile of random crud. His trailer had been like that.

"Ooh, the news is on," she said, handing him a collectible McDonald's glass featuring the Hamburglar. She turned on the TV and sat in a recliner. "I always watch the local news for the banter."

"For the what?"

"Banter. Like, small talk. You know when they're done with their serious reports, but then they need to segue into sports or weather? They try to smooth the transition by having banter. Like when they say things like 'Yeah, it's hot outside, but the heat isn't keeping people from going to see the Cats play, is it, Jeff?'"

As they drank their water and waited for the banter, some of the things that Jackie had said kept echoing in Blue Gene's mind. She had some nerve. He liked nerve up to a point, but not when it was being directed at him. He was not about to let a woman get the best of him. Even if it hurt his chances with her, he had to show her who's boss early on in the relationship, before this got out of hand.

"Hey, you said you wouldn't stand for sporting events, but wrestling, it's not a sporting event. So you should've stood."

"Well, it's *kind of* a sporting event, but yeah, you have a point. Why'd you bring *that* up?"

"I'm just sayin', sometimes you're wrong. You know you were sayin' earlier—"

"Oh, here. Sorry to interrupt, but here's some banter."

He listened as two newscasters had a pleasant but forced conversation about baseball. Jackie cracked up. "It's so fake and *awkward*," she said. "Isn't it great!? And look how they hold on to the papers on their desk. They clutch onto their papers like it'll protect them or something."

"That's funny," said Blue Gene with a laugh. "I hadn't noticed before."

A car commercial came on. "Ever notice how the volume goes up for commercials?"

"Well, yeah. Now that you mention it. Turn that down for a second." Jackie lowered the volume with the remote. "Listen here. You need to realize that I wouldn't be helpin' my family out with the campaign if I didn't *believe* in what they're doing."

"Okay. I realize that."

"You don't know John, but he's my brother, and I know that he would make a good congressman. You need to respect that."

"Okay."

"I'm just sayin', you act like you know everything about my family, but I know my family better than you, and if I say John would make a good congressman, then he *will*. Don't be questionin' my ass."

"He probably *would* make a good congressman, but good only for big business."

"No, now, you don't even know. He's good for family values, and he's good for American values, and he's my brother, and you need to show some respect."

"Maybe he does have values, but his main priority will be helping rich white people get more money. And that's the *truth*. *Values*, that's just a word."

"Maybe to you it is. But to me, it's what we're fightin' for."

"Would you *wake up*?"

"I'm wide awake, woman." Blue Gene suddenly stood. "Now, you need to watch your mouth." Jackie stared at Blue Gene and grinned. "*What?*"

"You talk so tough and macho," she said, "but you don't fool me. You have the kindest eyes."

A chill went through him, as if someone had blown in his ear.

"No, I don't," he said as he headed to the front door.

"Wait. Yes, you do. I wouldn't have let you in the house if you didn't."

"You're just so full of it, woman." He opened the door.

"You look tired, too, though. Kind but tired."

"Well, I'll give you that much. I'm tired, all right." He lingered in the foyer.

"But they're kind, too. Can't you even accept a compliment? Look— if we're going to be friends, you're going to have to stop acting like a tough guy all the time."

"Who said I *wanted* to be your friend?"

"Then what are you here for?"

"I was campaigning with my brother when I come up on you."

"Okay, fine. *I* want to be *your* friend."

"Don't do me any favors."

"I know. Lucky you, right?"

As mad as he was, Blue Gene still hoped for something more than friendship. He knew they were an unlikely pair, but he could see them watching wrestling together in a darkened room. He closed the front door. "I tell ya, I want to be your friend, too. But friends don't try to change who their friends are. They accept 'em."

"You're right. I'm sorry."

"That's okay, but also, you don't need to be puttin' my family down. And don't be talkin' down to me. I tell ya, some of the things you said, you're lucky you're a woman or I'd've beaten your ass."

Jackie rolled her eyes and walked back to the living room. She sat on the couch and folded her arms. Blue Gene came to the living room doorway. "What?"

"You would've *beaten my ass*?"

"Well, yeah, if you weren't a woman, I would've."

"Right. Be violent. Be a macho man. That's how they've duped you."

"Nobody's duped me."

"They know that in terms of the economy, they couldn't possibly get you behind them, so they appeal to your sense of masculine pride. You support the war because it's the manly thing to do, and only a sissy would back away from a fight, right?" Blue Gene stared at her. "That's a comfort to the servant class, because they might not have any money or a good job or a future, but they do live in the *greatest country in the world* that will never back down from a fight."

"Yeah, you got it all figured out, don't ya? All us servants are just a bunch of fools, and if we was only as smart as you, everything'd be better. Well guess what? If it wasn't for those stupid, macho guys you're talkin' about, you wouldn't be able to run your mouth like that. They fought so you could be free and say whatever you want."

"Do they hand out, like, *pamphlets* telling you what to say about these topics when all of you buy your pickup trucks? Yes, it is very free here. Fine, okay, I'll give you that. Freedom is great. But most countries have freedom regardless of their military records, some of them without being in a war for the last hundred years. This isn't the only free country in the world."

"No, but it's the freest, so it's the greatest."

"Maybe it is, maybe it isn't. I can't say. I've never even been anywhere outside of America. And most of the people who say that have never left America."

"Well, *I* have. I've been to almost every country in Europe." This shut her up. "Yeah, that's right, and none of 'em got anything on America. Their toilets can't handle American shits."

Jackie laughed. "The drummer from my band, his old band went on tour in Europe, and he said that in Switzerland, one of the cabs had an

Oriental rug in the floor of the backseat."

"Yeah, I don't doubt it. Over there the cabs are Mercedes."

"See, *that's* freedom. The fact that wealth is enjoyed not just by one percent of the population. Do you realize that *one percent* of the people in America have almost *half* of the overall money? It's crazy! Freedom from poverty is the best kind of freedom, and we could *easily* have that here, but instead of our riches going to people who need it, it all goes to military spending."

"Military spending is what protects our country in the first place."

"We spend more on our military than every other country in the world combined. Just think if that money went to *helping* people. Even a *fraction* of it."

"Okay, yeah, let's just stop fighting wars and let the Hitlers do whatever the hell they want. Get real, Jackie."

"There he is. He always comes up in these conversations sooner or later. He's the best thing that's ever happened for you warhawks. Well, second best. And fine, you're right, I can't defend Hitler, but I will defend the *opposite* of Hitler. The good Hitler." Blue Gene gave her a confused look. The TV was still muted, and John's campaign commercial came on. Jackie kept talking while John smiled in the background, soon joined by Abby and Arthur. "The world's had plenty of bad Hitlers who've ascended to power, but why can't we have the opposite of Hitler come into being, someone who rises to lead us but only uses his power to *improve* everyone's lives, not just the lives of the elite? Someone who refuses to start a war, who prevents death, who doesn't starve people but feeds them?"

"'Cause it's not that simple."

"I know it'll never happen, but the opposite of Hitler—and I realize that term might not work—let's call him Greg. Greg could only get so much in campaign contributions, because no corporations would support him. And let's say he somehow manages to have a successful campaign. Let's say he gets the common folk behind him and eventually manages to become president of the United States. Well, then, all of a sudden we'd have a man who goes against everything our government has stood for. He'd be the first nonimperialist president we'd ever had. He wants only to spread goodwill and help people and completely disregards the capitalistic urge for money. How do you think Congress would react to that? All his ideas would be shot down and fall to the Capitol floor. He'd be completely ineffective and probably end up being assassinated by the CIA."

"No. I tell you what'd happen. The other countries would take one look at Greg and see that he's a big ol' softy, and they'd say, finally, here's our chance! America's finally become weak! And that'd be the end of us. And I guess the foreigners would come in, and Greg'd just let 'em take over."

"God forbid we show weakness."

"You're damn right. We can't show any signs of weakness, 'cause that's when we get planes flown into our buildings. I tell you, you're living in some dream world where we don't get attacked. But it can happen now. We were attacked, and you're in, like, a little teenage-girl dream world where it didn't happen."

A ringing came from Blue Gene's shorts. He pulled out his cell phone.

"Mapother," he answered. "Yeah…a'ight. I'll be right there." Jackie stood. "That's my brother. I gotta go." Jackie got up and walked him to the front door. He turned after opening the door. "Thanks for the water." He extended his hand to Jackie. "Friends?"

She hesitated before taking his hand. "Friends," she agreed. But she winced and pulled her hand away.

"What?" asked Blue Gene.

"That hurt! You men and your firm handshakes. If you all took all the energy you use in impressing each other with your handshakes, and you put all that energy together, it would be enough manpower to feed every human being in history ten times over."

"Or you could put it all in one great big bomb."

"Why would you do that?"

"You say you hate war so much. I 'magine that's about all that'd stop it, kid."

VII.

Until this Labor Day weekend, no politician in Commonwealth County had ever attempted to advance his candidacy on the premises of a Wal-Mart. Henry Mapother
hypothesized that, as the commercial epicenter of the twenty-one
counties that comprised the district, Bashford's Wal-Mart Supercenter
would be visited by many of those stray denizens, rural or otherwise,
whom his son's campaign might have neglected. The Mapother for
Congress strategists agreed that maintaining a presence at the area's
most popular retailer over the holiday weekend could be the last big
push that would clinch this election for John. The latest polls showed
John ahead by twelve points, thanks largely to his staff's door-to-door
campaigning, which had left virtually no door in the entire district
unknocked.

The only problem was that political demonstrations on store property were a violation of Wal-Mart's corporate policy. But this particular
Wal-Mart's management allowed John some leeway because the
Mapothers had recently made some generous donations to Wal-Mart's
local charities, and also because the manager at the Bashford Wal-Mart
used to work with Blue Gene. He had never forgotten how patient Blue
Gene had been with him when he first started at Wal-Mart. Anytime he
made a mistake, Blue Gene turned it into a joke. The Wal-Mart manager told John's campaign manager that he would do anything for Blue
Gene Mapother, that he wouldn't even *bother* contacting the public re-

lations office in Arkansas. Therefore, campaigning would be allowed outside the Wal-Mart this one time, as long as the campaigner also displayed evidence of being there for the good of the community.

With no objection from the store manager, Blue Gene made the most of having the busiest piece of land in town as his platform for the weekend, and occasionally he even sold some baked goods that would profit the local hospice. Mapother leaflets were conspicuously placed among the white-chocolate macadamia cookies, petits fours, and turtle brownies that Elizabeth had baked, and anyone who came within five feet of the table would hear a voting suggestion for November just in case they didn't see the banner.

All weekend long, Blue Gene stood in the heat—which was still in the eighties even in September—outside this massive stronghold of commerce, with its light-gray and dark-blue exterior and its slogan written in slanted cursive on the façade: *Always*. Blue Gene would spend half the day in front of the department store side, and the other half on the supermarket side. In front of both entrances were slanted yellow lines marking the pedestrian crossing. For such a relatively small town, the flow of people at the Wal-Mart pedestrian crossings was amazing. At the store's busiest hour, it was the equivalent of the once thriving sidewalks of Main Street being compressed into two hectic rectangles.

$ $ $

In small-town America, if one person wanted to encounter any other person, the encounter would eventually take place, as long as one of them stayed put at Wal-Mart. At some point, whoever it is you're looking for will inevitably show up there. So it was no wonder that as Blue Gene stood outside Wal-Mart from nine to five on a Saturday, Sunday, and Monday, he saw a substantial cross-section of the people with whom he had grown up.

Mitchell Gibson—who had once filled Blue Gene's Saturday afternoons with Nintendo-playing, Nickelodeon-watching glee—appeared at Wal-Mart Saturday at around noon. They couldn't avoid each other, Blue Gene swelling out his chest with his MAPOTHER FOR CONGRESS muscle shirt, Mitchell walking right by in his orange polo shirt.

"Hey, Gibson," he said with signature gruff.

"Hey, Blue Gene." Blue Gene couldn't miss the sharpness of his tone. Mitchell kept walking.

"Hold on, man." Mitchell walked hesitantly over to Blue Gene's table. Blue Gene pulled the bill of his cap down almost over his eyes. "I want you to know that I *am* sorry about that guy at the Ambassador Inn."

"*Why didn't you hold up for me*?!" Mitchell said in a voice that to Blue Gene was suggestive of spike heels and housecats.

"I would've, but you know, I was there that night for John, and I promised him I wouldn't cause any trouble, and I just didn't want to get involved with y'all's argument."

"You always held up for me when we were little."

"We was kids," said Blue Gene. "People changes. Look at *you*."

"What do you mean by that? Because I'm *gay*?"

"Yeah."

"I was *always* gay, Blue Gene."

"Nuh-uh."

"Wouldn't I *know*?"

"It don't matter. Whatever pumps your 'nads."

Mitchell laughed. "You always could make me laugh."

"Don't get all emotional on me."

"You're *awful*." Mitchell tossed his head back and started off.

"Hey, man," said Blue Gene, taking his sunglasses from the bill of his cap and putting them on. "That guy at the Ambassador Inn—he didn't rough you up too bad, did he?"

"Not really."

"Look, I didn't like what happened, man. The timing was just so bad. When he was gettin' into it with you, my family was wanting me to be in a picture with 'em, and that's something that rarely happens, me being included with my family like that, you know?"

"Oh, yeah. Like I know nothing at all about that sort of thing."

$ $ $

Blue Gene Mapother was a wayward child who always laid his head down in class, and if the teachers in their holiday-specific sweaters questioned him, he told them he had a headache. His arms enclosed his head and darkened his view while daydreams sprouted from his fertile earwax, muffling the pedantic sounds between schoolbells. Mitchell, meanwhile, was a model student: quiet, conscientious, and serious beyond his years. Most of the other students hated him. The first week of first grade, a boy was picking on Mitchell so relentlessly that Blue Gene could no longer ignore it. When he saw that the teachers weren't going to do anything about it, one day at recess he took it upon himself to pin this bully to the ground and rub his elbows across the concrete. Mitchell then latched on to Blue Gene, and just like that, they were best friends.

Grade school eventually ended, and when junior high began, Blue Gene and Mitchell had to stop hiding behind their St. Katherine's uniforms and switch over to the locker-lined smorgasbord of pubescence that was East Junior High. It soon became clear that their friendship could not sustain the changes that a burgeoning social life causes in a weak, scared twelve-year-old. Instead of associating with the increasingly freaky, artsy, Kurt Cobain–worshipping Mitchell, Blue Gene situated himself within the orbit of the in crowd, a wild bunch of well-dressed junior socialites, some of whom he knew from Junior Pro basketball. Blue Gene's induction into the seventh-grade social elite happened naturally; they accepted him without question because of his last name, his sense of humor, and his appearance, which in those days he made sure was nothing but stylish.

Once upon a time, Blue Gene Mapother's hair had been a completely different creature. In those days, it sat obediently atop his skull and didn't even think about chasing down the back of his neck. Falling into the category of a Caesar cut for most of his teenage years, his hair was short all over and combed perfectly straight forward with gel that made the top of his head shine.

Meanwhile, Mitchell's hair seemed to change colors and styles on a weekly basis. By eighth grade, his and Blue Gene's friendship had been reduced to some "what's ups?" in the hallway. By their freshman year at Commonwealth County High, Mitchell Gibson was just another name in the yearbook to Blue Gene, who by then showed evidence in his every move that he thought he was God's gift to the school, and since his presence alone was an act of giving, he could behave as one who was constantly in the state of being repaid. Because he was always ready to take from the world, Blue Gene was constantly laid-back, like a sunbather waiting to be baked. In class he sank coolly into his desk, and his long legs sprawled forth wherever they pleased. He often rested one leg on the desk in front of him, tapping his brown Timberland boot on the book rack, to the aggravation of the student he sat behind. His other leg rested casually in the middle of the aisle, and his classmates were expected to step over the placid limb. He reached back far when he yawned, almost touching the face of the student behind him. Teachers could rarely earn his attention, as he mostly slept, popped gum, and threw things at people. When class was over, he walked the halls as though they were his. All this he did in spite of the fact that his true social ranking was only at the bottom of the top tier of preps (or the top of the bottom), because—truth be told—he wasn't all that handsome. He was plain and wore braces.

But again, he was rich and fit the part; plus, he played basketball. Though he wasn't put in games that often, making the varsity team did help solidify his place in the cafeteria hegemony. When he wasn't playing basketball, he could be found "chillin'" to rap music and partying with friends, whom he called "his boys." Back then, the word *blunt* was never far from his lips, and if he wasn't smoking weed, he was filling a toilet bowl with his alcohol-fortified urine. As for his lust life, Blue Gene went for the dirtiest of the clean girls. He easily managed to get what he wanted from these girls without actually having to date them. His spring breaks in Cancun with his girls and his boys approached orgiastic levels of ass-slapping hedonism, a veritable free-for-all of fluids.

Back then, Blue Gene had cases and cartons and Ziploc bagloads of fun doing whatever he pleased, which in itself was not so problematic outside the obvious health and safety concerns. But in this mindless pursuit of pleasure, he often hurt others. For instance, there was his careless treatment of his female companions. They were nothing but bodies to him, receptacles for his carnal glop, and once he grew bored of the bodies, he gave no consideration to the feelings within them. He dispensed similarly thoughtless treatment to any peer who didn't make the cut for the highly selective in crowd. Blue Gene wasn't particularly mean to classmates outside his social circle, nor was he nice to them. He seemed to look through them, never thinking a substantial thought about these lesser ones. He never bothered getting to know anyone who didn't sit within a ten-foot radius of his lunch table.

But there was something baffling about Blue Gene and his clique's one-way relationship with the majority of their socially inferior peers: despite the cool kids ignoring them, these nameless pygmies still came to the games and hooted and hollered for their superiors, and they still cheered as loudly as they could at the pep rallies. It seemed the less Blue Gene and his clique noticed the other students, the more these other students screamed in their support.

$ $ $

Blue Gene saw a considerable sampling of people he knew from high school during his weekend outside Wal-Mart. All of them were on the brink of their thirties, and most of them didn't recognize the tank-topped, flip-flopped, mullet-headed mustache man that Blue Gene had become. But some saw the Mapother sign and Mapother T-shirt and were able to put the pertinent numbers together.

"Blue?! Is that *you*?"

"What'd ya say, Stephanie?" Like most of the girls he'd dated in high school, Stephanie tended to look better from behind. She came to Wal-Mart Sunday morning, walking perkily with her ponytail tied tight and a silent frat-man at her side.

"What's *up*!?" she asked, her overtanned face showing that she could recall a boy in smarter clothes.

"Nothin'." He wanted to mouth off to her for looking at him like this, maybe tell her that she looked like a Chicken McNugget. But as she eyed his stringy hair curling slightly at his shoulders, he understood that it must have been hard for her to process the transformation he had undergone in the last ten years. "You have a mustache."

"No I don't. That's an eyebrow on top my lip." Stephanie and her man laughed. "Whatcha been up to?"

"I just moved back from Seattle. I finished up my master's in communication up there."

"Right on."

"What about you, Blue? What's new with you?"

"Helpin' my brother campaign. Here." He handed her a leaflet. He also handed one to the man, whom she didn't bother introducing. Blue Gene looked at him and nodded upward. It could've just as easily been him standing there with Stephanie. All he would've had to say after high school graduation was, "Bring on the suit and tie."

"Oh, yeah. My family and I both got an invitation to the Autumn Dinner Dance your brother's having. I guess I'll see you there."

Blue Gene had heard nothing about an Autumn Dinner Dance. It must have been something the Mapother team had cooked up to show the blue bloods that they weren't going to be forgotten in this scramble to get the working man vote. Miffed at first, Blue Gene brushed it off. He didn't want any part of an Autumn Dinner Dance, whatever the hell that was.

"Good to see ya, Stephanie," said Blue Gene in a timbre that made it clear he was through with the conversation.

She could have her dinner dance. They could all have their little dinner dances and choke on their dinners and break their necks on the dance floor, for all he cared. They could have high school all over again; Blue Gene would gladly be an outsider. At least outside you could still smoke.

$ $ $

In late October of Blue Gene's senior year, a neighboring county's basketball team was visiting Commonwealth County High, and by halftime it was clear that the visitors hadn't a hope in defeating the almighty County High Bobcats. Toward the end of the second half, both coaches put in their second-string players. This allowed Blue Gene a chance to play. As usual, none of his family members were there to watch, even though they had been the ones who made him play.

One of the benchwarmers from the other team was a short black boy wearing corrective goggles. The awkward-looking runt guarded Blue Gene tenaciously, and before Blue Gene knew it, the boy made a quick steal and rushed down the court in hopes of making an easy layup. His pride enflamed, Blue Gene chased the boy with all the speed his long legs could summon. He caught up as his opponent was jumping toward the goal, and he took a forceful running shove. As the referee's whistle shrieked in disapproval, the boy came down hard, contorting his body so that he wouldn't fall on some cheerleaders behind the baseline. He fell on his hip, and the side of his head bounced off the hardwood.

The home crowd couldn't help but boo. County High was up twenty-seven points, and Blue Gene's aggression was a show of extremely bad form. Meanwhile, Blue Gene was not concerned about the begoggled boy—who wasn't getting up—but was only irritated by the fact that he had still managed to make the shot. After shouting a few obscene reproofs at himself, he turned around to see eleven big basketball players charging his way.

Without a second thought, Blue Gene's body raged toward them, and in two seconds a human pit coalesced near the free-throw line, with tensed arms thrashing and clenched fists smacking their marks. Blue Gene's teammates fused themselves with the fracas, peeling opponents off him and starting their own side duels with the visitors. For over a minute, referees, coaches, a policeman, and even some parents from the bleachers tried to pull the frenzied teen-beasts off one another, but their efforts were like smoothing out the spiraling lines of a whirlpool, because at the center of this storm were two violent eyes that would not stop looking for the next target. This rare opportunity for continuous, rapid-fire attacks upon multiple foes unleashed some inner serpent that circulated Blue Gene's wrath.

But then something unusual happened. As Blue Gene lifted his fist to one of the visitors, one of his own teammates, the power forward named Darius Bledsoe, who was also County High's best player, hooked Blue Gene's arm from behind, spun him around, and laid him out on the hardwood with a punch to the eye.

Momentarily stunned, Blue Gene picked himself off the court and flung himself at Bledsoe. Both connected with vicious blows to the face before their teammates pulled them apart. But their anger made them stronger, and they were able to fend off the peacemakers and lunge toward each other again. This time, Blue Gene tackled Darius to the ground and attempted a cross-face choke-hold that proved ineffective. Darius retaliated with a hold of his own on Blue Gene's legs, but the two were pulled apart again. Before they could be completely separated, Blue Gene reached out for Darius and was able to grip his hand. As the teammates continued to yank Blue Gene away, he clawed into Darius's flesh, trying to pry his nails underneath the veins on the top of his hands. Blue Gene was shocked to see his nails gouging Bledsoe's skin, and he let go when he visualized where he was planning to go with this action.

After the maelstrom dissipated, Blue Gene stood panting with one eye closed, his head hunched menacingly beneath his shoulders, a rivulet of blood streaming from his mouth.

His hair was a mess.

$ $ $

On Labor Day morning, Blue Gene saw another old face from high school, one of his former teammates, Tyrone Castle. As he did with all the potential voters, Blue Gene gave Tyrone an upward nod and said, "Hidey. Vote for Mapother." This was met with a cold, hard look, which Blue Gene felt obligated to return.

Blue Gene knew that Tyrone was the type of man who wouldn't make a verbal response to anyone's greeting, acting as if saying "hello" or "hi" would be relenting something. It was like you had to *earn* a "hello" from a guy as tough as Tyrone.

Anytime Blue Gene ran into one of his former teammates, it was awkward, because they had all been on Darius's side after the brawl. It had always angered Blue Gene that no one had ever questioned why Darius turned on his own teammate.

But it only made sense. If you were to take any two high schools in the world and force them to combine, you would probably find that the alliances would not form according to who had been in which high school originally. Instead, the students would align themselves according to crowds. If Darius and the short, black, goggled guy had gone to the same school, they would have sat at the same lunch table. The fact that Darius and Blue Gene happened to go to the same school and happened to be on the same team hardly mattered, and it went against reason to expect them to defend one another because of how the school-district lines happened to fall.

Tyrone exited Wal-Mart in no time, throwing his white plastic sack away and immediately opening the box of ointment he had purchased. Blue Gene watched Tyrone as he walked across the parking lot, putting the ointment on a fresh tattoo. It was about time for Blue Gene to get a new tattoo: something big, something intimidating, something that would show the world that he was a man who meant business.

$ $ $

Everything was normal when Blue Gene returned to school after his suspension. His friends looked past what he had done because they couldn't fault a man for being so intensely competitive on the court. Blue Gene and Darius no longer spoke or even looked at each other, which was easy, since all the black students sat at one long table on the edge of the cafeteria, and he and Darius weren't chummy to begin with in the locker room.

But Blue Gene didn't forget how Darius had turned on him that night, and he held a grudge. And because he couldn't unburden himself of this grudge, he ended up with a leg so injured and arthritic that it hurt on rainy days ten years later.

It all started over a Tommy Hilfiger sweater. Darius came into algebra class one day wearing a Tommy Hilfiger sweater that, because of a distinctive steak-sauce stain on the bottom, Blue Gene immediately recognized as one he had formerly owned. After Elizabeth had seen the stain wasn't coming out, she had donated it to the St. Vincent de Paul thrift store. For the rest of the day, Blue Gene made it a point to tell all of his friends that County High's star athlete was wearing one of his crappy old hand-me-downs.

That day after school, when Blue Gene walked across the parking lot, he saw that Darius and seven of his closest, largest friends were leaning on Blue Gene's Range Rover. He looked around for someone—anyone. But there was no one, just a few guys and gals he had partied with, no one he could ask to go into a battle like this. He was on his own, and though common sense told him to go back into the school, he kept walking toward his SUV.

He wondered how he should begin what was sure to be a pointless conversation, but Darius was willing to do the talking. There was a salvo of *f*-bombs and something about "you talkin' 'bout me." All the other students in the parking lot turned to see what the commotion was. Blue

Gene stood and took it until it was his turn to talk. He looked at all those fists and thought about when he was little, how he had been shocked to see that the palms were white.

Blue Gene muttered a soft "sorry," and Darius called him a *pussy* for it. This sent Blue Gene cussing his lungs out in a diatribe that culminated with his saying that Darius was nothing without basketball and that the school used him. Just as Darius and all the other bodies started to spring into motion, a policeman came running across the parking lot. He was the cop hired to patrol the high school all day, and he quickly and deftly dispersed this hostile congregation.

The cop told Darius to leave the parking lot and go home. He then directed Blue Gene to do the same. Blue Gene felt safer in his vehicle. When he turned his key in the ignition, one of his Tupac Shakur CDs was playing. He immediately turned it off. He then realized that the parking lot was full of peers watching to see what would happen next, taking turns looking at Darius and his boys in a white '87 Lincoln Town Car and Blue Gene in his brand-new Range Rover.

Blue Gene pulled out of the parking lot and onto the highway. He knew his peers were still watching, and so he came up with the idea of swerving around Darius's car in order to beat him to the off-ramp so that it would look like Blue Gene had achieved the last laugh. Not to be outdone, Darius then swerved in front of the Range Rover before Blue Gene had a chance to pull out onto the bypass. Livid, Blue Gene drove dangerously fast in order to catch up with the Lincoln, not knowing what he would do once he did. He only knew that he couldn't let his enemy get away with pulling out ahead of him like that. No one could treat him like that without suffering for it in some way.

The bypass led onto the busy Highway 81, and Darius eventually had to slow down for a red light. His was the first car to stop for the light in the right lane, and Blue Gene made sure his Range Rover was the first car to stop in the left lane. As he pulled to a stop, he looked over to see Darius screaming "motherfucker" and "pussy" irately, repeatedly.

So fast that his actions felt automatic, Blue Gene threw open his car

door, ran around his Range Rover, and pulled at the Lincoln's door handle. It was locked. Darius looked up in disbelief as this madman fero-
ciously slapped his closed window. Blue Gene then turned to his Range
Rover, opened the back door, and pulled out an aluminum baseball bat.
He bashed in Darius's window. Then he swung at Darius, who blocked
the bat with his forearms. Freaked out, Darius stepped on the gas to get
away, but the light was still red, and as he sped into the busy intersection,
he came directly into the path of a speeding car that had to veer sharply
to avoid hitting him head on.

The driver of this other car received her second terrifying surprise
within two seconds, when she saw that in avoiding the Town Car, she
had veered into the path of a pedestrian who for some reason was in the
no-man's-land of an intersection. She hit her brakes but could not stop
her car from running directly into the young man, ramming his legs.

The remainder of Blue Gene's senior year showed him nothing but
delirium and pain. Blue Gene had multiple surgeries on both legs, three
on the left one alone. His left leg received the brunt of the car's force,
leaving him with little cartilage in his hip. After a blood clot formed in
his left leg, he was put on blood thinner and had to have bloodwork
done twice a week. When he came home, his room became a sort of vol-
untary sarcophagus. Ashamed and depressed, he would accept no visits
from friends. On into the spring semester, his presence at high school
was that of a spirit, wafting through the hallways by way of gossip. Henry
had kept all of Blue Gene's mistakes—his flagrant foul, the brawl, the
baseball-bat assault, and the accident—out of the newspaper, and without any proof to the contrary in print, there were rumors at County
High that Blue Gene Mapother had died.

Between his two broken legs and the disgust his parents communi-
cated to him with their every look, Blue Gene wanted to die. He hated
himself to the point of tears when he dwelled on one particular idea: the
short, goggled boy's parents in the bleachers, witnessing their son being
shoved to the ground.

His friends went to the prom and graduated. He watched back-to-back episodes of *Saved by the Bell* and visualized himself in a wheelchair, wishing he had a button at his disposal that could detonate not just himself, but the entire galaxy. Being completely immobile, he couldn't even gain access to the modest detonations of marijuana and alcohol, which had reliably blown his mind into oblivion on so many weekends in the past.

Through the spring and summer, Henry and Elizabeth forced him to attend physical therapy religiously, and in the fall they forced him to go back to school. Having a son who was held back a grade was shameful enough, but no son of theirs would be a high school dropout. Returning to his high school in a wheelchair was by far the most difficult thing Blue Gene had ever done. Even the physical act of entering the front door proved almost insurmountable. Once he was inside, he was self-conscious not only about the fact that he was in a wheelchair, but also because of the complete absence of stylishness in his general appearance. Because of the bulky casts that came to his knees, he had to wear sweatpants. And because of his general malaise, he had allowed his hair to grow out. It was not yet long, but it was getting there, and though Blue Gene found himself liking his longish hair when he looked in the mirror, once he was back in school, he worried about how people would react.

Most of his friends were in college now, but he had a few underclassmen pals who were now his fellow seniors. They greeted him cheerfully in the hallways, but the conversations that ensued were sad and awkward, because Blue Gene obviously tried to avoid talking about the specifics that had left him in this sorry state, and because, for the first time in his life, he felt like he was being condescended to. He hated having to look up to talk to people. He hated the strange spots where he was told to place himself in the classrooms so that he'd be out of everyone's way.

That first morning back at school, he spent the first four periods worrying about lunch. Having trouble getting around, he was late getting to the cafeteria, and nearly all the seats at the cool table were taken. He tried to figure out where he could squeeze his wheelchair, but there was no space for him.

After he paid for his lunch, Blue Gene set the tray on his thighs, but in concentrating so hard to balance the tray, he nearly ran into a girl he had slept with several times before exchanging her for a different bed-mate. To keep from hitting her, he stopped suddenly, causing the tray to slide off his lap and make that humiliating sound that only a tray hitting a hard cafeteria floor can make. Blue Gene never forgot that sound.

The girl quickly walked away, and feeling the pressure of everyone's stares, Blue Gene stretched down toward the scattered chicken rings on the floor and struggled to place them on his tray. He felt like he was in the middle of an ordeal that would never end, when he saw a pair of flip-flops approaching. The flip-flops contained a person who wore white socks and walked like a duck, but a duck with nice legs. She smiled sweetly and got on her knees to put the food back on Blue Gene's tray. He thanked her, and she said she'd help him with his tray and asked where he was sitting. He looked up into her dark-socketed eyes and asked where *she* was sitting.

They had been going to the same school for the last three years, but this was the first time Blue Gene had ever truly seen Cheyenne Staggs.

$ $ $

Amidst all the activity of Wal-Mart on Saturday—the deal-craving fam-ilies scuttling in to buy low-priced guns and leotards, the dazed con-sumers emerging from the store, trying to remember where they had parked while being pulled by glutted shopping carts, the busybody men pacing while yammering into cell phones—Cheyenne's daughter, Sa-vannah, showed up in bun-tight shorts and a chartreuse halter top. Blue Gene figured she was around thirteen, and as she duck-walked closer, the breakout of pimples on her sullen face confirmed she was a teenager. An older-looking, basketball jersey–wearing man with the demeanor of a warthog accompanied her.

"Hidey. Vote for Mapother," he said as they passed. He didn't know how to talk to her; it wouldn't feel right to say, "Remember me? I used to live with you when you was little."

Blue Gene had been visiting with Arthur at least twice a week. They played with their Transformers and G.I. Joes, collected lightning bugs, and had paper-wad wars, all the while keeping a close watch on Arthur's height, a topic with which he was currently obsessed. They also talked about his day at school, but they never stayed on this topic long, since Arthur didn't like school. The only thing he seemed to like about first grade was that it gave him a chance to be around "this one yellow-haired girl" he liked, which Blue Gene was glad to hear since it proved Arthur wouldn't wind up gay, despite loving *High School Musical*. Before the night was over, they always ended up in front of the TV, sometimes watching the Disney Channel, sometimes watching the reality show *Big Brother*.

Once Arthur asked Blue Gene why the people who were stuck in the *Big Brother* house treated each other the way they did, lying and hurting one another. Blue Gene said he reckoned it was for the money, which Arthur found hilarious. When Blue Gene asked him what was so funny about that, Arthur told him to "go up Santa's butt."

Not long after Cheyenne's daughter passed in front of him, Blue Gene's cell phone rang. Though he had tried to fight it, Blue Gene felt a flash of excitement every time his phone rang, thinking it might be Jackie. He had called her twice since their walk two weeks ago. They had talked at length both times, and he'd told her she could give him a holler anytime. She hadn't yet, but she knew he'd be outside Wal-Mart all weekend and had said she might stop by.

"Mapother," he answered, only to hear the scrambled murmur of a crowded public place on the other end. After yelling "hello" several times without reply, he could hear John talking to another man about tennis. Realizing that John had accidentally pressed the Call button, Blue Gene hung up and cussed. Jackie wasn't going to call and she wasn't going to stop by, but it was just as well. If there was one thing he had learned in life, it was that women had the power to turn a good day bad. But then, they could also turn a bad day good.

$ $ $

Through bowling alleys and the racetrack, through street festivals and the flea market, through Big Lots and bars, Blue Gene and Cheyenne walked through life with one hand deep inside the other's butt pocket. They bonded quickly. Her buxom body was what raised his attention in the first place, especially after she invited him to come see her perform at Sassy's Gentlemen's Club, where she was known as Heaven. But the fact that when he was with her he felt like he had entered some plush, Christmas-morning comfort zone—that was what made him devote himself to her. Within a week of dating her, he already felt at ease enough with Cheyenne that he didn't care what he smelled like around her. He had never felt this way with anyone before, and he easily overlooked that she was a manic-depressive mother to a child whose father was a whitish dope-dealing gangsta (thankfully out of the picture by the time Blue Gene met her).

As Blue Gene's second senior year scooched along, he traded his wheelchair for crutches, and Cheyenne became his one and only priority. Two months into their relationship, after noticing a certain laxness that her fuzz-faced male friends exhibited in their general appearance, Blue Gene worried that he wasn't visually interesting enough for his new mate. Unbeknownst to his parents, he got a tattoo of his favorite animal, the bald eagle, because Cheyenne had mentioned that she thought tattoos were sexy. She would later reveal that thick, manly mustaches were also a turn-on.

Blue Gene would do anything to ensure he and Cheyenne would ultimately ride off into the sunset together—though he realized his Range Rover wouldn't be quite the right car to ride off in with a girl like Cheyenne. The luxury SUV was Cheyenne's first clue that her new man was well-off. She didn't know the significance of the name Mapother because she had never read a newspaper, and she watched cartoons with Savannah instead of the news. In fact, it took her a while to even pronounce his last name correctly; it was *May*-pawther, not Maw-pawther. He concealed his wealth from her for as long as he could, afraid it might scare her off or attract her for the wrong reason. His plan was to make her like him so much with his kind but tough persona that once she *did* find out that he was not just well-off, but spectacularly rich, it wouldn't be an issue. As it turned out, that was precisely what happened.

Blue Gene ended up being more affected by Cheyenne's lack of wealth than she was by his surplus. In the end, it wasn't just a peroxide blond Blue Gene had fallen in love with. It was a whole new way of maneuvering through life: poor, and with neither pretension nor the burdensome expectation that you would ever amount to anything. There was no pressure around Cheyenne's circle of friends to be cool, because they weren't cool themselves, nor were they trendy. They were trashy and aggressively casual. His grammar would not be improving much around this new set, but he did learn some important things from them, especially how to enjoy the simple gifts of everyday life. While Cheyenne and her kind of people had never stepped inside a Saks Fifth Avenue, they were quick to point out things like the sound of cicadas, which meant the heart of summer had arrived; the reassuring sight of a pet pit bull sleeping on cold linoleum; or the gratifying first taste of an ice-cold Miller Lite after a hard day of work.

Blue Gene experienced this last sensation after he could no longer ignore the strange envy he felt for all his new friends, who had grueling adult jobs. All of them hated their bosses and their piddling wages, but when Blue Gene would see one of the men in a soiled workshirt with a personalized name tag sewn on, he couldn't help but feel like he was missing out. Everyone around him worked these exhausting jobs just to afford the few things they had, and not having a job made Blue Gene feel like less of a man.

Toward the end of his senior year, Blue Gene applied at Wal-Mart, and they hired him after two interviews, even though he had no prior work experience and was on crutches. Blue Gene's first great plunge in falling out with his parents came when he declared that he was taking this $6.60/hour job instead of going to college. Henry and Elizabeth pleaded with him all summer long, but all he could say is that he wanted to be his own man and make his own money.

Cheyenne bought a trailer that summer and was already asking Blue Gene to move in with her, but he knew the timing wasn't right. John was rehabbing at the Hazelden treatment center in Minnesota, and Blue Gene knew he should stay at home in case his mom needed him. When John returned, he said he had found not only God during his time away, but also a new woman, Abby. With things appearing stable at the Mapother house for a change, Blue Gene moved out shortly after he turned twenty-one, around the same time his cane became unnecessary, thanks to his weekly physical therapy.

Over the course of Henry and Elizabeth's arguments with Blue Gene, when it was revealed that his potential cohabitant was a stripper-mother, all Hades erupted in the Mapother household, which made it easier for Blue Gene to leave. For the next couple of years, Blue Gene did maintain a relationship with his family, at first popping in at his former home whenever he felt like it, then getting so he felt the need to call ahead. Only twice did he bring Cheyenne over for awkward family dinners in which Henry and Elizabeth detected the septic aura of "simple folk" coming from Blue Gene's side of the table. After Elizabeth told him over the phone that his girlfriend "even *looked* immoral," he vowed he'd never bring her over again.

The great estrangement leapt to a whole new level when Blue Gene announced to Henry and Elizabeth that he was going to be a father. This was the only time Blue Gene could recall his father using the *f*-word. Elizabeth kept saying how she had warned him this would happen, that this old floozy would see to it that she got pregnant so she could trap Blue Gene and take all his money. Henry told Elizabeth to let it go—that if their son wanted to ruin his life, it was his choice. Then he turned to Blue Gene and said if he continued this dissolute behavior, if he didn't straighten up and go to college, and if he decided to commit himself to a lifetime with this trailer-park whore, he would no longer be his son. If

Blue Gene went any further down this path of debauchery, Henry said he was not welcome in his home ever again.

Cheyenne's miscarriage ended the pregnancy, but Blue Gene was more determined than ever to be his own man. The estrangement lived on for the next four years, until Henry and John decided that Elizabeth should pay Blue Gene a visit. Meanwhile, after Blue Gene lost his baby, he gradually lost Cheyenne to her endless pursuit of twelve-hour highs. He saw that she preferred spending her days dodging German shepherds (both real and imaginary) to relaxing with him outside or in bed, like they used to. They broke up and got back together repeatedly, until finally he would not let her move back into the trailer, for which he had long been paying. Almost a year after this final breakup, Cheyenne overdosed, and while Blue Gene was not in the least surprised, her death caused her to evaporate into the ambience that would color his every move for a while thereafter. Of course, any semblance of zest that Blue Gene had once possessed had leaked out in his early twenties, mostly into unloading pallets at Wal-Mart. But after Cheyenne died, his spirits faded that much more, until he decided that the only way to climb out of this rut would be to do exactly what he had always wanted to do. And ever since Bernice had taken him to flea markets as a little kid, one thing he had always wanted to do was have his own booth. The decision of what to sell in this booth was easy because, more than anything else, he had toys.

$$ \text{\$ \$ \$} $$

Of all the encounters Blue Gene had that Labor Day weekend with the people who populated his jagged past, none were as significant to the rest of his days as the one that occurred at one thirty-three on Monday afternoon. It was then that he returned to his campaign post after a lunch break (a Number Two at the McDonald's that was conveniently located inside the Wal-Mart) and saw an old woman pushing an oxygen tank on rollers, making her way from her handicapped space toward the entrance. She moved so slowly that she was passed by one person after another, a scene reminiscent of a tractor creeping down a busy freeway. As she made it to the yellow slants of the pedestrian crossing, Blue Gene recognized her, barely. A guillotine slice of sadness dropped through him.

Her body had once been like a big loaf of meat, squooshy yet solid, warm and wholesome. It was now a bone-stalk wrapped in wrinkles and topped with hair aged to the color of oatmeal. Her face, which had once radiated such a plump butterball glow as she called him "hon," was now a gaunt, crinkled oval that seemed to openly declare, "I have lost."

She didn't seem to be aware of anything except for the few feet of concrete in front of her little oxygen tank. Life appeared to go straight through her, leaving her as a filter through which experience passed and left only the toxic residues of depression and illness, a specter in orthopedic shoes and compression stockings.

But something jarred her, causing her sunken head to snap up, filling her vacant face with activity, with what appeared to be anger. It was the bright red letters MAPOTHER FOR CONGRESS on the banner in front of Blue Gene's table.

Blue Gene was ready to say hello, but when she looked up at him she had such a scowl that he hesitated. She shook her head and mumbled something before the automatic doors admitted her into the building.

Surely she hadn't recognized him; she hadn't seen him since he was ten. Or maybe she did recognize him but hated him for some reason he didn't know—maybe the same reason why she had never replied to his letters or returned his calls.

He had actually seen her once since childhood, in his early twenties, coincidentally at the old Wal-Mart, where he was stocking shelves. He had been tempted to approach her then, but he wasn't sure if he even wanted to talk to someone who wouldn't write or call him back. Also, there was his fear that she might not remember him, and then he would feel like an idiot. So that day, he did nothing. But that day, she hadn't looked like *this*. She hadn't been lugging around an oxygen tank, and she hadn't looked so chewed on by life.

He stuffed the envelope full of bake-sale money into his shorts pocket and walked toward the bright lights of Wal-Mart's interior.

$$$

"Here," said Blue Gene. "Let me help you."

She was struggling to pull one shopping cart from another. She looked at him with annoyance. "I can do it," she said snippily. She jerked loose the cart and set her oxygen tank and big denim purse in it. When she saw he was still standing next to her, she looked at him like he was impaired and started to push her cart away.

"Ma'am, I'm sorry, but aren't you Bernice?"

"Yes." She had a drawl that often turned one-syllable words into two. That he knew her name caused her to look at his face more carefully. He could see her thinking, trying to work out how this long-haired, tattooed young stranger could know her.

"It's Blue Gene."

Her lips parted. She took a step closer and looked him in the eye, squinting. The incessant beeps of twenty-five price scanners filled the background like a gang of giddy pixies.

"Remember me?" he asked hopefully.

If someone in the back office had been watching the security monitor that showed the front of the store, they would have seen a frail woman pulling in a young man for an embrace of such drama that it would befit the silver screen.

"Of *course* I remember you!" The hug was weak, but he could feel her trying. She smelled like smoke and eucalyptus. She let go and looked him up and down. "Not a day goes by that I don't think of you, hon!"

"Thank ya. Me too."

Bernice continued to examine Blue Gene's person while Wal-Mart CEO Sam Walton watched over everyone on a banner hanging from the white rafters. "It's really you, isn't it?" Her bluish lips formed a contagious smile that Blue Gene's face caught. He nodded. "Oh, Blue Gene. My lands, I've missed you." When she spoke, she sounded like a hoarse person screaming.

"I've missed you, too. Been wonderin' about ya."

"I never would've recognized you if you hadn't told me." They had to scoot out of the way of some customers who needed to get to the shopping carts. Bernice continued to look Blue Gene up and down. "Now, why'd you have to go and do that to yourself?" she asked, no longer smiling.

Blue Gene laughed. "Do what?"

"All those ol' tattoos and that long hair. Look like an ol' barn rat. You'd be right good-lookin' if it wasn't for all that ol' mess."

"Take it easy on me," he said with a smirk. It was hard to take offense because he was so glad to see she still had some fight in her. She was in her late fifties but could have passed for seventysomething.

"I *declare*, I don't know why you'd wanna go around lookin' like that."

"Sorry." She didn't look much better, with her mannish haircut, sleeveless button-up shirt, and turquoise shorts that revealed veiny, chigger-eaten legs.

"Well," she said, irritated, and left it at that. "Baby Baby" by Amy Grant played in the background.

"You doin' okay?" he asked, but he knew it was a ridiculous question. He couldn't look at her without seeing the tubing routed up her nose.

"Oh, I reckon I'm doin' better today, 'cause this is the first time in forever that I even been out, 'cause my doctor says he's afraid I'll get pneumonia. I have that COPD. But I had been meanin' to check out this Super Wal-Marts here for a while, and I finally got the energy to come today."

"COPD?"

"It's a lung problem. Kind of like emphysema. I got that and congestive heart failure."

"I'm sorry."

"That's okay, hon. It's my lot, I reckon."

"Don't talk like that."

"Ain't no cure for it," she said matter-of-factly.

"Sorry."

"It's okay, though. It don't matter."

"You sure still seem feisty."

"I'm runnin' on fumes, hon. I lose my wind real easy. Littlest things take up all my energy. Like right now, I'm just drained. I want to talk to you badly, hon, but can we sit somewhere, you think?"

"Heck yeah." Blue Gene lifted Bernice's oxygen from the cart and accompanied her back to the vestibule between the two sets of automatic doors, where there were arcade games and Coke machines.

"Do I see you got a little limp?"

"Yeah. It's a long story."

They sat on one of the two wooden benches off to the side, next to the rack of *Thrifty Nickel* newspapers and free real-estate magazines.

"Was that you I seen out there with a Mapother sign?"

"Yep. John's runnin' for the House."

"Hmph. That's a laugh. I seen 'em runnin' his ads on TV, and I said, *yeah buddy*, he'll fit in just fine with that bunch in Washington. Is he still wilder than a buck?"

"Nah, actually, he's settled down here in recent years. Got him a wife and a kid. Seems to finally have his stuff together."

Bernice fidgeted constantly. She kept twisting her oxygen tube around her finger. "You watch out for that boy."

"Why you say that?"

"I know he's your kin, but he's got no scruples." She pursed her lips into a small circle when she breathed, as if sucking air through a straw.

"I used to think that, too, but people changes."

Across the vestibule, a man was watching a little boy in cowboy boots play a race-car game, yelling at him not to run into a tree.

"What do you do in life, hon?"

"What do ya mean?"

"How do ya earn a livin'?"

"Workin' on John's campaign right now. Worked at the old Wal-Mart for seven years. It was just a regular Division One store, not one of these big ones."

"What about college?"

"Didn't go."

Bernice reared her head back. "So this is *it* for you?"

"What do ya mean?"

"I mean, this is it for your life? You ain't pursuin' nothin'?"

"Well, I'd like to find me a good woman. I'm workin' on that right now, actually. Have some kids somewhere down the line."

"How you gonna *provide* for your kids?"

"I don't know. I'll worry about that later."

"Why didn't you go to college?"

"I ain't exactly college material. I barely even made it through high school, to be honest."

Bernice looked at him with eyes like November, cold and somber.

"What?" he asked.

"I expected so much more from you."

"Come on, now, Bernice. Don't you get on me now, too. I'm doin' fine."

"You don't *look* fine."

Blue Gene sighed. "Why you keep pushin' me?"

"You *need* pushin', that's why."

"I haven't seen you in, like, seventeen years, and you're all over my case."

"You was supposed to go far."

Blue Gene hunched over and cracked his knuckles. "Hey—I could be mad right now, too, if I wanted. How come you never would answer my letters or return my calls?"

"I couldn't return your calls 'cause I's afraid your parents would answer the phone, but I *did* answer your letters. Ever' one of 'em."

"I never saw 'em."

"I ain't surprised one bit. Your parents probably got ahold of 'em before you could see 'em."

"Why would they do that?"

"Oh, I'm sure they got their reasons." She coughed several times and was having trouble catching her breath. "It don't surprise me one bit."

"I'll have to get on them about that. I had no idea. All this time, I thought you was just blowin' me off."

"Lord no."

"Are you serious? You really wrote me back?"

"I swear I did."

"They had no right to do you and me like that. Why would they do that?"

"They don't have no scruples neither. I wouldn't put nothin' past 'em."

"Well, I'll just have a talk with 'em."

"You better not, though, Blue Gene. You better not do it." Her fidgeting increased.

"Why the hell not?"

"They'll end up gettin' on my case about it. We had such a fallin' out."

"What was your fallin' out over?"

"I don't know."

"What do you mean, *you don't know*?"

"Hon, you're gonna have to drop it. I don't have the breath to tell you." She coughed some more and was becoming breathless.

"I'm sorry. Here, what can I do for ya?"

"You do the talkin'." She started burrowing through her big purse.

"What do I talk about?"

"Tell me all about *you*. All about you since you was ten." She pulled an inhaler from her purse and took two deep puffs from it. "Come on, now. Get me all caught up."

Blue Gene told her about every hardship that had befallen him since childhood. Bernice listened closely and anxiously, distracted only by the need to deposit phlegm into a Kleenex every once in a while. After learning about each of his life-changing episodes, in which Blue Gene portrayed himself as the hapless victim, her eyes poured out compassion and understanding, and she patted him on the back. But when Blue Gene was done talking, Bernice's gaze changed from concerned to sore. She squeezed her thin lips together, making her mouth look like an asterisk.

"Why didn't those parents of yours *make* you go to college? Even if you was makin' bad grades, your parents could've paid your tuition."

"Lord knows they *tried* to make me. They offered to pay, but I was tired of livin' off them. None of my friends were living off their parents. I felt like I needed to go to work."

Bernice turned away. Her mouth creased in disapproval, and she shook her head. "They didn't care. They should have *made* you go to college. They just plain didn't care what become of you."

"They tried."

"Sounds to me like they just *let* you cut yourself off from them. They blamed it on that girl. But they were *ready* to cut the cord from you."

"It was a two-way road. Now, come on, now. You're gonna get your-self all worked up again."

"I took my puffer. I'm okay. I tell you, have those old parents of yours cared for you *at all* since I've been gone?" She looked Blue Gene up and down again and stared at his tattoos. "Have they done *anything* for you? I tried so hard to raise you right, made sure you had everything you needed, and the minute I'm gone, they just let you go to waste. What was that ol' John doin' while all this was goin' on?"

"He was doin' his own thing. Drinkin' and druggin'."

Bernice couldn't sit still. "I tell ya, I know I can't smoke no more, but I don't think I ever wanted a cigarette so bad."

"Why? Why you all worked up?"

"*Because* I don't like how they done you."

"But Bernice, everything's a'ight now. We made amends."

"Don't you let them do you wrong, Blue Gene. You hear me?"

"Yes, ma'am."

"Hey—you see those machines over there with the trinkets in 'em?" She pointed at the quarter machines filled with plastic containers that held cheap rings, Homies figurines, slime, and those sticky hands that have a way of quickly accumulating grime and carpet fuzz. "You remember how I used to bring you a bag full of 'em?"

"No."

"I guess you was too young to remember. 'Bout once a month I'd give you a paper grocery sack filled with those plastic bubbles. Ever' time I'd go to a store for your mom and dad, I'd get you some of those trinkets at the front of the store, and I'd let 'em build up in a bag and finally give 'em all to ya."

"That was mighty kind of you."

"Oh, you just thought it was the grandest thing to open one after another like that. But you seemed more interested in the plastic bubble containers than the trinkets themselves. You'd try to catch houseflies with 'em."

Blue Gene laughed, as did Bernice.

"Why'd I do that?"

"You said you wanted to capture 'em and keep 'em as your pet. You was always asking your parents for a dog, but they wouldn't let you have one after what happened with John's dog, so you figured you'd get the next best thing and get you a pet housefly. Couple times you actually caught one. You'd even give 'em names."

Blue Gene laughed some more. "Sounds like I was a funny little dude."

"Oh, you were so much fun. We had us a time. Say—am I keepin' you from your job?"

"No. Hey, let me help you with your shopping."

"Don't you have to be out there?"

"Oh, I've been doin' that all weekend. Come on." Blue Gene stood. "I ain't gonna let you be alone, the way you're havin' trouble breathin'. I reckon you need me more than John's campaign."

$ $ $

"Hello. Welcome to Wal-Mart," said an elderly gentleman in his highly-flaired blue Wal-Mart vest. Bernice and Blue Gene replied with a "hidey" at the exact same moment.

"Can you get me another buggy?" asked Bernice.

After Blue Gene pulled out a shopping cart, they proceeded down the opening aisle, where products were packed on both sides, bombarding the customers with low-priced temptations in colorful packages.

"It's so huge," said Bernice, looking up at the rows of bright fluorescent tube lights stretching out in every direction. She explained that for the past seventeen years, she had lived in Delacroix, a tiny town two counties over where her family was from. Delacroix didn't even have a Wal-Mart, and the closest city to Delacroix, Shibblesville, was far from progressing to the point of switching from a regular Wal-Mart to a Supercenter.

Blue Gene followed Bernice as she slowly pushed her cart down this opening aisle, past the Coke, Diet Coke, Cheerios, Slim-Fast, Tostitos, and refrigerated flowers on one side and the bottled water, Hawaiian Punch, notebooks, Fig Newtons, and bin full of cheap DVDs, such as *Willard* and *Kangaroo Jack*, on the other.

"I won't be in here long, hon, 'cause I hardly got none to spend. 'Bout spent all I had on the gasoline to get here. Somebody's gettin' rich off that gas, but it ain't us."

"I hear that."

Facing the jewelry department, Blue Gene had Bernice turn right, since she needed to go to the supermarket half of the store. Blue Gene offered to push the cart, which happened to be one with a wobbly wheel, but Bernice said she wanted to because it helped her walk. Over the PA, "Bring Me a Higher Love" replaced "Careless Whisper."

"Could you pick me up one of those *Stars*, hon?" The *Star* magazines were at the front of the many checkouts to their right. Blue Gene fetched the magazine, which featured Brad Pitt and Angelina Jolie's most recent sexcapades.

"I was thinkin' the other day," said Blue Gene. "That was weird, the way you used to read me these ol'-women magazines."

"Oh, I guess I just did it 'cause that's the same thing I did with my little girl. I didn't think nothin' of it."

Blue Gene had almost forgotten that Bernice even had a little girl. She had never made more than a passing reference to her daughter, saying it made her too sad to talk about it, since she had died when she was fourteen.

To their left, in front of the men's clothing department, was a display set up on two card tables paying tribute to local soldiers who had died. The homemade posterboard signs were covered in pictures and newspaper articles. In front of them was a sign that read: WAL-MART SUPPORTS OUR TROOPS.

"John had a big tribute for him on the Fourth of July," said Blue Gene, pointing to the display for Tim Balsam.

"Good for him."

"Wasn't your husband in 'Nam?"

"Yeah."

"Just so you know, if it wasn't for this leg of mine, I'd be defending my country, too. They wouldn't take me."

"*Good*. I'm *glad* you got your legs run over if that meant it kept you from fightin' in some ol' war."

"I ain't glad. After we was attacked, I was ready to enlist. I was rarin' to go."

"That don't impress me one bit. I guess your parents was just gonna *let* you?"

"No. I didn't tell 'em I was enlisting."

"If I'd've been in the picture and I caught wind of you doin' that, I would've whooped you into next week. You don't need to be goin' over there and gettin' killed."

"Least I'd've died tryin' to be a man."

"Pshaw."

"Why you so against it when your own husband fought?"

"It *ruined* Bart. He hated it from the get-go. When he first started, they was passin' out the boots for 'em to wear once they got over there, and when Bart got to the front of the line, they asked him his shoe size, and he said ten and a half, and the guy just laughed in his face. Said, 'This ain't a shoe store. We don't have half sizes.' And he gave him a ten 'cause they were low on elevens. His feet ended up gettin' torn up, all blistered and raw. And that was just his *feet*. He never was the same when he come back. He used to be so funny and silly-actin'. They took his smile away. I think it's why he killed himself. Well—they say it was an accident, but I think he was aimin' to die. And I'm still dealin' with it today. If Bart was alive today, I wouldn't be piss poor. He could be earnin' bread and I wouldn't have to be in some ol' shack in the boonies with no air conditioning."

"You don't have *air conditioning*?"

"Why, *no*," she said with a cough. "Broke down. Can't afford to fix it."

"No air conditioning *in this heat*?"

"Heat's what busted it. Pushed it to its limit."

"How are you even *alive* with your lung problem in this heat?"

"I don't know. I keep the fans blowin' on me all the time."

"That ain't no way to live."

"Tell me about it, hon."

$$\text{\$ \$ \$}$$

As the associates scurried to and fro in their dark blue vests with How May I Help You? written on the back, and as Toto's "Rosanna" played over the PA with frequent interruptions ("Tonya, line one"), Blue Gene and Bernice eventually reached the produce department, where she had him tear a plastic bag from a spool and fill it with only two apples. From there they went to get milk, bread, cereal, and deli meat, all the while reminiscing. Bernice reminded Blue Gene of things he hadn't thought of in years, like his childhood love for *The Dukes of Hazzard* and country music, especially Willie Nelson, Kenny Rogers, and Alabama.

Blue Gene and his parents rarely had any conversations that didn't pertain to John's campaign, and Henry and Elizabeth couldn't recall much of Blue Gene's childhood. For while Blue Gene was but an innocent babe learning the bare essentials for living, John was a teenager who drank so much that he'd try to swim on the floor. When Elizabeth wasn't volunteering at church, much of her time was devoted to disciplining John. Meanwhile, Henry stayed busy with work and wasn't home half the time, as the eighties brought his corporation's most astonishing growth spurt. Fortunately, Blue Gene had a special rapport with his nanny from the start. She watched over him even when she wasn't asked to, and he often played on the kitchen linoleum to be near her.

Bernice said she needed to sit down again before they made the long trek to the checkout. They sat in the McDonald's in the back of the store, and Blue Gene bought a cup of coffee.

"Are you okay?" Blue Gene asked.

"Yeah, hon. I reckon I shouldn't've come here. I'll never have enough energy to make it through one of these places. If this place were emptied out, you could have car races in here. It's grand and all, but I'd still take the little IGA like we used to have over this place any ol' day."

"I sure am glad you decided to come here, though."

"Oh, I am too, hon. I didn't mean it like that." She took his hand. "I've missed you so much. You don't even know." She examined his hand and started to weep, her already sad blue eyes filling with more sorrow.

"What's wrong?"

"Oh, nothin'."

"Hold on." Blue Gene went over to the condiment counter and brought back a napkin with a McDonald's logo on it. "Here. Did I say something wrong?"

"No."

"Then why you cryin'?"

"It's your finger. I saw it's turned yellow."

Blue Gene held up his right index finger, which was indeed jaundiced. "It's just from smokin'."

"I know what it's from."

"I was afraid you thought I had it up my butt or something." Bernice laughed. She sniffled and crumbled up the napkin. "Why you crying over my finger bein' yellow?"

"'Cause it's lookin' like you're gonna end up just like me." She held up her own shaky finger, which was also yellow, but mixed with light blue and purple, like a weird flesh-rainbow. She had been a smoker since she was a teenager, and when Blue Gene pictured Bernice, she was never without a long-filtered cigarette sticking out of her mouth.

"I had such high hopes for you. After my daughter died, you was like my own. I thought you'd amount to something more than us."

"You talk about me like I'm on skid row. I'm doin' a'ight."

"I bet you don't have a hunderd dollars in the bank."

"I do too. But who cares how much money I'm making? Money ain't everything."

"But it *is*, though. That's your parents talkin' there, 'cause the only people that say money ain't everything are the ones who *have* it."

"I'm just sayin' that it's possible to be happy without bein' rich. There are other things in life."

"You still got some growin' up to do." He snorted and then swallowed his phlegm and pulled the bill of his cap as low as it would go. "Look at me, hon." He tilted his head back to look at her. "I just don't want you to end up in a mess like I'm in. But maybe you'll be a'ight, 'cause you're a man. At least you got that goin' for ya."

"You know, I'm sorry, but if you hadn't quit workin' for Mom and Dad, maybe you wouldn't be so hard up."

"Is that what they told you? That I *quit*?"

"Well, yeah. Is that not true?"

"Heavens no, it ain't true. They *fired* me. I'd never have quit that job. Never."

"What'd they fire you for?"

"Basically said you was gettin' too old to need a nanny, which I could see, but it was more than that. Me and your parents had always butted heads from the time you was born, you know. The straw that broke the camel's back was when your mom went to one of those parent-teacher conferences at school, and she found out that you had been imitating wrestlers and passin' gas in class, and she blamed me for it."

"But you weren't the one that got me into wrestling. It was actually Dad, 'cause he bought me some wrestling figures. I was the one that got *you* into wrestling."

"Anyhow, her and your dad both said they weren't gonna have any kin of theirs reflectin' poorly on them. She said I encouraged you to pass gas 'cause she found out how we used to name your farts."

"I remember that! We used to name 'em like hurricanes, goin' down the alphabet."

"Yeah, and she found out you was doin' it at school—and you shouldn't have been doin' that at school, Blue Gene. I thought I taught you better than that—but she 'bout threw a fit, sayin' what a trashy thing that was to be namin' your gas. And I said I was sorry and that it was just something I did as a little kid, 'cause I grew up poor as a church-mouse, and we had so little that I'd give names to every little thing I had to feel like I owned it. Even my toots. But after your dad heard me say that, he said something like, that's no excuse. Sorry you were poor, but you had the same chance to come up in the world like anybody, so don't expect any sympathy from me! And then we got into it big-time. I told him he was wrong, that lots of times it's something somebody's born into. And here you were, born into money, and you *still* turned out like me. That's what makes me wanna cry."

"And they fired you after that argument?"

"Yeah. We had a lotta rows, but that was the biggest one we ever had, and they fired me. Wouldn't let me say goodbye to you. Said to never come back. Said if I contacted you again they'd have me arrested, and I believe your dad would've done it, too, 'cause I seen how tight he was with the chief of police."

"They told me you quit 'cause you was tired of working there."

"They lied."

Blue Gene readjusted his cap and sighed. "And all this time I've been kind of pissed, thinking you quit."

"Nope. Got fired. I wouldn't say anything to 'em about it, though."

"I can't *not* say anything. That's no way to treat you. No way."

"Well, I wish you wouldn't say nothin', but I'm to the point where I don't hardly care no more. I'll be dead soon enough anyway, so it don't matter."

"*Bernice.*"

"It's the *truth*. I'm to the point now where I can't even afford oxygen. Down to my last tank."

"Aren't you on disability?"

"Yeah, but it ain't enough. I get seven hunderd a month, and then I get ten dollars in food stamps a month. One of my medicines is free, but all the others come to nearly three hunderd, 'cause those inhalers I have to have are so expensive. I usually have to pick and choose my meds for which ones I'm hurtin' for the most. Like, I been goin' without my Zoloft for I don't know how long."

"I'm on Zoloft," Blue Gene blurted. He had never told anyone this before.

"Are ya?"

"Yeah. There's no shame in that."

Bernice laughed. "I didn't say there was. Most everybody's on something. But anyhow, it comes down to getting either my Zoloft or my nebulizer treatment so I can breathe—and, well, you gotta breathe. And between the medicine and my utilities and then all my bills—I owe the ambulance service and three—no, four—doctors, the hospital, and then some credit cards I had used to cover some prescriptions—after all that, all I have left is for groceries, and not all the groceries I need. I can't afford my Boost drink but ever' once in a while. That Boost helps give me energy, but I can't hardly afford it. And then there's this oxygen."

"Dang, Bernice. I'm sorry." It sounded to him like she wasn't living so much as she was holding on while the earth spun.

"And you're tellin' me money ain't everything?"

"I'm sorry." He realized that he said, "I'm sorry" a lot when he was around Bernice. "I guess you don't have insurance that'll cover your oxygen?"

"Oh, Lord no. Insurance would run me four hunderd dollars a

month. That's absolutely out of the question. I'll suffocate 'fore I get in-surance. That's what's the scariest about this COPD. You get so all you can think about is that you might suffocate to death."

"Damn. Here," said Blue Gene, standing up and reaching into his shorts for his wallet. "Let me help you out."

"Nuh-uh. I won't take it."

"Come on. Let's find you some of that Boost drink here."

"No. Sit down. That wasn't why I was tellin' you all this. I don't want your money. I'm telling you so maybe you'll get yourself together and go back to school, or even go to work for your dad. You sit down." Blue Gene sat down but kept his wallet out. "Has he even offered you a job?"

"Yeah, he and John both offered, but I ain't built for that kind of work."

Bernice nodded and coughed. "You're a grown man, and I guess I can't do nothin' with ya, but I'm tellin' ya, this world ain't for ya if you don't got money, and here you've had every opportunity laid out for ya, and you haven't taken a one of 'em. And you'll live to regret it. When hard times come a-knockin' at your door, you'll wish you had played it different."

As "Heaven Is a Place on Earth" played, Bernice went on to explain that she had become destitute in the space of only the last two and a half years. After Henry and Elizabeth fired her, she worked at a factory, mak-ing corrugated boxes for thirteen years, and because it was just her, her poodle, and her two cats, she was able to get by. But by the age of fifty-four, her lifelong smoking habit had led to the irreversible condition of chronic obstructive pulmonary disease. She had to start working less, which caused her to have less money, which added to her stress and de-pression about being so ill in the first place, which made her even less likely to be able to work or maintain a healthy lifestyle. When outsourc-ing caused half of the factory's employees to be laid off, she was among the first to go. For a year she searched for another job, but hardly any-one would hire her, which she suspected was because she was a woman in her fifties. The ones that would hire her wouldn't even provide poverty-level income. She tried to stretch out her savings by moving to a smaller house out in the sticks, but the move itself was expensive. Her money eventually ran out and her condition worsened, so she qualified for disability. She was diagnosed with congestive heart failure, and the medications she was on created a complex web of side effects that led to other illnesses and hospital visits. Because her disability benefit provided an income of over seven hundred dollars a month, she was ineligible for Medicaid. Furthermore, she wouldn't qualify for Medicare for another eighteen months. And as impoverished as she had become, she refused to lose her independence and go live in a nursing home, which was no place for a fifty-seven-year-old.

Blue Gene found Bernice's story as hard on his ears as her wilted face was on his eyes. Judging by everything she had told him in the last hour and a half, joy was something she saw only on TV.

"Bernice, let me help you." Blue Gene again opened his gray denim wallet.

"No. You probably ain't doin' much better than I am. Put that away."

"How much is oxygen?"

"I ain't takin' your money."

"I don't care. You *have* to. Look at all my family has, and here you are, not even able to afford *oxygen*?"

"That's your family, though. That ain't you. You ain't rich."

"Well, now..." He wanted to tell her about his trust fund, but it was something he had exiled so far from his own identity that he couldn't admit that it existed even to himself, let alone someone else. "I gotta do *something* to help you. I can't let you live like this."

"Well, I *will* ask you to do one thing for me, hon."

"You name it."

"Wait—before you agree, you oughta know it's gonna be the hardest thing in the world, though, what I'm gonna ask you to do."

"You was always good to me. You tell me what it is I can do."

"Stop smoking those cigarettes."

$$$

On that Labor Day weekend, Blue Gene also saw plenty of faces from his more recent past. He asked for votes from Bob, the one-armed veteran from the flea market; Steve and his family, whom he had seen at the monster-truck rally; several people he had talked to at the Ambassador Inn; and some of his friends from Heartland Championship Wrestling. On Sunday afternoon, Blue Gene saw Josh Balsam's pickup speeding dangerously fast down one of the parking-lot lanes. As was his custom, he skillfully backed into a parking space, a maneuver Blue Gene wasn't as impressed with this time. The spaces were slanted here, and backing into them was completely needless. Blue Gene realized that, in fact, the truck wouldn't even be headed in the right direction when Balsam pulled out.

As Balsam tramped across the parking lot in his baggy jeans, Blue Gene worried he would ask why no one had been calling for his help on the campaign lately. The truth was that after hearing how he had nearly attacked some innocent wrestlers, John wrote Balsam off as a liability. John hadn't notified Balsam that his services would no longer be needed, though, which would leave Blue Gene to break the news.

It was just like John to do something like this: use a gung-ho guy like Balsam and then abandon him the second something went wrong. Blue Gene decided he would play dumb if Balsam asked about the campaign. He would not do his brother's dirty work today.

As Balsam approached Blue Gene's table, his mustached and newly goateed face turned sour.

"Hey, Balsam. What's goin' on?"

"Nothin'. Had to get out of the house awhile. Amber and me just found out last night her number three is on the way. Birth-control baby."

"Well, should I say congratulations?"

"Everybody else does. What the fuck you doin' sellin' brownies and shit?"

"It's charity. For hospice."

"That's all good, but a bake sale? Did you bake all this yourself?" Balsam grinned.

Blue Gene fired off a defense without thinking. "No. I don't *bake*. They don't allow political campaigning here, and this is the only way we could get away with it."

"You're campaignin'?"

"Yeah," said Blue Gene with a sigh.

"I could be helpin'. How come y'all stopped callin' me?"

"Because." Blue Gene sighed again. "Shit. John oughta be the one tellin' you this. He didn't like how you got into it with those wrestlers, and he don't want anything like that to happen again. He don't want you workin' for him no more."

"What'd you do? Go and tattle on me?"

"No. Jesus, Balsam, what do you care for?"

"I don't care." He looked away and spat on the sidewalk. "Shut the fuck up."

"I'm just sayin', man, you shouldn't care whether or not my brother wants your help. You're the toughest son'bitch I know. You shouldn't be bendin' over backward for anybody, 'specially not my brother up in his ivory tower." Toward the end of the sentence, Blue Gene's voice cracked. Balsam looked as mean as a cold sore.

"I don't bend over for nobody, but I don't give a fuck 'cause this ain't about me. It's bigger than me, 'cause what your brother's doin' is about my country. This is the greatest fuckin' country in the world, and the fags are ruinin' it. And I ain't havin' it. I ain't so much for your brother as I am against fag enablers. Helpin' him out is the fuckin' least I can do cause they won't let me fight for my country, sayin' I'm mentally ill, but fuck that, 'cause I can sure as hell still fight for my country at home by defending us from fag enablers and fags."

"A'ight, Balsam. Chill, man. I hear ya."

"Just the other day, somebody said they was puttin' on a antiwar, pro-fag play downtown, and I said if I knew that was true I'd probably blow the fuckin' building up. And I mean it. This is my war and I will blow their asses off the fuckin' globe. All of em. We can't forget what's been done to us."

Not knowing what to say, Blue Gene nodded. He looked away at anything besides Balsam: at stray shopping carts that had been left sitting in parking spaces, at the red bikes for sale that were hanging upside down on metal racks like cattle. Meanwhile, Balsam decided to stand next to Blue Gene behind the table. His presence was heavy, and Blue Gene continued to avoid looking at him. He looked up at the security cameras perched atop the building like robotic cranes. He looked down and settled his eyes on the concrete, with its scattered sparkles, cigarette butts, and flattened black chewing gum. But no matter where his eyes focused, he couldn't avoid the thought that was as plain and bold as a billboard: he was afraid of another man.

It was Balsam's hatred that scared him, the raw openness of it exposed like a dark red nub of meat raised by a ripped-off scab. Blue Gene disapproved of homosexuals, too, but he had never wished them dead.

"What the fuck's got into you, Mapother?" Balsam asked after a weighty silence. "Puttin' down your own brother like that."

"I don't know."

$$\$ \$ \$$$

On Labor Day afternoon, about a half an hour after Bernice had left, Jackie finally made an appearance. Blue Gene was trying to figure out what he could do to help Bernice, concentrating on her problem so much that he was forgetting to tell passersby to vote for Mapother, when he heard some loud, hyper music playing. He then saw Jackie's sticker-covered Grand Am. He was insulted that she had waited until the last possible minute to show, but he couldn't stay angry when he saw she was carrying a gift. It was a small square wrapped in aluminum foil and a white bow. She told him to open it right away. It was a CD titled *Jackie's Gnarly Mix for Blue Gene.*

"Thanks, man." Written in sloppy cursive on the cover were the names of bands he had never heard of: the Go-Betweens, Built to Spill, the dB's, Arcade Fire, the Butthole Surfers. Out of all twenty-four artists on the album, he knew only of Bob Dylan and David Bowie. The Bowie song was called "Blue Jean," which Blue Gene had never heard.

"You're welcome. I *love* making mixes for people. This one's got some new and some old on there." As usual, she talked fast, sometimes so fast that she stumbled over her words, but it didn't keep her from continuing. "I put a lot of eighties stuff on there, but not like Hall and Oates or anything like that. Like, underground bands from the eighties. There was so much great music that was being made when we were little, but since we were, like, five at the time, we didn't really have access to it."

"Thanks a lot." Blue Gene realized his tongue must have been yellow from drinking so much coffee throughout the day. He stepped back from Jackie, fearing his breath might stink. She was wearing unmissable bright green pants and a vintage brown Polo shirt, and had her hair pulled back with barrettes.

"So how's it been going out here?" she asked.

"I feel like I've seen every possible voter in the whole district. If John loses, it ain't my fault."

"How were you even allowed to *do* this? They wouldn't even let me put flyers up here for shows or for wrestling."

"I knew some people from working at the old Wal-Mart."

"Oh, yeah. I forget you have connections."

"Yeah. They said I could have my old job back after I'm done workin' for the campaign, so I'm happy 'bout that."

"Why do you like working at Wal-Mart so much?"

Blue Gene considered the question as he stared into the brown bugeyes of the wild-child honor student. "The breaks."

"The *breaks*?"

"Yeah. Every two hours at Wal-Mart you get a fifteen-minute break. You haven't lived until you had a break at work. A lunch break, a coffee break, especially a cigarette break. Man. You can't beat 'em."

"You know, *other* jobs have breaks."

"Yeah. But I really got to be around some cool people there."

"Knowing Wal-Mart, they probably give you breaks knowing they'll make you work overtime without pay."

"Why can't you leave well enough alone?"

"I don't know. I guess I just instinctively question everything."

"You're the type of person that would proofread graffiti."

Jackie covered her crooked teeth as she laughed. Blue Gene went on to explain the appreciation he had for days off work, how every little thing he did on those days felt glorious. On his days off, every TV show felt like a gift for his tired mind.

Then they discussed the latest happenings in wrestling as well as in Jackie's band, which had broken up and gotten back together since their show at the armory. As much as Blue Gene enjoyed listening to Jackie talk and all the opinions coming out of her ass, his mind kept wandering back to Bernice.

"You look like you're worried about something," said Jackie, after Blue Gene had become less and less talkative.

"It don't matter."

"Yes it does. What's wrong?"

"Nothin'."

"You're not telling me the truth. You know I hate it when people don't tell me the truth."

"Well, let me put it this way. What if there was someone you cared about, and this person needed money in order to stay healthy and stay alive, but in order to get her the money, you had to use some money that you had never planned on touching?"

"Well, if it's a matter of a person living or dying, I don't see why there'd be any question about it."

"Yeah, but what if it went against your personal principles to use this money, 'cause you'd have to ask somebody for it, and you never ever wanted to use it, and now you gotta change your thinking on it?"

"It still sounds to me like a no-brainer. *Isn't it?*"

VIII.

To Blue Gene, the receptionist at his father's office looked like something that belonged only on his TV. She was so sophisticated and fresh-looking, not at all the type of woman he normally encountered in reality. Not surprisingly, when Blue Gene came flip-flopping toward her in his John Deere tank top the day after Labor Day, she looked at him as if he were the personification of a repellent odor, like aging taco meat.

"Can I help you?" she asked.

"I'd like to see Henry Mapother."

"Do you have an *appointment*?"

"Nah."

She smiled and laughed cruelly. "You can't see Mr. Mapother without an appointment."

"Even if you're his son?"

"Oh—you're Blue Gene. I'm so—I apologize. I didn't know."

"That's a'ight. Ain't no thang."

This exchange was a game Blue Gene liked to play with people if they talked down to him. It was the only situation in which he drew attention to his last name. Through the years he had revealed his last name to various snobs the way a detective flashes his badge, only to have them laugh in his face and give some generic retort like, "If you're Henry Mapother's son, I'm the queen of England." But since word had gotten around at Westway International that Henry Mapother's *other* son had been helping his family with the campaign, the secretary accepted that this hirsute skeeze was exactly who he said he was.

But that afternoon, despite the credential of his surname, Blue Gene still had to sit on a sleek black leather sofa in the reception area and wait ten minutes for admittance to his father's office. As impressive as it was to most people that he was Henry Mapother's son, it seemed to carry little weight with Henry Mapother himself.

$$$

As a rule, Henry always made his visitors wait before seeing him. This was so he could establish dominance before he even saw the person. In a similar vein, he sometimes called people only to immediately put them on hold. If they hung up, he assumed they didn't respect him enough, and he would no longer do business with them.

"Hello, Eugene. I'm sorry to have kept you waiting."

He and Blue Gene pumped each other's hands, their arms extended over his spacious, cluttered desk.

"You sure have a nice office." Blue Gene looked all around at 360 degrees of mahogany and burgundy. "Smells like a new car in here. You know, in all these years, this is the first time I ever seen it."

"Oh?"

"Yeah."

Henry was glad that the picture frames on his desk were facing him and not Eugene. There was a picture of Elizabeth on their honeymoon to the Riviera, one of himself with Elizabeth and John the day John graduated from Harvard, and even one of Arthur dressed up for church. But none of Eugene.

"Have a seat. Would you like a drink?" He nodded at the elegant ivory bar in the corner.

"No thanks."

"So, what brings you here today?" His hawklike face was serious and businesslike, and he was zeroed in on whatever topic was about to be presented, confident he could solve anything.

"Well, you know your dad's inheritance money I had comin' to me?"

"Yes."

"I been thinkin' it over, and I'm ready to collect on that now."

"I see. Are you in some kind of trouble?"

"*No*," said Blue Gene, agitated. "Why would you say that?"

"You yourself have said on several occasions that the only way you'd ever accept your inheritance would be if some sort of emergency arose."

Henry's father, John Henry Mapother the Third, had died when Henry was sixteen. The founder of Westway and also an heir himself, John Henry the Third left half of his fortune to his widow and Henry, their only child. The other half was to be saved and divided among Henry's future children. Henry had offered Blue Gene access to his inheritance years ago, but at that time Blue Gene was a proud new employee of Wal-Mart and intoxicated with independence, earning his own living for the first time in all his pampered life. He'd outright rejected his father's offer.

"Well, it ain't an emergency, but I need it now. I know you put it in a trust for me. Ain't that what you call it? A trust?"

"Yes."

"Then it might as well be in my bank account, right?"

"But you can see why this is curious to me, can't you? You suddenly ask for your inheritance after all of these years of never making a single mention of it?"

"Yeah. I can see why that'd seem curious to you. I sure can." Blue Gene looked down at his hands and dug dirt from beneath his fingernails. But Henry was not to be avoided.

"So?!" The word swooped down and up into Blue Gene's face, causing him to raise his head.

"Here's the deal: I have an old friend that's in need. Of course, I ain't plannin' on givin' her *all* the money. But just a little bit of it would help her situation out a lot. And like I say, I got that money comin' to me anyway, right? Now I got a chance to put it to good use."

"Who is it?"

"It don't matter."

"Your grammar is a disgrace."

"I know," said Blue Gene with a little laugh. But Henry was deadly serious. He hated that any relative of his could have the speech of a hayseed. He knew Eugene was not unintelligent, but it was so hard not to equate his complete lack of refinement with sheer stupidity. He knew Eugene could help it, too; he flaunted his white-trash proclivities, begging to be scolded.

"Who is it?" Henry repeated.

"Huh?"

"Who is the woman that needs money?"

"I'd rather not say."

"As the executor of my father's will, I have the right to know who will be profiting from his inheritance."

"Do you really have that right? 'Cause it's my money, and—"

"Eugene, at this point, you appear so suspicious that I couldn't possibly grant you access to that money. For all I know, you might be funding something illegal. Is it dogfights?"

"*No.* I don't do *illegal* stuff no more."

"At any rate, you're obviously hiding something."

"It's nothing shady, Dad. I know it must look that way to you, but it's nothing shady at all. And I kind of resent that. It's been a long-ass time since I even *done* anything shady. I oughta be gettin' credit for that."

"If it's another exotic dancer who's after your money, you should be cautious."

"It ain't a stripper!" Blue Gene sighed forcefully. "Here, fine, I'll just go ahead and tell you. It's for Bernice. She's in awful shape and I want to help her."

"Bernice Munly?"

"Yeah." Henry felt a hint of emotion pop onto his face, but quickly reset his expression to serious.

"See. I wasn't up to nothin'. I didn't wanna tell you 'cause I know you and Mom aren't on good terms with her, and I know you probably wouldn't want me giving her money, but she was so good to me when I was little. And you oughta see the poor thing now. She's pitiful."

"How did this come about?"

"Saw her yesterday when I's campaignin' outside Wal-Mart. I hardly even recognized her. She's got some breathing disease, and she's all skinny."

"What did she say?"

"What do ya mean?"

"What did you talk about?"

"Oh, we talked about old times mostly. But I'm worried about her 'cause she can't even afford oxygen. She can barely afford her medicines."

"I'm sorry to hear that."

"Yeah. So I'd like to help her out. Just so she can afford all her medicines and groceries. It wouldn't be for her to spend on like a trip to Hawaii or nothin' like that."

"Did she ask you for money?"

"No way. She wouldn't even take ten dollars to help her pay for her groceries. She'd hate it if she knew I was doin' this. But I can't stand by and let her suffer, can I?"

Henry finally looked away and scanned the room for his thoughts. His office was vast but sparsely decorated. There was an ornate globe on a metal stand in one corner, a bronze bust of his father in another, and on the far wall were the *Course of Empire* landscape paintings by Thomas Cole. He finally returned his stare to Blue Gene and paused before announcing his verdict.

"I think you've been taken in."

"No, I haven't!" Blue Gene pounded his fist on his thigh so hard that he winced. "I'm sick of people always telling me that!"

"I'm sorry to tear down the saintly image of this woman that you've built for yourself, but Bernice Munly is a liar—always was and always will be. Don't romanticize her. She was good to you, but she was good to you because she was your employee. She finagled her way into our money before, and she's doing it again. She saw you at Wal-Mart, and she saw an opportunity. She's too lazy to earn a living honestly, and she's hoping to get easy money out of a rich, gullible boy with the last name Mapother."

"Jesus, Dad, she was luggin' around an oxygen tank."

"I'm not saying she's not sick. I'm saying she's using her sickness to her advantage. She wants you to pity her, and that's exactly what you're doing. I know that woman. You should not get involved with her. No good can come from associating with that woman. Besides, it's not your place to help her."

"Why do you have it in for her so?"

"I don't have it in for her. I'm protecting your interests."

"She told me how she had been sendin' me letters through the years. I guess you was protecting my interests then, too, not giving them to me?"

"I don't know anything about any letters," Henry denied staidly.

"And all this time I thought she quit. But now I know you and Mom fired her."

"We didn't fire her. She's lying. She quit. She was lazy and stupid and she quit. Of course she wouldn't admit that to you. Are you going to take her word over your family's?"

Blue Gene hunched over and massaged his mustache. "I don't know."

"You don't know? There shouldn't be a moment's hesitation. You should never put someone ahead of your own family. What has she done for you? Where has she been all these years?"

"Well, she *tried* writing me."

"I don't know anything about that," Henry denied again. "I'll have someone look into that. But that's neither here nor there. You're not getting your inheritance for this purpose. I'm not going to let trash like her live off my family fortune."

"But the money's just sittin' there doin' nothin'. Besides, it's *my* money. You can't keep it."

"I can, though. There's a clause in the will that states you cannot receive any of that money until you're thirty."

"Bullshit!"

"You think I'm lying?"

"You've told me before that I could have it."

"I was just being generous. That was around the time you first started defecting. I thought if we sent some money your way, you'd come to your senses and go to college and stop dating that whore."

"No, now, like a month ago you said I could have it. That night you pulled a pistol on me."

"Yes, if I wanted to, I could waive the age clause, but now that this woman is involved, I want the clause to remain intact."

"So you're honestly gonna sit there and tell me I can't have my own money? I can't have what rightfully should be mine?"

"Not until you turn thirty."

"Let me see that will."

"I don't have it."

"Where is it?"

"Leonard Crosby has the only copy." Leonard was the longtime family lawyer.

"Well, either you get him on the horn or I will."

"I'm the executor of the will. I don't have to do anything I don't want to."

"Fine, then. I'm gettin' a lawyer."

Henry let out a silvery laugh. "I didn't realize you'd made any attorney friends at the trailer park."

"I'll look one up in the phone book, just like anybody would."

"I guess Leonard and I will see you in court, then."

Blue Gene sighed and got up. He paced on a black oriental rug that sprawled over the area between the desk and the door. Henry turned away when he noticed the limp. In all these years, they had never spoken about Blue Gene's injury or what had led to it.

Henry's phone rang. He pressed a button. "Yes?"

"Ronald Gray is on line one," the secretary's voice said.

"Keep him on hold. I'll answer in a minute."

"How 'bout this," said Blue Gene, taking his seat again. "How 'bout you just loan me some money? Like a few thousand. I'll pay you back. You know I'm good for it."

"I can't do that, Eugene," Henry immediately replied.

"Why not?"

"It's obvious that you'll give it to Bernice."

"Why do you *hate* her so?"

"I don't hate her. It's a matter of principle. I'm sorry that she's ill, but I won't be held accountable for the financial quandary she's in. I supported her for eleven years, and I don't owe her anything."

"Ten years, wasn't it? I was ten when she left."

"Yes, thank you for correcting me, Eugene. Ten years. At any rate, I'm firm on this. Now, I want you to promise me you'll cut off all communication with that woman."

"Hey—can I borrow a few thousand dollars? Not for her, but for me?"

"Eugene."

"You're just hoarding money, Dad. I'm not askin' but for a drop of what you have. All that money you got, you're just sittin' on it, when it could be out there circulating around, helpin' people that can't help themselves, like Bernice."

"Would you stop this? Whatever happened to *honor thy parents*?"

"I still honor you."

"No, you don't. I need to take this call. You sit there and think about what you've been doing to me here today. It's been a sin."

Blue Gene rolled his eyes. "I'm gonna smoke a smoke." Henry nodded, and Blue Gene exited. Henry then told his secretary to have the man on the phone call back later. He needed to regroup and think about how to handle this delicate situation. He had to make sure that by the time Blue Gene left his office, he would be convinced to never contact Bernice Munly again. But he knew this would not be easy, because, as usual, he had been cast as the uncaring corporate misanthrope, nothing more than an evil Versace suit blooming from a multimillionaire sphincter. It was nothing new. Through the years, he had gotten so he assumed that everyone he met hated him by default because he was impossibly rich. Since he was a teenager, he had gone into every human relationship thinking that the other person couldn't possibly like him. Even after forty years of marriage, he wondered if his own wife truly loved him. But, of course, a rich man wasn't allowed to have problems. The Bernice Munlys of the world had a monopoly on suffering. He would like to line up his childhood next to Bernice's and see who truly had it worse.

It then occurred to him that he had a good angle to work with when Eugene returned, since Eugene seemed to lap up the tears of a good sob story. It would be in direct conflict with another personal rule of Henry's: to never willingly show another person weakness. But he hardly had a choice in the matter, considering the effect that Bernice's resurfacing could have on John's campaign, not to mention the entire legacy of the Mapother family.

$ $ $

As soon as Blue Gene stepped outside, he remembered that he was no longer a smoker. He had quit twenty-four hours ago but had forgotten because his father had him rattled. Wishing he hadn't thrown his Parliaments away, he was left to snort up phlegm and spit across the parking lot of Westway, where one of the old downtown movie theaters had once stood.

He wished he had gone to his mother about this first, but she was currently away on a ten-day mission to Mexico with a bunch of women from church. She said she was going on the mission to seek answers to her dream and its new, foreboding vibe.

He cleared his throat and held up his broad shoulders. He had to fight back and keep himself from being cornered again by his father's fast talk. When his father laid into him like he had in his office, Blue

Gene felt like a kid in a courtroom. He told himself that he had to get tough and fight back against his father, even if it was a sin. There were all sorts of sins flying around this town like vampire bats, and disagreeing with your parents wasn't but a housefly in comparison.

Blue Gene took the elevator back to the fourth floor and returned to the burgundy leather chair in front of his father's desk. Henry got up from his desk and stood behind Blue Gene. Blue Gene turned.

"I want to tell you something that I've told very few people in this life," Henry began dramatically. "When I was a little boy, almost every single morning before I went to school, I had diarrhea."

Blue Gene laughed.

"Don't you laugh at me. It isn't easy for me to talk about this. I never talk about this." To keep from laughing, Blue Gene stared at the oriental rug. It still had lines from a recent vacuuming. "May I continue?"

"Yeah. My bad."

"As a child, I had a nervous stomach. I was nervous because I dreaded the school day I had ahead of me. I was the smallest, sickliest, scrawniest boy in my class. The other children intimidated me. They were so brazen and loud. They picked on me. The biggest ones would even pick me up and carry me. It was humiliating. My father was ashamed of me. I begged my parents to let me switch schools, and when I was old enough, I started going to Groton. Once I was at Groton, I vowed to myself that I would become the type of son my father could be proud of. Through my own willpower I built myself into the sturdy, solid man that you have always known. I adopted an intense exercise regimen and excelled in basketball, football, and tennis. I never felt inferior to another person again, and by the time my dad died, he was indeed proud to have me as his son."

"Right on."

"I'm not done. Listen, because I'm never repeating any of this again. My father died when I was sixteen. After he died, I was faced with returning to Bashford to be the man of the house before I could truly even be called a man. I spent my teenage years not going to parties or dating, instead studying my father's papers and law books because I didn't want anyone to take advantage of my mother. I'd stay up until the wee hours of the morning, stooped over my desk in my bedroom, studying these documents, only to have my mother die of a massive heart attack when I was twenty. Growing up was not an enjoyable experience for me."

Blue Gene waited for him to continue, but he didn't. "Why you tellin' me all this?"

"I'm telling you all of this because clearly, you were impressed by the difficult life that Bernice has had, and I wanted to show you that everyone, even someone like myself, has had his fair share of suffering. But some of us are strong enough to survive this suffering, to use the suffering as a motivation to rise above it, while others are not. I am sorry that Bernice is in such poor shape, but she had the same opportunity as all of us to build a more secure life. She could have saved her money. She could have led a healthier lifestyle. It is not your responsibility to use the family fortune to save her. You will only regret it, and I want you to forget you even saw her."

"I swear. You and Mom and John. All of y'all are scared to death of losin' a little money. It's like all you see is money, and the people aren't even there. Do you even *see* people? Am I here?"

"Don't start that with me." Henry returned to his seat behind his desk. "You talk about money like that, acting like it's so wrong to accumulate it, but let me ask you this. Do you think that the United States is the greatest country in the world?"

"Well, hell yeah."

"Finally, something we can agree on. What you are referring to when you point out our reverence of money is called the profit motive, and the profit motive is what makes the United States the greatest country in the world. Profit is the fuel that gives our country its power. Profit is what makes this country prosper the way it does so you and everyone else can enjoy it."

"Tell that to Bernice."

"Hmph. Bernice has benefited from my wealth as much as anybody.

If she had been born in any other country in the world, she likely would have died long ago. She wouldn't even have sustenance anywhere else in the world."

"But she wasn't born in any other country. She was born in America. The greatest country in the world. She deserves better."

Henry pushed his swaying gray hair off his liver-spotted brow and looked at his watch. "Why aren't you working, anyway?"

"Worked all weekend. John told me to take a couple days off."

"Do you have any plans to see that Bernice again?"

"Yeah."

"When?"

"I ain't sayin'."

"Where does she live now?"

"I ain't sayin'." Blue Gene *did* know where she lived. Since her phone service had been cut off earlier in the summer, he had asked her to write down directions to her house so he could visit her sometime.

Henry arose from his seat again and paced around the spacious office, his temples subtly bulging. As he walked, he jingled with pocket change. "You shouldn't associate with her."

"Just give me my money. I'll help her out, and that'll be that."

"No. I cannot do that."

"Listen to yourself, Dad. You're cheating me like I's one of your workers. I've overheard people talkin' 'bout you, you know."

"I don't appreciate you coming into my office and making me into the blackhearted corporate villain. If you think of me as money hungry, take a closer look at the blue-collared good ol' boys you emulate. In all my business transactions, never have I encountered a being as devious and greedy as the common building contractor. I personally witnessed one, as simple and slow-talking as he could be, who cheated my mother out of thousands because he knew she was a vulnerable widow. If you take a fair and balanced look at me, I've earned my money, and I don't owe anybody. I've already paid my debts. My wealth has been taxed away for the benefit of both my nation and the world. I've ensured the protection of the uneducated like Bernice in my own nation, and I've ensured the protection and well-being of the less fortunate all over the world. I've helped make America what it is. To insult me like you've done is to insult your nation. I thought you loved your nation."

"I do love my nation! Don't go sayin' that."

"See. You've only talked to her one time, and Bernice already has you questioning your own country. I told you no good can come from associating with her."

"I'm not questioning my own country. You know I love America more than anybody. I'm just— Well—"

"Well?"

"I lost my train of thought."

Henry stood next to Blue Gene, looked down at him, and gave him a poker-faced stare. Blue Gene sensed there was a smile somewhere underneath his father's face. Uncomfortable under his father's unshakable watch, he looked away at the floor-to-ceiling mahogany bookshelves with brass bookends in the shape of antique guns.

"Before you leave here today, I want us to have complete closure on the topic you've brought to my office. I appreciate your coming to me, and if it weren't for your poor timing, I'd be much more willing to help you with your request and waive the age restriction. But the fact remains that John has not won yet, and until he does, the election is my top priority. This is a pivotal time, and I will not have my family taking any risks right now—and you will have to believe me when I tell you that any dealings of any sort with Bernice Munly would be a risk. She is manipulative and conniving, and I'm sure she'd take pleasure in scandalizing you and your brother. We can talk about this again after the election, but until then, I want you to cut off all contact with that woman. Now, I want your word on that. Haven't I heard you say before that a man is only as good as his word?"

"You say we can talk about it again, but when the time comes, you still won't let me have my own money, will you?"

"When you turn thirty, it's all yours."

"I never ask you for anything, Dad."

"I know, Eugene. You're a good boy, and we appreciate all that you've done for the campaign. You really have made a difference in getting John support. But this is out of the question. Bernice Munly is an enemy to the Mapother family, and you are asking me to give assistance to the enemy. Now, I can't believe in my heart that you'd want to do that. Do you want to hurt us? Your own family? John has waited for this his entire life. Don't you remember your mother's dream? This isn't just for the Mapothers. Don't you want your mother's dream to come true?"

"I don't know about that dream."

"That dream represents all that is good. It—"

"I don't wanna talk about some ol' dream. This is about Bernice and getting her help. I think what this all boils down to is that you and me see Bernice in two totally different lights."

"True."

"You've made her out to be this evil, lazy thing, while I don't see her like that at all. And what I think—I'm sorry, Dad, but what I think is *real* evil is that only one percent of the people in America own 'bout half the money. One percent! That's what's wrong here."

Henry walked to the window behind his desk and turned his back to Blue Gene. "Where is this coming from?"

"Are you part of that one percent?" Blue Gene asked.

"Yes. Does that automatically make me a bad person?"

"No, but here's your chance to stop hoggin'. I ain't askin' for much—just enough to help her with her medicine and food and oxygen. Fuckin' oxygen! By God, I don't see what the big deal is!"

"You're out of line, Eugene. First of all, my own hard work and ingenuity put me in the top one percent, and damn you for turning that into something negative. My wealth is not just an accident of birth. I have earned my fortune. And if I hog money, as you say, I hog for all of you. I hog for your good and the good of your future children. I will not feel guilty about that. This is America, and everyone has the same chance to rise here, even Bernice Munly."

"But you had a head start. We was tobacco barons goin' way back—"

"I am speaking—"

"Even America is allowed to get things wrong sometimes, isn't it?"

"You're sounding more and more like a traitor to your own nation."

"Don't say that. I love it or I wouldn't even be—"

"Where is your patriotism?"

"It's right here!" cried Blue Gene, pointing to his chest through his John Deere tank top. "I'm not—"

"You are spitting in the face of every man who ever fought for this country."

Blue Gene jumped up from his seat. "But you didn't fight!" He found himself screaming, speckles of saliva shooting from his mouth.

"I pay for the fighting." Henry's nostrils were flaring violently. "You and all your people who treat freedom as a god—as you well know, that freedom must be protected and maintained, and it is maintained through money. Our military doesn't pay for itself. Are you saying we should allow our military to weaken and let another attack take place?"

"You and John say all that stuff, and it sounds all good, but still, y'all didn't fight. Y'all weren't even in the reserves, were you? I couldn't fight because I'm a cripple. What's your excuse?"

"If you can't act civil, I'm going to have to ask you to leave."

"I'm civil."

"I was too young to be drafted for Korea, if you must know. You shouldn't be questioning me."

"What about 'Nam?"

"I couldn't get drafted because I had a child. Had it not been for John being born, I would have gladly fought for my country, but instead I stayed behind and strengthened the interior. At any rate, you should not be questioning your father."

"You couldn't be drafted, but you still could've volunteered, couldn't you've?"

"No. I told you to stop questioning me. If you can't act civil, our time is up. I have a meeting to go to."

"You and John always pull that stuff, but y'all didn't practice what you preached." Blue Gene sat back down, breathing heavily.

"Why are you sitting? I told you our time was up."

"But Dad—"

"Conversation over." Blue Gene shook his head, got up, and limped toward the door. "And if you talk to Bernice again, you will no longer be a part of this family."

"Was I ever?"

$ $ $

Like flies in a bug zapper, thoughts darted all over Blue Gene's mind and disintegrated before landing on any conclusions. There were doubts, worries, suspicions, and random phrases from the Pledge of Allegiance, all flitting around because of his dizzying conversation with his father. His confusion over where he should stand with his family and Bernice and the campaign had led to such a mental tangle that the only action he knew to take was to just go home, or at least to the building he currently called home: his parents' poolhouse. But to get there required driving, a task on which his fluttering thoughts could not focus. Not too far from his father's office, he drove straight through a four-way stop. Later, when he turned onto River Town Road, he confused his turn signals, absentmindedly thinking that switching the signal up meant left and down meant right.

Once he managed to make it home, he threw off his shirt, since it had become soggy under the arms. He sat and drank a Diet Ski as he tried to figure out what to do with himself. He kept imagining Bernice spending her last moments on Earth terrified, gasping for air. His father and he both knew that he wasn't about to go through with his threat of getting a lawyer; Henry and his lawyer had proven on several occasions that they were unbeatable in court. He considered asking his mom or John for some money, but his pride wouldn't allow it.

Now that he thought about it, it made sense that his dad wouldn't let him have his own money. Blue Gene Mapother wasn't the only person who looked on in head-scratching frustration while a more powerful man withheld the money that by all rights and common sense belonged to him; Henry Mapother had *everybody's* money.

Blue Gene decided that for right now, all he could do was give Bernice his savings. He had been working for John for two months now, and though his wages weren't much, he hadn't been paying rent on the poolhouse (though he did offer). He had been planning to move out as soon as he could afford to, but he could put that plan on hold if it meant saving someone's life. It would be a siege to get Bernice to accept his money, though, and Blue Gene had already had enough arguing for one day. He decided he'd go out to Bernice's tomorrow. The rest of this day, he'd attempt to relax.

He called Jackie at three-thirty, but no one was home. He waited two hours and tried again, but still no one answered, and although he was tempted the rest of the afternoon, he would not let himself call a girl three times in one day, since she surely had caller ID.

He ate some leftover Papa John's pizza for supper and then settled himself across the sofa for the evening, wearing only his white briefs and his crucifix necklace. He knew the remote control buttons by touch alone and punched in his favorite channels, but since the fall TV season had not yet begun, there wasn't anything good on, and what *was* good he had already seen. For the next hour he flipped through the channels, hardly paying attention to anything he saw because he kept thinking about the argument he'd had with his dad. Things had been going so well with him and his family. It was bound to get messy again sooner or later. He guessed that was what he got for talking about money. His father had always told him to never talk about money.

At seven o'clock, he finally settled his TV on *Big Brother*. The way the people on the show fought made him laugh. But that night, nothing kept Blue Gene's mood from dipping into pessimism: everyone on the commercials looked so attractive, but their noses were full of mucus just like anyone's. He put his finger in his belly button to pick out the lint, which normally gave him a small degree of satisfaction, but he noticed his navel was harder to get to because his stomach had gotten fatter. He had never thought he'd care about getting old, but here it was, happening right underneath his eyes, and he cared. The baseball players he had watched as a kid were being voted into the Hall of Fame, and that just didn't seem right. Nothing seemed right. He badly wanted a smoke, but he gave his word to Bernice, and a man was only as good as his word. Bernice was good—good to him, at least, so how could his father treat someone who was so good as if she wasn't worth saving? Was it because goodness was weakness? Did that make badness strength? What would be better: to have paper cuts on your tongue, or to have an eye poked with one of those little points on umbrellas? And he knew that damn girl had caller ID, so why didn't she call back?

When the phone did ring at eight thirty-six, Blue Gene was jolted into the moment and popped up from the sofa. His heart sped, thinking Jackie might be calling him back, but on the caller ID he saw it was John calling on his cell phone.

"Mapother," he answered gruffly. On the other line, no one said anything at first. But then he heard two men talking hurriedly, agitatedly. Blue Gene couldn't distinguish every word, but he knew one of the speakers was John, who really needed to learn how to lock the keypad on his cell phone.

"John!" yelled Blue Gene. "Hang up your phone, dumbass!" But it was useless. There was a pause, and then the other speaker came through clearer. It was his father. Blue Gene considered hanging up, but couldn't after he heard his own name.

With the remote control, he muted the TV. Then he listened to the conversation as closely as he could. Bits and pieces of dialogue came through plainly.

"Twenty-seven............this...now......she......she....ruin...," said Henry.

"...had......happen eventually," replied John.

"...told you and............allowed.......with us."

"I thought........help!" yelled John. "He *has* helped!"

There was a long silence. Then there was a rustling noise. John usually kept his cell phone in his front pants pocket. He must have been moving around. Blue Gene heard his father muttering quietly, and then came a loud noise, as if the phone were shifting positions. After that, Blue Gene could hear the voices perfectly.

"I know, Dad. I've been apologizing to you all my life, and I'll apologize to you again. I'm sorry. And I'm sorry he ran into Bernice, but how could I have known that would happen?"

"You need to take care of this," said Henry. "He's your son. I shouldn't be having to deal with this, him marching into my office and putting me in that position."

A shock wave of confusion swept over Blue Gene, from the tip of his cowlick to the edge of his toenails. Questions instantly cropped up but had to be wadded tightly in the back of his throat.

"I'll take care of it. I'll have a long talk with him and make sure he never talks to her again."

"You can't guarantee that. If it gets out, we're through. All of our work goes down the drain."

"It won't get out. I'll get somebody to track down Bernice. I'll give a blank check to whomever I send. She can name her price."

"You cannot send anyone. You cannot involve anyone else in this!"

"Right. I know. I'll go to her myself," said John.

"You're damn right you'll go to her yourself. You got us into this, and you're going to get us out."

"I know. I will."

"Right now!"

"Okay. But how do I find her?"

"God, John. Are you that helpless?"

"I'm nervous."

"Call Information."

"I knew that. I'm just flustered over this." John's voice grew even clearer. "I thought she was out of the picture for good. Let's see. Uh—oh. *Hello?*"

Blue Gene froze.

"Hello? Is somebody there?"

Blue Gene hung up. He jumped off the couch and immediately searched the house for a stray pack of cigarettes, but he had thrown them all away last night. He threw his clothes on, grabbed his keys, and ran out of the poolhouse, but by the time he turned his headlights on, he knew where he had to point his dirty old pickup, and it wasn't to get cigarettes.

$ $ $

Maybe he hadn't heard them correctly. Or maybe when his dad said, "He's *your* son," he was talking about some illegitimate son who had some tie to Bernice, who had nothing to do with Blue Gene. But Jesus Christ—if it didn't make sense. That age difference. That age difference that had always seemed so unusual, having a brother who was thirteen years older. He had a sudden urge to hurt himself, to strip off his tooth enamel like an orange rind and expose the nerves of his pulp to the wind that rushed through the open window.

He feverishly tried to add it all up as he drove on a narrow back road in the hinterlands of Dixon County. His cell phone rang. It was John. He debated whether to answer. He was curious to see if John suspected that he had overheard the conversation.

"Mapother."

"Hey, Blue Gene. What's going on?"

"Nothin'."

"What are you up to?"

"Nothin'."

"What are you doing?"

"Nothin'. Drivin' around."

"Where are you driving to?"

"Nowhere. Just drivin'."

"Anything new?"

"Nothin' new at all."

"All right. I just wanted to check in on you. Oh—I was also calling to see how it went at Wal-Mart."

"Went just fine. I talked you up real good."

"Great. I thank you for that."

"You're welcome."

"Anything else?"

"Nope."

"All right. Why don't you come on home? Dad wanted to have you over."

"Don't feel up to it."

"Oh. Are you okay?"

"I'm fine as wine. Just don't feel like talkin'."

"All right. I guess I'll let you go, then."

"Bye."

After hanging up, Blue Gene shook his head, angered by how casually John had come across. But then he realized he had acted equally casual, and that he had just taken part not in a conversation, but in a charade. He threw his cell phone out the window and into a ditch.

He sure had picked a fine time to stop smoking. But if there were ever an instance in which a man could break down and go back on his word and buy a carton of Parlies, here it was. If what he thought he'd heard was true, then he had enough questions and concerns to fill a truck bed. Could a thirteen-year-old even do that? And he may have been twelve at the time. Blue Gene then realized that, just off the top of his head, he could name a couple of twelve-year-old boys he knew of who had fathered kids of their own. But those were some true lowlifes. Not Mapothers.

$ $ $

John had phoned Blue Gene from a cavernous upstairs bathroom in the Mapother mansion. He couldn't risk his father's overhearing him as he tried to ascertain whether Blue Gene had learned something he shouldn't have. Downstairs about an hour before, he had told his father that he was mistaken, that no one was on the phone line. But after seeing Blue Gene's truck speeding off the premises, and after talking to Blue Gene and catching a hint of angst in his voice, John assumed the twenty-seven-year-old secret had most likely escaped through the cellular waves.

If you looked for the seed from which the secret had grown, you might find it deep within a forest out by Lake Cobalt, several counties over. Ten-year-old John stood still, his bright orange cap sticking out of the brown-and-green surroundings, a twelve-gauge shotgun shaking in his hands as he wept. It was his first hunting trip, which he had been thrilled about initially, but which instantly lost its appeal in the moment he superimposed his crosshairs over a young buck. His father yelled at him when he let the easy kill escape, and John teared up. Henry told him not to cry, that this was supposed to be fun, that he had always wished his own dad had taken him on a trip like this. John cried even more. Henry yelled even more. John could barely breathe for sobbing, and Henry kept getting more frustrated, until finally he told John to get it all out of his system because he was going to have to become a man soon.

John sat on a log while Henry told him all about what Elizabeth had prophesied back when John was seven, even though Henry and Elizabeth had agreed they wouldn't tell John about it until he was an adult. Though the dream contained the ideals of hope and perfection, it was still visually apocalyptic and not suitable for a child to hear, especially when that child had a starring role in the vision as the usher for the Messiah.

For weeks after learning about the dream, John had crying spells. Elizabeth told him that it was okay to cry, just so long as no one saw him. She said she hated to say something so callous but believed she was giving him good advice that would spare him a fatherly scolding. Henry believed his son's conditioning for future leadership had already begun, and weeping would not be tolerated.

John took Elizabeth's advice to heart and made sure no one ever saw that he had become given to crying fits. He sobbed in secretive solitude in the darkness of his closet, cramping himself in its corner for up to an hour at a time. He eventually began to feel gratification sitting in the closet. He found the darkness comforting and learned that by simply sitting alone in his hiding place and becoming dead to the outside world, which didn't seem to miss him, he could experience the same catharsis that came from the act of crying. He felt like himself in the dark. He felt free, and he liked himself better there, too. At school, while gnawing on a number-two pencil, he looked forward to the soundless moments that would come later that afternoon in the excruciating splendor of the dark.

By the age of twelve, John saw that his own closet was running out of room because it was gradually filling up with toys that he found himself outgrowing. He was becoming more interested in sports than toys. Because of his lack of closet space, he began experimenting with other closets and found that his parents' closet was just as suitable for his morbid hobby, and it was even more enjoyable since it was a place he knew he probably shouldn't have been. It was a walk-in closet, but still confining, since it was filled with two adult lifetimes' worth of clothes, shoes, and boxes full of documents. In the back were several of Henry's shotguns and even a pistol that John liked to hold.

The fifth and final time John secretly crouched in his parents' closet, his heart hiccuped when he heard someone enter the room. Through the slight crack between the sliding closet doors, John could see Trish, their flighty young housekeeper, sitting on the edge of the bed. He had to stifle his laughter when he saw her sniffing her own armpits.

The laughter impulse died and would remain dead for days to come when John saw his father enter, closing and then locking the door behind him. What followed so petrified John that he couldn't turn away even if he wanted to, which he only halfway did. The lithe, dirty-blond housekeeper had taken off everything, allowing John his first vision of a fully nude woman. His father undid his belt with abrupt sharpness and let his pants and boxers drop, his shirt tails obscuring the key anatomy from John's view. John had seen only street dogs do this before. The dogs had been in a similar configuration but hadn't seemed so angry. John thought they looked and sounded like they were killing each other, dying in violent unison. He was scared by what he saw and what it implied and wanted to cry but couldn't. He felt himself stiffening. Soon they were finished, and Henry pulled up his pants and left without either of them saying a word.

These images plagued John without cease for the next week, but he managed to internalize the abominable emotion they gave rise to, a serrated beast of disgust, confusion, and curiosity. To Henry and Elizabeth, nothing appeared out of the ordinary with John, except that he started going on long bike rides, sometimes leaving for two or three hours. When they questioned him, he told his parents he had just been riding around exploring, thus beginning a sordid lifetime of half-truths.

$ $ $

"Blue Gene!?" said Bernice as she held open the screen door, wearing a faded old bathrobe. She smiled until she saw his tense face. "What's wrong?"

"Nothin.'" A deep smell of smoke clung to him the moment he entered the tiny, light blue–carpeted living room, where a manic poodle pounced on his legs. The house was cool enough, with three electric fans going in this room alone, but still stuffy.

"Shasta!" Bernice shouted at the dog. "You stay off of him!"

"Has my brother—has John been here?"

"Why, *no.* Why would he?"

A fat, gray cat was watching *Law & Order SVU*, which was blasting on the medium-size TV set in order to be audible over the hum of the fans. Once Blue Gene was within a foot of the cat, it disappeared into the nearby bedroom. "You mind if I turn this off?" asked Blue Gene, pointing to the TV.

"Go'r't ahead. Are you okay?"

"Yeah." He turned off the TV.

"You look like something's the matter."

"I'm fine."

"Want a Coke or something to drink?"

"I don't guess you got any beer, do ya?"

"No. I used to keep it on hand 'cause I have this hiatal hernia, and one of my doctors told me I should drink a beer 'fore supper and it'd keep me from chokin'. And I tell ya, it *did* help, but I haven't been able to afford beer lately. Got Coke, though."

"No thanks."

"If you're hungry, let's see, there's some shoepeg corn I fixed and—"

"I gotta talk to you 'bout something serious."

"Well, I *thought* you looked serious. What is it?"

"I'm comin' to you 'cause I know you're involved in this somehow, and I figured you'd be more likely to give me answers than my family."

"Involved in *what*?"

"Is my brother really my dad?"

Bernice laughed nervously, then coughed, then laughed again. "Where'd you get that?" She twisted her oxygen tube around both thumbs.

"Please just answer me. Just tell me the truth. Is John my dad?"

Bernice took a seat in a ratty orange recliner with cigarette burns on its arms. "Sit down," she said. The arthritic old shack creaked as Blue Gene took a seat on a brown-flowered couch. "I reckon you're more than old enough to know. Yeah, hon, he's your dad."

The United States, with all her time zones and logos, was the home to so many lonely souls, but none at that particular moment felt such an extraordinary loneliness as Blue Gene Mapother, who felt like someone had just signed the divorce papers that would separate himself from himself.

"Why didn't anybody tell me?" he asked solemnly, staring straight ahead at the wall, which was the beige shade that old newspapers eventually turn.

"I'm sorry. They said it would've been a scandal. How'd you find out?"

Blue Gene explained the cell phone accident before figuring out what question should come next. "So all this time, my mom and dad were really my mamaw and papaw?"

"Yes."

"Who's my real mom, then? Hold on—is it *you*?"

"Well, Blue Gene, I don't know what to tell you. I guess the cat's out of the bag, and you got a right to know. Your mom's name was Tammy. My daughter."

"Your *dead* daughter?"

"Yeah. She died in childbirth."

"You mean, givin' birth to me?" The black poodle was trying to get in Blue Gene's lap, but he pushed it away with more force than was necessary.

"*Shasta.* Stop that. Yeah, hon. I'm sorry."

"Well, I reckon I'm the one who should be sorry."

"No. It wasn't your fault. It was *a lot* of people's faults, but not yours. You're the only one in the whole mess that *was* innocent."

$$\$\,\$\,\$$

John had been feeling so sure of himself, so in control as of late. But with the push of a button, all control was lost. Maybe it was this new confidence that had made him careless. On multiple occasions, Blue Gene and Abby had both told him that he'd accidentally dialed them and that they could hear him talking. He had even learned how to lock the buttons to prevent this from happening, but he found that every time he wanted to use the phone, he had to *unlock* the buttons, which was inconvenient. He loathed himself as he drove into Dixon County, looking for a Delacroix sign. If there were a guardrail around instead of just a bunch of corn, he would have sent himself into it at ninety miles per hour in hopes that the metal would wedge him in two. "Everything that once was metal now they make in plastic," his father liked to say, as a euphemism for how soft society had become in the last fifty years. Guardrails were still made of metal, though, and if John could find one, he'd use it.

But there weren't any rails, and when John saw how fast he was going, he slowed down. Why did cars even go so fast if the speed limits were only so much? He didn't know what the speed limit was out here in the boondocks, so he took it down to forty. He had to calm down, or he'd botch something again. He had to turn this night around and make everything right. A checkbook pulsated with purpose within his blazer pocket. He would buy Bernice's silence at any cost. If Blue Gene was already at Bernice's, he knew how to play it. Blue Gene wouldn't take any hush money, because that wasn't his style. But John could offer Bernice a check in front of Blue Gene. He could tell her that she could name any amount, that all her medical expenses would be taken care of for the rest of her life, as long as she and Blue Gene both kept quiet about this insalubrious matter.

If Blue Gene had gone to ask Bernice about it, at least it might spare John from having to go over all the details. And Bernice could definitely tell Blue Gene more about his mother than John could.

There had been prettier girls than Tammy in John's seventh grade class, fashionable girls of good breeding. But John didn't care. He singled out the always quiet Tammy for reasons other than attraction, which wasn't to say he didn't find her attractive. Once he started studying her from across the classroom, he found the unhealthy-looking, scrawny girl with the out-of-style clothes to be interesting compared with the more sterile girls whose dads knew his dad.

Furthermore, John knew that the physical entanglement he sought—the kind he had witnessed his dad and the housekeeper doing—was something that could never be spoken of, and Tammy was the one girl in his class who never spoke. His courtship was carried out through the passing of secret notes, and when he invited himself to Tammy's house one day, she accepted. When he fondled her at her house, she didn't object. She didn't object to John's subsequent advancements, either, which took place in her dingy bedroom on the bed she had slept in all her life. As John came closer to the inaugural moment, his fear made room for excitement, because the kissing did feel good, and his excitement gave way to arousal, because he saw that this person was serving herself to him as she melted into the sheets. John later realized the feeling that allowed him arousal had little to do with the warm body underneath him. The feeling was power, domination over a weakling whom he considered lucky to even be deemed significant enough for him to visit her. He visited her five more times, and from this reckless swinging of newly discovered power, and from the complacency of a shy little low-class girl, came the cellular brew that would one day grow a mustache and mullet because it felt like the thing to do.

$ $ $

Blue Gene gained and lost a mother in the space of a single minute. He had also gained a grandmother in Bernice, which would be easy to adjust to since she had always been the mamaw type. But the bonus of a new grandmother was little consolation. He demanded to know how all this had happened. Bernice took some hearty breaths from her nebulizer mask. Then, in a voice that was tough yet warm, like that of a career waitress at a truck-stop diner, she told him of his origin.

"Tammy was thirteen years old when she got pregnant. She kept it a secret as long as she could, but I knew something was wrong with her. I mean, she'd always seemed pretty sad, ever since her dad died, but I noticed she wasn't just sad anymore. She started to looked *scared*. And she liked to have never told me, held out as long as she could, but I finally got it out of her that she wasn't getting her period. She cried her eyes out. At first she wouldn't tell the truth. She made up some yarn about aliens puttin' a baby inside her. Course, that didn't surprise me none 'cause she was real into UFOs, just like her dad, and she come up with this real long tale about this alien comin' in her room one night that could talk to her inside her head, and he wrapped his tentacle or whatever around her waist—but she said he was real nice about it. A real gentleman. And he led her out to a spaceship, and they hooked her up to these machines and—"

"How'd it *really* happen?" interjected Blue Gene, who felt a hot, liquid sting in his belly. He took some deep breaths until the feeling passed in the form of silent gas.

"Well, basically her and John met at East Junior High, and John'd ride his bike over in the afternoon, and I was workin' in the afternoons or I would've been there, and you know, I don't like thinkin' about what went on, but it *did*. I didn't think they was even old enough to know *how* to. But anyway, what happened was I finally got Tammy to stop talkin' all that alien business, and she told me the truth, so I took her to the doctor to make sure she really was pregnant, and she was. Doctor told me it happened more than he'd like to admit. He'd seen even younger, in fact. So anyways, I thought it over and decided I'd better go see this kid's parents. *Your* parents."

"They ain't my parents no more."

"Well, but they *are*, though. They legally adopted you. They're still your parents."

Blue Gene rolled his eyes. "Then what happened?"

"I hated to tell your mom what I had to tell her over the phone, so I went to her in person, to her house, and I just laid it all out on the table. She and that ol' husband of hers thought I was scammin' 'em. So they wanted to do a paternity test, and I said fine.

"A week later, the test come up positive, so me and the Mapothers got together at his office downtown and tried to figure out what to do. Right off the bat I told 'em there was no way that Tammy and me could raise you, and that's no offense to you, Blue Gene, but I could hardly afford to feed just the two of us after Bart died, let alone a baby. It just would've been impossible. But then Henry and Elizabeth, they didn't want that responsibility either of raising a kid, and plus it may have caused a big scandal for 'em to all of a sudden add a new baby to their family."

"If you say *money* was the reason you weren't gonna raise me, why couldn't Mom and Dad just *give* you money?"

"Well, yeah, we talked about that, maybe them sendin' checks until you turned eighteen, but that ol' Henry was really against that. Said it wasn't his place to pay. Just kept actin' like he was gettin' scammed. Like *he* couldn't afford it. And he kept sayin', what happens when the kid grows up and starts wantin' to know who his father is? He didn't want no part of it.

"So we finally decided that adoption was the only way to go, which I wasn't crazy about—havin' my daughter go through nine months of pregnancy and then labor on top of that, just to give up the baby to God-knows-who, but I reckoned it was still better than the kid growing up having its parents in junior high. So we planned on givin' you up for adoption, but in the meantime Tammy was gonna start showin' pretty soon, so Henry and Elizabeth come up with this arrangement. They owned a cabin out on Lake Cobalt."

"Yeah. We used to go there every once in a while when I's little."

"Nice, ain't it? It was to Tammy and me, anyway. So I had to quit my job for us to live up there, but your dad at least agreed to pay for our expenses while we was there, and he said when it was time for me to work again, he'd get me on at the Westway factory. Lookin' back, I cherish those five months I got to spend with Tammy on the lake. We'd watch our stories together all day and sit outside and talk at night. But anyway, you came a month premature, and Tammy, well, I reckon her little body wasn't ready for a little body of its own, which I had been afraid of. She was just skin and bones. I tried to tell your mother that, but—well, anyway, that was that."

The hot sting came back to Blue Gene's stomach. It felt like a wet swirl at the bottom of his gut, a brown disaster that would soon have to drop. "Where was John during all this?"

"Oh, they kept him pretty sheltered from ever'thing. I mean, he knew the basics of what was goin' on, but he didn't take part in nothin'. He wasn't there when you was born. The only one from your family that was at the hospital that night was Elizabeth. After I found out about losing Tammy, I lost it, and I went up to Elizabeth and right there in the waiting room I screamed, *I oughta tell the whole world what y'all've done to my little girl!* And of course she didn't know what to say but she was so sorry, she was so sorry. And she said she would do absolutely *anything* in the world she could for me 'cause she felt so bad for everything.

She said money, a new house, *anything* in the world she or her husband could do for me, I shouldn't hesitate and they would make it happen. And course I said there was nothin' that could make up for what had happened, but that night I laid wide awake, and I finally realized that there *was* one thing they could do for me, and next day I asked her, and I'll give her credit, 'cause she said yes."

"Well?"

"Well, next day at the hospital, while we was lookin' at you through the baby window—you was hooked up to a breathing machine—I told her I'd take her up on her offer of doin' anything in the world to help me. And I nodded at you and I said, make him a Mapother. And she said, what? And I said, make him a Mapother. Give him a shot at this world, 'cause God knows y'all've taken my daughter's. I said for 'em to adopt you and give you everything you ever asked for. Not just everything you needed, but everything you wanted. I said to spoil that boy rotten. Make him one of you. I said, he won't have a prayer as a Munly, and God knows what'll end up happenin' to him if we give him up for adoption, 'cause we wouldn't be able to see him grow up. I told her to give you the best life money could buy, to buy you whatever car you wanted, and to send you to the best college. Basically, I asked her to give you everything Tammy and I never could've, but also to love you 'cause you did have half their blood. And Elizabeth immediately agreed to it, and then she asked me if there was anything they could do for *me*, and I said I reckoned I'd take her husband up on that offer to work in his factory. And she said, is *that* all you want? And I said, yeah. And she started crying. I asked her what she was crying for, and she said, there's no way I'm gonna let you work in that awful factory. Next thing I knew, I was a nanny."

$ $ $

John turned up "Sleepers, Awake!" and tried to focus on what mattered most, the thing for which he was put on this planet. As monumental as the cell phone revelation had been, he would handle it, contain it, and push it back inside the shadows so that his higher order would be fulfilled. Nothing had changed, really. The scandal would be stifled, the dream would still come to be, the election would be won, as would the next and the next, until he became a man the size of Mount Rushmore, delivering the inaugural speech that would make him the last great forefather.

But as he tried to visualize this triumph, he couldn't stop seeing Blue Gene's face, that face that always seemed to be saying: "Lord, won't you toss some good news my way?" He wondered what the face looked like now, how low the mustache must be dipping, how far the rings underneath the eyes must be drooping.

John tried praying but couldn't stop worrying about how his father would react if he found out that because of one silly mistake, Blue Gene *knew*. Their lies had held everything together for so long.

Their lies began after Blue Gene was born, when the Mapothers casually spread the news that Elizabeth had recently had a baby. They said that the reason they hadn't told anyone she was pregnant was that she had a history of miscarriages and wanted to be sure this time. This lie was based in truth, since Elizabeth really did endure two miscarriages in the thirteen years after John was born. Further lending credibility to their story was the fact that the petite Elizabeth had hardly shown her pregnancy when she had carried John.

The paperwork the adoption required proved to be on sale upon Henry's clandestine inquiry and bidding. In Elizabeth's fit of sympathy, she allowed Bernice to name the child. Bernice named him after her father, a long-gone coal miner named Eugene, a name the Mapothers hated because it wasn't in vogue at the time.

When the baby was brought home, thirteen-year-old John instantly fell in love with him, and though he knew he was supposed to pose as nothing more than a big brother, he privately vowed to be a father to the boy. Within a week it became clear to him that such a great responsibility could not be taken on by someone with so little experience. He at least came up with a nickname that would survive.

Years later, when John experienced a religious reawakening, he considered putting an end to the lies and telling the world that Blue Gene was his son. His parents talked him out of it. His dad told him that lies weren't such a serious offense. One positive thing that could be said about lying, according to Henry, was: if you lie, it doesn't matter if the other person is lying to you, because how can you fault him when you've beaten him to the punch with *your* lie? And there was a good chance that the other party has already beaten *you* to the punch in lying in the first place, so what does it matter? This was business, Henry said.

Elizabeth said this particular lie was venial when compared with what *could've* happened to Blue Gene. On the rare occasions when the topic actually surfaced, Elizabeth reminded John that he should not feel like it was a sin to perpetuate this lie, because this lie was what allowed Blue Gene the good, stable life that he enjoyed. As long as he kept this in mind, it was not a lie. It was morality.

John turned onto the highway where Mapquest said the Munly house would be. He finally saw a speed limit sign and obeyed it, which seemed absurd to do because this night had become so *big* that it was unreal, but he obeyed it anyway because he was determined to be good. He had been bad for so many years, and it didn't take a therapist to explain why (though he had been to his fair share of therapists at his mother's insistence, and to his father's chagrin). He had impregnated a girl when he was twelve years old, and it had caused the girl to die. It was an unnatural sin bordering on demonic, and it inspired him to spend his teenage years and most of his adult life doing all he could to destroy himself—not to mention ejaculating on pillows, couch cushions, telephones—anything except an actual womb. That Arthur was even conceived was a miracle of millimeters.

He finally found the address: 718 Hwy. 38 B. It was a pathetic white shack. He pulled into the gravel drive. Seeing Blue Gene's muddy old pickup in the drive with the 110% BAD-ASS sign decorating its windshield proved that his quarter-century-old role as a brother was most likely over. John's face fried with prickly heat. He felt combustible, as if he were lethally allergic to the hair on his own head, the skin on his own bones. While part of him yelled, "Don't back down!" the other part was having chest pains, one symptom he had never felt until this moment. He was now faced with a decision: He could go inside and face Blue Gene and Bernice and write the check that would shut them up, or he could back out of the driveway and head home, where he could take five bars of Xanax and sleep, sleep, sleep.

$$$

After unburdening his volcanic stomach, Blue Gene looked at himself in the bathroom mirror to make sure he was still there. He felt like an alien who had fallen into a new world and was beginning the process of recovering from interplanetary jetlag. He walked back into the living room, where the poodle had settled down and Letterman was coming on TV. Bernice was in the kitchen, her head practically inside the refrigerator.

"I'm a lookin' for you something to eat."

"No way can I eat right now." Blue Gene pressed his fingertips to his eyelids, as if to rub off the tiredness. He opened his eyes and noticed that Bernice had just one picture on her living room walls: an old, white-haired, bearded man hunched over his daily bread, with a big thick book off to the side. He was either praying or meditating. Blue Gene liked the painting. Whatever that old man was doing, he was trying. "Get back in here. There anything else I oughta know?"

"No, hon," she said from the doorway, with her shoes and socks off. "That's all I can think of. I know it's a lot for you to chew on. Can I get you anything?"

"Nah."

"Would you wanna spend the night over here? I don't want you drivin' after havin' a shock like this. And we could talk it all out."

"Nah. I'm a'ight. I always knew something wasn't right with my family. Course, I didn't know it'd be *this* messed up. But there ain't nothin' I can do about it."

"If it's any consolation to you, I read in the *Star* once that pretty much the exact same thing happened to ol' Jack Nicholson. He spent half his life thinkin' the woman who was actually his *mom* was his *sister*. She had him when she was a teen, and that was a while back when that sort of thing wasn't talked about, and her family didn't want a scandal just like the Mapothers or me didn't want one. So they just passed his mom off as his sister and his grandma as his mom. Just like we did with you."

"I ain't no Jack Nicholson, though."

Bernice sat back down in her recliner, where a small electric fan that was clipped onto the coffee table blew on her.

"It's like somethin' off a soap opera, ain't it? Off *One Life to Live*. Remember watchin' that with me when you was little? That one and *General Hospital*?"

Just as Blue Gene dipped his toe in the waters of a childhood reverie, he was jostled back to the present by the sound of a car in Bernice's gravel driveway. He looked through the dusty window blinds and saw a big, black Escalade pulling out of the drive.

"It's John." Blue Gene spun around and stood with accusing posture. "I thought you said he didn't call you!"

"He didn't!"

"Then how'd he know where you lived?"

"I don't know."

"I bet you don't know. I bet y'all are all in cahoots."

"Blue Gene, please! How do you even figure that?"

"I don't know." He peeked through the blinds again, but John was gone.

"I know all this has got you thinkin' sideways, but you gotta believe me. I don't know nothin' that's goin' on any more than you do."

Blue Gene paced around the little room and fanned himself with his ball cap. He didn't know what to do with himself. He wanted to punch something, anything.

"He oughta have come in here," said Bernice. "He knows you know about him now, don't he? You say he knew you was on the phone listenin'?"

"Think so. If he can put two and two together, he knows I know, which is pro'ly what he just did."

"And just takin' off and leavin' you like that. You need him now more than ever."

"He didn't want to have to deal with me," said Blue Gene as he slid back onto the couch. "He was comin' to pay you off, but he seen my truck out front and didn't want to deal with me. I reckon I wouldn't either if I's him. But how I know y'all ain't plannin' something else on me?"

"Why would I do that?"

"I don't know."

"I haven't talked to him or the rest of your family in ages."

Blue Gene sat and looked at Bernice, rubbing his mustache.

"Don't you believe me?" she pleaded.

"I just don't know what to think. You were in on this, too, you know."

"I know. I know. If you never wanna see me again, I'll understand. I'll be brokenhearted, but I'll understand. It's gonna be real hard for you to trust again. I'm sorry, hon."

Blue Gene stood abruptly. "I'm gonna take off."

"What are you gonna do?"

"Get drunk."

"Oh, don't do that."

"Don't know what else to do."

"Well, if you gotta get drunk, get drunk here. Let me go get the stuff for you. You don't need to be out driving. That's how Bart—well, now I can say *your papaw*—that's how your papaw died. Driving around drunk. Stay here, why don't ya?"

"Nah. I wanna be alone. Here," he said, reaching out to hug Bernice. She immediately went for his arms. "You lost your girl in the deal. It's hard to be mad at ya."

Blue Gene patted Bernice on the back a few times and opened the front door.

"*Please* don't go."

"If John comes back here, he's gonna offer you some money so you'll keep quiet about all this. If he does, you take it. You hear me?"

"Won't do no good to pay me off. You already found out everything."

"It don't matter. He won't take *any* chances on his past comin' out, not with the election comin' up. I tried gettin' the money for you myself, but I couldn't swing it. So if he comes back and offers you some, just take it."

"Promise me you won't drive drunk, Blue Gene," said Bernice, holding the cat-clawed screen door open.

"I promise," he said, and he put his frazzled self in his pickup, pulled out of the drive, and sped away, never bothering to look in his rearview mirror. He turned his back on all and every, pushing his foot hard to the accelerator, wishing he could drive straight into a new day, or into yesterday, because this day had made him feel like such a flimsy-gutted, stick-figure twitch of a man.

IX.

"Sir, I'm gonna ask you to calm down and tell us what happened."

"I'm sorry, Officer. Let's see. It was about one-thirty when I got in my car. I started the engine, and as I got ready to pull out, I turned and saw *this man* sitting in the passenger's side. Naturally, it scared me half to death. I took a closer look at him, and I saw his eyes were just barely open, like two little slits. I said, 'Are you okay?' and he didn't answer. He looked dead. So I got out of the car and didn't know what to do."

"Did he have any weapons on him?"

"Well, no, but I didn't want to just immediately kick him out because—I mean, just to look at him, and the fact that he was high on God-knows-what—I didn't know what to do. So I opened the door and I yelled at him, but he wouldn't respond. Then I grabbed him by the shoulder and shook him. I kept shaking him until he woke up. Then I told him to leave, but he wouldn't move. He started speaking some gibberish. He kept repeating, 'Cut it off, cut it off.' Then, he said something like he was looking for his brother and asked me if I could help him find him. I asked him where his brother lived, and he said he was pretty sure it was somewhere in this neighborhood, which I doubt, but he begged for my help. So I felt sorry for him, and I told him he could use my cell phone to call his brother, but when I reached for my cell phone, it freaked him out. I guess he thought I was reaching for a gun, and he immediately hopped out of the car and became panicky."

"Where'd he go?"

"Oh, he's still in my car. He's lying down in my backseat right now."

The pair of police officers led the man across the lawn toward the BMW. "Anything else? Did he attempt to assault you?"

"No. I asked him how he got here, and he said he walked, so I told him he had better walk back to where he came from, or I'd call the police. Then he said really slowly, 'You know what? I'd 'preciate it if you'd just give me a ride,' and that's when I got fed up and said to get off this property right now or I'd call the cops. So he walked off, and I went back inside the house for a minute to tell my friend what happened, but it wasn't five minutes later that I came outside and he was in my car again. That's when I called you all."

"Full moon tonight," said the cop who was asking all the questions, a stocky thirty-something with a buzz cut. "Lots of crazies out." He opened the car door to see the perpetrator wearing only denim shorts. The cop shook the unconscious man's long, hairy leg. "Wake up, partner."

$$\$\ \$\ \$$$

Blue Gene didn't seem surprised to see a police officer hovering over him.

"What'd I do now?" he asked, blinking repeatedly as if it would improve the reception of the scene in front of him.

"Well, it *smells* like you've been drinking."

"What's goin' on?"

"I don't know what's goin' on with you, but we been trying to wake you up the last five minutes. Do you have any weapons on you?"

"No," said Blue Gene, still lying down. "Got thirteen—no, twelve—guns. Yeah. Twelve at the poolhouse, but I ain't gonna live there no more." He spoke in the breathy strains of someone who had just awakened.

"Do you have any illegal substances on you?"

"I resent you askin' that."

"I don't care. Is there anything illegal on you that I need to know about?"

"Uh-uh. Dickhead."

"Watch it now, partner. I'm gonna have you step out of the car for me."

Cussing under his breath, Blue Gene groggily pulled himself out of the car.

"All right, partner, what I'm gonna have you do is turn around and put your hands on your head with your fingers interlaced."

"My fingers *what*?"

"Like this," said the policeman, demonstrating with his hands.

"Oh," said Blue Gene, and he imitated what the cop was doing.

"Now turn around." Blue Gene obeyed. "You don't have any needles that are gonna poke me, do you?"

"No, sir." Blue Gene wasn't blinking so much now.

The cop frisked him thoroughly, up and down. "How much have you had to drink tonight, partner?" he asked as he frisked.

"Oh, I had a few Buddy Lights."

"A few?"

"Yeah. And what few I had I done pissed out. So no more problems."

"May I go now, officer?" the male-pattern-balding owner of the BMW asked the other, younger officer. "I really need to get home."

"Yes, sir. Wait just a minute. He's almost done."

"Okay, partner. Turn around. Do you have any ID on you?"

"No. Do you have any cigarettes on *you*?"

"No. I don't smoke."

"I don't neither."

"What's your name?"

"My name is Shawn Michaels. Please, could I ask you a question?"

"What?"

"Beat me up. I know you want to."

The officer laughed. "Partner, I don't want to beat you up. I want to help you. What are you doing out here tonight?"

It took a while, but the officers finally ascertained that he had been drunkenly searching for his brother on foot before giving up and going to sleep in the closest unlocked car he could find.

"Where do you live?" asked the older cop.

"With him," replied Blue Gene, pointing to the younger officer. Both policemen cracked up.

"Hey, Dave," said the older cop. "Didn't know you had a roommate."

"I didn't either," he replied.

"Do either of y'all got a cigarette on ya?" slurred Blue Gene.

"No. What I'm gonna ask you to do is turn around and put your hands behind your back."

"What the hell for?"

"You're under arrest."

"No I'm not."

"Yeah, trust me. You are. You're under arrest for drunk and disorderly conduct. Now turn around." The officer took hold of Blue Gene's shoulders and turned him around. "Give me your hands."

"Oh, man," cried Blue Gene. "I've lost all faith!"

"Give me your hands, partner," the older cop said firmly. The officer grabbed Blue Gene by both wrists and pulled his arms behind his back. Blue Gene's languid body suddenly jerked with vigor. He attempted to dash away, but the other officer grabbed him and forced him against the side of the BMW. Blue Gene struggled to get away, but within ten seconds, the policemen had him face-first on the driveway.

"I've lost all faith in the system!" wailed Blue Gene as he was being handcuffed, violently writhing as the younger policeman's knee pinned him to the ground.

"Excuse me, officers, but if this ends up in the paper, can we keep my name out of it?"

"Relax, Doc," said the older officer. "You were never here."

Blue Gene continued to squirm. "Please just let me talk to my brother!"

"What's this brother of yours up to?" asked the younger cop.

"I don't know. I don't know!"

"Yeah. Why you wanna see your brother so bad, partner?"

"'Cause he's my brother, and he's havin' a rough time at school. He's just started first grade."

$ $ $

Somewhere deep within the boondocks of Dixon County, at the bottom of a brown-grassed ditch, a cell phone had been ringing off and on throughout the night and into the morning. The calls originated from the Mapother estate, where Henry paced frantically in his burgundy silk pajamas, casting spastic shadows that whirled around the walls of his den. With John stuck in a medication-induced slumber and Elizabeth on her mission trip, Henry was left alone to face this long-averted problem. Here it was, throbbing in his face fifty-six days before the election.

At around 8:00 a.m., after he had given up and gone to bed, Henry finally learned where Blue Gene was. The chief of police, a potbellied old roughneck who many people said should have retired years ago, had called him personally. As Henry sped toward the Commonwealth County Detention Center, he recalled meeting Oral Haynes when he was but a rookie, and how their first encounter had been such a formative event in his life.

Henry was nineteen at the time, home from college for the summer. One day he got a call from his mother. She had been in a minor car accident and needed Henry to come pick her up. When Officer Haynes arrived, he got out of his car and immediately asked what had happened. The other driver, a grizzly bear-like man in a pickup, instantly jumped in with his version of the story. Then Haynes asked the man how fast he had been going. Satisfied with the man's reply, he asked Henry's mom how fast she had been going. After she replied, Haynes cocked his head sideways and gave her a funny look. He asked her if she was *sure* she hadn't been going faster. Henry's mom, shaken from the wreck and on the verge of tears, lifted her hands up helplessly and said she really didn't know how fast she was going.

Back then, it was not like Henry to be confrontational, but, red-faced and sweaty, he felt compelled to ask the officer why he had immediately accepted the man's answer but questioned his mother's. Haynes asked Henry who he was, and if *he* had been in the accident. Then he told Henry to go sit in his car. Dorothy asked Henry to be quiet and do what the officer said.

And Henry obeyed. He bit his cheek until it bled and walked back to his car. But as he opened his car door, Oral Haynes asked Henry just how many traffic accidents *he* had worked in his life. Henry spun around and asked the officer how much sense he had in his skull. Haynes suddenly reached behind himself for his handcuffs. He led Henry over to the police car and stood absurdly close to him, nose to nose, saying if he made one more smart-aleck comment, he would be taken to jail.

Dorothy pleaded with the policeman, saying she was J. H. Mapother's widow and this was his son, and he had never done anything like this before. He had never been in any trouble. He was a good boy, home from Harvard.

As he listened to his mom saying this, and as all the other cars sped by, Henry looked at his reflection in the cop's sunglasses, staring back at himself. Something about seeing himself in those sunglasses made him feel physically ill. Right then and there, he vowed that someday he would donate a check to the Bashford Fraternal Order of Police, one bigger than even his father could have written.

Within ten years, he did just that, flicking out the cursive of his name on that check like a generalissimo signing a treaty ending a war he had just won. His mom didn't live to see it, though; the day after the accident, her heart palpitations began.

When Henry arrived at the detention center, Police Chief Haynes was the first person he saw. Haynes's arms were folded and he had a grim look on his craggy face. Henry shook his hand.

"How long has he been here?" Henry asked.

"Since around two. But see, your boy, he gave us a fake name, and he didn't have an ID, so my arresting officers didn't know him, and then, see, I didn't come in till eight, and so I's the first to recognize him, but I called you soon as I saw him. I got on those officers, though, for not finding out who he was sooner, and they said they were sorry and wanted me to tell you they were sorry, but they tell me they been treatin' him all right. Said he vomited a good deal in the car and after he got here. I told him not to worry and got him some coffee. He seems pretty much sobered up now. Slept it off, I reckon. They just didn't know him."

"Please, Haynes. Let's move this along."

"Yessir, I'll have 'em fetch him for you. You let Donna take care of you there, and you just let me know if we can do anything for you."

After Haynes exited, with exaggerated warmth the receptionist handed Henry a form and kindly asked him to fill it out. As he took a seat, he almost laughed aloud when he thought about how sweet everyone was at this detention center, but then he reminded himself that they were only proving the same lesson he had been experiencing all his adult life: to be treated with respect or dignity, or even to be treated as a human being, you had to be rich, famous, or powerful. Henry assumed that his wealth was really the only reason he ever received a kind word from anyone.

He was filling out the paperwork for bail when the chief returned.

"He'll be out in a minute, Mr. Mapother. Can I get you anything?"

"No thank you. So you've been talking to Eugene?"

"I talked to him for a little bit, yeah. I was the one who woke him."

"What'd he have to say?"

"Nothin' much. Just small talk."

"He didn't say what his problem was or anything to that effect?"

"Nah. Mostly just talked about how he had given up smoking again, and he felt nervous 'cause of it. I offered him a smoke, but he wouldn't take it."

The door opened, and a tall, skinny officer appeared. "Excuse me, Chief. May I speak to you?" The chief left but returned a moment later.

"Well, this is a new one. Your son says that if you're the one posting bail, he ain't leavin.'"

Henry's small mouth smiled. "Oh. I see. We've been having our troubles as of late."

"I guess we can *force* him to leave, but only if you'd *want* that."

"Better not do that. May I speak to him? Do you have a little room where we can talk privately?"

"Sure." Haynes turned to the officer. "Go put him in 206." The tall officer left again. "Just so you know, I've already told Campbell to leave this one out of the paper."

"Good." Henry stared at the police chief, looking for any irregularities in his demeanor. He seemed to know nothing more than he ever did.

"John's lookin' real good for November, isn't he?"

"Definitely. It's his time. We appreciate your support, Haynes."

"Well, we appreciate *yours.*"

The tall officer appeared again. "I'm sorry, but he says he doesn't want to see you."

"You want us to *drag* him out?" asked Haynes with a half smile.

"No. Would it be a breach in your protocol if I just go back to where you're holding him and talk to him there? Privately?"

$$ \$ \$ \$ $$

On a concrete-slab bench that ran the length of one of the walls of the holding cell, Blue Gene sat Indian-style, resting his chin in his hands, wondering if he would puke anymore, hoping he could because he wanted to barf up all the bad. He heard serious-sounding footsteps coming down the corridor. He looked up and saw the police chief's bullfrog face through the little square window in the steel door. The chief slowly opened the door to reveal Henry.

"Take your time," said the chief of police.

"I need to have a father-son talk with him. Will you be able to hear us?"

"No, sir. Got cameras on him, but there's no audio."

Henry entered. He stood in front of the closed door and stared at

Blue Gene expressionlessly. "Are you okay?" he asked quietly.

"What do *you* care if I'm okay?" Blue Gene replied loudly.

"Let's be civil. Please. Are you really not going to come out of here?"

"Not if *you're* bailing me out."

"Well, then, do you mind if I have a seat?"

Blue Gene shrugged and scooted across the smooth, cold concrete that protruded from the beige brick walls, until he had himself planted in the corner. Henry chose a spot toward the opposite corner. Blue Gene had already planned what he'd say to his family when and if he ever saw them again.

"Guess what *I* heard."

"I know. John called me last night. He's a complete wreck over it."

"Well, *poor* John."

"Let's go home and talk about this. We'll sort things out and talk about your future."

"I don't *wanna* talk to you," said Blue Gene with a phlegmy cough.

"You sound sick. Are you all right?"

Blue Gene didn't respond. The fluorescent lights were giving him a badass headache.

"Are you sick?" Henry repeated.

"My throat hurts."

"Then come on. Please don't be this way. I don't want you to be in here while you're sick."

Blue Gene studied Henry's face. He saw concern on it, along with another rarity: the pinhead dots of chin stubble. Blue Gene remembered times, few and far between—but they'd still happened, or at least he *thought* they'd happened—when this man sitting across the concrete bench had held him in his solid arms, and Blue Gene had reached up and touched his face, and it had surprised him each time that the face felt like sandpaper. But the man who had once held him wasn't who Blue Gene thought he was. And now, the more Blue Gene looked at his face, the more he could not believe that the expression was one of concern, even though it did appear sincere.

"Leave me alone."

"I'm not leaving without you. Tell me what happened last night."

"Bought me some beer. Went down by the river. Laid in my truck bed. Got drunk."

"How did you end up in Vandalia Hills?"

"Walked there."

"You couldn't have. You mean you walked from the riverfront?"

"Yep."

"Did you drink alone?"

"Yeah, I drank alone. Oh—you're worrying I told somebody. Well, I haven't. Not yet, anyway. Hey—that's the only reason you want me outta here, I bet, isn't it? You wanna keep tabs on me and make sure I don't go tellin' nobody nothin'."

Henry crossed his legs man-style and checked his watch. "Hush. I want you to know I'm not mad at you."

Blue Gene jumped up from the slab of concrete, his stance unstable. The T-shirt they had given him was too big and made it look like he didn't have any pants on. He looked like a feeble-minded nursing-home patient in a nightshirt and no shoes.

"Why would *you* be mad at *me*?"

"For getting arrested."

"You're the one oughta be arrested. All the lies you've told me all my life, *that's* a crime. And never mind me. That little girl that died havin' me—"

"Be quiet!"

"They can't hear us. What y'all did to her was the biggest crime of all. You oughta be stuck in here right alongside with me."

"We'll discuss this at home."

Blue Gene sat back down in the corner. "I told you I ain't goin' with you." He sat Indian-style again. A film of dark brown dust stuck to the soles of his feet.

"I am sorry you found out the way you did, Eugene. I truly am. We were going to tell you eventually."

"When? When I turned forty?"

Henry sighed. He stood and took his black suit coat off and draped it neatly across his arm. He then sat back down, this time toward the middle of the concrete bench. He crossed his leg and leaned over toward Blue Gene.

"I was waiting for you to be ready."

"I'm twenty-seven!"

"But listen. I'm sixty-nine, and when you've lived as long as I have, you look back on the events that have made up your life, and each individual event looks so small. It looks small because your life has grown so big and long. On the other hand, there are children. Children do not have big lives. On the contrary, life is a small, fragile thing to them, and therefore every single thing they encounter seems huge and traumatic. That is why we've waited so long to tell you, so that these life events would take on the proper proportion."

"*Proper proportion.* Oh my God."

"I still consider you a child. Look at how you're acting right now. You're refusing to come out of the drunk tank."

"Rather be in here than livin' with y'all, fakin' my life away."

"Maybe this is where you belong, then."

"Right, 'cause I come from trash, and trash belongs in prison. Is that what you're saying?"

"You're not trash."

"Half of me *is*, though. That's why I am the way I am. That's why you hate me."

"I don't hate you, and it is not hereditary. You weren't born trash. You have chosen this for yourself."

"No, now, I thought about this down by the river. Half of me chose it, and half of me was born like this. That's what I think."

"I think you're wrong."

"Something else I come up with last night is that you're scared."

"Scared of what?"

"You're scared that something like *me* could come from y'all. Y'all helped make me. I'm half and half, but your perfect son contributed. That's why you hate me."

"You've chosen it." Henry grunted and leaned against the wall. "This is neither here nor there. I am still your father, you are still my son, I don't hate you, and I want us to go home and sort this out."

"I already sorted it out on my own."

"You couldn't possibly have sorted it out on your own. It's not that simple. I've known this day would come, you know. I've even known what I would say for a while now. What you need to do is start all over. You have to relearn everything. Think of learning as a mass of wire hangers, all tangled together, and your learning began as one single hanger, but as you grew up, other hangers—"

"Stop talking about hangers!"

"Let me finish. Each thing you learn is a new hanger that is hooked on to the bundle. That is, in order to memorize something, you must hook it on to something you knew before. Due to the youthful indiscretion that you've recently become privy to, I am sorry to say that your learning has been incorrect from the beginning. So what we must do is unhook one hanger at a time until we are back to a more manageable clot."

"What are you *talking* about?"

"We want to help you. We will help you through this, your mother and I, if you want us to. We'll help you relearn yourself, and once you do that, you'll be able to make a more well-informed decision about who you truly are. Then and only then will you be able to decide if you want to live like you have been living or if you want to live like one of us."

"I already know I don't wanna live like one of y'all. I known that all along. Ain't that obvious? And now I know for sure, 'cause y'all are just a bunch of liars. Now get outta here."

Henry stood. "Honestly, is what you've discovered about your family the most horrible thing? I look at people in your age group, and I see an entire generation of kids who were raised by their grandparents."

"It *is* the most *horrible thing*!" wailed Blue Gene. He jumped off the bench and slapped the cement walls. Henry stood back next to the stainless steel toilet coming out of the wall. The chief of police and the tall officer suddenly burst into the room.

"What's he doing?" asked the chief.

"Nothing. He's fine. He's fine. We're just having a squabble."

"Just a squabble, officer," said Blue Gene. He sat back down in the corner. "You know us Mapothers never have any problems."

"I need just a little more time here," said Henry. "Give me a few more minutes with my son."

"Don't you call me that no more," said Blue Gene. "Can't you make him leave me alone? I'm sick of his shit."

"Son, you need to show some respect," said Chief Haynes. "That's no way to talk about your father."

"My *father*," said Blue Gene with a bitter laugh.

"Eugene," Henry said sternly. "Haynes, leave us alone. Give me five more minutes."

"Whatever you say, Mr. Mapother."

As soon as the steel door slammed, Henry glared at Blue Gene. "If you ever want that inheritance you begged me for, you will never pull a stunt like that again."

"Hey, now, I didn't *beg* you for it. I don't beg. I—hold up." Blue Gene stood up again. He walked around the cell, rubbing his mustache, before standing in the middle where a drain was in the floor. He looked Henry in his narrow eyes. "You don't have the cards to be talkin' like that. That ain't right one bit. Uh-uh. This is how it's gonna be. You go ahead and give me my rightful inheritance, and I'll play along with you. I'll come out of here and everything'll be cool as can-be. I'll never say a word."

"No. Nothing has changed on that front. I concede that I will have to offer Bernice some money to keep the peace, if need be. But I wouldn't be comfortable with giving you that money yet. No telling what kind of damage you would do with four hundred million dollars. Just wait three years. When you're thirty, it will be yours, and all this will have blown over by then."

"I don't think you're hearin' me. If you don't give me my money, I'm gonna tell everybody *everything*."

Henry looked annoyed. "That will hurt John more than anyone. Don't be mad at him."

"I don't care anymore. Give me my money, and I never want to see y'all again."

"John wanted to tell you everything. In fact, on several occasions, he's wanted to. But I told him it would be best if he distanced himself from you because of his political career. It's my fault. Not John's. You have every right to be mad, but don't take out your anger on John."

"I don't care whose fault anything is. I'm telling you, this is the way it's gonna be. I want my inheritance. I just want what I got comin' to me and not a penny more. And if you don't give it to me, I'll start by tellin' the chief of police."

Henry smiled. "Are you serious?"

"Yes, I'm serious. What do you expect, doin' me like that all my life?"

"You wouldn't."

"By God, I'll holler for Haynes right now."

"You would be hurting yourself, too, if you did that."

"Do I look like I care?" He was so unkempt, even more than usual, his neck hair reaching out in all directions. The pantless look and the fact that his color looked a bit gray didn't make him any handsomer.

"What would you even do with all that money? Besides helping that woman?"

"Whatever the hell I want. You just give it to me, and you won't hear a peep from me, and I don't wanna hear a peep from any of y'all. Don't even *try* findin' me. I'm skippin' town. I'll be outta your hair."

Henry sighed and put his suit coat back on. He walked to the door, his back to Blue Gene.

"Fine," he said over his shoulder.

"You give it to me, and I don't ever wanna talk to y'all again," said Blue Gene, with the conviction of a man who had a PhD in everything that ever was.

"It's yours, but not a word about any of this will ever be spoken to anyone."

"You don't have to worry about that. I'm a man of my word. And my word actually means something."

"I'll have it transferred to your account this afternoon. Now can we get out of here?"

This was how Blue Gene Mapother became the third-richest man in Bashford.

$$\$ \$ \$$$

After they left the jail, to make sure that he followed through on his end of the deal, Blue Gene insisted that Henry take him to the bank immediately. On the way there, Henry suggested that Blue Gene allow him to set up an annuity for him, or even a tax-free foundation, if he planned on donating money to Bernice or any other charities. Blue Gene said he wanted to keep it simple; he just wanted the money in his account. He was afraid that if they got fancy, Henry would somehow swindle him, which he could easily do since Blue Gene knew absolutely nothing about business.

Once his puny bank account was instantly swollen with his inheritance, Blue Gene asked to be taken to his truck, which had been waiting for him at the riverfront. When Henry dropped him off, Blue Gene told him he was going somewhere far away for a while, but that he wasn't telling where, because he didn't want to see his family ever again. Henry didn't argue.

Blue Gene didn't actually go far, though, because he was hungover and still a little drunk and didn't have the energy to travel. One minute after Henry left, Blue Gene was pulling into the parking lot of the Ambassador Inn, which he chose simply because he was a multimillionaire now, and staying at the nicest hotel in town seemed like the thing to do. Yet at the front desk when he was checking in, he found himself asking for one of the less expensive rooms "down on the far end," instead of one of the upper-story suites that afforded scenic views of the river.

Before he went to his room, he had to close the thing that had opened this mess in the first place. He sat on one of the leather couches in the hotel lobby and wrote out a check for $700,000.00. Then, he went to the hotel gift shop and bought a stamp and an envelope and jotted a note that read:

Bernice—

This here's for you to go to the doctor with and get meds with and to take care of your bills with. Don't argue with me, I insist you take it and that's all there is to it. If you want me to forgive you for lying to me so much you have to take this money if you don't take it I'll also kill myself. *Take it.* Something I got to do. Don't try to find me but don't worry bout me neither. Take her easy, BG

He limped outside, and with a nervous laugh he dropped the plain white envelope through the long open slat of a big blue postal box. He peeked inside to make sure it went down. Then he reentered the hotel lobby with its atrium and made the four-minute walk to his hotel room, past the hotel bar, past the indoor swimming pool, down, down, down, then up some stairs and down a hall past the ice machine. He finally reached his modest, earth-toned room, pulled the blackout drapes shut, and stayed in bed for the next two days.

$ $ $

Once the sting of reality had begun to dull and spread in the form of a restless depression and profound disorientation of the existential order, Blue Gene went to Super Wal-Mart. Only time, he figured, would help ease him into his new place in the world, and he decided he wanted to spend that time alone, not on the grounds of his family's estate, not in a godforsaken trailer park, but holed up in the cheapest room within the most expensive hotel in Bashford. This would require supplies.

For the first time in his life, Blue Gene bought every single thing he wanted. After filling up his shopping cart with more toiletries than he could possibly need, he went to the electronics department, where he added to his cart a DVD player, *Smokey and the Bandit*, *Cannonball Run*, all the *Rambo* movies, all the *Star Wars*, all the *Rocky*s, anything with Adam Sandler in it, and every wrestling DVD the store had in stock. Then he picked out a boom box and a couple dozen CDs, including Aerosmith, Mudvayne, Bob Seger, Van Halen, Godsmack, Poison, Led Zeppelin, Black Crowes, Kid Rock, Jimi Hendrix, and Saliva.

He proceeded to men's clothing, where he bought an entirely new wardrobe from the underwear out. He bought tank tops, T-shirts, and shorts, as well as a few pairs of swimming trunks in case he decided to try out his new home's indoor pool.

His cart was eventually filled to the brim.

"Damn, you really went to town," said the elderly woman cashier, whom Blue Gene had worked with at the old Wal-Mart.

"It ain't for me. I wanted to get a head start on my Christmas shopping."

He paid with a check, unloaded the cart into his truck bed, covered his merchandise with a tarp, and reentered Wal-Mart to do his grocery shopping. Realizing his options for eating in his hotel room would be limited, he bought a toaster and a microwave. He stocked up on Pop Tarts, Spaghetti-Os, junk food, and bread. He concluded the Wal-Mart spree with one case of High Life, one case of Miller Genuine Draft, the biggest ice cooler he could find, a bottle of both Dayquil and Nyquil, and, in case he decided to take up smoking again, ten cartons of Parliaments. On his way back to the Ambassador Inn, he stopped in a Circle K convenience store.

"I want one copy of every magazine you got back there," he said to the cashier, looking down at the counter. "Except the ones with dudes in 'em."

He added a fistful of Slim Jim beef jerky sticks to the stack of magazines, paid, and hopped back into his merchandise-crammed truck.

$ $ $

Blue Gene took pleasure in the fact that nobody knew where he was. He made no attempt to call anyone, not even Jackie, and he thought only of himself. For the first couple of nights of his isolation, he mostly smoked and drank beer and watched movies or TV, though he had trouble concentrating on them. Life had given him way too much to suck on for him to devote enough attention to how Earl of *My Name is Earl* would atone for another sin.

Already tired of waiting for time to spread its Tiger Balm across his new sores, Blue Gene convinced himself that he could somehow *solve* the angst he was feeling if he could just think it through. But again, there would be no lightbulb pops of clarity that would provide him the light by which he could know himself. He already knew this, but it didn't stop him from trying. The beer didn't help his efforts, though it did help him forget that he had a cold.

After two days straight in the hotel room with a DO NOT DISTURB sign on the door, Blue Gene ventured out to the indoor swimming pool Saturday evening, holding a can of MGD inside a foam beer cozy. He hoped he would meet an unfamiliar woman he could chat with at the pool, but only little kids were there. Because he found the smell of chlorine so agreeable, he went ahead and parked himself on one of the reclining chairs. The smell of chlorine reminded him of his childhood, of the Olympic-size swimming pool he learned to swim in. He found the constant splashing and high-pitched giggles of the kids to be pleasant, and he also liked how the ceiling above the pool was a vast skylight that gave the evening sun a gray tint, casting everything in a surreal half-bright, half-dark light. Everything was overcast.

When some loud-talking, bikini-clad women showed up at the pool, Blue Gene made no effort to talk to them. They were weak substitutes for Jackie Stepchild. He decided to not even look at them, because that's what they'd expect him to do. Instead, he stared up at the skylight. He watched the stars come out and found it so enjoyable that when he finished his beer, he went to his room and brought his cooler and a pack of cigarettes back down to the pool with him. There he resumed looking up at the stars and attempted to reorient himself.

After twenty-seven years, Blue Gene Mapother had discovered the man who called him "Son" was actually his grandfather. The woman who called him "Son" was actually his grandmother. He had *two* grandmothers now. And the little boy he knew as his nephew was actually his little brother. This was the one development Blue Gene was excited about, except he assumed Arthur would never get to know the truth, so what difference did it make?

Then there was that poor little girl who was nothing but a name to him. That was the saddest part: he had never had a mother, but for the few moments she held him while she was dying.

But of course, the hardest adjustment was to think of John as his father. As a "dad" Henry had mostly been distant, and as a "mom" Elizabeth had not been half as nurturing as his "nanny"; to lose those two as parental figures wasn't completely devastating. But to think that his big brother John, the teenage boy who would pass gas to make him laugh, the hard-partying high schooler who popped in every once in a while, yakked on the phone, and drove too fast, the twentysomething frat boy who flunked out of life, the addict who could get lost in a bathroom stall, the professional kid—*this* was Dad? As he stared out the black skylight, Blue Gene saw that this was a fact he'd have to grapple with the rest of his life: Father was a child.

$$\$\,\$\,\$$$

He eventually went back to his room, where he stayed up late and absent-mindedly watched wrestling documentaries. He slept through most of the next day and repeated this routine the next two nights, returning to the pool at around five each day, all the while trying to arrive at some conclusion about how to think of himself and his family now that he knew he was a half-blood. The closest thing to a conclusion he reached was that at least he wasn't terminally ill, at least he had all his limbs, at least he wasn't some elderly prostitute standing outside all night on Story Boulevard, and at least he wasn't some mutilated body found by some stream or wooded area, which was where bodies tended to show up in Commonwealth County, if they showed up at all. And he didn't care what Henry said; the fact that he was born a half-blood could easily be the reason why he was the way he was, and knowing why you are the way you are is a luxury most people are never afforded.

At this point he had run out of beer, and though he could've bought some more at the liquor store conveniently located within the hotel, he didn't. He had drunk more than he should've the past week, and it had taken its toll on him. The thought of drinking any more depressed him.

The night he ran out of beer, Blue Gene realized he wanted to listen to music. When he got back to his plain box of a room after an evening of sitting by the pool, he knew exactly what he wanted to listen to. He had plenty of CDs that he had bought at Wal-Mart, but there was only one disc that he kept going back to during his stay at the Ambassador Inn: the one that had been made just for him.

For the first time since he had met Jackie, she was not foremost on his mind. His crowded mind had pushed her toward the back, but as the nights wore on, she inched back toward the front. He thought about asking her to meet up with him in a mysterious location that would make her laugh, something like: Meet me underneath the twelfth pew at the nondenominational church on February Boulevard. But he feared that if he didn't get the signals he wanted from her, his depression would be sent to even danker depths. It made him feel closer to her, though, when he listened to her mix CD.

As he lay down on one of the two twin beds, he thought about what the singers were saying, and he thought about what Jackie was trying to say to him by including these particular songs. It was clear to Blue Gene that the songs Jackie had chosen were meant to teach him something, that the song choices were inspired by the discussions they'd had about his views of the world. But now he didn't resent Jackie's trying to change his ways so much, because as much as he hated to admit it, she appeared to be right about his family.

In light of everything he now knew, some of the song lyrics hit Blue Gene in a way they hadn't before. "Only a Pawn in Their Game" now made perfect sense. Apparently, Jackie really wanted Blue Gene to appreciate Bob Dylan; she included two other songs by him: "With God on Our Side" and "Masters of War." Of course, he wasn't about to give up his long-held beliefs because of some songs on some mix CD, but he flirted with the idea of playing some of these disgruntled tunes for his family just to spite them, blasting songs like "Bastards of Young," "Making Plans for Nigel," and "Capitalism Stole My Virginity" on their state-of-the-art stereo equipment, set on repeat.

Once Jackie's mix ended at around midnight, he played it again as he wondered how, exactly, he should think of each of his family members now that he knew the truth. From now on, when he thought of the word *dad*, should he see an image of John? The man he had been calling Dad was Dad in name only. All these people and their names. And the names meant more than the people they belonged to, because the names were what held everything together.

If someone asks you, "Why do you put up with your dad, the way he treats you?" you say, "Because he's my *dad*, and I love him." So you love him and honor him because he's that word: *dad. Family* is another one. You might fight them, but they're still your *family*, so you always go back to them in the end. Because these people are those words, you set aside everything else. The words always take priority, because the words represent the ideas that you've been taught to value all your life. And all that's keen, but what do you do if you find out that words like *mom, dad, brother*, and *family* don't truly represent the picture you've held for a quarter century?

Maybe you start thinking about some other words that up to this point have *meant* the most to you. Maybe you pick those words up and dust them off and hold them up to the hotel room light and take a real good look at them. Maybe you take the words that are the most important to you, and the ones that are most important to them—and they must be important, because they sure do come up in their speeches a lot—and for the first time in your life, you really *look* at them. You poke your finger through their shine and peel off their golden coating, and for the first time you can see the inside of those words, and you are actually not too surprised at all to find that the insides of the words and the words themselves haven't got a goddamn thing to do with each other.

$$ \$\,\$\,\$ $$

When he first checked into the Ambassador Inn, Blue Gene had imagined himself living out some dark, solemn reclusion in which he would not speak to another human being, a hibernation that would end only once the length of his hair reached the bottom of his ass. In the end, it lasted a week.

"I been listenin' to that mix album you made for me a bunch here lately, and I was wonderin' if you could point me toward which records I should buy of the ones on there."

"Oh, wow. You really like it?"

"Yeah. I'll admit, I didn't at first. But I do now."

"Thank you! I mean, that's great. I love it when this happens. This usually doesn't happen. Who'd you like the most?"

"Bob Dylan."

"Yes!"

"Has he always sounded like an old man?"

Jackie laughed. "Yeah. He has. I had never thought of putting it like that, but yeah, he's always sounded like an old man. The songs I gave you, he would've been in his twenties then, I guess. Really, with him, you can't go wrong buying any of his albums made in the sixties. And they have tons of 'best of' collections for him that would be good to start with. Actually, they've made way too many of those collections for him. Who else did you like?"

Blue Gene looked on the CD cover Jackie had made. "The Clash.

Which of their stuff should I buy?"

"I love it when people ask me things like that. Let's see. My favorite Clash album is *Sandinista!*, but not everyone likes it because they try so many different styles on it, but I love it because they sound natural playing *any* style. Oh, but to be safe, I'd recommend *London Calling* since it's generally regarded as their masterpiece. Course, they have a lot of 'best of' collections, too, that would serve as good primers for you."

They talked about music for half an hour, about Pixies, Sparks, and the Smiths, the last of which Blue Gene asserted was too wussy for his tastes.

"Check this out. I've been living up in the Ambassador Inn."

"I saw that on the caller ID. I thought, 'Who would be calling me from the Ambassador Inn?' Why are you there?"

"I had a falling-out with my parents. Again."

"What happened?"

"It's a long story. I don't wanna get into that. It's just a big mess."

"So you're just going to live in a hotel?"

"Nah. I'll start lookin' for a place here pretty soon. Just needed some Blue Gene time. Know what I mean?"

"Yeah. Does this mean you're not helping out on your brother's campaign anymore?"

"Yep. Washed my hands of the whole mess."

"What happened?"

Part of Blue Gene wanted to tell her. He could educate her on the Mapothers and all their awful secrets, just like she had with him and Heartland Championship Wrestling. But he had given his word.

"Let me put it this way. You a night person or a day person?"

"A night person."

"Well, what if it turned out you only *thought* you were a night person, and you were really a morning person, but you never knew it 'cause you were always asleep in the morning?"

"Huh?"

"Never mind it. Just some bullshit I come up with when I was drunk.

Your band got any gigs comin' up?"

Jackie growled. "*No.* We can't find any place to play around here. I've almost decided to go on and play covers at the bars, but most of the people that would even want to come see us would be underage, so that won't work. I've called every place I could think of, from the American Legion to a karate dojo, asking if we could play there, but they won't have it. Nobody wants to give young people anything to do around here. Then they wonder why all the young people are high half the time."

"You still banned at the armory?"

"Yeah. No place will have us, not even in Donato Falls. So I don't know. We'll either have to break up or relocate."

"*Relocate?*"

"Yeah."

"Where would you relocate?"

"I don't know. New York or California. New York Angeles...Definitely one of the coasts. I have this theory that new ideas start in the oceans, and then they reach the coasts, and so Middle America ends up being the last to get the new ideas. Like, we always seem to be the last to hear that the wars are unnecessary."

"It's as good here as anywhere."

"I know, but there are more opportunities in bigger cities. Like, have you ever thought about how in this entire town, there's not a single building with a revolving door?"

"People have gotten killed in those."

"But my point is, I can't even find a job here. Anyway, this is nothing new. I've been thinking about making my move for years. I'm leaning toward California."

"Don't do it, man. Don't move."

"Why not?"

"'Cause everybody does that. I thought you were supposed to be different."

"I know. I hate that I want to be famous. Well—I don't want to be famous. I know I wouldn't get famous with this band. Or with my screenwriting. And it's not fame I want so much as the money. And I hate that I want the money so badly, but it would help my family and me so much, give us some breathing room. I can't get Sallie Mae off my back."

"Who's she?"

"It's a company. Sallie Mae is the student-loan company. I'm way behind on my payments."

"I could help you out."

"I wouldn't let you. I just need to make some changes. I'm not getting anywhere in Bashford."

"You're being serious right now, aren't ya?"

"I'm being *totally* serious. I'm devoting all this energy to the band and to my screenplays, but I'm never going to amount to anything as long as I'm here. I'll be a career substitute teacher."

"Ain't there anything here that makes you want to stay?"

"Sure there is. There are the people I care about. But you know how it is. What can I say?"

"I don't know. What *can* you say?"

"I'm dyin' here."

Blue Gene wished he hadn't made that call. Throughout all the sadness and frustration of the past week, he had always held Jackie Stepchild as the Miller Lite at the end of his tunnel. The family he had known was gone, but there was always the promise of a new family—not that he was hoping to impregnate the girl, but he had learned with Cheyenne that when two people love each other hard enough, a new sort of family springs up between them. And maybe Jackie would never be his; his expectations were low. But it was a nice thought. Even if they didn't end up together, the idea of her being in Bashford was comforting to Blue Gene. How bad could a place be if someone like Jackie Stepchild existed there? And here she was, raring to leave for someplace she thought would be better.

Then Blue Gene had an idea, one that he at first dismissed as stupid, but that ended up exciting him so much that he couldn't stop considering it, even after he went to bed. At eleven thirty-three, with a "what the hell," he threw off his sheets and found himself going down to the gift shop to buy a *Register*. He threw away all the sections except the classifieds, which he perused back in his room. Not finding what he was looking for, he grabbed the keys to his pickup and headed for Super Wal-Mart, where he walked into the vestibule, picked up a free real-estate magazine from the metal rack, and walked out. He scanned the magazine in his truck, still not finding anything that would suit his purpose.

When he returned to his hotel room, with Conan O'Brien on mute and the stereo playing Jackie's CD, he searched himself for possibilities. Downtown would be cool; he and Jackie both had an appreciation for its old-school feel. But so many of those buildings had residents upstairs who would complain about the noise. River Town Road was centrally located and had lots of big buildings, but which of them were vacant? He decided that the next day he would drive all over town and look for former businesses with FOR RENT or FOR SALE signs, because off the top of his head, he could think of only one empty building that was available for sure.

Then he realized there was no building in the world he'd rather own.

$ $ $

For the past year, the long building that had once contained the second Wal-Mart in Bashford's history had been just that: a building. Inside was one hundred thousand square feet of dirty white tile reaching across a sprawling expanse toward bare, mushroom-colored walls. There were no elderly greeters, no old friends from grade school running into each other, no everyday low prices, nothing. The doors were locked and not a soul came inside. Never. Fortunately for the consumers of Bashford and all surrounding counties, the abandonment of this Wal-Mart had occurred only because of the opening of an even larger one. Thus, the city's unofficial capitol was merely relocated and supersized, not permanently removed, which would be unthinkable.

It was a sad but familiar sight for motorists on Highway 81 to see that ghosts had so quickly established a new town at Bashford Commons, the shopping center for which Wal-Mart had been the anchor. The same thing had happened when Bashford's first Wal-Mart (now the Commonwealth County Flea Market) had closed in favor of this one. Bashford Commons had its business sucked out and spit up in the form of a new shopping center surrounding the Wal-Mart Supercenter on the edge of town, just as two decades ago it had sucked the business out of the Old Hickory Shopping Center, which had itself sucked the business out of Bashford's once thriving downtown. This shopping center, like all the rest, had it coming, and the cycle was continuing perfectly, allowing the city to grow and expand further and further away from its heart.

Ever since this Wal-Mart had closed last winter, no one had made the slightest move to put the emptied shopping center to use, unless you counted the old woman who lived in a station wagon that was always parked in the once flourishing lot. But then came the morning when Blue Gene Mapother woke up and wiped the slobber from his chin and the crust from his eyes and forced himself out of bed at 7:00 a.m. sharp. Overnight he had chosen a new business for himself, which he planned to treat as seriously as he had his previous jobs.

Herein lay another reason why his hibernation would have to be cut short: Blue Gene realized he was the type of person who *had* to work. Without work breaking up his schedule, the week had felt like a wasted, mashed-up dogpile of days. He didn't really like being around people, but after so many years of going out and earning a living, to simply lie back and relax atop a cushy mound of money would not do, especially since he had not earned that money.

He blew out his loose mucus—his cold was breaking—drank a cup of coffee, and drove over to Bashford Commons to see which realty company he should contact. Back in his hotel room, he placed a call at 8:00 a.m.

Though his deep, masculine voice never showed it, he did not go about this new endeavor with confidence. His wealth was still an unwieldy thing to him, and he wondered if he was using it incorrectly, swinging it at the realtor, and later the bank, to get what basically amounted to a one-hundred-thousand-square-foot empty gift box for a girl he had fallen for. But it wasn't just for her; he had so many happy memories in that building, back when things were still good with Cheyenne and people had just started looking at him in a different way with his impressively thick mustache. And maybe he and Jackie could really turn the place into something. You never could tell.

The realtor asked Blue Gene if he was messing with her. Here was an individual, representing only himself and not some corporation, who said he would like to buy the old Wal-Mart building. Immediately.

"Don't you want to *see* it?"

"Nah. I seen every inch of it at some time or 'nother."

"Who *is* this?"

"Name's Mapother."

$ $ $

Until one Saturday afternoon in September, the pedestrian crossings in front of the old Wal-Mart building at Bashford Commons had gone untouched for the past year, except by precipitation and the indifferent white splatters of bird droppings. Now Blue Gene and Jackie walked across the yellow slanted lines to the front entrance. Hot as it ever was, they both had T-shirts on, Blue Gene wearing a plain black one with the sleeves cut off, Jackie in a homemade one that said, YOU CAN TRUST ME in iron-on letters.

"Why'd you want to meet *here*?" she asked. Her hair was oily and messy and was the way Blue Gene liked most so far.

"You'll see. Hey, over there's where me and my friends used to bring our trucks out to see who had the loudest pipes." Blue Gene pointed across the parking lot.

"Why?"

"Nothin' else to do, I reckon." He paused at the entrance. Jackie cupped her hands and peeked into the window. He couldn't help but grin as he pulled a set of keys out of his denim shorts.

"What are you up to?" Jackie asked. "I've never seen you smiling so much."

He turned his back to Jackie and put the key in the front door.

"What are you doing?"

He swung the door open, held it with his leg, and gallantly motioned for her to enter. Jackie gave him a puzzled smile before covering it with her hands.

"I told you I'd be lookin' for a new place to stay soon. Here it is."

"You *bought* it?"

"Yeah. It ain't official yet. I gotta sign some papers at the bank next week. But yeah, it's mine."

Jackie playfully hit Blue Gene on the chest, as if to say, "Get *out*!" Her pimpled face showed childlike amazement. She hesitantly entered the building. Blue Gene followed. He had turned all the lights on in advance so she would feel the full effect of the enormous empty space.

"*How*?" she asked, slowly spinning herself around as she looked up at the ceiling.

"I come into some money here lately. I finally decided to collect on my inheritance."

"I've never even heard you *mention* your inheritance."

"My folks always taught me never to talk about money."

"How long have you had it coming to you?"

"All my life, I reckon."

"And you spent it on an old Wal-Mart building?"

"Not *all* of it. My granddad was filthy rich. I ain't spent but the tip of the iceberg on this place."

"So you're going to *live* here?"

"Well, hell yeah."

"That's *awesome*."

"I thought so, too."

"I mean, who else would do this with their money?" Blue Gene leaned against the railing where the shopping carts had once been kept.

He watched Jackie look around. "It's so wide open, it makes me want to run," she said.

"Well run, then."

She ran across the center of the room, across the two huge squares of carpets where the men's and women's clothing departments had once been. "Echo!" she screamed. Blue Gene laughed. She swung around one of the many poles that ran from floor to ceiling. One of them she tried climbing. Then she walked back toward the front. "You could have some *really* cool parties here," she said, her brown eyes wide.

"Yeah." He tried to play it cool, nodding casually and looking up at the black sphere halves that were placed throughout the ceiling. The spheres had once had cameras inside them. "Actually, I's thinkin' maybe I could put on some shows here."

"*Really?*"

"Yeah. You think Uncle Sam's Finger'd be interested in playin' here?"

"Yes! That'd be awesome. I've even written a song about Wal-Mart."

"I's thinkin' I could have a stage built over yonder," Blue Gene pointed to the back wall, "and we'd turn it into an actual club or whatever where bands could play."

Jackie suddenly looked concerned. "You really want to do that?"

"It's just an idea. I's just thinking about what you said about the young people not having anything to do around here, and this big building was just sittin' here, being wasted. So I thought maybe I could do something with it. Put it to use. What? Do you think it's a bad idea?"

"No, no. I think it's a wonderful idea."

They both looked around. There was at once a lot and nothing at all to see.

"I bought it for nostalgia, too, though. Like those marks right there where you're standing—that's where customer service used to be. There was this dude they always had working customer service named Crit, and he'd always be tryin' to get you to buy firewood—like, every time you saw him, he'd ask you about it. And over there is where I'd take my smoke breaks." He pointed to the café area off to the side that still had black-and-white square tiles on the floor.

"This is so cool. I'm seeing so many possibilities."

"I know. It's really big for a club, so I's thinking I could have other stuff, too. Like I's thinking I could put a wrestling ring up, and we could have wrestling shows here on occasion. But the main thing would be that we'd have bands play here."

"It would be an all-ages club, right?"

"Oh, yeah. Because it's to make kids feel like something's actually going on in Bashford."

"I love it!" Jackie ran over and hugged Blue Gene briefly. He tried to absorb the feel of her as much as he could. She felt straight and sharp. "This is great. It'll be a place for all the shy people to get together and scream in."

Blue Gene nodded.

"Also, though, Jackie, since you know more about this stuff than me, and since you know of other bands around here, I was wondering if you'd wanna be, like, the manager or whatever? The one in charge of puttin' the shows together?"

"Don't *you* want to do that?"

"No. I don't got the mind for that. I think I'll just work mainte-nance." Jackie laughed. "I'm serious. I tend to prefer physical work. I like jobs where I don't have to think."

"Be careful not to slip into a coma."

Blue Gene guffawed. "I'll pay you for managing it, by the way."

"Oh, no. You don't have to do that."

"No, now, you're always bitchin' about money. Now here I am, offer-ing you a good-paying job, and you won't even take it?"

"Well, okay, but you don't have to pay me much, though. When's the first show?"

"Soon as you can put one together."

"I used to could throw a show together at one of the park shelters in a week. But wait—we'll need to get a business license, because at the shelters we weren't supposed to charge money at the door. If the cops showed up, we'd put up a sign that said, DONATIONS ACCEPTED. We should really get a license for here, though."

"I wasn't plannin' on chargin' at all, actually. I was thinking every show could be free."

"Really?"

"Yeah. Why not? I thought you'd like that."

"I do, but the bands won't be happy about that. Especially if we get out-of-town bands that are touring."

"I'll pay 'em out of my own pocket."

"You would do that?"

"Yeah."

She gave him the "oh my God" look he had been hoping for. "Wow." Jackie smiled and covered her mouth. "This is so *exciting*. I get so sick of this town, but it's people like you that make me want to stay."

Blue Gene smiled. "Keep talkin', mama," he said.

Jackie laughed. "Seriously, there aren't many like you, but every once in a while I'll meet someone that makes Bashford special. Like that old man who always sits up front at Denny's. Every time he sees me, he asks me if he can touch my hair, and then he tells me he loves my hair because it's soft like a dog."

Blue Gene's mood plummeted as he was being compared to an autistic old man who petted people.

"And that's what's cool about small towns," she continued. "They produce genuine eccentrics, not run-of-the-mill artsy types or hipsters or people being different just for the sake of being different. One of a kinds. That's what you seem to be. I mean, I've seen people reject materialism, but you reject it with a *vengeance*."

"That ain't even true. I collect guns. I love cars."

"But still, most of the time when young people rebel, they, you know, go the freak route or get into weird music, like me. Like, look at this." Jackie pointed at herself, at her ripped jeans and Chuck Taylors. "This is so typical. I'm a dime a dozen. But you, you chose to become something that is so *not* cool or hip or trendy or even visually appealing. You—"

"Hey!"

"But that's good! You found something original."

Blue Gene sighed. "A'ight then."

"What?"

"Nothin.'"

"No. You look pissed."

"I ain't stupid, you know. I might look it, but I ain't."

"I didn't say you were."

"Yeah, but you talk about me like I don't see the humor in anything."

"I didn't say that."

"That's just the feeling I got, and you oughta know that I see the humor in my situation. I'm not stupid."

"Okay. I didn't mean anything. I'm sorry."

"That's okay. I need to smoke a Parlie." He started out the door but immediately came back and lit up inside. "Hope you don't mind," he said, holding up his cigarette.

"Not at all. It's your building."

"That's what I was thinking. But yeah, anyway, like, one time I's down by the river, and they had some Civil War reenactment goin' on there, and I's just there to watch, but this little boy come up to me, and he saw me with my hair and 'stache and my ragged clothes, and he asked me when the next battle was, and I said I didn't know, ask one of the soldiers, and he said, 'You mean *you're* not a soldier?'" Jackie laughed. "And I laughed. I see the humor in it. Don't think that I don't."

"Okay. I'll remember that. I'm glad you told me that."

"A'ight."

"So what do we do first?" She was always switching subjects.

"Well, first we gotta paint the outside of the building, and we also gotta knock that vestibule out."

"Why?"

"It's policy. They got a lot of policies I had to agree to. They wouldn't have even let me buy it, 'cept I made it clear I wasn't a retailer at all."

Blue Gene explained that the realtor had contacted the man who owned the land that this Wal-Mart was on and told him the surprising news that someone wanted to buy the building outright. This required that Wal-Mart's lease be terminated, and, as was the custom when a new establishment moved into a former Wal-Mart building, Wal-Mart's corporate office demanded that the building be painted so that it would not resemble its former identity. Blue Gene agreed to the company's demands without hesitation. He had several old friends who would get a kick out of painting the old Wal-Mart building, and they were always looking for work.

He could pay them well.

PART THREE

X.

After a stern pep talk from his father and an uplifting homily from his mother, John Hurstbourne Mapother made the decision that he would not shrink away from life. For an entire day after the cell phone accident, he had hardly separated himself from his bedsheets, but his parents reminded him that he had a job and—more important—a campaign on which to focus. His personal crisis would have to be cast off to contend with on some future date. For now, there was nothing anyone could do to improve the Blue Gene situation. Henry told John how Blue Gene had made it resoundingly clear that he didn't want to speak to his family, and John was relieved he wouldn't have to confront him. He was also relieved that at least Blue Gene now had the funds to choose any avenue of life he so desired, and maybe it would be good for him to leave Bashford for a while. Furthermore, as Elizabeth said, the revelation, as untimely as it had been, was God's will. So Henry, Elizabeth, and John agreed that at least until the campaign was over, the best thing to do would be to go on like nothing had ever happened, which was precisely what they had always done.

But when John returned to work, as he tried to smile and stand up straight through the obligations of a dismal Thursday, he couldn't help but feel like a well-dressed wretch whose madman soul was suffering convulsions. Just the day before last, he had sat in his office, daydreaming about staying in some charming old New Hampshire hotel for a primary that he would one day win, and how he and the whole family, even

Blue Gene, would vacation on Martha's Vineyard once he ascended to power. Today, he obsessively pictured Blue Gene lying shirtless and shoeless in the back of some old police car, covered in the acidic remnants of his own dinner. Disturbing images like this continued to fester within John on his nervous drive home from work, and everything around him took on the grimmest connotations. The trees turned to phallic symbols stabbing at the sky. All the flags flying half-mast looked as if they were drooping in shame.

That night, when Elizabeth called John, she could immediately hear the drink in his voice. He angrily denied it and then criticized her for being off on some mission trip when he had needed her the most. She apologized and said she had taken the first flight back as soon as she'd heard what had happened. He said it didn't matter now anyway, and to leave him alone, and that he hated all people.

$ $ $

When Henry and Elizabeth arrived at John's house, Abby told them they would have to take care of John, because she and John had agreed that if one of them ever had another episode, the sober parent would keep Arthur away. Abby and Arthur would be staying the night at her mother's house and come back once John was sober. Arthur's face was puffy and pink, and he wouldn't let go of his mother's thigh.

"It's okay, Arthur," said Elizabeth, leaning over her grandson in the white marble foyer.

"It doesn't even sound like Dad," Arthur said.

"Oh, I know, sweetheart," said Elizabeth. "It's *not* him. But everything will be fine. Don't be scared."

"John's more scared than Arthur," said Abby, tossing back her long, straight blond hair.

"What's he scared of?" asked Henry.

"You."

"Daddy *is not* scared," Arthur said in between sniffles. "He's not scared of anything. One time he saw a tornado, and he just *laughed* at it."

Everyone enjoyed this, except for Arthur, whose face crinkled as they laughed. After hugging Arthur goodbye, Henry and Elizabeth called for their son, but he didn't answer. They found him in the basement, leaning against the pool table, wearing a gray sport coat over a white undershirt.

"Hi, John," said Elizabeth.

"Hi." One of his arms was inside the bottom front pocket of his coat, clutching something.

"Does he have a gun?" Elizabeth quietly asked Henry.

"What are you up to?" asked Henry, cautiously walking across the spacious, cream-carpeted basement.

"Nothing." John walked away from his father and stood close to a Galaga arcade machine in the corner. He tried to be still, but he couldn't stop swaying. He had a strange, almost scary smile, and there was a quizzical slant to his perfect eyebrows.

"How much have you had to drink tonight?" asked Henry.

"None at all."

"Do you think we're that stupid? You're not fooling anyone. Now is a hell of a time for you to get weak on us, fifty-four days before the election."

"He had been doing so well," said Elizabeth.

"Yes. Until Eugene came along. I told you you shouldn't have included him."

"Uh-huh," said John. He still wouldn't take his hand from inside his front pocket.

"Who is that you're listening to, John?" asked Elizabeth.

"I don't know."

"It's Peggy Lee," said Henry.

"I didn't know you liked that type of music," said Elizabeth.

"I like everything Dad likes." He spoke carefully, as though his parents were just waiting for him to mess up a word.

"She performed at the Ambassador Inn," said Elizabeth. "Ages ago."

Inappropriately, John laughed and nodded. The song ended. He slowly made his way to the stereo and made it repeat the song "Is That All There Is?" As he leaned down to do so, his sport coat started dripping. He then leaned against a wall covered in baseball pennants as a wet spot spread across his front.

"Do you have a drink in your pocket?" asked Henry.

"No."

"You clearly do, though."

Henry and Elizabeth stared at the wet spot. John laughed and took a half-empty glass out from his coat. A clear tumbler with no lid, it contained a light-gold liquid with lots of ice.

"Oh, John," said Elizabeth.

"What can I tell you? I always did like to hear those ice cubes ring."

$ $ $

They couldn't make him go back to Hazelden; word might leak. After a long talk the next morning, it was decided that John and Abby would take Arthur out of school for a week—which thrilled Arthur—and the three of them would have something of a vacation out at the family cabin on Lake Cobalt. Henry would stay behind to watch over the campaign; he and Elizabeth would have to represent the family at the fifty-dollar-a-plate Autumn Dinner Dance that Saturday night.

At first, this plan seemed to work. John was able to relax, even without the aid of chemicals. Friday night, he and Abby watched the Disney version of *Tarzan* with Arthur, and the next morning he taught Arthur how to shoot free throws on a basketball goal on their private drive.

But Saturday afternoon, John disappeared. At two in the afternoon, he said he was going hunting. When he had not returned by eight, Abby could no longer contain her panic and called John's parents.

As it turned out, John had gone out to the woods without a shotgun, wearing black slacks and a white T-shirt. He spent most of the afternoon searching deep within the forest, not for wildlife, but for the precise spot where his father had sat him down so many years ago to tell him of his mother's prophecy. Once he found the spot that felt right, he got on his knees and prayed aloud, feverishly repeating himself as darkness overtook the forest.

"Heavenly Father, please hold me in your arms. Protect me from myself and uncloud my mind. Forgive me, oh Lord, for all that I've done. It was what I saw. It was too much, too soon, but this blight I alone have created. Please let me be born again again. Almighty God, I pledge myself your homunculus. I am your dust. I kneel on a spot where a great dinosaur once may have stood. I am as transitory as any of them, but I am told I am special dust, for you gave my mother true vision, as you did Joseph before her. But why, dear Lord, why did you let the truth out? Why now? Have we lost our way? In the end will we have to pry the cellular phones from our stiff, dead hands? Please forgive my trespasses. Please show me the way. God, I wish I knew where you were right now. It is right to give you thanks and praise, but why can't you give us your coordinates? Please let my heart be pure. I'm so sorry I fell back into the demon drink. I vow it will have been the last time. Please let the sirens stop calling, and if they must continue, give me strength to ignore them. Soothe my nerves with your loving hands. Please help me with my family. Please help me with Blue Gene. Please don't let this change anything. I accept my destiny the same as I ever did. Whoever is awaiting the apotheosis, I will clear the way for him, the greatest man who will have ever lived. I will drive a wedge between the harlots of power. And if a Californium bullet should strike me down, or whatever Mother's most recent premonition means should indeed come to pass, all I ask is that you allow this bullet to contain the meaning of this realm of consciousness so that I might receive your knowledge in my last moment, so that I might perish with a smile upon this face that I alone know is actually quite hideous. Please show me the way back. Please let me fulfill the plan and lead the people of the antebellum. Please forgive them. Oh, God, don't you know I'm trying? I'm trying! And if I am the one to bring the death of afternoon, please let the final twilight be one of your supreme grace. Dear Lord, watch over my family, and please favor our undertakings. Give us the strength and wisdom necessary to establish a new order for the ages."

John stopped only when he heard a noise behind him, stirring in the grass. He turned around. In the moonlight, he could see the outline of a great figure lurking with what was either eerie calmness or predatory menace. It appeared to be human, except for its head, which was bulky, angular, and robotic. The figure now stood still as death. Terrified, John thought about the angel that had once sat on his mother's windowsill. He told himself to be not afraid.

"Who are you?" John gasped.

"Shit," said the figure. "I hoped you wouldn't hear me so you'd keep talkin'. I liked all that you was sayin'."

"Is that *Josh Balsam*?"

"Yeah." Balsam came closer. He was wearing all camouflage and a helmet mounted with night-vision goggles, which he now removed. "I don't know what all you was sayin' just then, but that's why I liked you in the first place, 'cause you just talk like nobody I know of. Around here, at least."

"What are you *doing* here?" John asked as he arose from kneeling.

"Your dad called me. Said he needed somebody to find you out here. He and your mom's at some dance and they're all freakin' out, wonderin' what happened to you. Thought you was dead or God knows what."

"I was just praying." John brushed the knees of his pant legs. "Anything you heard me talking about just then—I'd appreciate it if you would never repeat to anyone."

"See, I wouldn't do that, though, Mr. Mapother. That's why your dad said he wanted me to hunt you up in the first place. Said he had no idea what kind of shape you'd be in if I found you, but said he thought y'all could trust me. And you can. I wanna help y'all out all I can."

"Thank you," said John, brushing his pant legs one more time before shaking hands with the brick-fisted hulk of a boy. "Thanks for coming all this way to find me. I needed to talk to God, and I thought He could hear me better out here. But I'm done now. Let's go back."

Balsam and John began walking through the labyrinth of trees. "Be careful," said Balsam, putting his helmet back on. "Land mines could be anywhere."

"*Land mines?*"

"Yeah. Dog shit. Stepped in some earlier." John laughed. "Blue Gene said you was pissed 'cause I got into it with those foreign motherfuckers at the wrestling match."

"Don't pay any attention to what Blue Gene said. I'm not mad at you."

"Where's he tonight?"

"I don't know. We haven't been seeing eye to eye lately. He's actually quit the campaign altogether."

"Shit. Let me take his place."

"We'd be proud to have you, Josh."

"It ain't like me, helpin' out with some politician like this, but—"

"I am not a politician. I'm a political agent for the Lord."

"Yeah. That's what I'm sayin'. You ain't just anybody, 'cause you actually stand for something. I still got the Blood Flag. It goes with me everywhere I go."

"You earned it."

"No. My father earned it. I'll earn it someday. Don't know how, but I will. Army was my only shot at gettin' out of fuckin' Bashford."

"I think you're right where God wants you to be. If you were in the war, right now you'd probably be teaching some foreign soldiers how to march. Instead, God sent you to me. I think the campaign needs you worse than some foreign country does, because this is a campaign for America. I think we're both exactly where God wants us to be. You do believe in God, don't you?"

"You must not have seen my cross tattoo."

$ $ $

John returned home in mid-September, but Henry told him it would be for the best if he kept a low profile, considering his erratic behavior the week before. The campaign was now in full swing, and Henry had become John's de facto spokesman, which ended up having its benefits. Henry was able to make statements of fatherly pride that might have come across as arrogant had John said them. For instance, the elder Mapother regularly told reporters that his son had always been destined for greatness and challenged them to find any other rising political star who, as a baby boy, had received a kiss on the forehead from both Nixon and Johnson. It made for an impressive sound bite.

Henry also used his status as CEO of Westway to appeal to the many smokers of the district, telling several reporters that he would make it a personal priority to push for a ballot referendum that would allow voters to reverse the smoking ban currently enforced in all public buildings. He failed to mention that it was already too late to include such an initiative on the November ballot.

That John wasn't out politicking himself seemed not to matter so much for the time being, as the machinery of the campaign was unstoppable at this point, completely wound up and grinding away on its own, grating on the public's nerves every hour of the day, giving rise to an oft-repeated complaint: "I sure will be glad when this election is over so they'll all shut up." TV spots from both Mapother and Grant Frick were now guaranteed to appear during what felt like every commercial break on what felt like every channel. The latest Mapother commercials had been filmed in the summer but were just now appearing, each one with a more highly buffed Madison Avenue veneer than the last. Henry had hired astoundingly expensive advertising wizards to weave their nuanced market targeting in hopes of catching the average viewer. The latest thirty-second spot showed overall-wearing bums smiling hopefully while a gospel choir sang "This Little Light of Mine."

The onslaught was altogether inescapable. Both Mapother and Frick bumper stickers, yard signs, and even billboards were seen by anyone who went anywhere. The Mapothers' latest innovation was to display a huge sign in the bed of a pickup and park it near the busiest intersections of all the towns of the district. Also, all the Sunday papers contained a quarter-page ad with a Fourth of July photo of the Mapothers—including Blue Gene—smiling away in front of the fireworks.

But most important, John's numbers were holding up. A phone canvassing showed that with only thirty-two days until election, John's lead over Frick had solidified into fifteen points. Thanks to John and Blue Gene's hard work throughout the summer, John's constituents no longer saw him as some snooty, heartless bigwig. At worst, they saw him as effete but electable. At best, they now saw him as one of the guys. Just better.

John's campaign manager warned him, though, that because of his ever-surmounting lead, his opponent was likely to resort to the most tried-and-true practice in all of politics: he would try to put John on the defensive. Grant Frick's people had undoubtedly already done opposition research on John as soon as he entered the race, which was precisely why John had gone out of his way to divulge his sordid past in his Fourth of July speech. But now all Frick could do to even put up a fight was to have his team work the oppo angle, which was even more likely to happen in the last month, since thus far, both teams had run surprisingly clean campaigns.

Therefore, the Mapother team in particular had to do everything *right* up through November 2. John vowed to his father that any alcoholic slip-ups or anxiety-induced flip-outs were out of his system now, and that he had regained his balance out in the woods with the help of God. As long as Blue Gene would remain quiet, there wouldn't be a clot of mud available for Frick to sling.

$ $ $

The respite from the campaign was good for John. When reflecting on this monumental effort that had seen him running for office for the first time, he imagined himself literally running with blistered feet through a marathon that had actually begun more than a year before, when Frick's sex scandal had broken and it was decided that it was time for John to start. Since then he had sweated through the process of becoming a public figure, jogged through his Fourth of July rally after nearly tripping over the hurdle of onstage humiliation, and chafed through door-to-doors and meet-and-greets. With Election Day in a month, the finish was in sight, though he knew only longer, tougher races would be ahead in what was destined to be a long career in governing.

During this short break from all the running, when he wasn't compensating for the previous night's insomnia by taking naps, John was trying to spend as much time as possible with Arthur. Strangely enough, Arthur's favorite thing to do didn't cost a dime. There was no other way he liked to spend an afternoon more than going to the airport and watching the planes take off. Bashford had only a small airport for private planes, so one day in late September, John took Arthur to the regional airport in Donato Falls, something they hadn't done together since the campaign had started.

John didn't watch the planes himself; he watched Arthur's wonder-struck face as each jet took off. He prayed to God in heaven that this child would never grow up.

"Arthur, I have to ask you something. I don't want to ask you, but I have to."

"What?" Arthur was taking giant sips from a large Sprite that he held with both hands. John took the cup from him and set it on the floor.

"Do you know where babies come from?"

Arthur looked away from the panoramic window and into his father's eyes. "Birds?"

"Sure. Yes. Birds. Actually, there's more to it than that, but you'll learn soon enough, I suppose. But I do want to tell you one thing, and it's what my dad told me. I know this is going to sound weird, but just let me say it, and I'll be done." John cleared his throat and looked around to see if anyone was watching him. Then he pointed to his crotch. "This thing is a lot like a gun."

Arthur laughed. He looked down at his feet, which he often complained were not growing fast enough. He was small for his age.

"I know it sounds funny, but I'm being serious. You know how I've talked to you about the guns we have at home, how they're dangerous?" Arthur nodded. "And this, it's like a gun because it's also a very dangerous thing."

"Because of the pee?"

"Well, no. There's more to it. Just listen. A gun is very dangerous because it has the potential to *take* life from someone. A penis—" Arthur giggled at the word. "Listen. I'm serious. Your manhood is very dangerous because it has the potential to *give* life to someone. Do you understand that at all?"

"Pee gives life?"

"No." John looked up at the ceiling and tried to get his neck to pop. "The important thing I guess I'm trying to say here is that you always have to use this thing carefully, just like you would a gun. If you go around using it carelessly, you'll end up creating a life, and that's a serious thing. That's a serious power that we men have."

Arthur nodded.

"So always, for the rest of your life, be careful where you shoot your gun. It's an extremely serious and powerful thing. Okay?"

"Okay."

"Okay" was all Arthur gave him, but the look spread across the baby-fat face seemed just serious and thoughtful enough to let John know that he understood the importance of what was being said. Henry had used the same metaphor with John the day the paternity test came back. John never forgot it. He was sitting on the floor of his bedroom, organizing his basketball cards across the carpet, when Henry came in and told him he would be a father at the age of thirteen. He wanted to cry but knew not to, and any tears that might have materialized did not once Henry started in with his gun speech. John had always considered the gun speech an effective analogy, but it had left him with one question for his father: what about *his* gun?

But John never asked this question, because doing so might have disrupted a bond that developed between him and his father. For the rest of their lives, they would be like two coworkers slaving off a payment for similar sins, one for his precocious experiments with a child, one for his shadowy lust for the help. Each man would allow the other his one life-changing mistake, because they needed the other's support in the face of the mother and wife who had every right to make them pay hell.

By the time Arthur returned his attention to the airplanes, John already regretted repeating his father's gun speech. First of all, it was nothing that had any place in the skull of a five-year-old. More important, what if it caused Arthur to start asking questions? John cringed at the thought of Arthur knowing about what he had done. Yet he had spoken out of the hope that this be the one son who didn't repeat his father's sins.

John realized he was sweating at the hairline. He prayed that Arthur would never find out, that Blue Gene would never tell anyone, and that the public would never know anything about it, because the kids at school would tell Arthur and tease him relentlessly. As he prayed repetitively that everything would stay the same, his heart pounded and his face turned red. And to think, someone in this condition was scheduled to have a live televised debate in just three days.

$ $ $

They were in the newspaper, the changes. At first they weren't in the headlines, or even in the articles explicitly, but they were in there, almost subliminal. If you bowed your head and took a deep breath of the newsprint, and if you had a mind to ask questions, you could tell there was something going on, something *off*. It started in the same issue of the *Register* in which an op-ed pundit speculated the reason John Hurstbourne Mapother had canceled his debate was that he was so far ahead in the polls that debating the more experienced Frick could only hurt him. On the back page of this section of the paper, there was a three-by-five-inch ad promoting a punk rock show on September 30, which in itself was unusual since the standard way for any garage band to advertise had always been to slap together a shoddy flyer, make copies at the convenience store, and tape flyers to storefront windows and utility poles. The names of the bands sounded typical enough (Constipation, the Ginsbergs, and Uncle Sam's Finger), but then there was the peculiar choice of venue: the former Wal-Mart building on Highway 81.

The day of the show, a brief feature ran on page A3 about this new club that would have free shows and be open to all ages. The person in charge was a young lady who insisted her last name was Stepchild, who also claimed to have bought the former retail building herself, even though in the same article she complained that she couldn't find anything to do with her master's degree in this area except be a substitute teacher. Alongside the article was a photo of a group of painters outside the former Wal-Mart, coloring the building a curious shade of pea green, and there was no trace of the WAL-MART letters, nor SATISFACTION GUARANTEED.

A couple of days later, a rare piece of good news popped up on A2, catty-corner from the Court Beat section: While playing outside the previous day, a little girl had found a shoebox containing a white envelope on which the words "Whoever finds this—it's yours" were written. Inside was five hundred dollars in cash. The girl had found the shoebox in the trailer court where she lived. It was left on top of a freestanding set of concrete steps.

Then a quarter-page ad for another show appeared, this one set for October 7, and this time the club had a name: the Commonwealth Building. Below this in parentheses was: "formerly the old Wal-Mart building." Again, the show was free and open to all ages.

The day after that, this time on the front page, there appeared a report of some more mystery money being discovered. An employee of the local Captain D's fast-food restaurant said that when he took out the garbage, just like he had done every night for the last six years, a miracle happened. When he went to reach for the big plastic lid of the Dumpster, he noticed that a white envelope with his name on it was sticking out. Inside the envelope was one thousand dollars in cash. There was no note. He said the money would allow him to have surgery on his back, which he had injured in a wrestling match this past summer.

Later that week, a half-page ad welcomed the public to the Commonwealth Building, simply stating that the venue was now: "FREE. Open to the public daily. Shelter, lodging, food, entertainment for all ages. Music, movies, games, etc. Bring your kids. Open twenty-four hours. Also—this Saturday—Live: Uncle Sam's Finger, the Decroded, and Filet Mignon and P-Bone. Free." Sure enough, speeding motorists on Highway 81 started noticing that the Bashford Commons parking lot, which by all rights should have been an asphalt void, was gradually starting to fill up with cars again.

In mid-October, John made his return to the public, speaking at a luncheon for the Bashford Chamber of Commerce, announcing a budgetary plan that he had titled "Drop Your Lowest Grade." Truth be told, he and his campaign manager had come up with the slogan first and adapted an economic plan to it later. Regardless, his announcement didn't even make the paper. The big news that day was the "mystery saint," as the paper now called him or her, who had left an envelope of three thousand dollars underneath the windshield wiper of a man who lived in one of the poorest parts of Bashford. Upon seeing this latest recipient's name, Henry called John to let him know that something might need to be done. It was a name they had seldom spoken in the last ten years, but it was one they had never been able to forget. That name was Darius Bledsoe, who openly wept before a TV camera that evening as he said, "Whoever did this—I *beep*-ing love you!"

$$$

The first person Henry called was Harold Campbell, CEO of the *Register*'s parent company, GFB, Inc., which had long had Henry on its board of directors. Henry asked his old associate to be on the lookout for any reports that came in involving his younger son, who went by Blue Gene.

Then Henry had John call Josh Balsam, who was now officially on the Mapother for Congress payroll, to assign him to a kind of reconnaissance mission at this Commonwealth Building. Later that afternoon, Campbell and Balsam gave Henry the same news, one saying that it appeared as though his son "had taken a sudden interest in philanthropy," the other saying that Blue Gene "was giving shit away like it was going out of style."

Explaining that his younger son was behaving so unpredictably, Henry asked Campbell not to run any stories on Blue Gene in any of his publications, at least until after the election. The CEO said that he would ask the publishers of the *Register* and all other area publications to neglect mentioning Blue Gene Mapother in any stories, and to make sure that no news regarding this young man went anywhere near the wires. However, Campbell added that honestly, it was a pretty incredible story and it would be hard to keep it from blowing up—even from going national—before long.

That night, Henry called for an emergency meeting at the campaign headquarters in the old JCPenney building. With the sleeves of their white dress shirts rolled up and Styrofoam coffee cups in hand, Henry, John, Mark (the bow-tied campaign manager), and two other campaign confidants took turns sitting and standing while anticipating damage control.

"But can't this reflect well on us?" asked John, checking the dampness of his armpits. "He's doing *good* for the community, right?"

"It *could* have reflected well on us," said the campaign manager, "but not if he no longer endorses you. Isn't there any way you can get him back?"

"I really don't think so," said John.

"But that would solve the problem right there. Just get him to come back on our side, and this shouldn't be a big deal. I mean, did you really have *that* big of a fight with him?"

"Yes," said Henry, his hawklike face tightening. "He won't speak to us."

"Have you tried speaking to *him*?"

"We've tried calling him, but we can't reach him."

"You said you sent that Balsam boy over there," said an elderly gentleman. "Was he able to find anything out?"

"He said that Eugene didn't even want to hear our name. But the good news is that there appears to be no political work at all in whatever he's doing. Balsam said there were a lot of young people there, and I was concerned about Eugene swinging the youth vote toward Frick. But apparently he won't even talk about the campaign at all."

"Twenty days till the election," said the old man. "Maybe he won't say or do anything that would come back on John."

"But Frick will spin it any way he can," said the campaign manager. "The *contrast* is what he'll probably go for. The problem is that the brother *not* running for office looks like a hero, and the brother who *is* running looks like he's standing off to the side, doing nothing. One lays people off; the other provides well-paying jobs. And then the obvious question on everyone's mind is: how can he afford to do this? It's his family fortune. How does his family fit in? Frick will try to make everyone see you as these rich corporate tyrants, and Blue Gene—he's like Robin Hood, giving your money away. It's the contrast that'll get us. And then if they find out he's estranged from you, that could be big trouble."

For the next hour, they all put their heads together and came up with a statement for John, should he be asked anything about Blue Gene at press conferences or stump speeches between now and Election Day. Henry made him memorize it then and there. They rehearsed until 1:00 a.m.:

> "Actually, it was my little brother's involvement with my campaign that gave him a social conscience in the first place. Before he worked on the Mapother campaign, Blue Gene was interested in little more than pro wrestling and monster trucks. He's told me that *my* cause awakened him to a new life of possibilities, and I will have the same effect on my constituents once I'm in the Capitol."

When asked the obvious question of "Then why won't Blue Gene have anything to do with your campaign anymore?" John memorized another statement:

> "It was my idea. When my little brother told me of this great idea to turn an abandoned, unused property into a refuge for the youth and the less fortunate of Bashford, I told him it was a great idea. But I said in order for it to succeed, he needed to stop working for me. I said that if he did this wonderful thing for the community and he was campaigning at the same time, it wouldn't feel as pure. So I told him to devote himself wholly to this project, which is exactly what he's done. I'm proud to call Blue Gene Mapother my brother."

$$\$ \ \$ \ \$$

Initially, thanks to Henry's behind-the-scenes connections, the area newspapers did not cover what the Commonwealth Building was doing for the community of Bashford, or the person truly responsible for its being established. But the Mapothers quickly saw that the internet would not so easily suppress such an unusual human-interest story, as random blogs began to appear, most of them teenagers telling one another they had found a new hangout. Then a TV report appeared on one of Donato Falls' three affiliate stations, which someone posted on YouTube. The blogs and the report exposed Blue Gene Mapother as the man behind the Commonwealth Building, though the proprietor himself was never quoted or on camera.

That Blue Gene completely rejected the attention only made people more curious. When reporters couldn't get the man himself to grant them an interview, they easily found alternatives in the townspeople, who saw an opportunity to contribute to a news story for the first time in their lives. Luckily, everyone had mostly positive things to say about

Blue Gene. Such was the case with his former boss at the very Wal-Mart building Blue Gene now owned.

"When I hired him I asked if he was any kin to the Mapothers that owned the tobacco company, and he said no. But then it came out that he *was* one of those Mapothers, and he told me he didn't want any special treatment, and if anything, he wanted me to work him *twice* as hard as I did anyone else. I offered him a promotion three times through the years, but he never would take one. Best worker I ever had."

The strangest tidbit came from a blogger whose older sister had gone to County High with Blue Gene.

"My sister says she remembers him being all snobby and preppy until he got in a fight or car accident or something and got hit in the head so many times that it caused brain damage, and that's why he completely lost interest in money and started acting like he was poor. Which I guess explains why he's doing all this, giving away free meals and stuff."

The news of Blue Gene's altruism started to spread, and in the third week of October, Grant Frick started giving aggressive stump speeches inside and outside every evangelical church he could find throughout the twenty-one counties of the district. He told these crowds that in case they hadn't heard about it, there was this *wonderful* building the Mapothers had set up in Bashford, a sort of teen hangout/shelter for the less fortunate. They may have heard it was a good place, a place of charity and good Christian values, a regular YMCA. But Frick assured these audiences that this "Commonwealth Building," as they called it, was not the utopian establishment the Mapothers would have people believe. Frick said that he had seen the inside of the building with his very own eyes, and in truth, he had never seen such a sordid den of debauchery.

Every speech was the same. After explaining that the Mapothers' new venture amounted to little more than a safe haven for depravity—drugs, alcohol, sex, and perhaps even homosexual orgies—he went on to remind the voters of the moralistic slant that John Hurstbourne Mapother had been using in his public appearances and TV ads. He never bothered mentioning that it was only one Mapother, the one uninvolved in politics, who even had any affiliation with the building. He concluded his speeches by suggesting that if Mapother was to win, this sort of wholesale hedonism was what could be expected all over the state. "Don't let his talk of faith and family fool you," Frick would say. "Mapother only stood for money, and his money would bring us all down like it was doing with those people in the Commonwealth Building. After all, the Mapothers didn't become the richest family around through their goodness."

With Frick's inflammatory accusations suddenly heating up an otherwise uneventful campaign season, the local papers could no longer ignore the possibly good/possibly bad deeds of one Blue Gene Mapother. Reporters started seeking John's response. He rebutted with cries of "lies and conjecture." But now the word *alleged* began to appear regularly in the same sentence as his last name. Some poll points had already been shaved from John's lead. Whether these accusations concerning Blue Gene's new venture were true or not, everyone in the Mapother camp agreed that the building would need to be either under heavy surveillance or shut down completely.

But before the Mapothers could even decide how to go about handling this, two men were arrested at the Commonwealth Building for distributing a controlled substance to minors. A TV crew was on the scene before Henry could even make a single phone call. After he saw the report, he called Oral Haynes and asked him with fiery politeness to please never arrest anyone at his son's place of business again. Haynes explained that it wasn't that simple, that he had been getting several complaints about the Commonwealth Building in the last day or two, complaints that he had originally intended to ignore, until it was brought to his attention that some guys were selling drugs to kids there, which he just couldn't allow in his jurisdiction. The conversation concluded with the police chief saying he'd turn a blind eye as much as possible, but that Mr. Mapother really should consider asking his son to close this place before something worse happened. Meanwhile, Frick was already giving gloating speeches and press statements that told voters that this was the sort of thing they could expect if a Mapother was given power over the people: the reckless throwing around of money for the sake of undermining their values.

The very next day, Elizabeth was sent to the old Wal-Mart building. It was agreed that Blue Gene probably hated her the least.

$$$

Elizabeth was having trouble finding a parking space Saturday afternoon, weaving her Lexus up one row and down the next, finally settling for a space in the back between a beat-up Ford Escort and a pristine Harley-Davidson. When she checked her makeup in the rearview, she caught a peripheral glimpse of a vehicle she knew. She removed her petite self from her formidable SUV to take a better look. As she had thought, it was Gene's truck, but she was surprised to see that the white lettering (110% BAD-ASS) across the top of the windshield was gone. Elizabeth had winced every time she had seen this message in her driveway this past summer. Only after moving out, of course, had he removed it.

She pressed the button that locked her Lexus, causing it to chirp attentively as always, and she wished she had worn something more comfortable than her black high heels as she began the trek across the parking lot. Curiously, there were no signs of any kind on the building. Toward the front of the row she had parked in, close to the pedestrian crossing, a tailgate party was in full swing, with seven rednecks holding cans of Coors Light and shouting at each other over a country song blasting from the truck's interior. She saw there was no way to avoid the young hellions, so she smiled as she passed and mouthed "hello." A couple of the boys smiled back and nodded, and that was the extent of their encounter. She couldn't blame them for wanting to be outside; it was finally starting to get cooler. It had even been raining off and on a bit since the middle of September, which was a great relief to this parched region.

As she reached the pedestrian crossing, the romantic sound of a saxophone was pushing its way through the country music. An older black man wearing a beret was playing in front of the building, between its entrance to the right and exit on the left. Elizabeth recognized the song as Gershwin's "Rhapsody in Blue."

The sax player reminded her of how Gene had always loved hearing street musicians when the family used to go on vacations to big cities like New York or Chicago. He would ask why they didn't have music outside like this in Bashford, to which Henry would reply that it was good that Bashford had no street musicians, as they were a reflection of the city's poverty.

Inevitably, Gene would then ask his parents for a dollar to give the musician. Henry would always say no; Elizabeth would always say yes. Like Gene, she loved hearing music out in the street. It made a city feel more human, the melody reaching out and reminding people there was more to life than buildings. Her favorite memory of New York City, where she had attended college, was a man on a crowded subway who serenaded all the rush-hour commuters with Louis Armstrong's "What a Wonderful World."

If God was Elizabeth's first love, music was her second. By the time she was thirteen, she was already a cantor at her church. In high school she sang "Camelot" in a talent show and won. And she still remembered the precise moment when, in her lonesome dormitory, she fell in love with the saccharine rasp of John Lennon's vocals. It was the same moment she realized she wanted to devote the rest of her life to singing.

With a serious, focused look, the sax player nodded at Elizabeth as she passed. She smiled and looked for the hat or case at his feet to see if he had accumulated many donations this afternoon, but there was nothing down there but his faded wingtips.

The front doors to the saxophonist's right were propped open with wedges of wood. Above the doors was a cardboard sign that said No MEDIA ALLOWED, written in black marker. Elizabeth entered. Her first surprise was the lighting. True, she had not been a loyal patron of Wal-Mart through the years, but she had been there enough to know that it, like all other retail stores, had always been ultra-brightly lit. Here, that sharp, fluorescent vividness had been replaced with much softer lighting, on the verge of being dim, dark enough that her Cartier sunglasses would have no place inside.

The entrance area was no longer partitioned; the second set of doors had been completely removed. As she placed her sunglasses in her black Louis Vuitton city bag, Elizabeth heard a voice from her past.

"Hidey, Mrs. Mapother."

The face was almost unrecognizable, much older and thinner than she remembered, and the tubes running from the nose were distracting, but unmistakable was the tired, warm voice that sounded far removed from any semblance of gentility. Elizabeth forced a smile.

"Hello, Bernice."

Wearing a colorful floral pantsuit, Bernice stood from her folding beach chair with a painful "oh." She offered a prune-lipped smile. "It's been years, ain't it?" she asked.

"It has." Elizabeth couldn't look at Bernice in the eye as she envisioned herself and Henry burning her letters. "How have you been?"

"Oh, I've actually been doin' a little better here lately. How 'bout you?"

"Fine, thank you. I've thought of you often."

"Me too."

Elizabeth started several sentences, but none of them felt right. She tried to think of things she knew about Bernice: her love of the blues, soap operas, and all things Burt Reynolds, but nothing felt appropriate.

Elizabeth looked behind Bernice and saw that the abandoned Wal-Mart had been completely rejuvenated. Only traces of the building's former occupant remained. There was still the white-tile flooring and white poles to which telephones were attached. But gone were the rows upon rows of shelves that had once divided this colossal room into departments. The result was that she could see from one end of the room to the other, making her realize how spacious these big-box stores truly were.

Instead of shoppers, there were scattered groups of people, most of them teenage, but all other ages as well. They wore baseball caps, cowboy boots, camouflage, piercings, and sweatpants, though by and large, it was a kingdom of denim. By the sound of it, they were apparently having a fine time. Some sat in circles, some stood with red plastic cups in their hands, some sat on blankets. In one corner some young black men were playing basketball, one tall white boy among them. In another, a large projector screen was set up and people were watching a movie, something with Steve Martin. The whole scenario was a lot to take in.

"I reckon you're here to see Blue Gene?"

"Yes."

"I'll hunt 'im up for ya," said Bernice as she unclipped a black walkie-talkie from her elastic waistband.

"Freedom Hawk?" She looked at the walkie-talkie as she awaited an answer.

"Here I am, Chumba Wumba," is what came from the little speaker in Bernice's veiny hand.

"I got a visitor here to see ya. Where you at?"

"Fixin' to go in the meeting room. Send 'im on back."

"It's your mama." Bernice again looked down at the device, waiting for a response, but this time a response didn't come. Bernice gave Elizabeth a look that said she wasn't responsible for his rudeness.

"I guess he's upset with me?"

"Oh, he's upset with the whole world. Upset with the whole situation."

"Do you think he'll even *speak* to me?"

"I *'magine* he will. Come on. I'll take you to him."

"Oh, you don't have to do that."

"I kinda do, though. It's my job. Follow me—oh, I'm supposed to ask you if you want anything to eat or drink." Bernice nodded at the café off to the right of the entrance. There was a dry-erase board out front that said, "Today—Barbecue." People were lined up with trays, waiting for their servings.

"No thank you."

"It's on the house."

"I had a late lunch."

"All right, then. Follow me."

With nothing in their way but some small congregations of casually dressed people here and there, Elizabeth followed Bernice and her oxygen tank as they slowly advanced in a straight diagonal line toward the back. Her eyes were drawn to a square section of the wall where a captivating mural had been painted. It was a beach scene with surrealistic palm trees and half-dolphin/half-doglike creatures leaping out of a lavender sea. She then saw that interspersed along the perimeter of the room were artists working on their own sections of the wall. Elizabeth couldn't see any of their faces, as they were all engrossed in their work, diligently painting in eager strokes.

Suddenly, an excited yellow Labrador retriever ran up to Elizabeth and smelled her with hyper delight.

"Labradoria! Stop that! You're gonna get hair all over her pantsuit." Bernice grabbed the dog by its collar and yanked her away, but Labradoria proved too strong for her. She continued to sniff Elizabeth, who was rich in the scent of Chanel No. 5 perfume. "Don't worry. She won't attack you. Might lick you to death, though."

Elizabeth laughed nervously and patted the dog's head with the back of her fingers before it pranced off to smell someone else.

"Blue Gene lets people bring their pets in here. Labradoria was a stray someone brought in, and he just let her stay." This explained why there were dogs and cats running throughout the great room. In the middle of the front corner was a sectioned-off area in which both cats and dogs were relaxing and sleeping. Not far from that was a gigantic trampoline on which some children merrily bounced and squealed.

"We never did let him have a pet after John's dog died," said Elizabeth, "so I guess he's making up for it." They kept walking, passing a camping tent with some teenagers inside, all of them dressed in black. "So does Gene *live* here?"

"Yeah. He's got 'im a little bedroom set up upstairs. Did you know that every Wal-Mart has an upstairs?"

"No."

"I didn't neither. I thought that was interesting. They normally have their layaway room upstairs and also a break room. Blue Gene sleeps in the break room."

"Do *you* live here?"

"No. There *are* some that live in the offices in the back that Blue Gene had turned into bedrooms. They don't have nowhere else to go, so he offers 'em room and board. But I just work here, if you can call it that. I greet people, sometimes show 'em around like I'm doin' with you now. But I won't let him pay me. It's the least I could do in return for all he's done for me."

"What has he done for you?"

Bernice stopped and faced Elizabeth.

"You should probably talk to him about that. I don't mean to treat it like a secret, 'cause it's not, but—you know what? Scratch that. He told me no more secrets from here on out, to just be out and open with everything, so there's no need for me to be beatin' around the bush like this, 'cause he'd tell you himself if you asked him. What Blue Gene did for me is, well, I got this breathing problem, and I was gettin' so I couldn't hardly pay the bills, and long-story-short, he took care of it all for me in one fell swoop. I don't got to worry about none of that no more because of him."

"How *nice*," said Elizabeth, with artificial surprise. She knew that Bernice's financial situation was the reason Blue Gene had asked for his inheritance in the first place, that it was in fact the origin of the campaign's current woes.

"*Nice* ain't but the start of it," replied Bernice, almost starkly. She glanced over Elizabeth's shoulder before she continued to the back. Then Elizabeth turned around and noticed that in the front of the room, there were several rows of people sitting on metal folding chairs. Some were black, some white, some wrinkled, some pimpled, some young and runny-nosed. All of them were clearly waiting for something.

"Why are all those people sitting there?"

Again, Bernice stopped in her tracks and turned to face Elizabeth.

"Well, now *that* I *really* can't tell you 'bout. It's something new Blue Gene's offering, but I'd rather let him tell you 'bout that, 'cause he told us all to keep quiet about it since the press keeps gettin' on us and they're liable to mess it all up."

Elizabeth nodded. They continued walking. At the back of the room was a small group holding tattered paperback copies of *Death of a Salesman*. Elizabeth recognized the actor reading the Willy Loman part as Gene's best friend from grade school, that nice Gibson boy who had chosen a certain lifestyle for himself, one with which she did not agree.

"What are *they* doing?" asked Elizabeth.

"They put on free plays," said Bernice. "It's real nice for people who don't normally see plays."

Elizabeth smiled and nodded, glad that someone was acknowledging that most of the people here, the adults more so than the teens, were from a certain walk of life. "People who don't normally see plays," was one way to put it. She had been around them earlier this year at the flea market and at the Fourth of July rally, but this was the first time she had seen them acting happy, though happiness could not erase a certain indescribable *look* they always carried on their faces. Still, everywhere she looked there were people enjoying themselves, drinking beer, playing with the dogs, laughing, and she could understand why they would come here. Blue Gene had created the opposite of a country club.

"Here we go," said Bernice. "Just down this hall."

At the end of the hall was a long, narrow room, nondescript except for an oversize American flag spread across one wall. In the middle of the room was a large, circular table at which nine men sat. The majority of them had scraggly, long gray hair and beards, though one clean-cut younger man and one clean-cut geriatric man were included. Several of them had earrings and plastic eyeglasses that were straight across the top, and they wore either leather or camouflage vests. Sitting against the walls were men and women listening to what the people at the table had to say. In the far corner, Elizabeth spotted Gene sitting with horrible posture. But his posture was the least of what wasn't right with his appearance.

He was wearing what was unmistakably intended to be one of Elvis's sparkling white jumpsuits. It fit him snugly, making no secret of his watermelonish midsection. As usual, he wore a baseball cap, but now his long hair was feathery and billowy, like wings that unfolded from the side of his neck. Out of his mouth hung something thin and white, what she feared would be a joint, but what turned out to be the end of a sucker. And to top this off, sitting next to him was an equally strange-looking girl who looked to be a teenager, whose hair had a streak of crimson and whose T-shirt had the Polo logo and bold black letters that said: RALPH LIFSCHITZ.

"Blue Gene!" hollered Bernice, interrupting the one-armed elderly man who currently held everyone's attention, telling them how they should hire some tutors to help kids with their homework. Elizabeth recognized him as the man who had sold her a fiber-optic Mary statue at the flea market. "Where are ya!?"

Blue Gene stood. His dark eyes met Elizabeth's from across the crowded room. Everyone took notice of the classy-looking woman standing at the threshold. She raised a hand that had pressed elevator buttons all across Europe and held salad forks in the company of quoted names.

"Well, hello there, Mrs. Mapother," said the one-armed man.

"Hi!"

"I'm Bob. We met at the flea market."

"I remember you! How are you, Bob?"

"Doin' pretty good. You all, this is Blue Gene's mother."

Everyone at the table turned around to see her, and after a moment of collective surprise came a release of enthusiastic greetings.

"Hi." "Hello." "Hi, Missus Mapother." "Hey." "Hidey."

"Hello," said Elizabeth with an uncomfortable smile. "I didn't mean to interrupt."

"Oh, you aren't interrupting a thing, Mrs. Mapother," said Bob. "Blue Gene, you want us to adjourn?"

"Nah. Y'all go on without me," said Blue Gene as he limped across the room in his sparkling Elvis suit. As he walked, his flip-flops made their noise, that noise that Elizabeth had always told him was the most unintelligent sound a human can make. Something dangled at his side as he walked. It was attached to a thin metal chain that was connected to his waist. The people sitting against the wall had to move their legs underneath their chairs to make room for him to walk through. "I'll take you to my room," he said. Elizabeth nodded. As Blue Gene got closer she saw the object attached to the chain was a checkbook.

She started to follow Blue Gene out the door.

"Wait! Mrs. Mapother, wait." A skeletal woman whose age could not be discerned stood from her steel folding chair and headed for Elizabeth. "I just wanted to tell you, you did a fine job raising your boy." She took both of Elizabeth's hands. She had a solemn look on her face. She looked down and shook her head.

"Thank you," said Elizabeth.

"I don't know what I would've done if it wasn't for him."

"Thank you," she repeated.

"He's helped so many of us, and in such little time. He's given us—"

"Thanks, Roseanne, but we've heard enough of your bullshit for today," said Blue Gene. The room burst with laughter, and he led Elizabeth up a nearby flight of stairs. As she thought about the reverence with which the woman had spoken, and as she watched his checkbook swing freely at his side, Elizabeth wanted to scream. Here was one more man she would have to watch have his greatness. Her husband was the nationally known CEO, her son was the rising politician-savior-man, and now the one role she had always wanted for herself appeared to have been taken.

In 1983, Pope John Paul II officially decreased the number of miracles required for sainthood from four to two, and only one for a martyr. Having already performed what she believed was one miracle by having a precognitive dream for twelve consecutive nights, she considered sainthood to be within her reach. She only had to perform one more miracle before she died; this was doable. For years, she exuded a perfected graciousness, and every sentence that came from her mouth was designed to ingratiate or uplift, and she assumed that eventually, another miracle would present itself to her. She felt foolish for having such an impossible goal, so she never said it aloud, but still, she committed herself to the idea and truly believed she would one day be looked back on as Saint Elizabeth Mapother. Now it appeared that another Mapother was more likely to take the position.

$ $ $

Blue Gene led Elizabeth to a medium-sized room with nothing in it but a twin bed, a chest of drawers, and a large stereo with some CDs on top. He used the room only for sleeping and occasionally for receiving people who wanted to either ask him or thank him for something.

"We've been worried about you," said Elizabeth.

"Hmm," he grunted.

"How have you been?"

"Can't complain."

"Why are you wearing an Elvis suit?"

"This one lady made it for me. Feel like I have to wear it every now and again."

When Blue Gene did favors for people at the Commonwealth Building, they often felt the need to repay him. But since most of them didn't have much money, they reimbursed him in other ways. He let the old lady who slept in her station wagon stay for free in a furnished room downstairs. Her only skill was sewing; she had worked at a locally owned garment factory for thirty years before it closed. When she asked Blue Gene if he liked Elvis, he didn't know he was saying yes to having a sequined jumpsuit tailor-made for him. Similarly, earlier that morning he had let one of the veterans' wives style his hair. She wanted to show him how grateful she was that he had given her husband a position on the newly established Veterans Committee, which paid extremely generously.

Elizabeth suddenly reached across and picked at Blue Gene's jumpsuit.

"Stop!"

"I was just picking some dog hairs off."

"I know what you were doing, and I said stop it."

"Don't be hateful."

Blue Gene snorted up phlegm and then swallowed it. "You can sit on my bed if you want."

Elizabeth sat on the edge of the unmade bed and placed her purse at her feet. She looked around the undecorated room, and then at Blue Gene, who leaned against the wall. "Want a Dum Dum?"

"No thank you."

"I suck on 'em to keep me from smoking."

"You're welcome to come back home. You know that, don't you?"

"I like it fine here."

"Where do you bathe?"

"I don't."

Elizabeth's mouth dropped. "*Gene.*"

"Jesus, you thought I was serious? You must think I'm the biggest skank ever lived. I had a shower installed downstairs."

"Wow. You've really fixed this place up. How did you ever get it all together so fast?"

"Money."

Blue Gene had quickly learned that with his riches he could make the impossible possible. He had hired two separate crews to work on the building, both crews consisting of old friends of his and Cheyenne's. He paid them such a wage that it made them downright giddy, and he offered each crew a bonus if they could finish the refurbishments in under a month, which they both did.

"What can I do for you?" he asked, assuming a squatting position and popping his knuckles one at a time, a thing that had always irritated her.

"I just want to talk to you."

"Well, here I am."

Elizabeth cleared her throat effeminately before speaking. "I know you're still mad at us, and I can understand that. I would be, too. But I hope you realize that your father and I, we always did what we thought was best for you."

"Best for me or best for John?"

"Best for both of you. Bashford was still such a conservative little town back then. It would've ruined both of your lives if we had been open about everything. I'm sorry I wasn't here when you found out, though. I hate that it happened the way it did, and I hate even more that I wasn't here for you, but for what it's worth, I *did* find understanding in Mexico. Of my dream." Blue Gene just stared at Elizabeth like he would a commercial, with eyes half-closed and an impatient pucker of the lips. "My dream—it stopped after I arrived in Mexico, and I prayed and meditated, and I came to realize that the ominous feeling I had been getting from the visions, they were trying to tell me that our secret was about to come out. That in itself was the danger."

"You had to go on a damn mission trip to figure that out?"

"The mission helped me find my center. And the dream *did* stop down there. It stopped the night before your father called me and told me what happened with you and the cell phone. I figured out that the danger—what I believe the dream was trying to warn me of recently— was that you suddenly came into possession of this great knowledge. If you were a lesser man, you could have *used* that knowledge to take revenge on John and your father and me. You could have completely derailed his fate. But you *didn't*, and I want to thank you for that."

"You don't have to thank me. Why would I wanna go around telling people I had a thirteen-year-old dad? Ain't nothin' cool about that. It's *gross.*"

"Well, I know you must have been tempted to tell since you blackmailed your own father over it."

"I wouldn't call it *blackmail.*"

"You pressured your father into giving you money by threatening him. It's the very definition of blackmail."

"Well, if you put it that way. But it don't matter, 'cause I wasn't ever gonna tell nobody mine and John's secret. I just wanted my inheritance to help Bernice, and this was one of the few times I ever had the upper hand over Dad—or Henry. What the hell am I supposed to call y'all people now?"

"Mom and Dad. We adopted you. I'm still your mother. Your father is still your father. That hasn't changed. It's official."

"A'ight, then. Why are you here, Mother?"

"Primarily, I'm here to check on you."

Blue Gene sighed. "I wanna get one thing straight. I don't want no more lyin'. Don't worry 'bout hurtin' my feelings or whatever. Just give it to me straight. If you're here because of the campaign, go on and tell me."

"I'm here for the campaign, but first and foremost, I'm here to check on you."

"Well, thank you. I'm fine as wine. Now, what can I do for you?" he snapped.

"Would you be nice?"

"Come on, now. What'd they send you here for? I'm not as dumb as you think."

"*Okay*. It's Frick. He's using you against John. It has to stop."

"I haven't been saying an unkind word about John. I haven't said a kind word about him, either. I don't talk about him, period."

"And I appreciate that, but the problem is that Frick has taken advantage of your situation. Do you know what he's been saying about this place?"

"About how it's wild?"

"Yes."

"That's just a few bad apples."

"But they *do* exist, these bad apples?"

"Well, sure, if you get enough people together in one place, there'll be some that misbehave."

"But now they're being arrested. This does not make John look good."

"I haven't done no wrong. You tell John it could be a lot worse for him if I wanted it to be. Jackie's been trying to talk me into starting up some campaign of our own here, like endorsing a write-in candidate. But I wouldn't do it. I was tempted, 'cause it would serve y'all right, but I wouldn't."

"Who's Jackie?"

"Nobody." Blue Gene felt himself blushing and adjusted his cap.

"We weren't going to bother you at all, Gene. But now that there have been *arrests* made here—you know we can't have that going on with the election so near. We can't have our name associated with that."

"What do you want me to do about it?"

"Can't you close this place down?"

"*No*," said Blue Gene, insulted.

"Just for two weeks, until after the election, at least?"

"No way. Too many people are dependin' on it."

"But John's numbers are down."

"I said no, and that's that."

Elizabeth opened her mouth to argue but closed it when she heard someone coming up the steps.

"Blue Gene?" said a deep, gravelly voice.

"Come on up, Charlie."

Blue Gene reached for his checkbook on a chain.

"Sorry to interrupt y'all," said the man as he entered the room. It was the saxophone player.

"Ain't no thing but a chicken wing." Blue Gene scribbled his signature on the check and ripped it out with a snap of the wrist. "There you go."

"Thanks, Blue Gene."

"Don't mention it. Oh, Charlie, this is Elizabeth."

"Why, hello, Elizabeth. So nice to meet you."

"Nice to meet *you*. I enjoyed hearing you play."

"Thank you. I'm glad to *have* somewhere to play. Blue Gene here's given me that."

"Ah, yeah. It's a good gig you got here, playing outside an ol' Wal-Mart."

"Well, hey now—it pays just the same." He laughed at himself.

"Charlie," said Elizabeth, "did you used to play at the Blue Room in Donato Falls, by any chance?"

"Why, I sure did. I thought you looked familiar," he said with a smirk.

"No, you didn't."

"I *did*."

"Oh, wasn't that the greatest place?" asked Elizabeth.

"It was."

"Why can't they have places like that around here anymore?"

"I don't know. I just don't know. Things ain't what they used to be."

"No," agreed Elizabeth.

"Say now, it was nice to meet you," he said to Elizabeth with a slight bow.

"Nice to meet you, Charlie."

"See you next week, big nuts," said Blue Gene.

"Thanks, Blue Gene," he said with a chuckle. "Be good, now."

Moments after Charlie left, Elizabeth was still smiling. Then she looked up, saw that Blue Gene was staring at her, and shook off the smile. "How much did you pay him?" she asked.

"I *knew* you would ask that. I pay him what I think's fair. Same as I pay everybody who works here."

"Those artists painting the murals downstairs—do you pay them?"

"Sure. And the actors, and the cooks. We've created all kinds of jobs up in here. And I pay everybody the same."

"Why the same?"

"It was Jackie's idea. She said if you have a pay scale, it divides people against one another, 'cause they'd all be fightin' for position. Seemed fair to me, doin' it like this."

"Was Jackie that girl you were sitting next to in there?"

"Yep." They always sat next to each other at the meetings. This enterprise seemed to have energized Jackie to a whole new level. Every day she arrived early and stayed late and constantly looked for ways to make the place better, all the while excited and overcaffeinated.

"But you're not bringing any money in, are you? Because every-thing's free?"

"That's right. Not for profit."

"And everything here is made possible with just your inheritance, right?"

"Yep."

"What happens when your money runs out?"

"Then I guess we'll have to shut it down. But until that happens, this'll help a lot of people out."

"Why are you doing all this?"

"'Cause I got the money."

"I think it's good that you're helping people. I do. But when I see you giving away all you have—all that your grandfather and his father and his father earned—to *these* people, just like that," she said, with a snap of her fingers, "and they take it, just like that," she snapped again, "I can't help but think that God helps those who help themselves."

"I think God would prefer someone to be doin' something like this over what John's doing, goin' around collectin' votes just so he can stick it in everybody and break it off."

"*Gene.* John will help the multitudes one day. He's going to make everything right. You know the things I've seen."

"I don't think you ever even had that dream."

"Of course I did!" Elizabeth's face was flooded with anguish.

"Y'all made up everything else about my history. How do I know you didn't make up your dream?"

"I swear to you that the dream is real. Tell me you don't really think I'd lie about that. You know how important it is to us."

"I just don't know anything no more."

"I swear to you I had that dream, and the only thing that can keep it from coming true is you, doing all this. Why do you want to hurt John's chances?"

"This place ain't got nothin' to do with John. I'm just trying to make people happy. Including myself."

"It's sweet that you want to make people happy, Gene," said Elizabeth. "I just don't want anyone taking advantage of you."

Blue Gene shook his head and rolled his eyes.

"What?" she asked.

"If they weren't taking advantage of me, y'all would be. So don't you dare sit there and talk to me about taking advantage."

"I don't know why you have to be so difficult," she said.

"If you wanna talk about taking advantage of people, how about John? How about all his big talk about America and how great it is and how he gets people all riled up so they'll vote for him, but then when he gets in there, you know he ain't gonna look out for America. You know exactly who he's gonna look out for."

"What has made you so cynical all of a sudden?"

"What do you think?! If somebody lies to you enough, you get so you don't believe a single word they say."

At this, Elizabeth picked up her purse and stood. "I'm sorry, Gene. I'm sorry you found out the way you did, and I'm sorry for everything. I've prayed for your forgiveness, but I can see you're not ready to give it. I'll be praying for you."

"A'ight, then."

"If you won't close this building, will you at least make sure that no one else gets arrested?"

"I already made a morning announcement about that. I told 'em to keep it all at home and not bring it in here."

"Will you at least walk me out?"

"Yeah. Hold on. How's Arthur?"

"He's fine. He asks about you."

"What do y'all tell him?"

"We tell him you're vacationing in Florida."

"Hey, I wanna send him some things by you. We got a bunch of prizes downstairs for the kids." Blue Gene reached behind himself and pulled out his walkie-talkie. "I'll have Bernice round up some gifts for him."

"That's *another* thing I'm not too happy about," said Elizabeth snippily.

"What?"

"You giving Bernice a job here."

"Hey, she come here herself when she heard on the news about me. She said she wanted to help, so I let her."

"I don't see why *she* would be offered a job here, and not I."

"Do you *want* a job here?"

"No."

Blue Gene sighed and rolled his eyes.

"You've clearly forgiven her," continued Elizabeth. "Why does *she* get off the hook so easily?"

"Way I figure it is, during that whole big mess when her daughter was pregnant, she was the only one looking out for me." Elizabeth looked shocked. "If it wasn't for her, y'all would've pawned me off on some orphanage."

"Is *that* what you think?"

"What?"

"That *she* saved you?"

$ $ $

Elizabeth told Blue Gene that they should probably sit down. Blue Gene groaned and lay down on his bed. The rhinestones on his suit snagged one of his throws. He pulled it off and threw it on the floor. Elizabeth returned to the edge of the bed and tried to ignore that Blue Gene's bare feet in their flip-flops were right next to her. She had always hated feet. She wore socks even in bed.

"I'm sorry in advance if this upsets you," she said, "but I think that I deserve some credit."

"Ain't nothin' much that can upset me at this point."

"I'm sorry. But I can't not say anything. I'm guessing when Bernice told you everything, she neglected to mention that when she first showed up on our doorstep, it was to ask us to pay for an abortion."

Elizabeth waited for Blue Gene to reply, but he only looked on with his tired, ringed eyes. Elizabeth waited some more, until finally Blue Gene said, "Yeah, I reckon Bernice failed to mention that tidbit."

"She said that it was her understanding that it was the father who normally took on the responsibility of paying for one. Of course, you know how I feel about this topic. I said, 'Let me make myself perfectly clear right now, Mrs. Munly. We will never, *ever* take *any* part in *any* abortion.' I told her we would help her out in any way we could, but not like that. She said that she and her daughter were barely getting by as it was and couldn't afford another mouth to feed, and naturally, she was worried about having a daughter become a mother herself when she was only in seventh grade.

"I told her I understood what a difficult situation it was for her and her daughter, but that abortion was never a solution. After the paternity test came back, she was still pushing for one, but I wouldn't budge. I would not agree to give her any money for one, and I pleaded with her until she finally agreed. And yes, originally we were going to put you up for adoption, but when the poor girl died, that changed everything. So I think you should know if it weren't for your father and me, you would never have been born in the first place."

"I doubt that Dad had a thing to do with it."

"Why do you say that?"

"'Cause he was never half as religious as you. I remember a lot of the times at church, it'd be just you, me, and John. Dad'd stay home and watch a ballgame."

"No. He agreed with me. We both pleaded for your life."

"I thought I told you no more lying."

Elizabeth uncrossed her legs and then crossed them again in the opposite direction. She was almost glad she had been caught. She, too, was sick of the lies. "Yes. All right. You guessed it. Henry agreed with Bernice. I had to fight for you."

"How'd you ever win?"

"I was in a position like you were recently. For once, I had the upper hand over your father."

She explained how when Bernice left after that first visit, she and Henry called upstairs for John. Henry demanded that John sit down for a talk. It took some interrogating; John wouldn't admit that he had even spoken to a girl with the last name Munly, let alone been to her house.

But when Elizabeth told John that the Munly girl was pregnant, she noticed him swallow, as though drinking a gob of air, before he said, "So what?" Then he started fidgeting to such a degree that it scared her. Henry came out and told John that the girl's mother claimed *he* was the one who had impregnated her. John said that was crazy, but his little Adam's apple revealed one nervous swallow after another.

Elizabeth started crying. Henry yelled at her to stop, but she couldn't. As the mascara flowed, Henry kept screaming for her to shut up. Then John told his dad not to yell at his mom. This caused Henry to turn his wrath toward John, telling him he had ruined himself, his future, his whole family, until John at last blurted, "I only did it because I saw you do it to Trish!"

Elizabeth abruptly stopped crying. Henry looked at John murderously. John fled back upstairs.

Though it felt cathartic to tell Blue Gene about Henry's affair, she felt obligated to explain that Henry generally *did* agree with her pro-life sentiments. It was just that he was very protective of his family, and now that the life in debate could have held damning consequences for his family's future, the abortion question had gone from being true-or-false to multiple choice and wasn't so easily answerable. But the fact remained that Henry had been unfaithful, and because of this, Elizabeth suddenly held their marriage in her perpetually manicured hand. During that time, her say held an unusual amount of finality. When she pronounced an abortion forbidden, Henry acquiesced and refused Bernice the funds that could terminate the pregnancy. He then joined Elizabeth in imploring that Bernice's daughter have the baby and give it up for adoption.

After Blue Gene's birth mother died, Elizabeth used her newfound bargaining power once again. She demanded that the Mapothers adopt the baby and give his grandmother a job as their nanny. Not without a battle, Henry finally agreed but swore that with this, his penance was paid. He said he would do as Elizabeth asked and make this child a part of the family, but he had a demand of his own: that his affair with the housekeeper never be used against him again. Not another word of it could ever be uttered from that point onward.

After Elizabeth was done telling him all of this, Blue Gene sat up and scooted down the bed to sit next to her. He picked at one of the loose rhinestones on his thigh. "I bet you're wishing they'd gone on and done me in, after all the trouble I've caused."

"Heavens no, Gene. Stop that. Don't even say that. But can you see now that Bernice hasn't been the only one in your corner?"

He nodded.

"So won't you close this building? For *me*? Just until the election's over?"

"No." He growled. "Just when I's feelin' you, you start in with that crap."

"But Frick's gaining momentum. What if he wins?"

"I don't care. We got some big stuff going on next week. Besides, after all you just told me, I don't get why you even *want* to help Dad."

"It's for the greater good."

"You might think that, but John and Dad, they don't really care about doing no good."

"Henry maybe, but not John. You're wrong about John."

"John's in it for the money, too."

"No. He's good. I believe that our world will finally have a good Christian man to lead it. I just hope I live long enough to see it happen."

"A good Christian man? Wake up, Mom. A good Christian man don't do a son like he's done me. A good Christian man wouldn't have screwed a little girl. And if he's so good, then why didn't he take care of my ass when I was growing up? He was never even around."

"That wasn't his fault. It was ours. We let him come and go as he pleased because we felt bad about all he'd been through. Look at what that child went through. There was my dream he wasn't supposed to know about, and then seeing his dad *in the act* of committing adultery, and then becoming a father so young. We wanted John to go out and have fun if he wanted. We thought it might be unhealthy if he stayed in with you too much, and also, I always wished my own parents hadn't been so strict with me. And I thought it was how Bernice wanted things, too, to take care of you herself. She hated John. And you always seemed perfectly happy with Bernice taking care of you. You always seemed to like her best. You definitely liked her more than you did me."

"Nuh-uh."

"You've given her a job here, and yet you haven't even spoken to me in over a month."

"You haven't spoken to me, neither."

"Henry said that you were quite adamant about not wanting us to contact you, and besides, half the time I had no idea where you were. For all I knew, you had run off to some other country."

"Fine. You're right. So do you want a job here, then?"

"No."

"Seriously, why don't you come work for me?"

"What would I do?"

"I don't know. But come on, I want you to."

"Why?"

"Well, first of all, 'cause you're acting like you *want* to work here."

"Oh, I just think that if you asked Bernice—"

"Second, though, I just wanna do something for you, 'cause I feel all guilty. Sounds to me like it was hardest on you. I mean, you found out that Dad was cheating on you and that your thirteen-year-old kid was going to be a father, all on the same day. You must be a tougher gal than I ever realized to put up with all that shit."

If John or Henry thought this, they never said so aloud, but then, they always avoided the topic. But just once, she wanted someone to acknowledge that this ordeal had been especially awful for her, yet she had survived.

"What job would you even give me here?" Elizabeth asked.

"Oh, I don't know. What would you be interested in?"

"Helping people."

"A'ight. I'll find you something. We can always find something. Oh—also, we're always needing people to sing the National Anthem. We have people sing it before the shows and sometimes even before the meetings, but we never had nobody that could sing good, like you. You think that's something you'd be interested in?"

$$$

Meanwhile, downstairs, a dozen more people had taken seats up front since Elizabeth had arrived. They had brought books and magazines and sleeping bags, and after they signed themselves in, they picked a spot and settled in.

"Don't you think this is too good to be true?"

"Yeah, that's what we was sayin'. 'Bout the only way we'll believe it is once we see the receipt that it's all paid for."

"Sounds too good to be true, but on the other hand, I can't afford no three hundred dollars for a doctor, so I was at least gonna *try* this. Where is he, anyway?"

"Don't know. They say he's around here somewhere."

"There's gotta be some catch."

"Well, that's what we was sayin', but somebody was sayin' something earlier like he had a death wish or something and wants to use up all his riches before he dies."

"Papaw, now, that was comin' from ol' Kingsize. You can't go by anything *he* says."

"I heard he gives away money 'cause it gives him, like, a natural high. Like, supposedly, when this place first opened and he had bands playing here, one of the poorer guys in one of the bands left his jacket sittin' on the floor. And what he did is he put a hundred-dollar bill in the boy's jacket, and when he saw how excited this poor kid got, supposedly just watching that gave him a nice little buzz. So he kept doing that sort of thing, only bigger and bigger."

"Well, he's gonna get a real good buzz offa me, 'cause I got asthma and those inhalers is expensive."

"It's just too good to be true. He must be workin' some kind of angle."

"Maybe so. But the way I figure it is, if somebody's willin' to help you, why not let 'em?"

XI.

If you knelt to the ground of Bashford and cupped your ear to its soil, which seemed to get less and less fertile with each passing year, or if you pressed your face against the windows of the low-income homes where withering insect exoskeletons clung to their dusty-webbed death-spots, you might have heard a dragging voice moaning the mantra of the exhausted:

"I'm sorry I've been in such a bad mood lately honey but they've about killed me at work but once I've finished this next job things'll get better because I'll have more time and when I have more time I'll start exercising and I'll get healthy and start feeling better and be happier and I've always wanted to learn to play the piano or learn to do magic tricks or maybe even learn to speak another language maybe German so when I have some free time I'm gonna learn and yes we'll go on vacation maybe to a beach somewhere just don't give up on me 'cause God knows I'm trying I'm just so tired my God I'm so worn out."

It was for the owners of this voice that the Commonwealth Building was a blessing, as it provided a new kind of freedom: a radical, almost *alien* kind of freedom where everything really was *free*. In general, it was a godsend for those whose every single move in life was predetermined by how little was in their bank account.

For teenagers, particularly those of skewed fashion choices made for either originality's sake or the lack of funds, it was a place where they could congregate on the weekend and listen to music of their peers' creation without a cover charge. For the old, though they were shy in coming at first, it was like the porch of an old general store where they could sit and talk without having to buy anything, and where they could get a hot, down-home breakfast, lunch, or dinner, always all-you-can-eat, always free. The building could also accommodate the bored at no charge through various forms of recreation, eventually serving as a go-to place where they were bound to see someone they knew and maybe even liked. There was even free beer on tap if anyone wanted to wet their throats, but the counter that served Miller Lite did have a sensible, law-abiding list of stipulations that some guests found ways to tiptoe around.

For the Bashford destitute, the Commonwealth Building was so good that they naturally assumed it couldn't last. Here was a place that offered three quality meals a day (not one of them soup), lodging if you needed it (though the rooms were limited to five), and that would supposedly even house a free doctor's office soon, in the room where the Wal-Mart pharmacy had once been. And if that wasn't enough, the building also provided jobs that paid well above minimum wage.

There were others, however, who had no intention of working at the Commonwealth Building or anywhere else, who did nothing but *take* from this institution of giving, thus ensuring that the rest of the town saw them as a collection of slovenly limbs slacking off a pumpkin-truck headed toward the cliff of dissolution. Furthermore, a small but significant sampling of the population saw nothing more than opportunity at the Commonwealth Building. Instead of charity or goodwill, they mainly noticed a healthy smattering of possible clientele for their illegalities. Crime was inevitable, the Veterans agreed, but they would keep a closer eye on it, especially after those arrests, and they stressed that at the first sign of violence, the nine of them would act as bouncers, using the firm but polite ejection method they had learned from Patrick Swayze in *Road House*.

So this place where money was not welcome possessed no immunity to serious flaws, and the unsavory was in fact savored there by those who sought it. But all those who enjoyed and approved of the Commonwealth had a similar view, which Mitchell Gibson most uniquely articulated at the venue's first (and last) Poetry Night. Mitchell, whom Blue Gene initially invited to bring his theatrical expertise to this plain, unsophisticated white room, had quickly become one of the building's most visible denizens, behind only Blue Gene, Jackie, and the Veterans Committee in active participation. That first and last Poetry Night, he stood on the stage where the bands normally played, and dramatically recited a prose poem titled "Inevitable Acne Vulgaris":

"A man at the mall told me that even Elvis had acne. This was when he was just starting out, at his freshest, purest stage of black velveteen handsomeness, before he had discovered the power within his hips and when his face was at once cute and pustulate. But you don't hear much about that. I think the people should know that the King had bad skin. Backwards a century, I'd like to call attention to the melancholia of Lincoln, how he'd sit alone in a darkened corner thinking about his dead loved ones and what their corpses must have looked like. His morose statues were accurate representations of a spidery form overwhelmed with sorrow and syndrome. Deeper still into the national memory, I might find myself a spectator at an oral report for the ages, witnessing forefather qualms. George Washington nervously shook as he read America's first-ever inaugural address. I can see his alabaster hands tremble as they hold on to a speech he can hardly read. In the end, given enough time, the King's skin did clear up... only to bloat. But on this we will not dwell. Let us look back in praise of the immaculate pompadour and the defiance of his lips and the revolutions made by his good holy hips."

Unfortunately for the Commonwealth Building, the twenty-one counties of the fifth district contained a considerable number of voters who had made up their minds—under incessant advice from U.S. Representative Grant Frick—that the blemishes young Gibson alluded to were actually budding buboes of a plague that would have the quaint streets of their small towns running with the toxic pus of immorality.

Once these concerned citizens were convinced, their voice was more audible than those exhausted voices from underground or from the low-income homes, because the voice of the concerned amplified more ardently, and they didn't hesitate to share it everywhere they went or to broadcast it with letters to their town's newspaper:

"Last Saturday, I allowed my granddaughters to attend a so-called 'punk rock show' at this Commonwealth Building. I regret this decision. They came back with a new education given to them free of charge by ex-cons, deviants, and other adult elements who had no business being around youths in the first place. I am tired of hearing that millions and millions of dollars (riches which likely originated from the historically unstable Mr. Mapother's various slush funds) are now being appropriated to teach area youth all about cussing, gambling, drinking, drugging, and sexing. Mapother, despite his best intentions, is not earning points in the eyes of the Lord by doing what he's doing. He is paying for our decline and funding our downfall. He is stripping our community of its values, and he's doing it in the worst possible way: under the guise of charitable godliness. He does not fool me. It needs to be put to a stop. The first step would be to make sure that he does not have his brother to do his bidding in our government. Do the right thing and vote for Grant Frick on November 2."

These ejaculations often appeared on the same page as letters like this one:

"Maybe I'm old-fashioned, but I still believe that America is the greatest country in the world. This is the one place on the planet where if you work hard and long enough you *will* make your dreams come true. I don't care what anybody says. This is the one place in the world where we can take any little boy or even girl and tell them that if they work hard and are good to their country, they can become anything, even the president of the United States. That is what freedom is, the ability to take our lives as far as possible. What is going on at the Commonwealth Building is purely un-American. Mr. Mapother is spitting in the face of what we tell our children. He is just giving it all away. Want food on the table? Here you go. No, you don't have to earn it here. And now we don't have to pay our doctor bills? Why should any of us ever work a day of our lives? Now we have the Commonwealth Building! America is not about being lazy and letting someone take care of you. America is about being strong and being all that you can be. Apparently, Mapother and his family would have you think otherwise. Vote for Grant Frick, who still abides by the rules that make us a proud people."

But there was one more voice, one that carried farther than any other because it came from a much higher place and could be projected over the steeples and across the land. This voice belonged to men who rode in the sky, who saw Blue Gene Mapother's grandiose altruism as a threat to the force that held up humanity's backbone so that it could even walk upright in the first place, that force which gave the powerful their posture and allowed them to hold up all the bent-backed people. The force, had it been some mythical elixir or all-powerful spell uttered confidently from the lips of a wise old cigar-clenching wizard, would've been called *emmo anywhy*, the man-made magic potion that allowed the taxpaying organism to sustain its existence. In Blue Gene Mapother, they believed that this power had fallen into the hands of a demented millionaire rogue.

For its immortal success and for its invincible energy, this last voice relied upon a great irony: the voice that is the most likely to be heard and obeyed is the one coming from the tiniest amount of people. Somehow, the most microscopic cluster of men can shoot their words straight through the garble of billions.

So it came to be that one typographical whispering from one rich man's computer to another's was all it took to end the Commonwealth discussion altogether.

$ $ $

The last day that the Commonwealth Building remained open to the public began like any other, with Blue Gene sitting in the back where the layaway counter had been, gnawing the stick of a Dum Dum sucker into pulp, wearing a pair of gray sweatshorts and his black Stone Cold Steve Austin T-shirt, reading off his morning announcements into a microphone:

"Mornin', everybody. Thought it was gonna stay cool, but here we are comin' up on Halloween, and it feels like summer again. It's nice, I reckon, but I miss the good ol' days when we had seasons, don't y'all? Anyhow, everybody here for the clinic, I wasn't intendin' on it being like this, with y'all camping out and waiting, but word just got out so quick and I guess everybody kind of jumped all over it. The good news is that Dr. Wharton and two other doctors will be in at nine tomorrow morning. So until then, welcome, and I'm sure you've noticed there's plenty for y'all to do while you wait. Employees, as always, thanks for comin' in on a Sunday. And in honor of Sunday, we got something special planned today, because in an hour here, at eleven, we're gonna have a little prayer service in the back for anyone that wants to attend. So you're all invited. Let's see...got a choice of ham or fried chicken for lunch, with cornbread and collard greens. At two o'clock the Veterans Committee is gonna have a meeting in the meeting room. Open to everybody, as usual. Tonight for dinner is breakfast food. Then at seven, in the main room, we'll be showing *The Wedding Singer*, starring Adam Sandler and Drew Barrymore. In the back room we got karaoke tonight. And to give you something to look forward to, next weekend we got a monster truck that's gonna be parked in the parking lot. All right, y'all. If you see me, wish me luck on stopping smoking. Five days straight without smoking one, and I'm smellin' better all the time. Last but not least, did you hear the one about the naked man wrapped in cellophane? Walked in the doctor's office. Doctor said, I can clearly see you're nuts. All right, y'all. Take her easy."

The previous afternoon, Blue Gene had talked Elizabeth into staying awhile and singing the National Anthem before the bands started playing. The raucous reaction she received from the audience pleased her so that she asked what else she could do at the Commonwealth Building. Blue Gene said she could do whatever she wanted. She suggested she lead a prayer service, saying that maybe it would silence some of Blue Gene's critics who considered this place so naughty.

So Blue Gene invited Elizabeth back the very next morning to lead the service. He asked if she would bring Arthur along, but she arrived alone, saying John had already asked Arthur to be a ball boy for his tennis match that morning.

"Aw, man," said Blue Gene. "You see that there?" Blue Gene pointed to the former Lawn and Garden room, where children and some adults were enjoying a game area full of arcade games, Skee-Ball, small rides, and even an enclosure full of plastic balls to jump in. Most remarkably, a sign outside the room's entrance read: FREE TOKENS FOR GAME ROOM HERE. There were even little tickets and prizes, just like any venue of the Chuck E. Cheese variety had. "I set that up with Arthur in mind."

"Maybe next time," said Elizabeth.

"Yeah, right. John don't want me around his boy."

"Oh, sure he does."

"Well, I ain't hidin' anymore. John knows where I am, and he still hasn't come to see me. I think he's done with me, but that's a'ight, 'cause I'm done with *him*."

"He is not *done* with you. He just doesn't know where to even *begin*. The things you two have to talk about, they're so *big* to John. You'll need to pray for him."

"Hell nah."

After the prayer service, which about forty people attended, Blue Gene invited Elizabeth to eat lunch with him. They sat at a corner table at the café. As they unloaded their plastic trays, Blue Gene noticed that Elizabeth looked distracted.

"What's wrong?"

"Bernice is over there all alone. Why don't you go ask her to join us?"

"Really? I was gonna, but I didn't think you'd like that."

"You might offend her, eating with me and not inviting her."

Blue Gene brought Bernice over. She and her oxygen tank sat on Elizabeth's side of the table. As Blue Gene watched one woman eat her chicken breast with a fork and knife, the other with her hands, he held a naïve hope that his maternal and paternal grandmothers would become friends. He envisioned future holidays with both of them. Where Henry and John fit into these holidays, Blue Gene could not visualize at all.

Jackie suddenly appeared, wearing a red Ramones T-shirt. Blue Gene had been eating with her several times a week. His feelings for her were growing by the day, but he could feel their relationship solidifying into friendship.

"Excuse me," she said. "I just wanted to tell you that now both Duderonomy *and* the Cult of Stedman have canceled for next Saturday."

"Well, I'll be," said Blue Gene. "Band people sure can be unreliable. Oh well; just go ahead and book some replacements. Whoever you want."

"Would you like to sit with us?" asked Elizabeth.

"I don't want to intrude."

After encouragement from both Elizabeth and Bernice, Jackie went to get a coffee and came back and sat next to Blue Gene.

"You sure sounded great last night," Jackie said to Elizabeth.

"Why, thank you."

"She used to was gonna be a singer," said Blue Gene. "Went to Juilliard, even."

"Oh, wow," said Jackie. "But you stopped singing?"

"Oh, I decided it wouldn't be the right career for me. Just one of those things. Wasn't God's plan, I suppose."

"It was Dad's fault," said Blue Gene. "She met Dad, and at the time Mom was dating—weren't you dating some hippie?"

"Were you really?" asked Bernice, who was wearing a faded old T-shirt with the Olympic rings on it.

"Well, yes, I guess you could've called him that, but we don't have to get into that, Gene."

"It's funny, though. Dad fought some hippie for her. Hippie dude was fixin' to go on tour with his band, and my dad said, you go on that tour bus and you'll never see me again."

"That's not quite how it went, Gene. But I wouldn't have wanted that kind of lifestyle anyway." Elizabeth stared at her tray as the others stared at her.

"So, Jackie, what do you do?" she asked.

"I'm a substitute teacher."

"Oh. That must be rewarding."

"Every once in a while."

"Oh. It must be frustrating."

"Chicken sure is good," offered Bernice, licking her thumb. "This sure is a nice place that Blue Gene's got set up, ain't it?"

"Oh, isn't it, though?" said Elizabeth. "It's just a shame it can't last forever. A lot of these people will feel like the rug was swept out from under them once he runs out of money."

Blue Gene gave Elizabeth a quick scowl.

"Actually," said Jackie, "I'm looking into getting a grant so that maybe we can make it last longer. A little while longer, at least."

"That's nice," said Elizabeth.

"I think it's the best thing that's ever happened to this town," said Bernice, with rural attitude.

"Oh, yes, I do love what he's done with the place," added Elizabeth. "He's had some great ideas."

"Shoot, they're mostly Jackie's ideas, and Bernice's, even. Bernice helped me come up with having a free clinic here, 'cause she kept goin' on and on about how I lifted such a burden off her when I paid her medical bills. And Jackie come up with how I do a lot of the things. She come up with having, like, meetings, and letting everybody be involved with everything."

"I just didn't want him to become a fascist."

"But I did come up with the Veterans Committee making the decisions," said Blue Gene. "I'm proud of that. Anything I do goes through them first."

"Where'd you find them?" asked Elizabeth.

"Well, quite a few of 'em come in for the free food. And that got me thinkin' about how they had risked their lives for America, and I thought they deserved better. And so I decided to turn over the whole operation to them. I'd still be the owner, and it'd still be my money making things go, but they would decide how my money would be spent, and they'd run everything."

"You should be proud of your son, Mrs. Mapother," said Jackie. "I thought patriotism was nothing but bullshit until I met him. You see all these magnets on peoples' cars that say SUPPORT OUR TROOPS? Well, here's one rich man who doesn't just say it. He's genuine."

"I *am* proud of him," said Elizabeth.

"He's been so good to me," said Jackie, standing, looking at the atomic clock on the wall that helped Commonwealth activities run smoothly. "One of the reasons he started this place was so my band would have somewhere to play." Jackie patted Blue Gene on the back the way she might have patted a little brother. He could hardly hide his disappointment. "I gotta go. Nice talking to you all." Blue Gene watched her small butt as she walked away.

"What's wrong, Blue Gene?" asked Bernice, licking chicken grease off each of her fingertips.

"Nothin'."

"Blue Gene, where did you meet that girl?"

"On the campaign trail."

"She seems nice enough, but I heard some of her band's lyrics last night, and I found them to be *very* offensive."

"I reckon I better go check our email." There were several computers set up throughout the building that offered free internet.

"You ain't done eatin' yet," said Bernice.

"I didn't appreciate that tirade on abortion she gave, either," said Elizabeth.

"Well, you gave one yourself this morning at the prayer service, didn't ya?"

"You told me I could say whatever I wanted."

"I know." Blue Gene angrily scraped meat off the chicken breast. "But dang, all you talked about was either abortin' babies or sinnin'. Sin, sin, sin! Like you're all high and mighty."

"What's wrong with you?" asked Elizabeth.

"If you really listen to what Jackie said, it makes sense. Everybody's so worried about the unborn. I'm for the unborn, too, obviously. But what about the *born*? I know you're pro-life, but you're also for the war. So what about the troops? What about them getting aborted? 'Cause they're getting aborted on the battlefield. And these are people who have memories and loved ones. They actually have a life to lose. What about them?"

"You're preaching to the choir," said Elizabeth. "I feel awful for our troops. I wish they didn't have to fight, either. Wait—since when are you not for the war?"

"I didn't even know you was *for* the war," said Bernice.

"He doesn't sound like he is," said Elizabeth.

Blue Gene took his camouflage ball cap off and ran his fingers through his oily hair.

"Oh, I don't know anything no more. I don't know if I'm comin' or goin'." He put his cap back on and looked Elizabeth in the eye. "Sorry I got cross with you. I'm just havin' a hard time lately, pro'ly 'cause I quit smoking again. And look there, see that woman waiting for the doctor to show up over there? That's a fifty-four-year-old with stage-four lung cancer. Now, what if it don't work out here for her? Where else would we send her? I don't know what I've got myself into here."

Elizabeth reached across the table for Blue Gene's hand, but he shook his head and kept it to himself.

"Don't be like that," said Bernice, as she grabbed his hand and forced it into Elizabeth's. Then she held his other hand. Blue Gene felt self-conscious holding hands with the two women and felt an overwhelming need to say something, to break the silence, as both his grandmothers stared at him.

"I'm sorry, y'all," he said.

"You don't have to apologize," said Elizabeth. "You've been through so much, finding out about John. You've handled it all really well. You're entitled to feel confused."

"But it ain't just that. That's the sad part. That's not even what's occupying my thoughts the most. You'd think it would be, but it ain't." When he realized how much he had divulged, he took his hands back and kept them in his lap.

"Well, you've just taken on too much here lately," said Bernice. "You didn't know this place would take off the way it's done, and it's done taken off in no time."

"It's not that either, though."

"Well, what is it then?" asked Bernice.

"Oh, I don't like being all gay, talking about stuff like this."

"Tell us what's wrong," said Elizabeth. "We might be able to help."

"You know we won't let up till you tell us," said Bernice.

"What's wrong?" repeated Elizabeth. Blue Gene pulled his ball cap down over his face and let out an exhausted man-growl.

"I'm in love."

$$$

Meanwhile, in their Nike whites, Henry and John played tennis on a clay court within the Mapother estate, with Arthur scurrying to and fro, retrieving their stray balls. Henry had suggested they play in order to release the frustrated energy of what had been a stressful week. Their friendly match ended up causing stress, though, because three separate times, Henry accused John of letting him win a point, which he considered an unpardonable insult. John swore he hadn't done so, and to prove his point, he took the last set six-zero, finishing his father off with two aces that whizzed past his squinting hazel eyes.

As always, at the match's conclusion, they met each other at the net and shook hands. Arthur included himself in the ritual, giving both his father and grandfather some impressive little hand-throbs, even though this wasn't required of the ball boy. As they walked off the court, Henry panted and sweated effusively.

"You okay?" asked John.

"I'm fine," said Henry, his nostrils enlarged. His father's nostrils had always intimidated John. They were hairy and commanding.

The three of them sat on a bench and drank bottled water. Half of what Arthur attempted to drink came out the sides of his mouth. Henry toweled his face and his hair until it was dry and preppily swayed to one side, like it had been for as long as John could remember.

"You had better not have given me those points," said Henry.

"Arthur, could you go get those balls that were hit outside the fence?" asked John. Arthur made his own sound effects as he ran off.

"Dad, you hate it if someone lets you win—which I wasn't doing— but I'm just saying, you hate that so much, so it seems like you could understand why I didn't want to get my membership like *this*."

"How do you think all the rest got in? Most of the world has been built behind closed doors."

"But I wanted to *earn* it."

"You have earned it. So have I, and my father, and his father. Believe me, the Mapothers have earned it."

"You could've at least consulted me first."

"Stop it." Henry's face suddenly took on the appearance of a jagged rock formation. "Stop whining. You made a mess of your campaign, and now I've guaranteed a way for you to still succeed in spite of yourself, so stop questioning me."

"How did *I* make a mess of the campaign? Blue Gene is the one who's caused the problem."

"You unceremoniously handed him the truth over a cellular phone."

"It was an *accident*!"

"I know that was an accident, but let's be honest. It's not just the cell phone. You destroyed your future the day you decided to hump that little girl. I've been having to clean up your messes ever since."

John shot up from the bench. "You were right. I *was* letting you win!"

"I knew you were. I knew. You had better watch it, Son. Maybe some-day you won't have me to solve all your problems."

"I can solve my own problems. I'll still win this election." Arthur re-turned with the tennis balls, looking at the adults with his head askance.

"I've seen how you solve your problems. You just cut and run, like you did with that debate. Do you know what that made you look like, John?"

He knew exactly what it made him look like. He had taken a small hit in the polls and felt a great shame that reached to the bowels of his character. But he didn't fire back because Arthur had returned.

"You need to calm it down, Grandpa," said Arthur. "Your breaths are too heavy."

"Thank you, Arthur, but I'm fine."

John saw that Arthur was right. Henry tried to hide how out of breath he was. And this, John decided, was why going through with the deal was the right thing to do. He had to get as far as possible while his father was still living and still had the health to enjoy his son's success. Westway International had made the Mapothers super-rich, but tobacco wasn't a tenth as important as it had once been—a fact that neither man verbally acknowledged—and its profits were only lessening. With an offer to be nominated for lifetime membership in the Wormland Group and to be sponsored by one of its senior members, John's political career had an instant growth spurt that would benefit the family for genera-tions to come.

John and Henry zipped up their racquets in black cases. Arthur ran off after a rabbit. He was always asking for a pet, and John told him if he could catch one of those rabbits, he could keep it.

"Well, I suppose this was all meant to be," said John. "Blue Gene in-advertently led to this offer falling into my lap."

"Apology accepted," said Henry.

"I didn't apologize."

"It was implicit. For you to change subjects like that, the apology was implicit."

"Whatever you say, Dad."

"I will accept your apology, though. I'll admit, this is misdirected anger on my part, too. I fought with your mom all last night and all morning over her going back to that building. You mustn't tell her that we had anything to do with its demise. She'd tell him, and he'd come out against you."

"He could figure it out without Mom, probably. Mom said she noticed a change in him yesterday."

"What kind of change?"

"He's just not as accepting as he once was. He said no to her from the start and wouldn't budge."

"Don't worry. When all is said and done, he'll be a footnote in your presidential memoir. He's a human-interest story. Human-interest stories aren't put in the history books. People are eating this up because it's a riches-to-rags story. People love riches-to-rags stories because they suggest that wealth isn't all it's cracked up to be. They like to see a rich man lose his way and say that money can't bring happiness, that money is no good. But they'll see how foolish he's been once his building closes."

"Mom said those people in there just adore him."

"Those people are idiots."

"They seem to have won Mom over."

"Your mother looks for the Virgin Mary in her pasta." John laughed. "Those people in there are idiots or they wouldn't be in there in the first place. The problem is that even though they're idiots, their votes count the same as yours or mine. I've always felt that was a big mistake. It makes no sense to me. Why should someone who is obviously uneducated, unintelligent, sometimes even criminal, who does nothing but avoid the death instinct, be on equal footing with his superiors when it comes to something as important as selecting our leaders?"

"Because there're so many. You have to let them have a say. I thought Blue Gene would help."

"I did too, or I would never have agreed to send your mother into that flea market in the first place."

"I'm still going to win the election, though." Henry didn't reply. "I will. I'm still ahead. Don't think of the Wormland Group as a substitute for Congress. I am still going to win that seat, and the Group will be the icing on the cake. I'll show you, Dad."

"I hope you do, Son."

$$$

"You gotta do it," said Bernice. "Just let 'er rip and ask her out. What are ya waiting for?"

"I agree," said Elizabeth. "You have no choice, really, when it comes to love. You'll only regret it if you don't."

Blue Gene was relieved to hear Elizabeth say this. She had shown concern just minutes before, saying that the petite young lady with the ragged shoes was a criminal in the making, and that her strange, angry music was a bad influence on Blue Gene. But Bernice vouched for her, explaining that she was a really bright girl—she had a master's degree in political science—and she didn't do drugs. And she was just as sweet as she could be, once you got to know her. Then, after Elizabeth learned Jackie's mother's maiden name, she encouraged him to make his move.

"I thought you didn't like her," said Blue Gene.

"Samson is a good, old Bashford name. And really, after all you've endured as of late, I only want you to be happy, and I know that when you embark on a relationship with someone, it *will* make you happy."

Elizabeth went on to explain how Henry had easily stolen her from the musician because he had made her feel as though anything was possible. Bernice talked about her Bart, how she and he had been two poor, lonely teenagers whose hard-luck lives had finally led to a moment of relief in which they met and instantly fell in love in the middle of an axle-shaft factory. Before long, Elizabeth and Bernice became like teenage girls goading their platonic guy-friend on at the high school lunch table. Blue Gene's leg bounced sporadically at the mention of asking Jackie out, and he started sucking harder on his candy.

"What if she says no? Ain't nothin' worse than a girl sayin' no."

"You're going to scoff at this," said Elizabeth, "but listen to me. You go up to your room and say a prayer that everything will work out one way or another. Then walk up to Jackie and ask her out."

Blue Gene looked at Bernice.

"Yeah, it's worth a try," said Bernice. "Give her a go."

Upstairs in his bedroom, his prayers evaporated into daydreams. He pictured himself and Jackie on a motorcycle, which was funny because he had never even ridden one, though he would never admit that. Nevertheless, he pictured them cutting across America down a silver highway that ran through perfectly lined cornfields. He imagined that this was their home: open road, thunder-thighs, crotch to rump, chromium coming from their bottoms, his hip bones as her handlebars. Their love was a roaring, four-legged, two-wheeled beast that chewed up the interstate. They would eventually settle down, though, in a modest home in downtown Bashford, but a home with all the excitement of Bourbon Street passing through the bedroom hallway. It wouldn't matter where he and Jackie lived, though; he knew from experience that he could be happy in a dinky, rust-bitten trailer, as long as the catnip of love was there to roll around in. But why even have thoughts like these? He used to daydream about Cheyenne like this, too, how they'd have a child of whom *he* could be called the father, and maybe they'd name him Freedom, or Liberty if it was a girl.

He unclipped his walkie-talkie.

"Bumblebee?" he asked.

"Here I am, Freedom Hawk," replied Jackie.

"Could I see you upstairs, please?"

"Yaish."

Within the minute, Jackie appeared in his doorway, her messy, barretted hair looking like some abstract work of art that Blue Gene didn't understand but knew he liked.

"What's crappenin'?" she asked.

He stood from his bed. He already knew how he would say it; he had actually known for a couple of weeks now.

"Jackie, you pro'ly already know this, but I like you. I like you man-and-woman style, and would you want to watch wrestling with me on a private basis sometime?"

He was good at making her laugh, and if he had any chance at catching her, he figured his humor would be his strongest weapon. Also, the topic of wrestling was something that would remind her that they had something in common, other than coming from "good" families and suffering from depression.

Jackie did laugh. She smiled and almost forgot to cover her mouth. She wouldn't say anything. Blue Gene reached for his bag of Dum Dums, which he kept next to his pillow. "Well?" he asked, as he fumbled with the wrapper.

She uncovered her mouth, exposing a frown.

"I don't know how to say this," she said, timidly. "I mean, sure, I'll watch wrestling with you sometime. I'd enjoy *that*."

"No more banter." It came out more like a projectile than he intended.

"Okay. I'm sorry. I just don't see you like that. I like what we have already. I think you are an *amazing* guy, but—"

"I said no more banter!"

Jackie's body language became frightened, curved like a question mark. "I'm sorry. I'm sorry, Blue Gene. I *do* like you. I can't help it. Please don't be mad."

"Get outta here."

"*Blue Gene?*" Her voice reached an octave higher.

"It's a'ight. I knew this is how it'd be. Get out."

"No." She took a step further into the room. Blue Gene hurled his bag of suckers at her with all his might, hitting her in the stomach. She let out a fragile "oh" and ran down the steps. For ten minutes he stared motionlessly at all the little suckers with their colorful wrappers scattered across the floor. Twice over the walkie-talkie, Bernice asked him what was going on, but he didn't answer. Bernice and Elizabeth finally appeared at his door.

"I need some alone time," he said without looking up.

"Do you want to talk?" Elizabeth asked carefully.

"No."

"I oughta whoop that girl," said Bernice. "You forget her, Blue Gene. Your ass would make her a nice face."

"A'ight. Just leave me alone."

"I'll pray for you," said Elizabeth. "And you should pray too. Don't lose faith."

"I'm sorry you're havin' such a rough time, hon," added Bernice. "But just remember: it's never so bad that it can't get worse." He turned away.

"Maybe it just wasn't meant to be," said Elizabeth. "Pray that it works out in the end, and that you end up with the right girl. And if that doesn't work, maybe it's time to get a haircut."

"Y'all, I'm fuckin' *serious*. Get out."

"Ooh, buddy. He's for real. We better get out."

"I'll call you later," said Elizabeth before she and Bernice headed down the steps. Blue Gene lay back on his bed and again got out his walkie-talkie. He demanded that one of the teenage boys he had hired as a gofer come upstairs immediately.

"You eighteen yet?" Blue Gene asked gruffly.

"Nineteen," said the buzz-cut boy with an oversize basketball jersey.

Blue Gene reached inside his shorts, pulled out his gray denim Velcro wallet, and gave the boy a couple of bills.

"Here. Go to the Thornton's across the way. Buy me two cartons of Parliaments."

"I thought you quit smoking."

"I ain't payin' you to ask questions."

Blue Gene spent the rest of the night chain-smoking in bed, wearing nothing but black briefs and a ball cap. He rudely turned away anyone who attempted to talk to him, whether it was an old vet on the walkie-talkie or a troubled teen at his door. Bernice tried to get him to come down and see some kids for a local charity, but he replied in his slow, deep monotone, "I already gave to their cause. It didn't seem to help."

He eventually turned off his walkie-talkie and threw it across the room. He stared at the smoke above him and thought about pushing Jackie's nose in with the heel of his palm, which immediately made him feel guilty. From his stereo, he pulled out Jackie's mix CD and broke it in half, shooting shards of hard plastic across the room. Doing this cut his hand, and he rubbed the blood on his underwear. He lay back down and absolutely refused to cry.

All girls were the same, he decided after bleeding awhile. Jackie, Cheyenne, the cheerleaders he dated when he was a basketball player—all the same girl. Jackie was supposed to be so unique, such an individual, but she was just like all the rest. No matter what style of clothes they wore, they were all shallow and would simply choose the handsomest, most superior boy they were capable of getting. It was as simple as that.

So maybe he'd say goodbye to all this. Maybe he would say, "Bring on that suit and tie," after all. He was better than this and better than her, anyway. He could buy her. He could buy her family. Her ancestors probably worked for his. His parents' house could swallow hers whole.

How dare she! How dare she reject him just like that after leaving him hanging all summer to guess whether she liked him. No one would ever treat him like that again. A few changes on his surface, and he could have any shallow bitch he wanted. All he had to do was clean up and cut the mullet. And damn her for asking if he knew what a mullet was, like he had some kind of disease. People like Jackie were supposed to be so tolerant and freethinking. They were the same smart alecks who spoke so highly of acceptance, yet bashed Christians like his mom without thinking a thing of it. It's funny how they'd throw a fit if you said a single negative word about Jews or blacks or gays, yet Christians were fair game for bashing. Jackie was as two-faced as anyone. Let her have her city with its rap and glass and smoke and people yelling, "Go!" and the way the city people always said, "Excuse me," in a certain way that sounded so hateful. She'd fit in just fine.

Maybe he'd wake up tomorrow, cut the mullet, shave, and spend the rest of his days like John, buttoning and unbuttoning his sport coat every time he stood and sat. He'd stop this stupid working man's dream, take an office job at Westway, and find himself a hot, classy chick, maybe one of those pharmaceutical salesgirls who were always bringing samples to the doctor's office. They were always so clean and put together so solidly in their form-fitting business suits. He could buy one with ease. Plus, that would mean free Zoloft for life. Or maybe he'd forego the woman route altogether. Maybe he'd buy himself a Venus flytrap and train it to satisfy him. What difference did it make?

He hid himself in his room on into the evening, doing nothing but smoking cigarettes in bed, refusing to see anyone and refusing to come out, even when he was told that a pair of cops had arrived and arrested one of his workers for providing beer to minors. The cops also left word for Blue Gene that they'd be paying him another visit soon. He didn't care.

$ $ $

At eight o'clock the next morning, Blue Gene awakened to what he thought was the sound of someone yelling for him. He dismissed it; he was such a popular guy at the Commonwealth Building that he always heard his name being called, to the extent that sometimes he only imagined it.

Then, at ten after eight, one of the men who lived downstairs shook him awake.

"Blue Gene, man, you need to get downstairs, fast. This time there're *a bunch* of cops. We seen 'em pull into the parking lot. Something's up."

"What do they want?"

"I don't know, but I figured you'd wanna know what was going on."

"A'ight. I'll be down in a minute."

But after the man left, Blue Gene didn't make a move. He had no desire to stay conscious.

Ten minutes later, Bernice was waking him.

"Let me sleep!" he yelled at her.

"But the cops say they're here to shut us down."

"Have the Veterans deal with it."

"But—"

"Please, just let me sleep!"

And with that, he turned over on his belly and stayed in bed. A bed had always been there for him: when he had his accident in high school and couldn't walk, when his bedmate Cheyenne would disappear for days at a time, and when the waking life did nothing but take stabs at him, like it had done yesterday. He didn't care what was going on downstairs. What could he say to the police, anyway? The idea of everyone suddenly leaving him alone sounded so appealing. Part of him was glad it was happening, because he knew he was about three-quarters of the way through his money and would eventually have to close the doors anyway. Now there was the chance it would be done for him. He concluded that the Veterans could deal with the problem, and if the place had to be closed, the place had to be closed. For now, he just wanted to sleep forever.

The third time he was awakened, it was to a forceful banging on his door and the words "Police! Open up!"

Blue Gene drowsily untangled himself from the bedsheets and opened the door to see two serious faces sitting atop black uniforms.

"What'd I do now?"

"You're the owner of this place, aren't you?" asked one of the cops.

"Yeah."

"Put some clothes on, guy."

"What for?" asked Blue Gene, scratching his protruding belly.

"Your business has been shut down. We're going to have to ask you to vacate the premises immediately."

Still half-asleep, he didn't even think to ask why the Commonwealth Building was being closed. Only when the officers led him downstairs did his droopy face lift with surprise. The great room was completely empty except for a few ownerless dogs and cats, whose barks and meows echoed pitifully. The bright fluorescent tube lights were on, and the room looked much like the abandoned retail store it once was: nothing but cold white tile and stiff white poles. The cozy smell of bacon remained in the air, and there were half-eaten meals left in the café area. Strewn about were red plastic cups and steel chairs, and in the background were incomplete murals.

Blue Gene and the officers walked out of the building and into the parking lot, which was already emptying except for a couple of news crews from Donato Falls, some police cars, and a handful of devotees. A defeated line of beat-up pickups was heading out the exit lane.

"There he is!" yelled one of the reporters, and the cameras swung toward him. "Blue Gene! Blue Gene!" He pulled the bill of his cap over his face and walked past the reporters, who swarmed him with microphones drawn.

"What do you have to say about your business closing down?"

"Do you condone the drug use that was going on here?"

"Did you know anything about the alleged prostitution?"

"Do you plan to reopen?"

But his mustached mouth would not provide any sound bites that morning. Once they made it past the reporters, one of the cops continued to walk with him.

"I don't like having to do this, but I have to escort you off the premises," said the young officer. "You have to completely leave the parking lot."

Blue Gene nodded, and they walked toward his truck, which was parked in the back. All the while, he looked around for Jackie.

"Blue Gene!" Blue Gene turned to see one of the Veterans, a sphere-shaped bearded man named Larry who always wore a black leather jacket that said 'NAM VETS on the back. "What are you gonna do?"

"What *can* I do?"

"Gotta keep walking," said the officer, taking Blue Gene by the elbow.

"What did the cops tell you?"

"Nothin'."

"They were tellin' me they were closin' it 'cause they were getting so many complaints. But can they really close it just 'cause of complaints?"

"I don't know, man."

"No, I don't think y'all can do that," Larry said to the cop. "Look. See those people? They were supposed to see the doctor today."

A small group of people was still standing in front of the building, some of them being interviewed, some of them looking like they were waiting for something to happen. A few still held clipboards on which they had been filling out their patient histories. The officer shook his head and looked sad and apologetic.

"What are we supposed to tell those people!?" asked Larry, addressing both Blue Gene and the cop.

"Sir, you're going to have to settle down and go home. There's nothing we can do about it."

"This is *wrong*!" said Larry.

"Sir!" shouted the cop, and Larry turned away. A couple of other Veterans had been walking behind him.

"*What*?" asked Larry. One of the other Veterans, a short man wearing a Billy Ray Cyrus T-shirt, was smiling. "What are you smilin' at?"

"Nothin', Larry! Cool it, man."

"At least I tried."

"Sure you did."

"Is that sarcastic?"

"No. Jesus, Larry."

But Larry was already in the other Veteran's face, their stomachs touching. They started taking swings. To break them up, the officer had to abandon Blue Gene, whose mouth hung open moronically. He had felt this way once before, when poor old Cheyenne had a seizure at a bike rally. Part of him said to do something and do something fast, but the other part pointed out that he had no idea what to do.

He was hooked back from his daze when he again heard his name being called.

"What do we do?" Now Bernice was at his side.

"Nothin' we *can* do."

"Did you know they arrested Jackie?"

"They *did*?"

"Yeah."

"What do I care?"

"I don't know."

"Why'd they arrest her?"

"She wouldn't leave the building. So they made her. Ol' turkey buz-zards. Should we go to the police station? See if we can pay her bail?"

"No. She can call her mom or stepdad."

"Where you gonna go?"

"I don't know." The nondescript room in the upstairs of the Wal-Mart building had been his home for the last month and a half.

"Do you want to come home with me?" she asked.

"I reckon so. Won't be any reporters to bug us out in the boonies."

By this point, the cops were actively making everyone leave. Blue Gene left his truck in the parking lot and let Bernice drive them away in her half-reliable 1987 Buick Regal. All the while, Charlie stood in his spot out front with his saxophone, playing "Happy Days Are Here Again," though its peppy melody came out slow and mournful, like a dirge.

$ $ $

"Send her in," said John, and he took several deep breaths, which every-one always said to do when you're stressed, but which only made him lightheaded. He started to get up from his desk to hug his mother, but as he had feared, she was clearly not in the mood for affection, her face as tight as the hair pulled back at the base of her skull.

"What's wrong?" he asked, standing behind his desk.

"I just came from Gene's building. It was closed."

"Yeah. I heard something about that."

"I'm coming to you first because I know I can't get the truth out of your father. Did either of you have anything to do with this?"

"No," said John, but he couldn't say it without looking at the top corner of the office.

"*John.*"

"Mother, please. I've got so much work to do."

"You two had me go in there and ask him to close it down, he says no, and then it ends up being closed anyway. I'm not an idiot."

"The police closed it."

"Don't I deserve to know what's going on!?" She threw her black purse at the floor.

"Mom, I wish you'd just trust that we're doing what's best for everyone and leave it at that."

"Stop condescending! I am not naïve. I know how politics works. But you don't have to keep *me* in the dark. You don't have to treat me like I'm just another voter."

"We're worried that you might tell Blue Gene," said John in a soft, tired voice. There were ten days left until the election, and he didn't know if he was going to make it after all with his psyche stretched to a near snap. "You spent so much time with him the last couple of days, and he has you leading a prayer group, and—"

"You put a stop to that, though, didn't you?"

"See. You're holding up for him right now. We obviously can't trust you on this topic."

"*You* can't trust *me*? You're both being awful to me. Just awful."

"We had to do it the way we did it, though. Your dream is what's most important, isn't it?"

Elizabeth took a deep breath and sat in front of John's desk. "Yes."

"It's what's most important to me, too, and now, it looks like it's starting to come true."

"How so?"

John glanced at his computer screen, which showed a picture of Arthur and Abby on the beach. "I'm not supposed to tell you, but it was *your* dream. I think you have a right to see it coming to fruition."

John sat at his computer. After a few clicks of the mouse, he invited his mom to sit in his seat.

"Dad forwarded this to me," he said. "Don't tell him I let you read this." Elizabeth read the email:

Dear Henry,

We hear the rumblings coming up from Bashford and are sorry the source is your son. We've been briefed on the situation and think it would be best to nip this in the bud, especially before this health clinic idea takes off. As our source explains, your son appears to be undermining us all, and his operations need to cease immediately.

We realize John's current run for office complicates this issue for you, but I am respectfully asking that you take care of this. After talking it over, we agreed that out of respect for you and all you've contributed through the years, we should let you handle this however you want. But we do hope that you will take care of it as soon as possible.

Our source has explained to us the impossible situation you've been placed in, and we do hope this won't hurt John's chances. (And perhaps it won't, considering the angle Frick's been playing!) To soften the blow that this may cause to John's congressional bid, you have my word that when I retire from the Wormland Group in two years' time, I will personally sponsor him to be the one to take my place. I will nominate him for lifetime membership, as I know this was what you always wanted.

Call or write back as soon as possible.
Sincerely,
Sen. Lawrence Pendergraft

Elizabeth turned to John after reading it.

"What do you think?" he asked.

"I don't know. What's this Wormland Group?"

"It's the most influential think tank—I guess you'd call it that, a think tank. Anyway, it's basically one of the most elite groups of executives in the world. Former presidents have even been in it. Supposedly only two men from each time zone in the world are in it. I'm not sure if that's true, though. It's basically a collection of some of the most influential men in the world. They help shape the world economy. All world leaders, even the United Nations, *listen* to what Wormland has to say."

"I've never even heard of it."

"They're kind of secretive—not secretive, but they don't advertise themselves. The most important thing for you to know, though, is that they carry a lot of influence in shaping foreign policy."

"What's that even mean? *Wormland Group?*"

"It's the name of the ski resort in Switzerland where they first met. They meet once a year at the finest hotels in the world, but the meetings are top secret. People don't even know where the meetings were until after the fact. But that's not what matters. What matters is that I'm one step closer." Elizabeth smiled and nodded. She got up from John's chair and stood at the window overlooking downtown Bashford. "Aren't you happy for me?"

"I am, but I wish this didn't have to happen at the expense of Gene's building."

"But Mom, it's for the dream. Don't you see? I can take Senator Pendergraft's spot in this group. I'll have lifetime membership, and maybe I can use it to help make your dream come true. I'll be able to influence people and put an end to war."

"By having a war."

"That's what your dream meant, right?"

"Yes. The last war. What we've all been building toward." She said it with a little laugh. She kept staring out the window, appearing to look at some image decades away in the distance.

"Good *Lord*, Mother, don't tell me you're questioning yourself *now*."

"No." She shook her head rapidly and walked away from the window. "I am *not* questioning myself. I wouldn't do that. You just keep saying, it's for the dream, *it's for the dream*. And that's what your father always says. Anytime I've ever doubted myself and said it was just a dream, your dad always says no, that it's a prophecy. I started having the dream the day America pulled out of Vietnam. He said that had to mean something, that it was a sign from God, sent when our country needed it the most, and that I was prophesizing how the world could be made right again."

"And I *will*. I will make the world right again. Mom, why can't you be happy for me? I thought you wanted me to follow my destiny more than anyone. So here you go; it's waiting for me on a silver platter. At this rate, I'll be president in another decade. And you know, I can still win this election. I will."

"I know. I just don't think it's right what you all have done to those people that Gene was helping. I'm not happy about that part one bit."

"I'm sure I'll make it up to you."

Elizabeth laughed. "Maybe that should be your new campaign slogan."

$ $ $

When they arrived at Bernice's house out in Dixon County, Blue Gene went to the guest bedroom, stripped down to his underwear, and collapsed in bed. The bedroom window was open, something he was unaccustomed to, and he soon found that he enjoyed hearing the occasional *whoosh* of a car zooming down the country road outside, because it reminded him that he was settled in for the day, while the people in their cars still had a ways to go.

He dreaded whatever would happen next. Reporters were likely to track him down at Bernice's, as well as some of the people he had gotten to know at the Commonwealth.

Right at 11:00 a.m., Bernice yelled for him.

"Blue Gene! Come here. We're on the TV!"

The whole scene from that morning at the Commonwealth Building played out on Bernice's dusty old TV set. A ceramic-looking anchorman explained that due to "continuous complaints" and reports of "illegal activities," the Bashford Police Department had evacuated the Commonwealth Building on Highway 81. Its doors would be padlocked indefinitely. Chief of Police Oral Haynes looked old and crabby as ever as he explained on camera that he had no choice but to close the building.

"It was getting really out of hand," he said. "Getting so we were having regular reports of all kinds of disturbances, and then last night we confirmed that someone on the premises was giving alcohol to minors, and that arrest led us to some more information about some narcotics and other potential problems. It had to be put to a stop."

As footage was shown of the police ushering people out of the green building, a voice-over explained the establishment was closed just an hour before the opening of its free health clinic.

"The clinic itself wasn't even legal," said Chief Haynes. "We got a full report from JCAHO saying that the clinic is below standard for patient treatment, infection control, and safety risks. It was a nice idea, but it's just not how to do things."

Then the bodiless, professional voice said that one arrest was made *during* the evacuation. Jackie was shown being dragged out by two cops, her short legs scuffing the pavement. "All we're trying to do is help people, and you want to demonize us for it!" the camera captured her saying. Her eyes bugged out, and she looked shaky. Then Blue Gene was shown walking past the crowd out front. With his head hung low, he looked like a baseball cap with long hair attached.

"The owner of the operation," continued the voice-over, "'Blue' Gene Mapother, left his controversial venue without incident, though some employees from the Commonwealth Building say their rights have been infringed upon."

"If Blue Gene doesn't fight back for us, I will," said one of the Veterans, the one young man of the group. He had a high-and-tight hair-

cut. "Closing us down with no notice, just kicking us out, it should-
n't have happened in the first place. This is supposed to be the land of
the free. Regardless of what Blue Gene does, we're not going to accept
this."

Before the report ended, Blue Gene was already on his feet.

"After all I done for them, and *that's* how they thank me?"

"No, now, that's just one of 'em talking. Most of them appreciate
what all you done."

"What do you mean, *most of them*?"

"I didn't want to upset you, but some of 'em thought you should've
got more aggressive. But I don't think so."

"What'd they say about me?"

"Well, they thought you should've been doing something to keep it
from closing. I don't wanna repeat what they called you, but—"

"Was it a pussy?"

"Yeah."

Blue Gene thrashed at the sofa cushions furiously.

"Calm down! I held up for you. I told 'em you weren't feeling well.
I knew you was still hurtin' over that Jackie."

"I don't give a care about her. What did *they* do to stop it from happening?"

"Nothing."

"Then screw them! Those guys think they're so badass. I'd have been
in the army, too, if it wasn't for my stupid leg."

"I wouldn't have let you."

"What else did they say?"

"It don't matter."

"Bernice!"

"They was sayin' maybe this was your true colors shinin' through,
that maybe you were just a rich boy and didn't care about none of them.
I held up for you, though."

"Can I use your phone?"

"What for?"

"I'm gonna call my mom and ask her if I can get a lawyer or something."

"Oh, Blue Gene, they ain't gonna let you open that building back up."

Blue Gene called Elizabeth's cell phone and asked her if she could recommend a lawyer who could help him reopen the Commonwealth. After a minute of what he could clearly identify as hemming and hawing, she let it out that there would be no point in his taking legal action, that Henry had this case won before it had even begun. She confessed to him over the phone everything that she wasn't supposed to, and ended the conversation by telling Blue Gene to let it go, because Henry and John would win no matter what. The best he could do, she said, was make himself a part of their agenda, but don't try stopping them, because nobody could.

"Bastards," muttered Blue Gene after he hung up.

This sent Blue Gene back to bed, this time not to sleep but to think. His first instinct was to point his pickup in a random direction and drive far away from his problems, but he winced once he realized he had even considered leaving town. How dare his own family get him in the state of mind where he would consider leaving Bashford! He loved his old hometown. They were the ones who were always putting it and its people down. He was only trying to make Bashford better with the Commonwealth Building, and they had taken it from him—not just him, though, but all those people who needed it. The cruelty of the whole situation, the fact that John and Henry were hurting hundreds of people who had nothing to do with their political affairs, soon exposed itself to Blue Gene.

He bounced out of bed and returned to the living room, where Bernice was watching *All My Children*.

"I'm going over there 'round suppertime."

"Over where?"

"Mom and Dad's."

"Why?"

"'Cause that's when I know John'll be there."

"I mean, why you goin' over there at all?"

"I'm gonna confront both John and Dad and tell 'em to give me my building back."

"You're liable to just make it worse."

"I ain't lettin' us go down without a fight. I'm gonna take both of 'em on."

"It don't matter. They got more money than you. They'll whoop you."

"You saw what I looked like on TV. I can't let that be the way I'm remembered. I can't just let this go."

"Can't you, though?"

$$\text{\textit{\$ \$ \$}}$$

John stared at his brine-cured roast turkey. Arthur nibbled on his chicken tenders, which the housekeeper had made especially for him. Abby stroked Arthur's straight, sandy hair while Henry and Elizabeth fought, as they had been doing since dinner began.

"Elizabeth, don't you see that if I didn't take care of it, someone from the Capitol would've? I handled it a lot better than anyone from up there would have. I told Haynes not to arrest Eugene. I told him not to arrest anybody, and the only one he had to take into custody was that girl, but that wasn't my fault."

"But why would the senator even *care*? What harm is Gene doing?"

"Aside from the social problems he's been causing, the senator asked himself why a man would do what Eugene is doing. We spoke about this on the phone. He said he didn't mean to cast judgment on my son, but as he saw it, what Eugene had done, in effect, was bring a lot of hard-up people together, and because he had provided so much for them, they might feel beholden to him. That could be dangerous. After all, Eugene is a red-blooded American man like any of us, and therefore he should not be trusted to have so many people at his personal disposal."

"That's ludicrous. Gene isn't like you men. He doesn't think like you do. The *senator* said that?"

"Yes. The senator said that these changes that are developing in a single, humble Wal-Mart building might lead others to follow by example, and that these changes have a way of creeping up on societies."

Just as the housekeeper, a big-boned old Mexican woman named Margarita, was bringing in the dessert—pears in raspberry-cabernet sauce and dark chocolate—there came a repeated, staccato ringing of the doorbell. Margarita set the tray down on a credenza and rushed to the foyer. A moment later, everyone heard some determined, uneven footsteps coming their way.

"Did you know he was coming?" asked Henry.

"No," said Elizabeth, "But I'm glad."

John threw his white cloth napkin on his half-eaten plate of food. He considered rushing out of the room. As he started to scoot his chair back, he looked up to see Blue Gene at the threshold, tendrils of his long, oily hair reaching out wildly, a shadow cast over his face by the bill of his ball cap, and a mustache frowning in scorn.

"He came in as soon as I opened the door and would not take off his shoes," said the housekeeper.

"That's all right," said Elizabeth. "He's okay. Go back to the kitchen." Elizabeth walked across the oriental rug but stopped when she saw that the sour look on Blue Gene's face wasn't changing.

"Hey, Blue Gene!" said a joyous, high-pitched voice. His features suddenly lost their angry slant. Arthur was already out of his seat and standing in front of him.

"Oh. Well, hey there, Arthur," he said. "What do you say, big nuts?"

Arthur giggled.

"Hello, Blue Gene," John made himself say, as plainly as possible.

"Hey." Blue Gene wouldn't look at him.

"Do you wanna make some paper airplanes?" asked Arthur.

"Arthur, not now," said Abby.

"I'll play with you in a little bit," said Blue Gene. "Okay?"

"Okay," said Arthur, pouting.

"Hey, man, don't be down. I'll play with you in a little bit. I promise." He squatted down to speak to Arthur face to face and even mustered a smile, though Arthur wouldn't return one. "Hey, let's see. Halloween's comin' up next week. Whatcha gonna dress up as?"

"Harry Potter!"

"Are you all letting him be Harry Potter?" asked Elizabeth.

"Yes," said John. Abby nodded.

"Have a seat, Gene," said Elizabeth, and Henry cut his eyes at her.

"I don't want to," said Blue Gene.

"Can I get you anything?" asked Elizabeth.

"No. Look here, I ain't here to socialize." Blue Gene arose from his squatting position and faced Henry. "That building, it was real important to me, and I want y'all to have the cops open it back up. You can wait till after the election, but I want your word that you'll do it."

"What are you talking about?" asked Henry.

"No more lying," said Blue Gene firmly. "I know y'all were behind it closing, so I know you can just as easily have it opened back up."

John and Henry both turned to Elizabeth. "Don't look surprised," she said. "I told you I wasn't going to lie anymore, either."

"Maybe Arthur and I should go to the other room," said Abby.

"No, let's let Arthur stay. Let's let him in on everything from now on," said Blue Gene, finally looking at John. "So he won't turn out as clueless as me." John felt hot blood instantly simmer beneath his face as he looked Blue Gene in the eye.

"Yes, both you and Arthur stay, Abby," said Henry.

"Have a seat," John told Blue Gene quietly.

"I don't want to."

And with that, silence engulfed the spacious, dim room. Arthur got out his Game Boy and sat on the rug, and the only sound was that of his fingers hitting the plastic buttons.

"So, I want y'all's word that you'll tell the cops to let me open it back up. I don't want any hassle from any of them or any of y'all."

"Let's not forget there were a lot of unsavory characters setting up shop in your building," said Henry. "That's the main reason I stepped in like I did, and that's why the authorities will make sure it remains closed."

"Aw, man, don't give me that. Maybe we had a few people that shouldn't have been in there. Fine, I'll give you that. But even so, I'm trying to help 'em."

"At any rate," said Henry. "I don't think my father would've wanted the family fortune being squandered on those people."

"You're probably right. Your dad, if he was anything like you, probably wouldn't have wanted but half of me to have the money—the rich half. But that's ass-backwards. It oughta be the other way around. Only half my blood deserves all that money, but it's not the rich half. It's the other half that we don't talk about that deserves it. The money was in your dad's name, and I don't want to take anything away from your dad because I didn't know him, and I'm sure he had some good points, but he didn't make that money. Well, he *did*, but not but a piece of it. It was all of his workers that really made it for him, and then he took it and put it away for me and John, even though we didn't do a damn thing for it but be born. And so here I was, finally *using* it, giving it back to the people that really deserved it."

"And look at what they did with it!" Henry shot back. "They turned it into a crack house and a fornicatorium."

"Just some of 'em!"

"But Blue Gene, you know it was interfering with our campaign," said John. "You say no more lying, so there's your truth. You know that the things you were doing were causing me some serious PR headaches. People started associating our family name with the negative things that Dad's talking about. And then the ones that may still have voted for me—you wouldn't even endorse me anymore. It put us in this unsolvable predicament. I needed those people's votes, and all of a sudden, you wouldn't have anything to do with me."

"Only 'cause I found out you been lying to me my whole damn life."

"All right," said Elizabeth. "This isn't accomplishing anything."

"It was complicated," said John, who unbuttoned the top two buttons of his white dress shirt and fanned himself with his undershirt.

"Eugene," said Henry, "you have to look at the bigger picture here.

This is John's whole life. You know we'd been planning on this since he was a boy. Meanwhile, you've just taken an interest in helping people in the last summer, and it was at the expense of John's campaign. So, yes, John's entire career is more important than the fate of your little Wal-Mart building."

"It wasn't little. You always call things *little* when it's someone else's thing. It was *huge*. It kicked ass."

"But at John's expense! You were hurting his chances. That boy has worked so hard to get where he is. I know you want to think you've got the monopoly on the work ethic, but John has worked hard to make himself a leader. And you were ruining all of his hard work just because you had this whim to buy an old Wal-Mart building."

"Buying a Wal-Mart wasn't a whim. If you had ever bothered getting to know me, you'd know it was a longtime fantasy of mine."

"When I let you have your inheritance, I thought you'd help pay Bernice's medical bills and go buy an exotic pet snake or something," said Henry. "But you had to go and make yourself look so big, right at the height of campaign season. It was really poor form."

"If you're saying that I's trying to steal John's thunder, you're wrong." Blue Gene turned to John. "God's honest, the original reason I bought the building was to impress some girl, but she turned out to be a bitch anyways, so screw her."

"Don't give up so easily," said Elizabeth.

"It don't matter," said Blue Gene.

"Have you talked to her today?"

"No."

"But in the long run," said John, "what we did was the right thing to do, because I will help more people than you could ever imagine."

"Yeah, yeah, yeah."

"I will," said John. "Listen to me, Blue Gene. I *will* help people someday. But I have to make my own dreams come true before I can make their dreams come true. I have to secure my own position, but once I have everything in place for us, then I will use my position and my power to help everyone else."

"I don't care, man. I ain't gonna let y'all bully me and all those peo-ple. I tell you that right now. You're making me look like a chump. I can't have that."

"What exactly do you plan on doing, then?" asked Henry.

"Doing what I gotta do. If you don't reopen my building beginning of November, I'll go to the press with everything. My whole deal."

"Why would you want to ruin your own family?" asked Henry.

"'Cause y'all made me look like a damn fool, and you've lied to me all my life, and I'm not taking anything off y'all anymore. You can't keep doing this to people and expect them not to do something back. Enough is enough."

"If you do it, you'll have hell to pay." said Henry.

"Both of you stop it!" said Elizabeth. "Don't you all see that all of this happened because of Grant Frick? Blue Gene, what you were doing for the people of this community *was* a good thing, but then Frick turned that against us. We should be mad at *him*, not each other. If it weren't for him, we never would've *had* to close down your Wal-Mart."

"She's right. We had to get on the offensive," said John, "and I'm sorry that meant hurting you, but Frick forced us into it."

"He used me, y'all used me, everybody's using everybody."

"This is exactly what he wants," continued John. "He wants our fam-ily divided. And this goes for you, too, Dad. You have to remember that Blue Gene isn't the enemy. Frick is the enemy. He's the one that wants to destroy our values. We need to remember what we started this campaign for in the first place: faith, values, freedom…all the things that make us who we are."

"That's true," Elizabeth chimed in.

"No, no. Stop it, y'all. I know big talk now when I hear it," said Blue Gene. "And that's big talk. They oughta call you Big Talk Mapother."

"Oh, knock it off," said John.

"It's true," said Henry. "Here we are fighting, when we should be de-voting our energy to defeating that whoremonger, Frick. If you go to the press about John's—" He paused, cleared his throat, and looked over at Abby. "Eugene, if you talk about John's mistake as a youth, you'd only be helping Frick win the election."

Abby suddenly got up from the table and exited.

"Abby, wait," said John.

"I don't want to listen to this," she said over her shoulder. John sighed and remained seated.

"Do you really want to help that immoral man succeed?" asked Henry. "He'll take our guns away and have the gays marrying and God knows what else."

"He definitely won't be building a kingdom of God," said John. "But I will. It's my destiny."

Blue Gene stomped his foot on the floor, causing Arthur to take notice and pause his video game. "Big talk!" Blue Gene yelled.

"It isn't big talk," said John. "I mean the things I say."

"How am I supposed to believe anything you say ever again?" asked Blue Gene. "Honestly. I mean, come on, John. How can you expect me to believe you? How can I believe any of y'all?!"

"All right, boys," said Elizabeth. "Let's talk about something positive." There was a long silence. "Anybody?"

"All's well that ends well," said Henry. "John is looking stable in the polls—an eight-point lead, as of yesterday, anyway. And Frick can no longer use your establishment against us."

"What about the people who were depending on *my establishment?*" asked Blue Gene.

"I'll see to it that the policies I set forth once I'm elected will help them," said John.

"They need your money more than anything, John."

"They need my leadership."

"They need your money. My money helped 'em more in a month than you have this whole time you've been campaigning. Let me ask you this. How much money you spent on this campaign?"

"You don't have to answer that," said Henry. "You do not have to defend yourself, John. And how many times do I have to say this? You provided for those people, and look what they did to pay you back. And don't tell me the people you were helping weren't criminals. Just turn on the news, any day of the week. Look at who's committing the crimes. Have you not seen the pictures of the people who kill each other and deal drugs and shoot and stab one another over nothing? Did you see the man who shook his girlfriend's baby to death? That dumb look in his eyes, on his face? Is it such a sin to point that out? It's the poorest, scummiest trash that you see in those mug shots, is it not?"

"The ones that look like me, you mean?" asked Blue Gene.

"I didn't say that. But why do you insist on helping the very people that are the abscesses on our society to begin with? They commit the murders, rob the stores. Why reward them? I tell you, it burns me up that I play by the rules of society, and I'm the one who is supposed to pay for their mistakes?"

"Look at John! Look at all he's done! Look at you!"

"Hold it down," said John.

"You don't judge us," said Henry. "That's not how it works."

"Look at you!" Blue Gene repeated.

"Stop fighting!"

The voice that said this was not yet mature, but because of its high pitch, it was able to penetrate the deeper tones of the adult males. Everyone hushed and looked down at Arthur, whose face was covered in anguish.

"Sorry, Arthur," said John. John got up from the table and sat on the floor next to his son and put his arm around him. "I'm sorry we're fighting. We're having a rough time, but don't you worry. Everything will be all right."

"You men should be ashamed of yourself," said Elizabeth. "Arguing like that with Arthur listening."

"Sorry, Arthur," said Blue Gene.

"That's okay," he said. "You still haven't played with me, though."

"You're right. I haven't."

As Blue Gene got down on the floor, John got up. "I'm going to go check on Abby," he said. Henry, meanwhile, got up and left the room without saying a word.

$ $ $

Within fifteen minutes, Blue Gene and Arthur's paper airplane–making had deteriorated into a paper-wad fight, which left Blue Gene sweaty and out of breath, reminding him how out of shape he was for a man in his late twenties. Eventually, John and Abby reappeared in the dining room doorway.

"All right, Arthur," said John. "Time to go home."

"Oh, John," said Elizabeth, still sitting at the dinner table. "Don't go yet. I think you and Gene need to talk for a while. Just the two of you."

"Abby's really tired," said John.

"I'm sure she wouldn't mind you staying behind, would you, Abby?"

"That's fine," said Abby.

"It's okay," said Blue Gene. "We don't need to talk no more."

"But you do," said Elizabeth.

"I've said all I've come to say," said Blue Gene. "I just wanted to let them know that they can't do me that way and get away with it, and they had better let me open my building back up or else."

"You're obviously still angry. You boys need to talk."

"Mom, he said he didn't want to," said John. "Now leave him alone."

"Come on, Arthur," said Abby.

"Can I stay?" he asked.

"No," said Abby. A swing of her long blond hair seconded her response as she headed for the door. Arthur moaned and got up from the floor.

"Hey, man, we'll play again sometime soon," said Blue Gene, also getting up from the floor. "I can still play with him sometime, can't I?" He looked at John and Abby.

"Of course," said John. "I wasn't sure if you'd want to—I mean, that would be fine."

"The way I figure it is that Arthur has nothing do with any of our stuff," said Blue Gene.

"Sure," said John.

"I'm gonna take off, too, then," said Blue Gene.

"No, you're not," said Elizabeth. "I'm serious. This is important. You and John need to talk. You boys have a seat. I'll have Margarita make you some hot tea."

"No, thanks," said John. "I don't want any."

"Neither do I," said Blue Gene.

"John, I'm going home," said Abby, curtly. He nodded. "Good night, everyone."

"Good night, Uncle Blue Gene," said Arthur.

"Good night, big buddy." Elizabeth walked Abby and Arthur to the front door. John and Blue Gene, not knowing what else to do, followed.

"Okay," Elizabeth said, after closing the door. "I'm going to go upstairs and give you two some privacy." Elizabeth turned before going up one of the curving ivory staircases with its wrought-iron rails. "I know that the two of you can't sort everything out in one night, but I just want the lines of communication to be open. Gene, tell him how you're feeling. And John, listen. Oh, and Gene, forgive John and Henry for what they pulled on you with the Commonwealth Building. Follow the Lord's way and forgive. Please don't go to the media about our secret. Offer it up to the Lord."

"A'ight. I'll take that under consideration."

"Good night, boys."

"Good night," both of them said. They walked into the living room and sat on opposite sides of the dark brown leather couch and stubbornly looked straight ahead.

"I know you hate me," John said finally. "But I assure you that my opinion of myself is lower than anyone else's could be."

Blue Gene nodded.

"Do you want to talk?" asked John.

"Do you?"

"I'll talk if you want to talk."

"I don't want to, really."

"There's no quick fix to something like this," said John.

"Nope." And that was the extent of their conversation for a silent stretch of two minutes. When someone finally spoke again, it was Blue Gene, only to say, "The room feels like it's dead without the TV on." He turned on the TV, then flipped through channels until he saw wrestling. With all the turmoil of the day, he had forgotten it was a Monday night. "Go ahead and make fun of me for watching wrestling."

"I'm not saying a word."

After five minutes of watching Vince McMahon praising himself in the ring, Blue Gene broke the silence.

"Y'all never really had me fooled."

"I didn't think we did. I knew that you knew, at least on a subconscious level."

"I knew I never was a gentleman. I knew that much."

"You're a gentleman."

"No. I seen how y'all gentlemen act. I ain't no gentleman."

"Come on, Blue Gene."

"All those years you been lying to me."

"What can I say? I mean, seriously, what's a guy supposed to say in this sort of situation?"

Blue Gene considered the question as he continued watching wrestling. It really wasn't that complicated, what John should've said. He should've said, "I'm sorry and I love you and I'll be here for you from now on." That would've been enough for Blue Gene, but he could already see that this new father figure would be just as cold as the old one.

"Why Tammy?" he shot off, hoping it would burn.

"What?"

"That was her name, right? *Tammy?*"

"Yes."

"Why her? The way Bernice talked about her, she didn't seem your type."

"Don't lay a guilt trip on me. Believe me, I've already put myself through a bigger guilt trip than you ever could."

"What do you remember about her?"

"I don't want to talk about that."

"Do you not remember, or are you just being a bastard?"

"Nothing has given you the license to talk to me that way." John stood and acted as though he was going to leave the room.

"Do you know *anything* about her? How 'bout her favorite color? Favorite colors are real important to little kids."

"She wasn't a little kid."

"Yes she was."

"She was old enough to not care about her favorite color. She wasn't altogether a child. You do know that I was traumatized by catching Dad with the housekeeper, don't you?"

"Yeah. So it's his fault?"

"*No.* But that's a part of it. That's an *important* part of it. And when you're around that age—" John turned to the fireplace. "Oh, God, I don't know how to say it, except that when you're that age, your genitals are like animals. They're these unclean, stupid things that you're curious about, and she—well, it was just like two animals rubbing against each other."

"*Gross.*"

"That's all it was. You asked me what she was like, but that's all it was. I don't know what else to say. We didn't talk much."

"So you didn't even *like* her?"

"I *liked* her, but...I don't know."

"But what?"

"I liked her, but she liked me more."

"Right. 'Cause you're so damn good-looking, aren't ya?"

John turned and stood over Blue Gene. "Why are you being such a child?"

"Let me ask you something. Have you ever in your whole life liked a girl that didn't like you back?"

"Well—Abby, when I first met her, she hated me because my opening line was 'Someday I'd like to get perfectly drunk with you.' It was in rehab."

"Yeah, but you ended up marrying her. Have you ever asked somebody out and they straight-up told you no?"

"No."

"Then you haven't lived. I guess you dumped Tammy, then?"

"We weren't even dating. I just stopped going over after it happened."

"But so she knew what it was like to be rejected, right?"

"I guess so."

"So that's where that part of me comes from. I knew I didn't inherit it from *you*." John sat back down. For the next minute, they didn't watch wrestling so much as look at the images on the screen. "You ain't even gonna *ask* what I'm referrin' to?" Blue Gene burst.

"What do you mean?"

"I mean, I talked about being rejected by a girl, and you ain't even gonna ask me the specifics?"

"Well, who rejected you?"

"Oh, like you really care. All I know is, you're lucky I was bummed out over a girl or I would've been raising hell this morning when y'all sent those cops in there. Which makes me wonder—did Mom tell you I was feeling under the weather because of that girl?"

"No."

"Wait a minute. I bet she did. I bet Mom told y'all I was all down and out and how I wouldn't come out of my room."

"She didn't."

"And so y'all knew I was at my weakest, and that's when you made your move."

"She didn't say anything to me about that."

"I'm gonna get to the bottom of this right now. Mom!"

"It was Balsam," blurted John.

"Huh?"

"I've been sending Josh Balsam into your building."

"I seen him in there."

"I've had him keep me posted on everything that goes on with you. He told us last night that you suddenly seemed to not care about anything."

"Y'all are just downright *mean*." Blue Gene turned off the TV and stood. "I mean, I'm your own *kin*."

"It wasn't Mom, though."

"You could send *Balsam* in there, but you couldn't come see me yourself? You are unbelievable."

"I had to send him in there. I had to keep an eye on you and stay on top of things. If I lose this election, I will never hear the end of it from Dad. That's what this comes down to. Don't you know how he is? I *have* to win."

"What about *me*?"

"What about *me*?"

"You ain't supposed to ask that. I'm the kid here."

"Well, what do you want me to do, Blue Gene? Help you slide on your diaper?"

"Go straight to hell." Blue Gene headed to the foyer. John followed. In the hallway where the family photos hung, Blue Gene stopped before the picture of him and John together. He snorted up his phlegm and spit on the picture of the brothers they had once been.

"Oh, so mature, Blue Gene. You're pathetic. Twenty-eight years old. Arthur acts more mature than you."

"Twenty-seven!" cried Blue Gene. He hurried out the front door. John followed him out. "I'm opening my place back up whether y'all like it or not," he said as he opened the door to his pickup.

"They won't let you."

"I'm doing whatever the hell I want from now on, 'cause that's what you do, and you're supposed to be my role model, ain't you?" Blue Gene got in his truck and slammed the door as violently as he could.

"Hold on," said John, approaching the driver's side window as Blue Gene started the engine. Blue Gene rolled down the window. It looked as if he had forced John into the apology that would end this.

"Yes?" he asked, his circled eyes looking up into John's.

"You haven't told anybody about you and me, have you?"

Blue Gene slapped his steering wheel so hard that John jumped back. "That's all you care about!? Whether or not this shit's gonna come back on you?"

"No, that's not all I care about. But did you tell anybody?"

"No."

"Are you? Are you going to tell the press?"

"Don't know."

"Blue Gene, I'm telling you, you better not. I'm going to make it, okay? As a leader, I mean. The dream is coming true. But you could ruin me with what you know, and I'm asking you—no, I'm begging you— don't do it."

"You, you, you," said Blue Gene, and he put the truck in drive.

"Don't you embarrass me!"

"Wouldn't think of it." Blue Gene took off. But when he heard John screaming, he hit the brakes. John ran up to his window again.

"Yes?" asked Blue Gene.

"Whatever you do to us, we can do back," he said.

Blue Gene shook his head. "Her favorite color was pea green." And he sped away before John could reply. This was war.

XII.

"You *say* you're not mad," said Jackie, "but then your voice has this sullen, pissed-off tone to it."

"That's just my voice. Ain't you noticed by now that's the way I talk?"

"See. Like just then, you sounded pissed."

"Jesus, woman. If I wasn't, I would be."

Jackie laughed; Blue Gene ached. She seemed determined to make him whip out his hurt. He had already explained that he wasn't calling her first thing in the morning to talk about their relationship. The only reason he was calling at all, he said, was because he needed her help to figure out if there was any way he could legally reopen the Commonwealth.

As it turned out, Jackie said she did have what she thought was a perfect solution, one she had been obsessing over since yesterday morning, after she was thrown in jail. She invited Blue Gene over, saying her plan was so momentous that it warranted discussing in person.

When Blue Gene pulled up to Jackie's house that morning, she was waiting on her front porch. He quickly switched off his radio so she wouldn't hear him listening to the Vindictives, a band she had introduced him to. As he took his time getting out of his trusty Chevy, Jackie was already halfway down her shrub-lined walk. She wore a plaid pair of Chucks, the usual ripped jeans with the cuffs rolled way up, and a jumbo-size white T-shirt that said BOOTYLICIOUS.

"Hey, Freedom Hawk," she said, sporting a ponytail that Blue Gene had a strange urge to pull.

"Hey."

She blocked his way with her skinny frame and stared at him. He looked around the suburban landscape and finally spoke. "Where's y'all's Halloween decorations?"

"That's really what you want to talk about?"

And there she went again, trying to scratch off his surface like a lottery ticket.

"Everybody else in your neighborhood seems to have 'em," he said.

"Are we seriously not going to talk about what happened between you and me?"

"No need to."

"But how can we go on like nothing happened?"

"That's how it's done."

"But that's not how *I* want to do it. At least let me say I'm sorry."

"Go'r't ahead."

"I'm sorry if I hurt you, and I'm sorry if I misled you. I'm sorry for everything. I suck as a person."

Blue Gene nodded and mumbled, "Nobody hurts me," as he pulled his Parliaments out of his Wrangler shorts.

"I thought you quit." Blue Gene rolled his eyes and lit one up. He jokingly offered her one. "I hope what happened—I hope it didn't drive you to start smoking again."

"Don't flatter yourself," he said, as he blew smoke from the side of his chapped mouth, away from her. "Anybody'd smoke after all that happened yesterday. My own damn place being taken away from me."

"Oh, yeah. That's understandable." She spat her next sentence out. "I don't smoke because I'm allergic."

"That's fine. I was kiddin' just then when I offered you one. I know how you're against it so."

"But that's what I'm saying. Probably the main reason I don't smoke is because I'm allergic. It gives me awful headaches, and it's not worth the buzz. I feel bad for not telling the truth. All that other stuff I said in front of everybody at the wrestling matches, I meant all of that. But I'm as weak as anybody. I probably would smoke if I could."

"Okay. I don't give a care."

"But I wanted you to know that about me, because a big part of the plan I have for us, for what we can do to get the Commonwealth back, is telling the truth. So that's the truth for why I don't smoke, in case you care."

"I don't."

After he finished his cigarette and flicked it to the street, Blue Gene followed Jackie down her front walk. "We have tons of Halloween decorations, actually," she said. "But we didn't bother getting them out this year. I hope we'll have the energy to at least decorate for Christmas, though. That's how you know when you've really given up, you know? If you don't even put up a Christmas tree." She turned to open the front door.

"Sorry I threw that shit at you."

"It's okay. We don't have to talk about it."

Her house hadn't changed at all in the two months since his last visit. The front room was still immaculate, but all the other rooms looked ransacked.

"You want something to drink?" she asked him in the kitchen, where food, dishes, and glasses hid every flat surface.

"You got Coke or Pepsi products?"

"Coke."

"Nah. I don't want anything."

"If it had been Pepsi, would you have said yes?"

"No."

Jackie laughed, covering her mischievous lips. "I want a Coke," she said, and she got herself a Sunkist from the fridge. Blue Gene leaned against the kitchen counter.

"Was your mom or stepdad mad at you for getting arrested?"

"No. They were mad at the cops."

"Yeah, I seen you on the news mouthin' off to 'em. You can't argue with the cops, man. That's one thing I've learned in life. It ends up being an unfair argument, 'cause at some point in the argument, they won't know what to say next, so they'll just threaten to take you downtown if you say one more word."

"Yeah. That's exactly what happened yesterday. And I said one more word."

"Ain't a level playing field. It's rigged."

"Where were you when the cops closed us down?"

"Sleepin'."

"How could you *sleep* through it?"

"I just did. Get off my back about it. There wouldn't even have *been* a damn place to close down if it wasn't for me."

"I know that. You don't have to tell me that. Come on. I want you to read what I've written. It's in my room." She rushed him through a large room with a pool table covered in clothes, newspapers, hangers, and boxes, then down a hallway with yellow stains all over its carpet, and finally to her bedroom.

Her bedroom was a colorful wreckage of books, vintage toys, antiques, and clothes, though after a few moments, Blue Gene saw that all the items seemed to be in carefully chosen spots. The room looked small with all the objects crammed into it: a record player on top of an electric organ, a file cabinet covered in magnets of the fifty states, pink flamingo statues, fake palm trees, lots of old-fashioned, tacky lamps, and a bed pushed into one of the corners. Posters of old movie stars and bands like the Dickies and the Dead Milkmen, as well as pictures cut from magazines, covered her walls completely. The magazine pics were mostly unflattering shots of famous people doing something stupid or wrong, such as Angelina Jolie screaming at a child.

He wasn't surprised to see a picture of the cast from *Saturday Night Live* hanging over her bed, one from the early nineties when Farley, Sandler, Spade, Rock, and MacDonald reigned. She had told him that one of her many pipe dreams was to stand up on the little stage at the end of an episode of *Saturday Night Live*, when all the cast members hug and wave at the audience.

On her ceiling, random phrases were written in marker, like "If you think your boss is dumb, wait until you meet his," and "Mama, my Powerball is *never* comin' up, is it?"

"That's my rock music," said Jackie, pointing to a rustic old bookcase with a black stereo on top.

"Damn." Stacks upon stacks of CDs in no particular order completely filled the three shelves.

"Yeah, I keep getting more and more of 'em, looking for my favorites, but the best ones I guess I'll never find, because the best ones will actually never get record deals. We'll never hear a peep from them. I think the greatest musicians ever will never even be able to afford instruments, so they'll never know it. I have too many CDs. I remember when I only had three of them. I was like, twelve, and all I had was one Nirvana and a couple of Green Days, and I would spend so much time with them. I'd study the artwork, and when I put them away, I'd make sure the CD was in its jewel case just so, and I'd prop them up to display them. And the CDs themselves are all scratched up because I listened to them so much. Now I just buy them like it's nothing."

"Huh. What's the deal with that?" Jackie's bedroom inspired a lot of questions, but there was one thing hanging on the wall that was most curious: an Abercrombie and Fitch shirt with ink splattered across the front, neatly displayed in a frame.

"Oh. That's evidence of the only crime I've ever committed—well, I guess I've committed *two* now, since they arrested me yesterday. It's stupid, I know. It's like, *hey, look at me. I shoplifted.* But I only stole it because I thought once I took off the security tag that would blast ink all over the shirt, I'd be making some sort of artistic statement."

"I used to wear shirts like that."

"That's hard for me to picture."

"Without the ink stain, I mean."

Jackie laughed. "I never shoplifted again, though. It made me so *nervous* to do it. That wasn't me at all. I think that's what makes people nervous, when they go against their instincts. Here—I want you to read what my idea is."

She turned away to click her mouse and told Blue Gene to sit at her desk. "Read this," she said. "It's a possible statement for you to give the paper." He sat at the desk, cluttered with papers, notebooks, snow globes, and Post-it notes with jotted-down ideas like "What was Holden Caulfield like as an adult?"

On her computer screen, he read:

"Yes, I do plan to get the Commonwealth Building reopened, and let me explain how. The way I see it, both of our local candidates for Congress have manipulated me to further their own political agendas. My brother used me all summer long to help him get votes. Then Grant Frick used me this fall to make my brother lose votes. Since both candidates have been using me for their own selfish reasons, I think it is now time that I use myself for the right reasons. That's why I'm recommending myself as the write-in candidate for the House of Representatives, District Five. If elected, I will make it a priority to get the Commonwealth reopened, as well as to recommend some of the ideas we tried at the Commonwealth for use at the governmental level."

Blue Gene swiveled around. "Forget it."

"But hold on. Don't you see? If you got into office, then you could secure funding. Not only could you get us up and running again, but you could have the government subsidize us, and you could maybe even get *other* shelters opened across this whole district. If you got into office, there would be so many *possibilities.*"

"I told you I ain't no politician."

"That's precisely why you should do it. Your brother and Frick are one and the same. You'd be giving people a choice."

"I wouldn't know what I was doing if I got in."

"You'd hire people to show you the ropes. Come on. Think of all the people you could help."

"I wouldn't win."

"You could, though. The other two aren't that far apart in the polls. You'd have a chance. And you know the people love you. You did so much for them. The least they could do is cast a vote for you. You've got so many people behind you, and here's one chance to finally get a genuinely good man to represent us."

"I ain't that good."

"Well, you're a better man than the other two running, at least. Plus, you're a bona fide man of the people, not a demagogue, not a poseur who puts on cowboy boots or rides on a motorcycle when the press shows up, and yet you're wealthy."

"If I throw my hat in the ring, first thing they'll do is dig up dirt on me. Why would I want to put myself through that?"

"What have you done that's so bad?"

"Nothing *that* bad, but it's nothing I'd want people to read about on the front page of the *Register*."

"What is it? What'd you do?"

"I got into drugs, okay?"

"Yeah, so? So did your brother, and he admitted it. So have most all politicians at this point. Now they're all from the generations that did drugs."

"Yeah, but with me, it's different. Back when I was with Cheyenne, she got me on meth for a little while—just a little bit—and I even helped her sell it a coupla times. Just for a very brief period."

"Oh. Well, that's still forgivable."

"But see, I led my mom and the rest of my family to believe that I didn't touch any of that stuff, and if it comes out, they'll be like, oh, we were right all along. He's just a druggie. And I'm *not* anymore. I never was, really. And you've seen how I've kind of got closer to my mom here recently, and this would mess everything up. And Bernice would read it, and—just forget it, Jackie! I'm not gonna let them make me look bad, and that's exactly what they'd do."

"Okay, okay. You're right. I don't blame you for not wanting to. But what about suggesting someone else as a write-in candidate? With all the contacts we made, we could mobilize people around *anybody*."

"Like who?"

"I don't know. It would have to be someone who would represent *our* values and not some giant corporation's."

Blue Gene turned his head sideways at Jackie, who sat on her unmade bed with its snowball-patterned quilt.

"What?" she asked.

"You said *our* values."

"Yeah. The minute you started using your money to help people is the minute we started having the same values. To me, that's the only value that matters. That would be the cornerstone of your candidacy, if you ran."

"Not runnin'."

"I know. But yeah, I definitely think we have the same values. Except that every once in a while, you still get up in my face and yell, 'Love it or leave it.'"

"It's true."

"I can't afford to leave it."

"I could. I easily got enough money for plane tickets. I could take you anywhere in the world."

Jackie laughed. Blue Gene abruptly got up, turned his back, and looked at the pictures on her walls. The border was made of punk rock flyers like the one he had seen on the music store window on the Fourth of July. "You got any other bright ideas besides having somebody running for us?"

"There's taking legal action, but you already said that wouldn't work."

"It won't."

"Why not?"

"It just won't. My dad wanted us closed, and he's got all the judges in his pocket."

"Then no, I don't think there's a better solution than getting someone with our ideals elected. It would have to be somebody whose past wouldn't haunt him, because, like you say, they'd try to bring him down a notch right away. It would be awesome to have a person run who doesn't have any dirt on him at all. Like, somebody who acts like a good person, but for once he actually is. Maybe somebody who has somehow managed to not run around on his wife, someone who hasn't been in on any shady business deals, someone who seems like a good person but *for once*, he actually *would be*."

"We ain't ever gonna find a person like that. Especially on short notice."

"Maybe we could put, like, an ad in the classifieds. It would say, 'Looking for just one good man. We're calling you out.'"

"Tell you the truth, in this whole district there probably isn't a single trustworthy man."

$$\$ \$ \$$$

It looked as if all of Bashford had left their houses for the first official campaign rally of the Have-Not Party. Run-down cars and trucks packed the back half of the old Wal-Mart parking lot, while the front half, the one closest to the defunct Commonwealth Building, was sectioned off with yellow rope to allow space for the gathering. A small stage of cinder blocks and plywood had been constructed in front of the building's entrance. By quarter after five, the rally popped with electric hubbub, with loud and loose folks enjoying an eclectic mix of music, catching up with one another between bites of free hamburgers, swallows of free beer, and drags off their cigarettes, all the while waiting for the evening's speeches to begin. Further adding to the spectacle was the fact that it was Halloween. Interspersed throughout the crowd were children and adults dressed as vampires, witches, hippies, zombies, Spider-Man, nuns, devils, and Darth Vader.

With hairspray to keep his hair in place, a mint to keep his breath from smelling, and deodorant to keep his armpits from stinking, John was all set. He had to place himself out among the voters one more time, to present himself to them as a realtor would a home. Election Day was the day after next, and this was the last crowd situation he would have to endure unless he counted Election Night, when he and all his supporters would gather at his campaign headquarters to either celebrate or commiserate. According to the latest polls, John was only two points ahead of his two competitors, who were virtually tied.

John followed his father, who squeezed along the edge of the audience to the front, saying John should be where the news cameras could see him. Behind John followed Josh Balsam, who wore tan combat fatigues, but not for Halloween. John had told him that wearing the desert fatigues would remind voters of the sacrifice that Josh's father had made, as well as the true ideals of this campaign. Once the three of them reached the front, Henry positioned himself at John's side and told Balsam to stick to John's other side.

"CNN van pulled up," said Balsam.

"CNN wouldn't cover this," said Henry.

"Except he's right, Dad," said John. Sure enough, the national cable news channel was present.

"Then losing," said Henry, "is even less of an option than ever."

Then the trio penetrated the crowd with all the cocksureness they could summon, shaking hands with everyone in their path, smiling, nodding, spurting out slogans, passing out pamphlets, forcing out maximum goodwill in one last stand of electioneering wherewithal.

Elizabeth had stayed home. She wished John well and still called herself his number-one supporter, but she refused to take part in campaigning for him at this particular event. She advised him against it, saying that openly campaigning at an opposing party's rally looked too antagonistic. She had also advised Blue Gene against putting on the rally in the first place. Since his statement and subsequent full-page ads had appeared in all the district's papers in the past week, she had been the only family member to contact Blue Gene, only to urge him to drop this third-party idea before somebody got hurt. Blue Gene had refused, telling her that somebody had to hold up for the people, not to mention himself. She told him what he was doing was not what Jesus would do.

Abby wasn't at the Halloween rally, either; she had opted to take Arthur trick-or-treating. Arthur had wanted both of his parents to take him trick-or-treating; he always liked to have both his mom and dad present for pretty much everything that happened to him, so this campaign had made his year a lousy one. John had broken the news to Arthur that morning as they nibbled on hot cherry Pop-Tarts. He told Arthur he couldn't take him trick-or-treating because he had to campaign, because his own dad had said so.

"Dad," John said between handshakes, "I don't think Frick is here."

"He should be," said Henry. "He'll be made a fool of, too, if he loses to them."

John, Henry, and Balsam had to stop campaigning when a heavy-set black woman (who got a huge laugh when she said her Halloween costume was supposed to be Keira Knightley) took the stage to sing the National Anthem. As soon as she finished, John went right back to meeting and greeting, but seconds later he was again interrupted when the crowd exploded with "woos!" and applause. John turned to see Blue Gene taking the stage.

Both strength and hesitation marked Blue Gene's movements. He approached the microphone stand and shooed his hand at the receptive crowd. Instead of his usual shorts and flip-flops, he wore baggy red sweatpants and clunky, generic white sneakers. The autumn air did not prevent him, however, from wearing his trademark sleeveless T-shirt that begged attention to his tattoos. This evening, his green shirt shouted in white iron-on letters: THE HAVE-NOT PARTY.

"Thanks," he said, and he cleared his throat and adjusted his navy blue Coors Light cap. "I wanna thank all you people for comin' out here tonight. This whoops ass."

John was impressed by the turnout, though he imagined Blue Gene had learned a great deal about political galvanization from working for the Mapother campaign over the summer. He knew for a fact that Blue Gene had the good sense to keep lists of the names and phone numbers of all the people he had come in contact with while running his building. And the ads in the paper that invited voters out for free burgers and beer also helped entice the largely blue-collar crowd.

"Happy Halloween, y'all." He cleared his throat again. "I ain't much on talkin', but I just wanted to let y'all know I wasn't happy about this building behind me closin' down."

The crowd booed. John looked around to make sure no one was looking at him or his dad. "Let's stand over there to the side," he said, and his dad agreed. Balsam followed, his chest puffed outward, his arms held in rigid curves, his shaved head turning from side to side as if expecting someone to try him.

"But I also want to let y'all know that the bottom line is...I ain't about to let it *stay* closed."

Applause and every variation of "woo!" filled the air. John felt conspicuous as he, his father, and his bodyguard stood lackadaisically next to the trolls and fairies, who clapped and cheered.

"The good news is we think we've found a way to get her goin' again. That's the reason we made up the Have-Not Party. We need to get one of our own elected, and with y'all supportin' our 'nads, we think it's actually possible. Our candidate's gonna talk here in a second about it, but basically what sets us apart is, well, the other two guys runnin', they stand for profits. The Have-Not Party, we stand for people. So if you're for people over profits, you need to get out to the polls and vote for our candidate. And now, I'm gonna shut up and let her talk, 'cause she can sure talk prettier than I ever could. Here she is...Ladies and gentlemen...Hailing from Bashford for the past twenty-five years straight... Jackie Ripplemeyer!"

John and Henry and all the rest of the Mapother team had cursed the United States Constitution for not being stricter. This old document allowed her to become electable because she was a resident of the state in which she was running, because she had been a U.S. citizen for at least seven years, and because she was the minimum age of twenty-five. She was highly educated in the way of politics, she was comfortable onstage, and she had been the key architect of the Commonwealth Building. If she won, she would be the youngest female in Congress. John and Henry shook their heads at each other as the crowd whooped for her. A girl was giving them a run for their money.

$ $ $

"That was good, hon," said Bernice, in a peach-colored sweatsuit, as Blue Gene took his place next to her behind the stage.

"It *was* good," said Mitchell, in a Frasier Crane costume. "You have an interesting stage presence. I mean, the way you carry yourself, it's like, I don't know, tired but commanding at the same time."

"It sucked," said Blue Gene. "I hated it. Here. Let's listen to Jackie."

Jackie unfolded the speech that she and Blue Gene had cowritten over the weekend at her place, in the wee hours over pizza and coffee. For the rally tonight, she wore a black pantsuit, an off-white blouse, and black closed-toe pumps, and her hair was pulled back in a bun. Blue Gene thought she should wear what she normally wore, but Jackie said that if she expected people to take her seriously, she had better look the part. So for Halloween, Jackie dressed as an adult, and Stepchild would not be her last name tonight.

Jackie speedily adjusted the mic stand to her height. "I want to talk to you all about only one thing, really," Jackie began in a bold tone similar to that which she used while fronting Uncle Sam's Finger. "Money." As Blue Gene and she had planned, she let the word simmer for a bit. "I'll admit, money isn't everything. But it *does* keep everything moving. Money can't buy love, but it *can* help move love along. You know, the love of your life might be walking around *right this minute* on the other side of the planet, but you might never meet this soul mate of yours because neither of you have enough money to afford the plane tickets that would allow you to meet. Not being able to afford plane tickets is in itself a travesty. I've always thought that *any one person* should be able to visit *any one place* in the world, but for most people, money won't allow it. But let's not dwell on plane tickets. Let's dwell on love. Maybe you'll never reach the man or woman of your dreams because you can't find him or her on the internet, because you can't even afford a computer. No, money can't buy love, but how else are you going to pay for your dates?"

Blue Gene watched to see how the audience responded to the little joke he had written. Half of them laughed. Then he saw John, Henry, and Josh Balsam standing on the western edge of the crowd toward the front, which immediately made his good spirits fade in favor of the surly demons of fear.

"Some people treat money like a god. I don't think money is a god. I think of it more as a guardian angel. Money provides us with a guardian angel who always watches over our shoulder, quietly protecting us, secretly nudging us away from the path that leads toward suffering and death. For instance, if you become seriously ill, your guardian will see to it that you have the best medical care available. If a hurricane is headed straight for your house, he'll make sure you're able to evacuate safely and rebuild a new life somewhere else.

"My candidacy, as well as the Have-Not Party itself, revolves around *one* problem, and that problem is that some people have much, much better guardian angels than others. Only one percent—*one tiny, miniscule percent*—of all the people in this country own *thirty-eight percent* of the total wealth. Therefore, that enormously, absurdly wealthy one percent can afford to be defended by the biggest, strongest, most capable guardian angels the world has ever seen. These are top-notch, upper-echelon angels, and anyone who has one of them watching his back should feel blessed. There are less and less of them these days.

"Most of us belong to that other ninety-nine percent, and because we are not so elite, our guardian angels are more run-of-the-mill and don't work as hard for us. They're good to us, but they're weaker than the top one percent, some of them even scrawny and anemic. But they do, generally, keep us on the right path. They see to it that we have steady food, shelter, and clothing. And they help us avoid incarceration. For instance, I recently learned firsthand that while my guardian angel can't pay off my student loans, he *can* afford to post my bail."

The crowd laughed and applauded, knowing Jackie had stood up for the Commonwealth in its final hour. Blue Gene wished he would've. "Damn, girl," he quietly cursed at her butt in its black slacks.

"But then there are the poor. If you are poor, you are assigned the most pathetic variety of guardian angel, one who doesn't even show up half the time. He fails his human defendant over and over again, and it seems like the more a poor human needs him, the less he comes around, until finally, one day this angel leaves the human to fend for himself, and he never, ever returns.

"The saddest case of them all, though, is the soul that is breathed into a newborn baby, who, for no fault of his own, for no reason whatsoever, really, is never assigned a guardian angel in the first place. The only hope a person like this has is that some other kindly guardian will somehow take notice of him and offer his help. This almost never happens.

"The Have-Not Party is based on the belief that we could *all* be afforded better guardians, if only we elected the right kind of leaders. John Hurstbourne Mapother and Grant Frick are *not* the right kind of leaders."

Blue Gene looked across the crowd at John, who looked at his black dress shoes, a kind but slightly worried look on his soap-opera-lover-man face. Henry stared ahead frigidly. Balsam spat.

"The kind of leader *I'm* talking about is one whose every act, whose every stroke of the pen, would be directed toward one simple concept, and that concept is this: since that first type of guardian angel I spoke of has more than enough power to spare, we take *just a fraction* of his resources to increase the less fortunate people's chances of survival and prosperity. That was the idea that the Commonwealth Building was based on, and for the Have-Not Party, the Commonwealth Building would only be the beginning. Reinstituting the building behind me is only the beginning of what we can make the mind-boggling wealth of this country do."

The crowd applauded. Blue Gene was glad they had gone with his idea. "The Have-Not Party" had a much better ring to it than "the Neo-

Anti-Imperialist League" (or NAIL).

"The candidates I'm running against don't ever mention the words *wealth* or *money* or *class*, but that is because they themselves are wealthy, and they don't want anything to change. They would not want to call attention to the serious flaws and moral shortcomings of the institutions they represent. Therefore, in the last few minutes I've already talked more about money, and all the good it can do and all the harm its absence can cause, than both of my opponents combined."

Now there were three separate television cameras pointed at Jackie. Blue Gene had heard the Veterans buzzing that, because of the unusual circumstances of this race, the Halloween rally might get picked up by the national news. Sure enough, a red CNN logo was in plain sight.

"Instead of talking about money, all my opponents want to talk about are big, bloated but pleasant words that sound really good over a PA but in reality serve as nothing more than vote-getting tools. So if you're the type of person who needs to hear these types of words, here is the part of the speech where I can accommodate you. Since apparently I'm a politician now, first let me tell you a story, as I've noticed politicians like to do.

"When working at the Commonwealth Building, I met a single mother who had two children and was only paid minimum wage at the warehouse where she worked, right here in Bashford. She told me that because of her financial situation, she and her kids were eventually reduced to living in a cheap hotel room. One night, when she was about to fall asleep, the mom heard a horrifying noise. It sounded like someone screaming outside, or maybe some animal, maybe a cat, shrieking in pain or fear. It turned out that the sound was coming from the very hotel room where she and her kids were staying. The sound was the growling and gurgling of her five-year-old son's stomach. So if you want me to use a nice word like *morality*, I think nothing shows less morality than a Congress that rejected and rejected and rejected an increase in minimum wage, while the cost of living continued to rise steadily, and while the congresspeople repeatedly gave *themselves* a raise! You want to hear me talk about a huge, grand word like *freedom*? How about freedom from hunger? You want to hear me talk about *family*? The United States of America has no laws guaranteeing paid vacation days or paid sick days. Every other major country in the world—127 of them, to be exact—*requires* its employers to allow paid vacation and sick days so that the workers can actually spend time with their families. So how's that for family values?

"Also, when I was helping run this glorious green building behind me, I met a woman with chronic obstructive pulmonary disease. Her medical expenses had become so overwhelming that she could no longer seek treatment. She had to give up on the idea of ever having good health, and she said one of the saddest things I've ever heard a person say. She said, 'Maybe I was just *meant* to be sick.'"

Bernice looked up at Blue Gene with questioning eyebrows. He gave her a wink.

"So if you want to hear me use a word like *faith*, I think it is not our faith but our sinfulness that allows the world's wealthiest country to be the only industrialized country that *does not* ensure that each and every citizen has access to health care by right of birth. You want to hear me talk about how *free* we are? Fine. We are the *freest* country in the world, but our worst-off citizens have the same life expectancies as citizens of developing third world countries, which we presume to be so unfree.

"The excess wealth of the super-rich could help people like these. I'm not saying each rich person needs to go all Blue Gene Mapother and make it his mission to feed and employ everybody in town."

Blue Gene pulled his cap down. She must have improvised that line.

"What I'm saying is that if our government would only ask a little more of that richest one percent, it could bring us a world of change. The problem is that the majority of us seem to have this masochistic desire for self-defeat. I say this because we repeatedly vote for men who are determined to use their power to make sure the structure of wealth remains intact, all the while hiding behind the flowery language of *faith*, *freedom*, and *patriotism*.

"I care deeply about this country or I wouldn't bother doing this. Still, this entire speech may be misconstrued as sounding unpatriotic, which is a risk I'll take. Patriotism casts a shadow over the truth. Patriotism declares in boldface letters how the Thirteenth Amendment freed the slaves for all eternity, but in fine print at the bottom of the page mentions how that same amendment allows a corporation to call itself a legal person and therefore get away with murder.

"With all that said, I agree that the United States is the greatest nation on Earth, but I also believe that it is the nation that has failed the most in living up to its own potential. After all, the sole superpower of our planet should be held to a pretty high standard. Therefore, I cannot toss around words like *freedom* and *democracy*, and I cannot hide behind the pomp and circumstance of patriotism, because to emphasize these virtues would be to belittle the truth, and the truth *is* that we Americans are just as capable of committing sin, just as complicit in allowing inequality, and just as thoroughly flawed as any other piece of geography on this globe."

The audience offered a half-hearted response, some screaming in agreement, most remaining quiet.

"The Have-Not Party runs solely on the fuel of truth. The truth is that Coca-Cola was invented by a morphine addict. The truth is that baseball was invented by a bunch of rich New York snobs, who were known to refuse to play with men of a lesser social station. The truth is that MTV originally refused to air videos by black musicians. The truth is that your favorite celebrity was probably mean in high school. The truth is that one of the reasons I want to become a congresswoman is because it pays way better than what a substitute teacher makes."

Blue Gene laughed and was surprised to see John laughing, too, until Henry turned toward him.

"That's the true America that I know, yet I still wouldn't want to live anywhere else, because after all, other countries have hypocrisies and inconsistencies of their own. One of our many enemies hates us because they think we're a bunch of sex-crazed hedonists, yet their primary motivation is the possibility of banging seventy virgins in heaven. Obviously, the leaders on the enemy's side also know how to use those big, bloated words to manipulate the people. It's the same all over the world, I imagine, with people having to choose between very similar political parties, all of whom represent the interests of big business, who are only interested in attaining more, more, more, who direct the wealth of the nations toward all the wrong things, who are obsessed with comeuppance, who want global domination and might just be able to buy it someday, only to find that the globe itself has some competition, because our tallest mountain range is dwarfed by the Olympus Mons of Mars.

"The Have-Not Party, for which I am the *first* but hopefully not the *last* candidate, absolutely *does not* represent big business. It represents the ninety-nine percent of the people whose wallets go ignored and untouched by big business. Blue Gene Mapother showed us all what one man's wealth could do for the have-nots. Just imagine if that sort of attitude toward money could become a part of our government.

"So many of us, myself included, are scared to death we're going to get ripped off, yet when it comes time to vote, we have a tendency to cast our ballots with our hearts instead of our wallets or our heads. We reject wealth. When the lower classes vote for men like John Hurstbourne Mapother or Grant Frick, in effect this is what we are doing: rejecting the possibility of more money for ourselves.

"If you write me in as your candidate and I win, I can guarantee you that the rest of Congress will try to ruin my ideas with what they'll call *compromise*, but at least you will have one representative who pledges to get money to those who truly need it, and whose ultimate goal will be nothing less than having as many people living the good life as possible."

The applause was thick, and Blue Gene had to let out a "woo!" of his own.

"Before I finish, I'd like to return one last time to those guardian angels I mentioned. I believe that the greatest guardian angel of them all, the one who has such an abundance of nurturing, warmth, care, and love to spread out among her children, is the one we call the world's last remaining superpower. Please write me in as your choice for Congress so that I might distract that almighty superpower from her incessant coddling of the rich and hold her attention for at least just a moment in order to say, *psst*. Hey. Come here. There are some people I'd like you to meet who need you much, much worse."

$$\$ \, \$ \, \$$$

The conclusion of Jackie's speech was met by a hearty mixture of cheers and applause; a few jeers here and there were drowned out by approval. Blue Gene then climbed onto the homemade stage and raised Jackie's arm in the manner of a referee raising a wrestler's arm after he wins a match. The crowd cheered even more.

"I was hoping her speech would be awful," John said to his father.

"It was awful," said Henry.

"But the crowd's so into it. This could be bad."

"Say the word and I'll beat her ass," said Balsam. "I don't care if she is a girl. Me and her's done got into it once before. She's got it comin'. The things she said."

"Balsam, please," said John.

"The least we can do is put up a fight," said Henry. "Let's shake some more hands."

Soon after John resumed campaigning, a doll-faced woman wearing a tight sweater approached him.

"You're one of Jackie Ripplemeyer's opponents, aren't you?" she asked.

"Yes. John Hurstbourne Mapother." He shook her hand quickly, since he could already feel his palm sweating. He recognized her from TV.

"I'm Christina Cadbury from CNN. This is a *great* story, and I was hoping to get an interview with you and her."

"Oh. You mean both of us simultaneously?"

"Yes. Could you?"

"I—" John's heart was already racing. "Our other opponent isn't here."

"That's okay," she said. "This will be great exposure for you, and we need a counterpoint."

He looked at his father. "You had better do it," said Henry.

"Will it be live?" asked John.

"Yes. Is that okay?"

"I guess. When?"

"About five minutes. Your opponent has actually already agreed to it." She pointed toward the CNN news van, where Jackie stood talking to the crew.

"I'll have to, then," said John, and he followed the newscaster to where the camera and spotlight were set up. His hands went clammy and his armpits gushed. A man with a headset told him to sit on a canvas chair. At arm's length sat Jackie Ripplemeyer. They looked at each other, and John felt sweat trickle down his back.

"Hey, Mr. Mapother," she said with a smile. John smiled back, relieved by her decorum.

"Hi. That was a really good speech," he said. As if by reflex, he checked to see if his dad had heard him, but his dad was off to the side, talking into Balsam's ear.

"Thank you. Blue Gene helped me write it."

"He *did*?" Jackie nodded. Before John could say anything else, a ponytailed woman wearing all black was leaning over him with a small canister of powder.

"Makeup," she said.

"Why?"

"So you won't look so pale."

"I look pale?"

"No. I mean, everybody looks pale on camera in the lights." She dabbed her brush in the powder.

"No. Please. Don't."

"But—"

"I sweat. I'll sweat it all off. Trust me."

"Okay," said the woman with a shrug. When she left, John looked to see how Jackie had reacted to this exchange, but she was only looking at her fingernails and her numerous, cheap-looking rings. It angered him, how calm she was. What could she possibly know about life when her armpits were bone-dry?

A crowd had gathered behind the camera, and Blue Gene stood next to Bernice, who looked a century older than John had remembered. To see the two of them talking to each other bothered John, but he had no time to tidy up his disconcertment. The anchorwoman was already seated across from Jackie and him, already poised for her segment. A man behind the camera counted down as seriously as he would have a blast-off, and soon the well-styled doll head was talking.

"Many congressional seats will be decided all across the nation on Tuesday," the newscaster enunciated into the camera, "but what makes this one special is that in the last week, a twenty-five-year-old female write-in candidate has emerged as a contender. Her name is Jackie Ripplemeyer, and judging by the response she's gotten at a rally here tonight, she stands to possibly ride the dark horse to victory come Tuesday. One of her two opponents is president of Westway International, John Hurstbourne Mapother. Now, Mr. Mapother, your opponent delivered a speech tonight that scolded politicians for luring in voters with buzzwords like *values* and *freedom*, and then doing nothing to improve their voters' lives once in office. What's your response to that accusation?"

"She must be referring to her other opponent, who didn't even bother showing up tonight. I don't think she could've been referring to me when she made those statements. Values are important to me, but I've actually already practiced what I preach. My family's tobacco company is the largest employer in the area. So if you take a look at me, and then you take a look at her, only one of us has provided money for the community, and it's not her. My family and I have provided more money for Bashford than she could ever hope to."

"Ms. Ripplemeyer?" asked the anchorwoman.

"It's true that he's provided a lot of jobs, but two of his favorite business moves are paying minimum wage and laying people off. The woman I spoke of in my speech who couldn't afford to feed her kids—she was actually one of John Mapother's employees. So if he treats his own employees like that, how is he going to treat his constituents?"

"I do not set the wages, nor do I control the climate of job security," John butted in as the reporter started to ask another question. "And I'd like to ask Ms. Ripplemeyer what she's done for the community besides putting on concerts that promote antifamily lifestyles and putting down the very troops that protect the freedom that she so obviously enjoys."

"I beg your pardon," said Jackie, "but you are such an *understudy*."

"Ms. Ripplemeyer—" said the anchorwoman.

"He is such an *understudy*."

"What do you even mean by that?" asked John.

"You're learning some other actors' lines."

"Well, if supporting our troops is just a line, it's a line I'm glad to have memorized."

John was pleased to hear a few "woos!" for himself.

"Oh, come on! *The troops protect our freedom*? What the military does is protect an *establishment* that spends trillions on the *military*. Why can't we take just *one* trillion out of the many trillions, and use it to help hungry children and sick old people? During wartime, our tax money goes toward death and destruction when it could be going toward life and prosperity. All of our money is going toward the wrong things!"

Some scattered "boos" surfaced.

"To get back on topic," said the interviewer, "tell us why you decided to become a write-in candidate just one week before the election."

"Because, strangely enough, it was about one week ago that the authorities of this town shut down a philanthropic organization that I helped create. A lot of people benefited from our organization, and we think if those *same* people would write me in as their candidate of choice, I'll be able to help them even more through my office. John

Mapother's own brother started this organization, actually."

"The story has yet another twist," the newscaster noted. "Is that true about your brother?"

"Well, Christina, you said it yourself. Jackie here has made herself a candidate one week before the election, and she's done so because she's an opportunist. She puts down politicians, but she's as shrewd as any politician I've seen. She knew she could get votes from people who supported my brother, who *has* done a lot of good for our community, and she's trying to take advantage of the situation and steal this election. If anyone is cunning here, it's this young lady. She's trying to steal this election without going to the trouble of having a campaign."

"Maybe I am opportunistic," Jackie said quietly and with a slight stutter. "But someone had to do something, and I was chosen as the right person to do it."

"And Jackie," John said, "I know you'll find this hard to believe, but when I talk about values and patriotism, I *mean* what I say. You act as if voters are so dumb for voting with their hearts instead of their heads or their wallets. I say, what's wrong with that? You say government should be more nurturing and warm and caring, but don't these things require heart?"

"Yes, but you won't have a heart once you're elected. You're a stereotypical politician. You're a wealthy businessman. He comes from one of the richest families in America."

"Back to—" attempted the interviewer.

"My money has nothing to do with my values. Believe it or not, but rich people can show kindness and compassion, just like anyone."

"Then prove it once you're in office. Hey—I'll drop out of the race right now and tell everyone not to vote for me, right here on live TV, if you'll promise to run your political office the way your brother ran his charity. I'm serious."

"An unusual offer," commented the newscaster, taken aback. "How do you respond?"

"Well, I'd like to point out that this idea of my brother's is nothing new. The sort of thing that he's done by throwing a bunch of desperate people together—it's called a phalanstery, and they used to have them in the 1800s, but they didn't work. Then there was the Hull House in Chicago and the Salvation Army and the Red Cross. Look, I think some of the ways my brother and Jackie ran their business would not be practical in government, but I could try my best to incorporate *some* of their better ideas."

"But listen," said Jackie. "His brother took his own money—it was his own inheritance from *their* family fortune—and he used it to provide for this community. He paid for their meals, he provided shelter, he created jobs and paid everybody equally—all with his excess wealth. He was even going to set up a free medical clinic."

"Which is all great," interjected John, "but you look at the world the way *a child* would."

"Yes! I do." The crowd cheered.

"As an adult *I* know this isn't a perfect world, and because of this fact, your operation did more harm than good. You provided a home base for criminals and freeloaders. Your ideas have consequences. They could be detrimental to the morally responsible people of this community, to the families who play by the rules. You are basically trying to dismantle the family values of Bashford."

"I'm sorry, but he *really* doesn't have any business talking about family values."

As if on cue, John blushed. Did she know? Was she so close to Blue Gene that he would tell her? Droplets of sweat popped out on his temples. The lights suddenly felt hotter than ever.

"What do you mean?" asked the woman.

John worried about people noticing that he was blushing, which caused his face to feel even redder. And then there was the camera staring directly at him. His forehead began to sweat. Maybe if he didn't talk anymore, there would be no close-ups of him and the interview would end sooner.

"His brother is a common man," said Jackie, "and he used his own brother to help him get the lower-class vote. *But* he hadn't even spoken to his brother in *four years* until this election came along."

John looked down at his lap. He thanked God that she hadn't revealed anything more. But the biological harbingers of his particular neurosis had already begun to spread. His heart was pounding dangerously fast. He glanced up to see Jackie and the interviewer staring at him. He wiped his brow with the back of his hand, and the hairs on his hand stuck to his skin.

"I don't know," he said, but the words came out sounding weird because his throat was so dry. He cleared his throat and then worried that by doing so, he would sound guilty. "I don't know what she's talking about."

"Getting back on topic," continued the reporter, "Ms. Ripplemeyer, you just offered to drop out of the race if your opponent adopts some of your views. What would you like to see Mr. Mapother do once he's in office?"

"Basically, I'd like to see him and all of his colleagues replace their empty rhetoric with meaningful actions. For instance, they're always praising our soldiers and talking about patriotism, yet they treat our veterans like second-class citizens."

John felt the blood prickling within his face.

"His brother, on the other hand," continued Jackie, "not only praises our soldiers, but he also handed over the leadership of his organization to them. He called them the Veterans Committee, and they made all the decisions. So that's something I'd like to see John Mapother and all the other career politicians do. If they love our troops as much as they say, then why not give them extra power in terms of governing? Maybe something as simple as letting each of their votes count as two."

"Mr. Mapother, do you think that's an idea that you could propose to Congress?"

John opened his mouth to speak, but his throat felt so dry that he couldn't get anything to come out. He suddenly felt a tight, sharp pain in his chest and immediately assumed he was having a heart attack.

"Mr. Mapother?" asked the reporter, tilting her head slightly.

"No, no. It wouldn't work," John blurted, praying the interview would just end.

"Why not?" asked Jackie.

"Why *not*?" repeated John, squirming in his seat, sweat streaking down his face and into his eyes.

"You okay?" the reporter asked out the side of her mouth. John realized that if she had noticed, everyone must have noticed.

"Yes!" said Jackie. "Why wouldn't you want our veterans to play a more important role in making our decisions?"

He swallowed before he spoke. "They're not capable of governing. They're not intelligent enough for decision making. That's *our* job."

The crowd suddenly went ballistic with boos and taunts. John looked out at them, past the lights, and their faces merged into a cyclone of scowls.

"No, no," he said. His body fried as though allergic to itself, gripped in neurotic thrombosis. "I didn't mean it like that. But their job is to fight, and—I'm sorry. I'm not well." John unclipped his microphone and got out of his seat as fast as he could.

The startled newscaster turned to the camera and stammered out a sign-off. John walked away from the crowd as fast as he could, not knowing where he was going. As his walk turned into a run, he threw off his suffocating suit coat. Somebody chasing after him grabbed the coat from the ground. He felt light-headed, and his chest felt so tight, so he sat down behind one of the news vans, resting his back and head against it. He looked up and saw Blue Gene holding his coat, brushing it clean. John undid his tie and unbuttoned his dress shirt.

$ $ $

"You okay, John?" Blue Gene found himself squatting at John's side with his hand on his shoulder.

"I'm having a panic attack."

"You have those?"

"Yeah."

"I'm—we—I didn't know. What can I do?"

"Nothing," John said as he dug around his pants pocket. Henry and Josh Balsam appeared.

"John!" said Henry. "What happened back there?"

John shook his head as he opened a little piece of aluminum foil. He pulled out a tiny white tablet and chewed it as fast as he could, which gave him a bitter expression.

"You need to pull yourself together and get back out there," said Henry.

"Damnit, Dad!" yelled Blue Gene. "He's having a panic attack." Blue Gene witnessed a flash of compassion in Henry's eyes as he took a step closer and leaned over his son.

"It's only in your head," said Henry.

A few random people were coming around behind the van. Henry turned his back to John and stood directly in front of him. "Stop looking at my son," he said, but people swung their necks to try to see what kind of condition John was in. "Balsam, keep everyone away."

"Everybody get the fuck away!" Balsam barked, walking toward the spectators like he was ready to strike, easily scaring them off. Then Jackie appeared next to Blue Gene, looking down at him and John.

"Is he all right?" she asked.

"Yes," said Blue Gene, irritated. "Go away, Jackie."

"You get the fuck away from him, bitch!" yelled Balsam, already heading toward Jackie. "You caused this to happen!"

Blue Gene got up from John's side. He stood next to Jackie and folded his arms. Balsam stopped a few feet in front of her.

"You won't say it to my face."

"Say what?" asked Jackie.

"You want to tell it to my motherfuckin' face that you don't support our troops?"

"I will not support anything that results in children dying violent deaths."

"Fuck you. Ain't just children. My dad was a grown-ass man."

"But the way modern warfare is—it kills *far* more civilians than soldiers. It's not like they meet on some far-off battlefield and just shoot at one another. *Everybody* dies. The soldiers die the *least*. The ratio is fucking twenty to one!"

"Shut the fuck up!"

A crowd started swarming toward the ruckus.

"Twenty innocent civilians die for each combatant, and how many of those do you think are women and children and the elderly? I will *never* support something that explodes innocent children. You can slap any words on it you want: *patriotism, freedom, democracy—*"

"Shut the fuck up! I'll slap you so hard—"

"I will *not* support anything that kills children for the sake of imperialism. This world belongs to the children."

The commotion magnetized more and more people who wanted to see a fight brew.

"I'm warning you. Shut up!"

"Children are the only ones who truly know how to enjoy it. The adults should be the protectors of the children. When we have these wars, we fail our children in the worst possible way. We kill them."

"I'm gonna kill *you*." Balsam became a rush of tan-camouflage rage. Blue Gene stepped in front of Jackie and held his long, tattooed arms out to block him.

"What the fuck do *you* want?!" roared Balsam.

"Calm down, Balsam man," said Blue Gene.

"I oughta beat your fuckin' head in, holdin' up for some bitch instead of your own brother."

"He doesn't care about you," said Blue Gene. Balsam's mouth seemed to drop in slow motion.

"I've had about enough of you, Mapother," said Balsam, and he spat on the pavement.

"Don't be all mad at me," said Blue Gene. "He's the one you should be mad at. The Blood Flag—he had his secretary do that. It was ketchup. So just settle down, and let's—" Before Blue Gene knew it, his baseball cap had been slapped off. Before the cap hit the ground, Blue Gene's body shot forward. His muscles clenched as he stood as close to Balsam as he could without touching. His hair looked funny, flattened on top.

Then Balsam, who had the height advantage by about a foot, craned his neck and pressed his forehead against Blue Gene's.

Even with the crowd screaming, "Fight! Fight! Fight!" even with Balsam's cigarette-stink-breath invading his nostrils as he growled, "Come on, bitch! Let's go!" even with Jackie pulling at his arm, even with another skull forced against his own, Blue Gene was somehow able to picture what this must have looked like from the outside. Two adult men had their foreheads pushed against each other. Honestly, he thought only professional wrestlers did this sort of thing.

"Blue Gene, come on," said Jackie, pulling his arm. "Don't. Let's go."

And then it occurred to Blue Gene that these were not two adult men. One was just a teenager. A kid, really.

Blue Gene broke himself away from Balsam.

"Pussy," Balsam said venomously.

Blue Gene snapped back into position, face to face with Balsam.

"Blue Gene, stop it!" said Jackie.

"*Blue Gene, stop it*," said Balsam, mocking her. "*Don't fight, Blue Gene!*"

"For Christ's sake," said Jackie. "This is so *stupid!*"

A second time, Blue Gene broke away from Balsam, because that was what felt natural. This did not, however, stop Balsam from shoving Blue Gene once his back was turned. Almost simultaneously, Blue Gene felt a jolt through his spine and his open palms scraping across the horrible concrete.

Blue Gene turned his head enough to see the camouflage coming his way. He felt his hair being pulled like no hair should ever be pulled, and he felt a sick, tearing sensation at the base of his skull that no person should ever feel. Then he heard some sort of hard, brutal spank.

Balsam let go.

Blue Gene looked up and saw Jackie's terrified face, her awkward mouth open and her chin shivering. Josh Balsam was laid out on the concrete next to Blue Gene.

"Hey! Cameraman!" yelled Henry. "Ripplemeyer just attacked someone!" But the news crew was already packing their equipment into their van. "Of course they don't get that on tape."

Blue Gene and Balsam both got to their feet as soon as humanly possible.

"Run," Blue Gene told Jackie. "Run!" She darted through the semicircle that had gathered, and Balsam started to follow.

"Balsam!" yelled Henry. "Stop acting like an animal and do your job. Take John home immediately." Balsam simply nodded and marched away with John at his side. The crowd disassembled with low-pitched mumbles.

"Are you okay?" Henry asked. Blue Gene looked down at the shredded flesh of his palms. "That looks awful. Go wash up."

"I'm a'ight," said Blue Gene, picking tiny bits of rock and dirt from the raw skids. "Is John okay?"

"He's fine. Just a little stage fright, but he'll outgrow that."

"Should we be with him?"

"Oh, spare me. Why are you suddenly so concerned about John's well-being?"

"Aw, come on now."

"I hold you responsible for what happened to him tonight. I hope you're happy."

"Y'all shouldn't have come out here in the first place."

"Oh. I suppose we should just lie down and let you people steal an election from us?"

$ $ $

John rested his forehead against the window, his handsome face staring morosely out at the lights of River Town Road. The Xanax was massaging his frayed nerves, but nothing could stop the worry. Meanwhile, in the driver's seat, an absolutely wrathful Josh Balsam muttered cuss words every other breath. "I'll fuckin' kill the bitch," he said out of the side of his mouth, with its misshapen teeth. "You don't fuck with me and just walk away from it."

John made no response, because the only words that mattered to him at that moment were "You need to find a way to fix this, and you need to fix it fast." It was the last thing his father had said to him before sending him home.

But how could he fix it? He had fallen face-first into the realm of worst-case scenario: a panic attack on national television, not to mention the political suicide of accidentally putting down the soldiers. He was ruined, destined to be a punch line. There went this election. There went all the elections. There went his lifetime membership to the Group, who now had televised proof he was not of their league.

"Bitch got a lucky lick in is all that was."

He never should've run. He knew he wasn't able. But they made him. They made him and he failed, just as he had failed at everything else in life. No! God help him! This was his entire life, tonight. His parents' whole life. Dad would hate him until the day he died for how badly he had botched it; Henry had looked so disgusted when he saw John chewing up that pill like a starved animal.

"I'll take my .45 and end it. Say *bam*! Let's hear you talk now."

He was not going to let himself go to ruin. He was not! This was *his* destiny, and he was in control of it, by God. All destinies. He would not let his own trifling mental problem—his own *weakness*—get in the way of God's plan.

One day between now and the election. It was too late to stop the interview from airing. He had humiliated himself on live TV, and it was probably already making the rounds on YouTube. But he could turn it around. He just had to divert the heat onto them. But how? He had turned into a rippling puddle of sweat and said the troops were dumb; how do you divert attention from *that*?

He couldn't do anything tonight. The medicine made him numb, and he couldn't think straight. He'd have a good night's rest, and then tomorrow morning he could explain to the media what had happened. He could say he had a horrible stomach problem while he was being interviewed, so bad that he didn't know what he was saying. He'd say that he adored the troops. And his stomach was much better now.

"I'll put a bullet in her temple. See how smart she is with a bullet poking out her skull."

But what if she won? What if the Wormland Group was watching to see how he handled this? What was he thinking, waiting until tomorrow morning? There was the ten o'clock news on tonight. It was six-thirty. He would have to kill this story before it began. The local stations would play clips at ten o'clock. They would play the clip, all of the district would see it, and it would all be over. A young woman write-in candidate would end his political career. Then there was tomorrow's local newspaper. Who was he kidding? There was no way out of this. He was finished.

"Shit. If I blew her head off, it wouldn't be just for me. It'd be straight-up justice for us all."

"*What?*" asked John, annoyed.

"Bitch treasoned. She should be executed. I'll execute her personally. Blow her head in two."

John shuddered. Then he turned and looked at Balsam's hard young face that was focused intensely on the road.

John was already asking God for forgiveness. But it was so perfect. Could God not have aligned this for him, for the dream to come true? Jackie had publicly humiliated Balsam; Balsam could do it for retaliation's sake. There were witnesses; people had seen her deck him. He had a simple, apolitical motive. It would have nothing to do with John Hurstbourne Mapother, nothing to do with politics—just a cold-blooded act of revenge. It could happen in the next hour. Jackie would still be at the Wal-Mart parking lot. The ten o'clock news and the morning paper would have murder—even an assassination—as the lead story. John's TV appearance would be forgotten, buried in the Local-Regional section if it made the paper at all.

How could these thoughts even be in his head? This was a human life! But God couldn't want that heathen girl to win. The things she said about her country! God couldn't want that girl to defeat John, not with John's sacred relationship to his maker, not with the dream waiting for him on some dark, unknown date in the far-off future, not after all the hell he had been through. In fact, maybe this was a test from God.

If it didn't kill her, it would at least scare her enough that she wouldn't go through with her candidacy. And if she did die, that would be up to the Lord.

John looked over at Balsam, who was still horn-mad, breathing heavily and shaking his head. What about him? If he were caught, if he were chased by the police—he could even be killed. What about that, Lord? Could the Lord want that?

"Turn left right there," said John, pointing to the entrance of Vandalia Hills. Balsam turned and accelerated. "Jesus, slow down," said John. "The kids are still trick-or-treating."

Balsam said nothing, but slowed down his oversize Dodge Ram. "I didn't mean to snap at you. It's just that we get an absurd amount of trick-or-treaters in this neighborhood—they say the most of any neighborhood in Bashford. They're not supposed to be doing it after dark, but they always do anyway. Turn right here."

"My kids are out trick-or-treatin', too."

"You have kids?"

"Yeah. Two."

"How old are you?"

"Nineteen."

John looked the bellicose man-child up and down, and for the first time he took in the surroundings of his truck. A solid stench of cigarette smoke hung in the air, and rap played on the radio. On the dashboard lay unopened toys from McDonald's Happy Meals, mechanized goggles, a hunting knife, and some classified ads.

"Here," said John. "It's this one on the left. Turn into that drive."

"This one?"

"Yeah. Wait! Let those kids pass."

"My bad. I got my mind elsewhere."

Balsam waited for a small group of pirates and Hannah Montanas to walk past the drive before turning.

"Thanks for the ride."

"You're welcome."

"So what do you plan to do?" asked John.

"About what?"

"About Jackie Ripplemeyer."

"All's I got to say is she better watch it next time I run into her."

John sighed heavily. "That's all?"

"Yeah. Why?"

"Nothing. Say, has anyone from my campaign team paid you lately?"

"No. Said they'd pay me the fifteenth."

"Why don't you come inside? I want to give you an advance."

John led Balsam into his house through the back door in the kitchen, then through the living room. "This is the nicest building I ever been in," said Balsam, as he looked up at the high ceilings. "Y'all *live* here?"

John laughed. "Yes."

"'Cause it don't look like anybody lives here."

John's office upstairs offered more decorations than the other rooms. The walls displayed framed certificates and photographs, most of them of John posing with important-looking men. John went behind his ornate mahogany desk and got out his checkbook. Balsam casually looked around but whipped his head in John's direction when he heard the quick rip of a check being torn from a checkbook.

"Thank you, Josh," John said, handing him the check. The doorbell rang. "Probably just trick-or-treaters. I don't feel like dealing with any-body."

John sat down behind his desk. Balsam stood staring at the check with his mouth hanging open even wider than usual.

"Damn, Mr. Mapother. Thank you."

"You're welcome. You're a fine worker. And tonight you were a great security guard. And you even got injured on the job, so consider it your hazard pay."

"Oh, that wasn't nothin'. I didn't get injured. Bitch got lucky. That's all that was. And all's I know is she better hope and pray I don't run into her."

"I know how you feel. She made a fool of me, too."

"Nah. She didn't make no fool of me. It ain't over either, you know? I get mad, but I get even."

"I don't know, Balsam. I think she made us both look like fools."

Balsam touched the imprint of Jackie's ring that had been left on his cheek. "I respect you and what you have to say and all, but she didn't make no fool of me."

"Oh, I know. I didn't mean anything by that. I hope that you do get even with her, though. I really do. Because that girl stands for everything our country is *not* about. Well, you heard her talking, putting down America. I don't have to tell you about it. It would be a crying shame if she ends up winning this election. Why don't you sit down?"

Balsam sat in one of the two dark-brown leather chairs in front of John's desk.

"I'm afraid after that interview tonight, she's going to pull out a victory on Tuesday."

"Might not."

"You think people will still vote for me?"

"I think a lot of 'em still will 'cause a lot of us didn't like what she had to say."

"Will you still vote for me?"

"I never did register, but I would, yeah."

"Why do you still believe in me?"

"Basically 'cause you're all I got." Balsam sat silently for a moment, his mouth open. "That and the Blood Flag."

"The Blood Flag? Is that all I've got going for me?"

"That's all you need. It shows what you're all about, and that's what

I'm all about. An eye for an eye, know what I'm sayin'? I ain't forgettin' it, and I will defend it and everything the Blood Flag stands for. That bitch that's running against you, she ain't about the Blood Flag at all. If it was up to her, she'd have all the fuckin' sand-people over for dinner. She ain't American. And it shouldn't be held against you that you said one bad thing about the troops, 'cause the way I see it, that bitch gave a whole motherfuckin' sermon putting down America. I'd fuckin' blow her head off if I had the chance."

"Would you?"

"Yeah."

"I want you to know, Josh, that I did *not* mean what I said about our troops. It came out wrong. That girl, she got me so riled up that I didn't know what I was saying. That's what her kind will do to you. *They* put down America, and meanwhile, here *I* am, for America, yet they turn *me* into the bad guy. You know I have only the utmost respect for the men and women who serve in our armed forces. Look at the tribute I put on for your father on the Fourth. People like Jackie, they think they're so much smarter than regular guys like us—they're the ones who hate our troops. Not me. And to think it's looking like she's going to win this election."

Balsam shook his head. John looked into Balsam's eyes, those dullard eyes that had likely never read a book.

"I wonder if it'll be in the paper about you and her getting into a fight," said John.

"You think it will?"

"I'd say so. Yeah. Sure it will. She's a newsmaker now. It'll probably be in there that she punched you out."

"Fuck that. I'll just go back there right now and settle the score."

"Josh, let me ask you this. Do you even own a gun?"

"Of course I do." Balsam pulled a handgun from his pants, and John reared his head back. "Had it on me for security for tonight."

"Do you think you could do it without getting caught?"

"Do what?"

"You know."

"Probably. Are you being for real right now?"

"Are *you*?"

"I mean, yeah. I'm always for real."

"You really think you could do that?"

Balsam nodded. "I mean, I *could*, but—"

"Then you better get out of here. If you're going to do it, you better do it quickly, before they print the story about her beating you up. My wife and son will be home soon. I don't want anyone seeing you here. I don't want anyone thinking I had anything to do with it. Because I didn't have anything to do with it, right? This is between you and that girl, right?"

"Right."

"It has absolutely nothing to do with John Hurstbourne Mapother. You agree?"

"Well, yeah."

"It's about you settling a personal score, because if you don't, for the rest of your life you'll be known as the guy who got his ass kicked by a girl."

Balsam and John stood at the same time. Balsam restored the pistol to his pants.

"Here. Give me that check back."

"What for?"

"I don't want any ties to you in case you get caught. I'll send it back to you after everything blows over." Balsam hesitantly gave John the check.

"I don't know 'bout all this. I mean, I was gonna give her a talkin' to. I don't know 'bout all this."

John walked out of his office and motioned for Balsam to follow. "Come on, Balsam. You say you love your country so much. Here's your chance to defend it, and to defend your own pride. Don't you want to defend your country against someone like her? You want to let her get into office?"

"No. But you know, I carry a piece but I never shot nobody. I mean, yeah, I'm pissed, but I don't know if it's worth—"

They quickly headed down the steps.

"What would your father say about what happened to you tonight, losing that fight, and to a person like *that*?"

"I don't know." John led Balsam down the hall and toward the back door.

"Would he have wanted you to just *take* it?"

"No."

"This is your chance to finally defend your country. It's your moral obligation. You have to do something. Don't wimp out."

"I ain't wimpin' out."

"When I make it to the White House, you will be rewarded, but for right now, it's your honor you have to defend. God wants you to do this. Will you stand up and be a man and do it?"

Balsam stiffened his posture.

"I will."

"God bless you. Now go! Hurry! Don't tell anybody you were ever here!"

John hurried Balsam out the back door. The boy's shorn head shone in the moonlight. He started his engine and lingered a moment, but then he was gone. John went back inside and started praying, frantically.

$ $ $

After Jackie was done greeting everyone and personally thanking them for coming to the rally, Blue Gene had her burrow her fist into a tub of ice in which one of the beer kegs rested. "Leave it in there till you can't stand it."

"You oughta be taking care of yourself," said Jackie.

"Nah. That ain't nothin'." Blue Gene set his can of Cherry Ski and his cigarette down and held the jagged red scrapes up to her.

"Ooh," she said with a wince.

"Hurts worse from where he yanked my hair." Blue Gene turned for her to see.

"Oh my God. A great big chunk of your mullet is *gone*."

"Is it?"

"Oh, wow. I'm so sorry that happened to you. Thanks for stopping him the way you did. He looked like he was going to kill me."

Blue Gene picked up his cigarette and Ski. "I would've gone on and fought 'im if I'd've known you were gonna."

"I didn't know I was going to, either."

"Why did ya?"

"I guess I'm not as good as I thought I was." Jackie looked away after saying it. The parking lot had become a herd of cars and trucks leaving at the same time. "That was the first time I've ever hit anybody. It'll be in the paper. I'll look like a hypocrite, talking about how we need peace and then getting into a fight. I just got so mad."

"It's okay," said Blue Gene. "Shut up about it." He took one more long drag from his cigarette before flicking it to the concrete.

"Is your brother okay?"

"I don't know."

"Was I too hard on him?"

Blue Gene shrugged his shoulders. "Too late now anyway. What do we do next?"

"Nothing," said Jackie. "We've done all we can do for tonight. Tomorrow we'll do some door-to-doors."

"A'ight. See ya tomorrow, then."

"Wait. Are you mad at me?"

"No." Blue Gene wondered if he truly was or not. He wanted to help the people, but he hated that John had looked so pitiful.

"I think we really have a chance now," said Jackie.

"Yeah."

"Aren't you happy? We could actually *win*."

"I can't win, Jackie."

$ $ $

John continued to pray that he was doing the right thing as he put on a dry undershirt. Then he plopped down on his bed and called his father's cell phone.

"Hey, Dad. I was just calling to let you know I have everything under control."

"How in the world did you manage that?"

"Oh, I pulled some strings, got some things lined up. I have a statement in mind for the paper."

"What?"

"I'll tell them I had a stomach virus, and that's why I acted the way I did on camera."

Henry paused, then laughed. He wouldn't stop laughing.

"I've taken care of everything, Dad. Please, have some faith in me. What's going on at the rally?"

"It's winding down. I'm getting ready to leave."

"Anything else happen?"

"No. There were a couple more speeches. Some veterans spoke. That Ripplemeyer girl's mother fussed at me because she thought I was the one who put Balsam up to trying to attack her daughter. We'll need to fire him, by the way. He's obviously unbalanced."

"Her *mother*?" asked John. His heart started speeding again.

"Yes. We know her, you know. She works at our bank. Angela Samson."

"I know. I *think* I knew that."

"Yes. We told you that was her mother when we were trying to find something on her."

"Maybe you did, but—oh, God. Oh, Dad. I have to go."

John hung up. His clean undershirt was already beginning to dampen under the arms. He pictured Angela Samson, this older woman whom he'd always see around town and at the bank, always so friendly, always so kind. She had probably been out there cheering Jackie on tonight. She probably called up all of her lady friends to tell them her daughter was running for office. She might still be there. John grabbed his cell phone.

What had happened to him only five minutes ago? What had snapped his mind in that direction? He started to call Balsam. But Balsam didn't even have a cell phone. The idiot. No—he wasn't an idiot. He couldn't help it that he was poor. Oh God, he'd said this was the nicest building he had ever been in. And John got to live here. The boy hadn't seen a thing of this world and probably never would.

John slipped into some house slippers and bounded down the steps. The phone rang. Maybe it was Balsam, telling him he couldn't do it. He checked the caller ID. It was Abby. There was no time to talk to her. He would have to drive after Balsam. It was his only chance. As he ran toward the garage, he wondered if he was doing the right thing, and then he pictured the older woman again, only now she was younger and Jackie was a little girl, just a cute little girl, and Balsam was a baby and his teeth were fine because they hadn't come in yet. As John grabbed the car keys, he heard someone pounding at the door but immediately dismissed it as some more trick-or-treaters.

He jumped into his Escalade and pulled out of the driveway before the garage door was even up, banging the top of his vehicle. He sped out of the driveway and saw one of his neighbors at his front door, but there was no time. He thought he heard a woman screaming as he headed down the road.

Then he saw a crowd gathered around something in the middle of the street. There were cars backed up going both ways, and he heard sirens and saw that an ambulance was headed his way. He pulled into a driveway so that he could turn around. But as he started backing out, he heard his name being screamed.

He put the car in park and got out. Abby was running toward him, waving her arms hysterically.

"John! John!"

"What?!" He grabbed hold of her shoulders. "What's wrong?!"

"Arthur was hit by a car."

"No."

"He was hit. It was a hit-and-run."

"No."

Down the road, the crowd parted so the paramedics could get to the figure in the middle. In the light of the ambulance, all John could see were little black shoes, the toes pointing to the sky.

"We walked out in front of a truck," said Abby. "We didn't see him because he didn't have his lights on."

ELECTION DAY

"**B**ut they're so *skanky* in there. Isn't there, like, a *private* waiting room or something where we can sit alone?"

"Oh, stop being so uppity."

"But I don't want to sit in there with—"

"Shh. They might hear you. Here's a dollar. Go to the basement and get a Coke or something."

The prissy teenage peacock snatched the dollar and was gone, already on her cell phone before her father turned away. The father took a seat in the waiting room off to the side, leaving the rough-looking quartet of half-dead folks to their own little section. Situated in the vinyl seats as if guarding one another, they looked familiar, but their clutched body language warned, "Stay away," and their drawn faces said, "Don't ask." Two sat on one side and two on the other, an ideal configuration for conversation, though their faces stayed directed at the floor. Occasional noises came from their side of the room: an uncouth snorting of the sinuses, a nerve-racked tapping of fingers, a stern clearing of the throat, and a pathetic rattle of a rosary.

$ $ $

This was the third day straight that Blue Gene was wearing the sweatpants and the green Have-Not Party muscle shirt that he had originally donned for the Halloween rally. Next to him was a scruffy, fidgety John, who had spent the night at the hospital for the second night in a row—the first as a patient, the second as a relative of a patient—and had not yet bothered changing out of his cotton sleeping shorts and the old Yankees T-shirt he obsessively wore to bed. Henry uncharacteristically wore no suit coat or tie, and his thick white facial stubble made him look like a professorial hillbilly. Elizabeth had her hair pulled back as tightly as ever but for once wore no makeup, making her look as exhausted and beaten-down as the three men, even a bit hard. All their eyes were puffy and gray as raindrops on newspapers.

The surgeon whom Henry had flown in from Chicago said that the operation could go on for eight to ten hours, and that he really wouldn't know how long the procedure would take until they started. For the family, there was nothing to do but whither the day away in the waiting room. Too tired to pace, they mostly just sat dumbstruck from the morning on into the afternoon, breathing the hospital air that was so thick with magnitude.

Occasionally a doctor would rush past, looking important with his surgical mask undone and flapping about. Sometimes from the nurses' station came a joke-sassy comment or a merry chortle, and all four Mapothers would shoot a dirty look their way.

As they had the previous day and the night of Halloween, the Mapothers did attempt to converse every once in a while, when the silence pressed down too hard, but every time they tried, the beat was off. Early that afternoon, Henry made the first serious attempt of the day.

"If any of you want to eat, go ahead. I'll stay here."

"No thank you," said Elizabeth. John and Blue Gene mumbled the same.

"I hope I won't be showing poor form if I point out—" said Henry. "No, I don't think it's poor form at all, because I'm merely stating the obvious. At any rate, what I'm trying to say is that today is Election Day, which I realize, Election Day holds no sway inside this building, but I think it would be germane to acknowledge—"

"If you need to be out campaigning, that's fine by me," said John.

"No. That's not why I mentioned it."

"It's your campaign now," said John. "You do whatever you need to be doing."

"No. I don't even plan to go vote, which is ludicrous considering all we've endured, but given the circumstances—regardless, do I look like I'm in the mood to campaign?"

"Maybe John is trying to say he doesn't *want* you here," said Elizabeth.

"*No*, that's not what I was saying," said John. "I said what I meant."

"Do you not want me here, John?" asked Henry.

"He just said he *did*," said Blue Gene.

"I didn't mean just you, Henry," said Elizabeth. "Maybe he doesn't want *any* of us here. If you need to be with Abby, we understand."

"I was only making conversation," said Henry. "Now I regret doing so."

"I'm exactly where I want to be right now," said John. He had started picking off the edges of his fingernails. He put the nail clippings in his pocket.

"We want to do whatever you want us to do," said Elizabeth.

"Y'all, just leave it alone," said Blue Gene. "Just cool it. You know the doctor said John has to stay calm. Why you gotta rile him up?"

"That's why perhaps it would be best if we left him alone," said Henry.

"Okay," said Elizabeth. "We'll be quiet."

"If he *hadn't* had a nervous breakdown, y'all'd *give* him one," said Blue Gene.

"He didn't say that I needed to stay calm," said John. "He said I needed rest."

"I'll let you rest, then," said Henry, getting up. "I'll be back in an hour or so."

"Where are you going?" asked Elizabeth.

"I'm going to go vote. Do you want to go with me?"

"No."

"Fine. Can I get you anything while I'm out, John?"

"No. Take your time." Henry left. "Mom, if you want to go with him, you can."

"Are you saying that because you *want* me to leave?"

"Oh, come on! I'm saying it because I *mean* it. If you want to go vote, go vote."

"Well, I honestly don't *want* to go vote."

"It *is* ridiculous not to vote after all we've been through," said John.

"Yeah," offered Blue Gene, "but if I voted and she voted, my vote would cancel hers out, so we might as well not bother."

"That isn't the way you should look at it," said John, "but I don't care what either of you do."

"I ain't goin' nowhere," said Blue Gene.

"Neither am I," said Elizabeth. "But John, if you need to be with Abby, Blue Gene and I understand."

"He *can't* be with Abby," said Blue Gene. "Doctor's orders. He can't watch the surgery. He's gotta stay calm."

"No, I just need rest," said John.

"I *know* that, Gene," said Elizabeth. "But maybe Abby could step outside the observation room to be with John."

"I'll go see her after a while," said John. "She has her parents in there with her."

"Oh, yes. She made *that* clear. She doesn't need us."

"*Mom*," said John.

"Just make sure you go be with her at some point. I'll get her out of observation if you want. I'm not going to have them think you're a negligent husband."

"*Mother*," John said, loud enough to make Elizabeth look to see if anyone was watching. "Stop it. I've got a child who will probably never see daylight again."

"Oh, what a horrible way to put it," said Elizabeth. "That just goes all through me to hear you say that."

"How am I supposed to put it? Would you prefer *brain death*?"

"Are you *trying* to make me leave?" asked Elizabeth.

"No."

"Either it goes all through you or it all goes through you," said Blue Gene.

"What?" both Elizabeth and John asked, half a second apart.

"Either it goes all through you or it all goes through you. You said Arthur'll pro'ly never see daylight again, and Mom said that goes all through her."

"But what do you mean?" asked Elizabeth. Blue Gene opened his mouth to speak but then just ran his fingers across his mustache and shrugged.

"Shit. I don't know. Let's everybody shut up."

And they did just that for a minute, until Elizabeth suddenly got up and looked out the window, and her shoulders shook as she muffled a whimper.

"Mom," said John, but he didn't make a move. He looked at Blue Gene helplessly, his handsome face fuzzy and lifeless. Blue Gene sighed and got up. He stood behind Elizabeth and patted her on the back twice.

"The river," said Elizabeth, but she couldn't finish her sentence. The waiting room was in a tower that overlooked the river. "Everybody talks about how great it is that our town is on a river, but our river, you have to admit, is so muddy and brown and ugly. Every once in a while, though, when the sun shines on it just so, and the sky is a certain shade, and there's a current in the water, it actually is quite beautiful."

"I don't know *where* you're gettin' that," said Blue Gene, now standing next to Elizabeth. "Sun isn't shining now at *all*."

Before Blue Gene had even finished the comment, Elizabeth sobbed.

"Sorry," he said, and he patted her shoulder. "I'm sorry, Mom. Come on. Let's you and me go to their little chapel. You want to?"

"Okay," she said. "John, is that okay? Do we need to stay with you? Oh, Lord. Now we're *all* abandoning you."

"Please just leave me alone," he said, all out of fight.

$$$

At any given moment of any given day, a million people were sending prayers out of their minds, a million transmissions going out at once to one omnipotent satellite. Elizabeth conceded this fact, and therefore to the end of her silent prayer she appended a P.S. that asked the Lord not to consider her conceited for requesting that her prayer take precedence over all others. She normally wouldn't make such a request, but she was desperate. She admitted that she and her family were clearly not special in His eyes, no more deserving of His divine mercy than the most sordid vulgarian, though part of her reasoned that maybe even *this*, the atrocious, preventable death of a child, was part of His plan, part of the intricate design that would give birth to the earthly manifestation of her prophecy. But any which way her frenetic prayer turned, it always crashed back into the undeniably wicked fact that a little boy could simply be no more, irreversibly flicked from the earth to never come running into a room again. No god of hers could want this.

Elizabeth knelt as long as she could. She finally made the sign of the cross and sat back in the pew. She was surprised to see that even after she sat down, Blue Gene showed no signs of stopping his own prayer, which was apparently being dispatched with intense concentration, his head buried in his interlaced fingers. She could even hear a syllable being whispered aloud here and there. She picked up his Coors Light cap that he had left in the pew, and thought about smelling the inside but didn't.

As Blue Gene's prayer went on and on, Elizabeth couldn't stop staring at the back of his head. It was so ratty, more uneven than ever before, since some had been pulled out.

"Surely you'll get your hair cut *now*," she said suddenly.

"Shh," he said. "I'm not done prayin' yet."

"You've prayed enough, dear." Blue Gene turned around and snarled his lip. "Really, you have. You'll drive yourself crazy. Sit back here with me." Blue Gene made the sign of the cross and sat. They were the only ones in the sorry little velvety chapel, but Elizabeth whispered to maintain the solemnity. "We've offered it up to the Lord. There's nothing more we can do."

"I think I need to tell you what I was praying just then," said Blue Gene, just above a whisper.

"You don't have to."

"Yeah, I do." With his foot in its unfashionable basketball sneaker, Blue Gene propped up the kneeler, then dropped it, then propped it up again. "I'm sorry for everything."

"What are you sorry about?"

"Are you asking that 'cause you really don't know or because you want to make me say it?"

"Because I really don't know."

"Oh. I'm sorry for going against y'all and putting up Jackie against my own family. It ended up causing John to have an attack on TV, and maybe if I had just let things go, he would've been with Arthur on Halloween and could've protected him somehow."

Elizabeth ran her hand through the front of his greasy hair, which was matted from wearing a cap. "That's sweet of you to apologize, but you don't have to. It was beyond your control. But yes, you're right. I wish it hadn't come to what it did with you against John. I tried to stop you."

"That's why I'm apologizing to you," said Blue Gene, becoming cross. "I'm sorry."

"It's okay. Shh."

"But you're trying to make me feel worse."

"That wasn't my intention."

"And it wasn't just me wanting revenge on John."

"I didn't say it *was*."

"I really want Jackie to win 'cause I believe in all the things she's for."

"What's going on with you two?"

"It's just professional now."

"You're not even *friends* anymore?"

"Hardly. She's s'posed to stop by tonight after the results are in to check on me."

"That might upset John."

"I'm gonna meet her outside. Why we even talking about her? Just know that I'm sorry."

"I forgive you, but really, though, you shouldn't blame yourself. You can't stop fate. It was just some fool who forgot to turn his lights on. I prayed for him. You should too, if you haven't already. Whoever it is, even his soul wants peace. Can you imagine what he must feel like right now? He couldn't have *meant* to run somebody down. He probably just got scared and didn't know what to do but keep driving."

"You say *he*. It may have been a woman."

"Abby said it was a great big pickup truck. I just assumed." They heard the door behind them open. A feeble, skeletal old man in a suit entered and knelt at a pew in the back. "Let's go." Gene held the door for her, and they walked side by side back into the stark white hallway. There was so much she would've liked to say to Gene, but when the man entered, she took it as a sign to be quiet. If the man hadn't entered, she would've said that if anyone should be feeling sorry, it was she. If she had just kept the prophecy to herself, maybe none of the family's tragedies would've come to pass.

But whether it was real or not, the idea of the dream had always *felt* right to Elizabeth. It was the strong, righteous axis on which the world of the Mapothers had revolved the last thirty years. As the days had gone by, they had spun on this axis so slowly that it all seemed safe, like no one could possibly be thrown off, but if she elapsed time she could see that all the while their sphere had actually been spiraling out of control, regardless of the good intentions that composed this central pole around which they flailed, no matter the ultimate perfection the dream represented. For so long she had strived for an absolute goodness, only to find herself staring at the worst kind of wrong. No, none of them were to blame, not even she, but she had to admit she was no saint and probably never would be.

"I know you're partial to Bernice," she said as they walked down the hall, past a janitor mopping the floor who seemed to know Gene, "but have I been a horrible mother?"

"You've been a lot better here lately. Hold on—I ain't partial to Bernice."

"It's okay if you are."

"I'm not. Why you askin' that?"

"No reason."

"If it's because you think you had a hand in me and John turnin' out the way we have, I wouldn't worry about it. I think with a dad like ours, we would've ended up messed up no matter what."

"Oh." But Elizabeth had to laugh. "Don't say that."

"You know it's true."

"You should know, though, that Henry's father wasn't good to him. You'll never hear him talk about it, but his dad was actually quite brutal."

"I know. The number of times I've heard him talk about his dad, I mean *really* talk about him and his dad, I could count on one finger."

Elizabeth laughed. Blue Gene pushed the button for the elevator, and she was glad when she saw they would be the only ones in it.

"Gene, you remember in my dream, those angels?"

"The ones without faces?"

"Yes. I can still see them running across the lawns on Main Street, and sometimes I think, 'What if John was wrong?' What if they weren't angels? They could've been monsters or aliens. Who could really know what they were?"

"Why you askin' all this serious stuff?"

"Well, I can't ask John or Henry. I thought I could talk to you since you got serious yourself back in the chapel. I'm just trying to find understanding in all this."

"You can ask me whatever you want, but what do I know? All I know is that we'll get through this just like we get through everything."

His sweetness and his simplicity made her want to cry again, but she got ahold of herself as the elevator door slid open. They turned to the wing that would lead them back to the waiting room. "You're right," she said. "We *will* get through this, and I still think everything happens for a reason, and if nothing else, maybe what has happened to Arthur will bring you and John together."

"Doubt it."

"*Gene.*"

"It's just so messed up. Was from the time I was born. How could it ever be different?"

"You know, one thing I've learned to do through the years is, when I feel myself getting really mad at someone, or if I even start to feel hatred toward them—"

"I don't hate him. I just can't get over things so easy."

"Listen to me. If you want to be good to someone whom you're having problems with, what you should do is visualize them in a hospital gown, lying in a hospital bed, because you know that if they live long enough, that's where they'll end up someday. And I've found that if you visualize them like this—sick or weak or dying—you won't feel any more hatred toward them."

"That actually sounds pretty cool."

"It really works. And I think that's how heaven will be. You'll be able to see everything as a whole, so you'll be able to see someone in their saddest moment, like lying on their deathbed. Or maybe you can see someone in their most embarrassing moment. Anyway, my point is that all of your grudges will go away in heaven. You can't have any enemies, and you can only love everyone else, because how could you not sympathize with them after seeing them in moments like that?"

"See, now, why the hell couldn't you have talked about that kind of stuff when you led that prayer service?"

$$$

When he returned to the hospital, Henry settled for a parking space in the very back, which he didn't mind, since he liked walking, though he couldn't help but laugh that the longest-serving member of the hospi-

tal's board of directors didn't have a better space. At least the chill of November had not yet arrived; it was nice outside, cloudy but back to being
unseasonably warm, like it had been for most of the fall.

What was supposed to be a quick trip to his polling place at the Lincoln Elementary gymnasium had ended up turning into two and a half
hours of business. After he voted, he had called to check in with Mark
Howard, the campaign manager, who had talked him into coming to
headquarters to take care of a few last-minute details. He had provided
a statement for the press concerning his grandson's condition, met
briefly with some district bigwigs and precinct captains, and recorded a
message to be phoned in to all the voters listed as undecided.

The day before, Henry had announced to the press that if John won
the election, he would serve out his son's term for him, as John couldn't
possibly take on the position while coping with his own son's devastating accident. All the Mapothers agreed that this only made sense, considering Henry's bureaucratic expertise and vast collection of
government contacts, not to mention the tacit understanding that this
had been largely his campaign from the beginning.

Because he never used elevators, Henry took the steps to the third
floor, where he found Eugene sitting alone in the waiting room, reading
Field and Stream.

"They finished the surgery 'bout half an hour ago," he said, still
holding the magazine open.

"And?" Henry asked impatiently. This was no time for Eugene's slow
talk.

"The surgery went the way it should, but they said the next twenty-
four hours will be critical."

"Will he live?"

"He'll live, but in the next day they'll see whether or not he'll be a
vegetable. Is that wrong of me to say it like that? I mean—that's the only
way I knew how to say what they said. He could end up a vegetable."

"You said it fine, Eugene. Where is everybody?"

"Mom and Abby are with Arthur, and John's in one of the patient rooms. They had to sedate him."

"Why?"

"'Cause after the surgery, they finally let him go in and see Arthur, and he couldn't handle it."

"Oh." Not knowing what else to do, Henry took a seat next to Eugene. "Did they have to readmit John?"

"No. They just offered him a bed. How was the turnout at the polls?"

"There weren't nearly as many as you'd think there would be, considering all the hoopla."

For the next forty-five minutes, save for one cell phone call from one of Henry's campaign workers, they sat in silence. Then Elizabeth and Abby appeared with wan faces. Henry stood immediately. He gave a hard look to Eugene, who set his magazine aside but remained seated; he had been taught better. As the women gravely approached, Henry wished that men still wore hats, just so he could take his off.

"He's gone into a coma," said Elizabeth.

"I'm sorry," said Henry, looking at Abby. She mouthed a "thank you."

"Can he come out of it?" asked Blue Gene.

"The doctor said he didn't know," said Elizabeth. "He could come out of it at any time. Hours, days, months, years, or not at all."

"I'm going to go tell John," said Abby.

"Have a seat," said Henry, and Elizabeth sat across from him. "I got tied up downtown."

"I don't care," said Elizabeth.

"Now what?" asked Blue Gene.

"I don't know," said Elizabeth. "I guess you can go home if you want. I'm not ready to leave yet."

"I'm not either," said Blue Gene.

So they sat in silence until ten after six, when Henry's cell phone began to ring.

"I wish you would turn that cell phone off," said Elizabeth the second time it rang.

"What am I supposed to do?" replied Henry. "They don't have a radio or a TV in here. How else am I going to hear the results coming in?"

"I don't think you're even supposed to have a cell phone in here."

"Let me take this one, and then I'll turn it off," said Henry. "Mapother," he answered. As he listened to his campaign manager, he watched Elizabeth roll her eyes at Eugene, who shrugged his shoulders. Henry soon hung up. "I'm sorry about that, but I do at least have good news. Twenty-five percent of all counties are in, and we're way ahead. Over thirty thousand ahead, according to exit polls."

"Congratulations," said Blue Gene, barely.

"No offense."

"It don't matter."

"Maybe I'll go find John," said Henry.

John lay in bed in a room down the hall. Abby sat at his side. "He fell back asleep," she whispered. Henry considered telling her the good news but didn't want to seem insensitive.

"Let me sit with him for a while," he said.

Abby left without much coaxing, and Henry took her seat. He badly wanted to wake up John, but the ombudsman in his mind said to let the poor boy sleep.

Henry wasn't in the room when John had his collapse on the night of Halloween, but Elizabeth said that upon hearing the doctor say there was a fifty-fifty chance Arthur could be permanently brain-dead, John started bawling, dropped to his knees, clasped his wife's leg, and then, in a sort of frantic delirium, lay himself down on the hard, white hospital floor and cried some more. The doctor called it nervous exhaustion.

After about ten minutes, Henry turned the TV on, muting it so as not to disturb John. All the TV channels had to offer were occasional updates on the election, nothing Henry didn't already know. He kept the TV on one of the local channels anyway and kept an eye on John.

Henry saw that in spite of his current state, and in spite of all he had endured, John still made a handsome figure, though his open mouth offset his good looks. Also, he was snoring, which Henry considered one of the basest noises a human could make. Henry felt bad that he was seeing John in such an unflattering condition. He would never want anyone seeing him like that, which was why he had always told Elizabeth he wanted a closed casket, to which she always replied, "Oh, Henry, you'll never die."

John's mouth wouldn't stay closed, even when Henry pushed his chin up. He looked dumb with his mouth open, and Henry could not abide letting this go on much longer. He called the campaign manager and asked for the latest numbers.

"John," he said after hanging up. There was no response. "John!?" Henry shook John until he awakened. John looked disoriented at first, then calm. "I thought you might want to know that the election results have started coming in. They have been for a while."

"Oh."

"About forty percent of the counties are in, and we're winning by forty-two thousand. The biggest counties haven't reported yet, but we're looking good."

"Anything new on Arthur?"

"I'm afraid not."

"Is he in a coma? Is that what Abby told me? I've been having trouble lately separating what I've dreamed and what's really happened."

"Oh, you can't get much out of the doctor or the nurses."

"Please tell me."

"Well, you weren't dreaming."

John looked out the window. Henry looked up at the TV.

"I hate myself," said John.

"Stop it."

"You don't understand."

"John, you're going to have to get ahold of yourself. I'm sorry, Son, but you just have to. I know this is the worst thing imaginable, but you have to stay strong for Abby. You can't be losing it every time something bad happens."

"I know. I know. But when they let me in there after his surgery, it was his little feet. They had the sheets and blanket over him tight, and his feet, they came to a point, a real skinny point, so his body under the covers was in the shape of a dagger, and I don't know why, but it just bothered me to see his feet like that. It looked stupid. So I tried to slide my hand in between his feet through the covers to get them apart, but they had the covers so tight that I couldn't separate them, and so then I was going to undo his covers and reach down to his legs, but Abby told me to stop, but I started to do it anyway and Abby grabbed ahold of me and she started crying and said, 'Stop, stop, you can't touch him,' and that's when I lost it."

"John, grace under pressure. I know it's the hardest thing in the world, but grace under pressure."

"I know. But if you could've seen his pointy little feet."

"You have to stop it. You're just hurting yourself." Henry's cell phone rang.

"You're not supposed to have those in here."

"Excuse me," said Henry, and he took the call. "Mapother...You have to be kidding me...Who's left to report?...Let me know the second you hear anything." He put his phone back in his dress-shirt pocket. "Heyburn County and most of the other eastern counties went to Frick. We're losing ground, and the five counties left are the biggest ones." Henry's nostrils flared.

"I ruined it all with that interview," said John.

"They didn't even mention your interview on the news. All they talked about was the hit-and-run."

"I ruin everything."

"John, stop feeling sorry for yourself. Let's just be quiet. You're not supposed to get excited."

"Can I see Arthur?"

"No. It might be too traumatic for you."

"If I stay calm, will they let me stay with him?"

"I don't know. You would need to prove that you can stay calm first."

They watched TV in silence, until finally another election update appeared. Commonwealth County had gone to Ripplemeyer, who received

7,300 votes to the Mapothers' 5,500 and Frick's 3,100. Henry growled.

"Good for her," he said. "But that's all she's getting."

"Sorry," said John.

"Don't say you're sorry."

"I don't think I was meant to be a leader."

"Of course you were. What about the dream?"

"I always secretly wanted to be a magician."

"That would be a waste of your talents. You're better than that."

"I'm too nervous to be a politician. I love people, but I hate them, too. I'm relieved it's you and not me now. Do you love people and hate them, too? Or do you just hate them?"

"I love them. You're loopy acting."

"I just don't care anymore. I don't care who wins or loses."

"That's understandable with all that's going on right now, but you have to remember the bigger picture. Don't forget your mother's visions. Don't you know what we have in store for the world? You have Worm-land, and we're still going to win this election and prove your mother a prophet."

"When you say *prophet*, how are you spelling it?"

"What do you mean?" His phone rang again. "Yeah...Call me when you hear about the last two." Henry hung up and said nothing.

"What?" asked John.

Henry stood and started pacing around the foot of John's bed.

"Is it over yet?" asked John.

"No."

"What happened?"

Henry wouldn't answer. He felt himself boiling and walked out to the hall. He had lost two more of those trashy, godforsaken counties, both to Frick. And only two more, even trashier, poorer counties were left. The lower-class counties! The lower classes that they had fought and scratched and clawed for—that they had even enlisted Eugene to help them win. Those mouth-breathers and their numbers! They could not provide for themselves a promising future. They had no prospects except for reproducing; that was their only power, so that's what they did, as much as they could, and he was paying for it at the polls.

He returned to John's room and looked up at the TV. He flipped through the stations, looking for election news, but there was none. He stood at the foot of John's bed and stared at him.

"What's happened?" asked John.

"John, you and I and your mother, and people like us—smart people, strong people, people that make it in the world—there's a theory that says all of our kind of people, we're called *Homo superiors*, and what that means is that we are of a higher species that has already evolved."

John took turns looking at his father, who was growing more excited by the second, and the TV.

"Everyone else, all those stupid, weak people, all the criminals and morons and all the rest, they're still just *Homo sapiens*. They only abide by what stimulus response dictates. We will never progress as a civilization until they evolve. This is our primary problem."

"Dad, hold on," said John.

"Oh, I know it sounds awful. It's just an idea. All I really want to do is bring the old days back. Is that so wrong? I want the days when I was young, before those long-haired, trashy, dirty losers arrived on the scene and ruined our country. I swear, I just want the good old days back."

"Dad, you've won."

"What do you mean?"

"You won. They just flashed it on the TV. The last two counties must've gone your way."

"Are you certain?"

"Yes."

"Let me call Mark."

His campaign manager confirmed it. The last two counties had both had huge turnouts and both heavily favored John Hurstbourne Mapother, who in the end had won by a convincing sixty thousand votes. Grant Frick was second and the write-in candidate had come in a solid third, thirty-seven thousand ballots behind the incumbent.

Elizabeth and Blue Gene entered, Elizabeth with a strained smile, Blue Gene apparently trying to look nonchalant by running his fingers through the back of his hair.

"We just won," said Henry.

"We heard," said Elizabeth. "One of the nurses told us. Congratulations."

Henry hugged and kissed Elizabeth. Blue Gene slumped against the wall. Then he offered his hand to Henry, and Henry took it and squeezed it tight and thanked him. John got out of bed and shook Henry's hand.

"You did it," he said. "I'm happy for you."

"No. We did it. This is your victory, son. You won. I'm merely representing you for a term, and I vow to do my best. I know I'm off to a late start, but I am not yet too old to make my mark. You're still so young. And let's not forget, you still have Wormland down the line."

While Henry was saying all this, John got back in bed and moaned. Henry knew that he couldn't expect much excitement with his grandson somewhere on this very floor, lying in critical condition, but John had better not be thinking about turning down the Wormland offer. It was a far more lucrative and powerful position than that of a congressman, and only Henry knew the under-the-table maneuvering it took to get that privileged spot open for John.

Now nobody said anything at all. It wasn't the victorious moment Henry had always pictured, and judging by everyone's downcast faces, maybe he wasn't even welcome in his own victory scene. It was understandable. They had to make him the villain, the profit worshipper who harbored perverted wishes of being so powerful that he would no longer be expected to say "hi" or "bye" to another being, a world traveler who could blame all his foibles on jet lag. They would never buy that he was looking only for peace, a peace he had never known but liked to think of as the serenity of an afternoon baseball game, with its leisurely pace and the hypnotic drone of the people in the background.

$ $ $

After ten minutes of debating, Henry and Elizabeth decided that they should at least make an appearance at campaign headquarters, since it might offend their supporters not to show up, and since there was little they could do for anyone at the hospital. Elizabeth balked at first but finally agreed to go, on the condition that they stop by home so she could put on some makeup. Meanwhile, for Blue Gene, the decision not to be with his supporters came easily. He knew they were supposed to gather in the old Wal-Mart parking lot, but if they lost, the plan was for Jackie to say a quick thank-you, and then the Have-Not Party would be over, at least for now.

Elizabeth kissed John goodbye on the forehead, and John congratulated his father. "I hope you can enjoy it," he said. "I really am glad it's you instead of me."

"Oh, come now," said Henry. "You're just in a slump, rightfully so. I'll serve out this term, and you can run again next time."

"Oh, Lord," said Elizabeth. "Let's not even think about that."

"For real," said Blue Gene. He invited himself to walk out with Henry and Elizabeth, saying it was time for a smoke break. After they walked through the automatic doors, Elizabeth hugged Blue Gene underneath the sheltered area where the ambulances parked.

"You really should change your shirt, at least," she said, and she brushed something off his shoulder. "Are you going to stay much longer?"

"I don't know. Pro'ly."

"You'll sit with John, won't you?"

"I reckon."

"I have to hand it to you, Eugene," said Henry. "You and your little ragtag team—that was a hell of a campaign you threw together on such short notice. If you had had more time, you might have been able to reach the other counties better. Congrats on Commonwealth County, at least. I trust there are no hard feelings?"

"Nah. I don't got no feelings at all."

"I know what you mean," said Henry.

"We'll be square, though," said Blue Gene, "if you just promise me you'll be a good leader."

"Of course I'll be a good leader."

"I mean a *good* leader, as in *good* to *everybody*."

"Of course I'll be good to everybody. Don't insult me."

Blue Gene sighed and got out his pack of Parliaments.

"And you say you'll keep John company, won't you?" asked Elizabeth.

"Yeah. Y'all go on."

They walked off to the back of the parking lot, holding hands.

Blue Gene stood next to a slim plastic receptacle, called a smoker's post, outside the hospital entrance and lit his cigarette. After he finished his first, he started another, all the while staring across the well-lit parking lot and occasionally glancing at the stars, thinking about how unfair it was that Henry would be in the House of Representatives and how he pretty much hated him but would miss him when he died. After a third cigarette, he went into the lobby and decided he could kill some time by calling Bernice on the courtesy phone. She had said to keep her posted.

When she answered, he could immediately hear her breathing problem acting up again.

"Are you okay?" he asked.

"Yeah, yeah. I'm fine. I'm just huntin' for a channel."

"But your breathin's funny. Have you not been taking your meds?"

"No, hon. I'm fine. Don't worry about me. How's Arthur?"

"He's in a coma. He's stable, at least, but they don't know if he'll ever wake up."

"My lands. Oh my, hon, I'm so sorry for all y'all. What can I do for you?"

"I'm worried about *you*. You don't sound too hot."

"I'm fine, hon. You just worry about that little boy. Don't you be worryin' about Bernice none. I'm doin' pretty good at the moment, actually." But she panted between sentences.

"What happened after y'all found out we lost?"

"Jackie gave just a short little speech, then a bunch of us left. Guess that dad of yours is happy."

"Yeah."

"How you holdin' up, hon?"

"Tired, but I just want Arthur to be okay."

"Ain't nothin' in this world worse than losin' a child."

"I'm sorry."

"No, don't be. I didn't mean nothin' by that."

"You know I'll always feel like it's part my fault."

"What?"

"Nothin'. I swear, life is just one thing after another."

"It's a bunch of *dust* is what it is."

"I hear that."

"I'm talkin' about the dust that the dustpan can't get. You know when you're using a whiskbroom with a dustpan, no matter how much you work that little broom, there's always gonna be a little line of dust left over?"

"Yeah."

"When I'd see that little line of dust, I'd always get so frustrated, but that there's life. Hard as you try to clean it up and get it the way you want it, there'll always be one more line of dust. Oh, fart. Listen to me. I'll come out and say it: we had us a coupla Wild Turkeys after we done lost the election, and I always end up talkin' like that when I drink."

"You drank and then you drove? You're always tellin' me not to do that."

"No. I had it after I got home."

"How—"

"My point is that you can't never get rid of that last line of dust, so don't try. I come up with that when I was cleanin' the floor of y'all's crapper."

Blue Gene laughed but then decided he shouldn't. "I gotta go," he said. "Now, if you keep havin' breathin' problems, I want you to go to the doctor, a'ight?"

"I'm fine, hon."

"No, I mean it. I'm gonna be worrying about you. I know you can afford to go to any doctor you want now, so that's no excuse."

"Just don't you worry. Whatever you heard in my breathin', it ain't what you think."

"You're in denial, Bernice. I know I heard you breathin' hard."

"Hon, I don't want you worryin' 'bout me on top of everything else. I have company, you see?"

"Why didn't you say so?"

"I don't know. It's Larry."

"Larry from the Veterans Committee?"

"Yeah. I didn't want to tell you, 'but don't think I'm havin' trouble breathin'. He was the only reason I was havin' trouble breathin'."

"Oh. *Oh.* I better let you go, then."

"You let me know if anything happens with Arthur."

"A'ight."

"I hope that didn't upset you—what I just said."

"No. I'm the opposite of upset. Have fun. Bye. Love you."

"I love you, hon."

Blue Gene smiled for the first time in days.

The clock said eight twenty-two. He went back outside and smoked some more, all the while looking across the parking lot, until finally he saw a sticker-covered Grand Am pull in. Jackie walked across the parking lot, under the lights and between the cars.

"Hey," she said sadly. She still wore her professional clothes, but with her hair down.

"Hey."

"How's your nephew?"

"He won't wake up."

"Oh, God."

"In a coma."

"I'm sorry. And your brother?"

"He'll be all right. Just needs to rest. I'm out here smoking when I should be up there with him, I guess, but I don't know what to say to him."

"I'm so sorry. I'm so sorry this has happened to you all."

Blue Gene nodded. For once, he failed to blow his cigarette smoke away from her. "One of my ol' friends is a patient in there, too," he said. "Got in a bad brush-hoggin' accident."

Jackie laughed.

"Don't laugh. That ain't funny."

"I know. Sometimes my wires get crossed. Sorry. I guess you know that we lost?"

"Yeah. How'd everybody take it?"

"Some of them were mad; some of them kind of just accepted it and left. You know what ended up putting your brother over the top, don't you?"

"Sympathy vote?"

"No. The smoking ban."

"Where'd you hear that?"

"There was a news crew filming us tonight, and I heard the reporter say they had exit polls asking people why they voted the way they did, and the smoking ban was by far the biggest issue. When people saw *Mapother* on the ballot, which is synonymous with tobacco, I guess it was a no-brainer, because meanwhile there I was, spouting off against smoking every chance I got. You were right. I never should've come out in favor of the ban."

"Yeah, but like you said, the truth's the truth, and that's what you believed."

"Yeah. That's what the truth gets you. They turn on you over something like that."

"You never can tell where you really stand with people."

"Yeah." Jackie's sharp features suddenly winced. "Gimme one of those cigarettes."

"Nuh-uh."

"Why?"

"You don't smoke. You're allergic."

"Who cares at this point?"

"I care. I don't want you hooked on 'em like I am."

"You're right. I'm just disenchanted with everything right now. Actually, I think I've been disenchanted since the day I was born."

"Aw, come *on*, Stepchild. Look at all I got goin' on, and you don't see me talking like that."

"You're right. I'm sorry. I shouldn't be complaining. You have it way worse than I do."

"That's not what I meant, though. I meant, everything's bad right now, but you just gotta keep on keepin' on and give yourself something to look forward to."

"Like what?"

"I don't know, like some of the bands you turned me on to—you can look forward to their new records coming out, can't you?"

"Most of those bands are broken up."

"Now you're just being contrary."

"No, you're right. I do have something to look forward to, I guess. It scares me, but I look forward to it."

"What?"

"I'm leaving Bashford."

"Whoopdy-doo."

"*Blue Gene.*"

"Where you going?"

"There's a college in San Francisco, a new one—"

"San Francisco?"

"The head of their political science department saw me on CNN, and he emailed me just to say he liked what we were doing, and we emailed back and forth yesterday, and he said that there was a teaching opening there if I wanted it, and I wouldn't even have to have my doctorate. He said I could just *say* I was pursuing my doctorate. I want you to know my plan was that if we won the election, I'd stay here, but if we lost, I'd go ahead and do it. So I'm going to go ahead and do it."

He barely opened his mouth as he said, "Good for you."

"Can't you at least *pretend* to be happy for me? I'm fed up with this town. Half the people here *hate* me with a passion now. I have to get out. I've been wanting out all my life."

"Life is what you make of it, no matter where you live."

"I know. But I can't just settle for being a substitute teacher the rest of my life. I want to be the *real* teacher. They should be substituting for me. You know, some of those students at the high school—they don't even know their middle names. I'm serious. I had to fill out a disciplinary form on one of them, and I had to ask his middle name, and he didn't even know. He finally said, just put Wayne or something. But listen. The best part is the *pay*. I'll finally get paid well. Full-time work. I have to take this job. I can help my mom. I'll finally get to stop worrying about money."

"Like I wasn't paying you good."

"You were, but you got closed. And that whole thing, it felt like a dream. It was hardly work."

"When you goin'?"

"School starts January 14, and I have to get moved. So, soon."

"Well, as long as it'll make you happy."

"It might not even do that, but at least it will be a change."

"A'ight, then. I better go in there and sit with John. Thanks for coming." He flicked his cigarette hard at the pavement.

"Blue Gene, wait. What are you going to do?"

"Don't know. Look for a job."

"You're not going to try to get the Commonwealth going again?"

"Don't know. Before you know it, I'll be startin' to run low on fundage."

"People still like you. I pissed a lot of them off with what I said during that interview, and with some of the other things I've said. But they'll still get behind you."

"Right now I really don't want to think about that. I'm just worried about my nephew."

"I'm sorry. I know. I know you need to get back in there. Let me hug you, at least."

He resisted at first and considered not hugging back at all, but when he felt her hair against his face, he gave her a bear hug that could've taken place in a wrestling ring, squeezing her as hard as he could until she let out a little yelp. He let go of her and she smiled, as always, with her mouth covered. He tried to return the favor but couldn't push a smile through the sadness he was feeling. This was the Bottoms, but without a four-wheeler.

"I still say you have the kindest eyes," she said. He turned away with a "pshaw."

"It's true!" she yelled.

"I wish you wouldn't say that crap. Nobody's ever said that kind of crap to me."

"What do they know?"

He couldn't look at her anymore. He turned to the automatic door. "So long, Jackie."

"So long you couldn't handle it."

"That's my line," he said, jerking around.

"I'm still going to use it, if that's okay."

"Whatever pumps your 'nads."

"I'm going to use that one, too. I'm sorry about your nephew. I'll call you tomorrow to see how your family's doing."

"A'ight."

"Bye," she said, and she started to walk away.

"Bye, pardner." He walked inside.

He hated that she had to give him that line about his eyes. Anyone could see his eyes were nothing but tired. He thought about repaying the compliment. He could go back outside and yell across the parking lot, "I think your teeth are pretty!" She would smile and run zigzags in between the cars, straight for him. He would start running toward her. They'd kiss from then on out.

But even in his fantasies, he looked funny running because of his limp. He was already in the elevator, wondering if he should take back his old job at Wal-Mart or try someplace new. It seemed like he had heard somewhere that you had to go to college for only two years to become a substitute teacher.

$ $ $

John insisted that his wife go home and sleep; he would sit with Arthur. He felt better now, less shaky. He told her he would not flake out again. His rest earlier in the day had renewed him. After a while, once he saw that no one was going to come into Arthur's room, he loosened the bedsheets and situated his son's legs in a more natural way.

He wished he could change Arthur into his play clothes. His Grandma Elizabeth made sure even his play clothes were nice: Ralph Lauren shirts and Armani dungarees. John laughed when he thought about how quickly Arthur always sullied his clothes with ketchup or grass stains.

John stared compulsively at the single tuft of sandy hair poking out from atop Arthur's bandages. He used the tuft of hair as a focal point as he prayed the hardest he had ever prayed in all his life, in hopes of brokering one final deal with God.

"My dear sweet Lord, please listen to me," he whispered, but with force. "If you've never listened to a word I've said, please let this be the time you start. Please hear me, because I've never meant words more than the ones I'm about to say. If you let my child John Arthur Mapother live, and if you let him heal and grow up and be healthy, I swear to you that I will never do another thing to harm another soul. I'll stop thinking of myself. I'll devote the entirety of the rest of my life to helping others. If you let my Arthur live, I'll take all the earthly riches I've accrued and I'll use them to help people. I will take for myself only what I need, and the rest I will give away in order to help you help people. My wallet will throb for all mankind. I'll open Blue Gene's building back up. I'll open a thousand buildings up for the people, if you let this one child live. One thousand mansions, I will buy. None for me—all for them, your meek.

"If that's not enough, then take me. Take my life instead of Arthur's. Send the pathogens into my body at this very second. Drop a hydrogen bomb on *my* head only and let me bear the brunt. Obliterate me.

"If we have misinterpreted your message, and if I am not destined to show the way for your planetary prince to redeem us, then allow me to offer you my insignificant soul for my son's. Plunder my destiny. Make me the mayor of some lowly necropolis in the darkest corner of your universe. Make me nothing at all. Just let him live.

"Dear Lord, forgive me. All my many trespasses. You humble me. I've let the old sins engulf me this year. I've been misguided. That awful dream. It kept coming for my mother, night after night after night. I still do not have lucidity. I still do not know what it means, nor can I hope to. But I'm seeing now that our little family is but one teardrop in the bucket of the cosmos. Even we can be swept up and swallowed by the behemoth of history. We were led to believe that I was a true man o' war, but is this not the folly of every epoch? A dream is but wish fulfillment, and we thought this was your divine wish, but as I look at this slain child, my eye sockets feel like nothing more than Judas holes.

"Arthur is too young for this. Is this the lesson you keep trying to teach us, that we are too young for everything? If that is the case, then age me, Lord. Make me timeless."

John stopped when he heard someone entering the room, but whoever it was immediately left. He quickly looked up to the ceiling and whispered, "I swear, dear Lord, if he lives, I will do nothing but provide for the rest of your children for the rest of my days." He then got up and looked down the hallway.

"Blue Gene." Blue Gene turned, his dark eyes and thick brown mustache drooping forlornly.

"Hey, John."

"Did you need something?"

"No. Just gonna see if *you* needed anything."

"No. You want to come sit with me?"

"I guess."

Blue Gene took a seat in the corner and looked everywhere except at Arthur and the tubes.

"How you doing?" asked John.

"Can't complain. How you?"

"Exhausted. Like I've run a marathon. Of course, I usually feel that way."

"Me too."

"You know, I wonder if you inherited that from me."

"Can you inherit tiredness?"

"I think you can inherit anything. I've worried that you would end up an alcoholic, since they say that's inherited. Are you?"

"What? An alcoholic?"

"Yes."

"No. If I am, I didn't know it."

"What about social anxiety disorder? Do you have that?"

"I don't think so. Is that what that was on Halloween? Social anxiety disorder?"

"Yes. I mean, that among other things."

"How long you had that?"

"It's hard to say. I remember the first time I noticed my nerves was at church when I was little. You know how you have to hold hands with whoever you're sitting next to for the Our Father?"

"Yeah."

"My mom was holding my hand on one side, and some guy I'd never met before was holding my other, and my hand that the man was holding started shaking. I was so embarrassed. From then on I got nervous going to church, and then in school it kept getting worse."

"Huh. No, I don't reckon I do have that problem, then."

"That's good. I have so many health problems. I *guess* you'd call them that. I've always worried that they'd be passed through my genes to you and Arthur." Blue Gene looked startled, his brow raising the bill of his cap. "I know. You probably find that hard to believe—that I've worried about you. But I have. You're my son just as much as Arthur is."

"No. It's not that. It's—what if he can *hear* you?"

"He can't, but if he could, I wouldn't care. I can't take the lying any-more."

"Yeah, right."

"What?"

"If Arthur wakes up, you're telling me that you'd tell him that me and him are brothers?"

"I mean, I wouldn't spring it on him. I guess I'd wait for the right time."

"Yeah, but when *is* the right time for something like that? When's the right time to say, 'Hey, you know that tattooed dude you thought was your uncle? He's actually my other son. Y'all are brothers.'"

"Do you not want me to tell him?"

"It don't matter. When it comes down to it, you wouldn't tell him."

"Why?"

"Sayin' and doin' aren't nowhere near being close to each other when it comes to this family."

"I know you have no reason to believe me, but I mean it when I say I intend to be as truthful as humanly possible from now on." John turned his chair away from Arthur to face Blue Gene. "I need to tell you some-thing right now, actually."

"Oh, jeez. What'd I do now?"

John cracked a little smile. "Nothing. You didn't do anything." John took a good look at Blue Gene. Like John's eyes, Blue Gene's eyes were dark and sapped.

"Well, what is it, then?" asked Blue Gene.

"It's my fault that Arthur got hit by a car."

"I know how you feel, but you can't blame yourself, man. You can't blame nobody but the guy who did it, and even then it was an accident."

"But I know who did it. He had just been at my house. I was the one who sent him out, and I was the one who told him to hurry, and I was the one who told him to make sure nobody saw him."

Blue Gene hunched over toward John and crossed his arms, as if to make himself less visible. "Are you serious?" he whispered.

"Yes. I don't know what to call it except temporary insanity. He wanted to shoot Jackie Ripplemeyer. And I encouraged it. I said go ahead. And look what happened. I'm evil. Blue Gene, I'm so evil that I'm surprised that gravity even applies to me anymore. I should float off to hell. I should be fried alive in the sun."

"Was it Balsam?"

John nodded.

"He was gonna kill her?"

"He acted like he would."

"Oh, man. John." Blue Gene readjusted his cap several times, to the point that it made John nervous.

"I don't know if I was half-crazy from what had just happened at the rally with the interview, but I was desperate, and I was at the end of my rope. But I should mention that not even five minutes after I let Balsam leave—not even three minutes, probably—I already regretted it. I lost my mind after what happened at that interview, but I got it back. I swear I regretted it, and I tried to stop him. I wouldn't have let him go through with it. But he hit Arthur, and he kept going. He's probably clear across the country by now. And now Arthur's going to die because of me. That's my punishment."

Blue Gene let out a few false starts and scratched his mustache before he finally said what he needed to say. "You know, still, it was a freak accident. But if you gotta blame yourself, you're gonna have to blame me, too, 'cause I was the one who put you in that situation at the Halloween rally in the first place. I was the one that had somebody running against you."

"We could go on all night over who started it. Like, I could say that Dad and I were the ones who shut down the Commonwealth Building and provoked you."

"I think everybody needs to cut everybody some slack."

"I do too, but I'm taking all the blame, and I told you because I had to confess to somebody. I wanted it to be you because the family had been keeping that secret about you and me all your life, and I wanted us to have a secret of our own that nobody else in the world would ever know about."

"Well, I 'preciate you telling me. I won't tell nobody."

"I know you won't. I had to tell somebody. It's between you and me and God."

"And Arthur, if he can hear you."

"If he lives through this, I'll spend the rest of my life making up for what I've done to him. I swear."

"What if he dies?"

"I'll kill myself."

"Come on now, John."

"All I've done all my life is cause people grief."

"Stop feeling sorry for yourself."

"You sound like Dad."

"Sorry."

"I just cause people to die. Like Arthur. And your mom."

Blue Gene stared at John speechlessly.

"I was the one that did it to her. I took her childhood. I might as well have put a bullet in her. But I'm glad you came out of it. Don't get me wrong about that."

John scooted his chair back next to Arthur. There was a moment of silence, which Blue Gene finally broke with a question. "What was she like?"

"Your mother?"

"Yeah. Can I ask that?"

"Sure. She was quiet. Shy, I guess you'd say. She was the quietest girl in the whole class. And she had this trick. It was so cool. She could always guess exactly what time it was without ever looking at a clock." Blue Gene smirked. "What else do you want to know about her?"

"Huh? Oh—that's enough for the time being. Did you hold her?"

"Did I *hold* her?"

"Yeah."

"Yes. I suppose I did hold her once or twice. I remember she wasn't much to hold. I mean, she was so skinny. Just skin and bones."

"So then why *her*?"

John started, then stopped. He felt a horrible shame welling up inside, and as he looked at Blue Gene he felt pressure building up behind his eyeballs. They felt like they were fattening. "This," he said quietly, "I don't want to risk him hearing." John stood and motioned for Blue Gene to follow him out of the room.

"That's cool. Forget it. Wanna watch some TV?"

"No." John, still wearing his gray cotton sleep shorts and a T-shirt, led Blue Gene out into the hallway. At ten after nine, the hallway was quiet except for the distant mumble of people on TV. A single nurse strolled from one room to the next.

Then John spoke, slowly and carefully, like a man learning a new language. "The reason I picked Tammy Munly of all people was because I looked at every girl in the class, and she was the one I thought mattered the least."

Upon hearing himself say it, a severe emotion disgorged itself from John's insides. Blue Gene looked at the white tiles below. He seemed afraid, the dark area around his eyes looking cavernous. As John's fat-feeling eyeballs wettened, the image of Blue Gene became a liquid haze. John held the tears in, and through the haze he saw what he thought to be Blue Gene taking off his cap. After John blinked a few times, making a pair of tears roll down his unshaven cheeks, he saw that he was correct. Blue Gene held his cap and ran his fingers through his hair.

"Cap makes my head hot sometimes," he said grumpily.

"Jackie said you helped her write that speech."

"Yeah."

"It was a good speech."

"Thank ya."

"You all talked about guardian angels. Mom said once that Tammy was yours. She said she watched over you and saved you from your wreck." Blue Gene nodded with pursed lips and put his cap back on. John became aware that his jaw was trembling. "I hope Arthur has someone watching over him."

"Sure he does. Dad said that specialist he flew in was the best in the country. Come on, man. We'll get through this just like we get through everything."

John nodded. His chin quivered as he said, "Arthur never hurt anyone. He was so *good*. Even animals knew it. Anytime he was around animals, they took to him." His words shook as he kept himself from crying. "If he lives, I'll get him a dog. He's wanted one so badly. Hey—maybe I should say that in front of him, just in case he can hear us." John started back inside the room.

"Hold on," said Blue Gene. "Maybe we should sit out in the waiting room awhile. Take a little break."

"But somebody needs to be with him."

"Just for a little bit. Come on." On the way to the waiting area, Blue Gene stopped at the nurses' station.

"May I help you?" a plump, big-haired, middle-aged nurse asked.

"If we sit out in the waiting room for a while, will y'all keep an eye on Arthur Mapother for us?"

"Of course, sugar. We got him monitored at all times. Don't y'all worry."

"Thank ya."

"Mr. Mapother," she said, looking at John. "I wanted to tell you I voted for you."

"Thank you," said John.

"No offense to you," she said to Blue Gene.

"That's a'ight."

"I've been following you alls's story in the paper. I hope your son will be okay."

"Thank you," said John. "That's sweet of you to say."

John and Blue Gene sat in the empty waiting room.

"You need anything?" asked Blue Gene. "Coffee or food or anything?"

"No thank you. Here you are, taking care of *me*. That's not how it's supposed to work."

"Shh," said Blue Gene.

As they sat in silence, John decided to make the most of this time by continuing his prayer mentally, but he was having trouble concentrating, and eventually he resorted to simply shouting the same thoughts over and over to heaven: "Lord, let him come back to us!" Before he could stop himself, he let out a ghastly wail and shouted aloud, "Lord, let him come back to us! I'll do everything I said. Oh, I just want him *back*!"

"Shut up, John."

And John would've been mad that he was being told to shut up, except that he felt his hand being grabbed. Blue Gene gripped his hand firmly, looking the opposite direction as if something big was going on down the hallway. John stopped crying and wiped the tears with one hand as his other hand, the one being held, started to sweat and shake. Blue Gene must have felt it shaking, because he squeezed it even harder, so hard that the hand couldn't tremble even if John wanted it to, until finally John had to say something.

"That kind of hurts." Blue Gene let go and wiped his palm on his sweatpants. "No—you didn't have to stop. I didn't mean—"

"Forget it."

John took Blue Gene's hand back anyway and held it for one long minute, until they both agreed it was making them too warm.

They sat in silence until a little after ten, when they heard someone yelling, "Mr. Mapother! Mr. Mapother!"

They both sprang up and headed toward the voice. It was the big nurse from earlier. She met them halfway down the hallway. Her face had turned pink.

"What is it?" asked John.

"It's your son! I've never seen anything like it. He's awake and talk-in'! It's a miracle!"

John gasped. He and Blue Gene rushed toward Arthur's room.

"Mr. Mapother! Wait!"

"What?" asked John and Blue Gene simultaneously.

She ran over to them and said quietly, hurriedly, "Before you go in there, you should know he's kind of talking out of his head. I think he's delirious."

"That's okay," said John, smiling. "That's okay."

"He keeps saying he wants to see his dad and his brand-new brother."

John and Blue Gene looked at one another. A boyish, downturned grin swept beneath Blue Gene's mustache.

"Keeps hollerin' for his daddy and his brother," the nurse continued, "but ain't he an only child?"

"No. Blue Gene here is actually his brother."

"He *is*?"

"*Yes!*"

"Oh. Well, then the both of y'all better get on in there," said the nurse. "He's a-waitin'."

$$\$ \, \$ \, \$$$

Fireworks or gunshots?

Whatever the noise was, Elizabeth's subconscious self followed it as she climbed the craggy insides of a wormhole out through her deepest orifice and into her childhood bedroom, where an angel sat on her windowsill.

"Is that fireworks or gunshots?" she asked the angel, a sexless shapeshifter that took on the appearance of everything from eggnog to Paul McCartney to a beach. The angel told her with its mind that she needed to go outside, and, as if on cue, all of outside bowed down before her.

The *pops* turned into *bangs*, and loud as they were, they were overpowered by a monstrous industrial rumble. An ominous convoy of incandescent tanks rolled down Main Street, creeping forth in a crooked line that began beyond the horizon. The cloudless sky took on an otherworldly mauve glow, and there was a dark red clot where the sun should have been. Lightning struck but stayed so that the heavens looked like they had permanently exposed their white-hot nerves.

Elizabeth, now a cowering little girl, turned to ask the angel what was happening, but the angel was gone. Then she realized she was standing on top of her house, which towered over the earth and hurled its shadow across the rest of the formerly quaint Main Street, whose houses looked like shoeboxes and whose gutters ran thick with diarrhea.

All cars stalled. They must have been stalled for years, because they were entirely shrouded in rust, rusted onto the concrete so that they had no choice but to let themselves be slowly crushed by the sluggish tanks.

Then all the tanks stopped at the precise same second, allowing for an unearthly silence. From the turrets poured an unlimited amount of soldiers, all of whom had the size, shape, and earth-toned fatigues associated with humans but otherwise were not. They moved with mechanical spasms and their faces were nebulous blurs of skin and night. Eerily quiet and wraithlike, thousands of them dispersed with rifles in hand across charred lawns, all of them knowing exactly where to run with not a whisper of communication.

All the ant-size people came out of their shoeboxes and onto their lawns. When she saw that they were all naked, Elizabeth looked at herself and saw she wore the sparkling evening gown of an immortal starlet. All the nude people turned to her and hissed, which scared her, until she realized this was their way of asking for help, and the hisses were actually coming from under the ground, which had started to develop yawning chasms that would never be sutured, over which syphilitic harlots were caught doing the splits. The hisses became louder and louder, until finally an explosion blew them away and released so much energy that the river ran backward.

In a state of terror, Elizabeth floated away from the scene and into some flawless white space that pulsated with the secretive vibe of someone's inner sanctum. She saw someone sitting on a king-size bed, and at first felt she was in the presence of her father.

The man turned out to be a baby. The baby was so gigantic that his crown was New York City and his rectum was Los Angeles. He had long hair made of gold and wore a diaper of silver and beams of light emitted from all twelve openings of his body. Despite being somehow ancient and deteriorated, all his purple veins ing. He looked down languidly and smiled at Elizabeth

"Hey, Mom," he said.

"John, is that you? What's wrong with you?!"

"Nothing is wrong at all. I caught the victory disease."

"We've got to get out of here!"

"Why?"

"We're at war. We're under attack. They're swarming us."

"Mother, we're not under attack," said the baby, as if Elizabe a moron. "Those soldiers are on *our* side."

"But they're aliens."

He coughed up a cute child laugh.

"They're angels. And they're following my orders."

"But you're just a baby."

At this, he banged his child-fist against the great white bed, and somewhere another explosion went off, powerful enough to jolt Elizabeth back into her bedroom. She was back inside her adult self in 1973, with a snoring Henry lying by her side, but the angel still sat on her windowsill, faintly glowing and now in the shape of a completely hairless young man with soft features.

"I don't understand," she said. "I'm scared."

"Don't be scared. Those soldiers down there are here to help you."

"But if they are here to help me, why does it look like hell on Earth outside?"

"It has to take on that appearance to attract the attention of the one who will save you."

"Who will save us?"

"The Monkey Who Mends Destinies. Your son will orchestrate the deal that brings Him back."

"But those people said they needed my help."

"They're fools. They're wasting, but they will be saved. Their mechanisms will all be shut off automatically. They will suffer no pain, no sorrow, no suffering. They will be given sudden and absolute peace."

"What does my son have to do with this?"

"He will represent his superiors for their highest agenda."

"What's their highest agenda?"

"To resurrect God."

Upon hearing these words, Elizabeth felt the dawning of a warm, soothing buzz in the center of her brain, similar to how she had felt in the past when she had drunk a martini on an empty stomach.

"God isn't dead," she said, as the buzz slowly rotated and snowballed.

"Of course He is. Of a broken heart. But we've found the science to resurrect Him. Our Father who had to leave us."

Elizabeth felt the buzz blossom into full-blown bliss. She had become high from within, no artificial chemicals present, her brain producing natural euphoria of its own accord, and as the explosions resumed outside, she was absolutely certain that everyone everywhere was on the verge of becoming perfect.

With the explosions came radiant lights that must have looked like mayday flares to alien eyes.

THE END

ACKNOWLEDGMENTS

I want to thank these people:

My mother, Nancy Goebel, my sister, CeCe, and her husband, Michael Bruner, and my heart, my bride, Micah. While I'd like to think I write for everybody, it is primarily for these four people.

Everyone at MacAdam/Cage, especially David Poindexter, Kate Nitze, and (alphabetically) Dave Adams, Scott Allen, Julie Burton, Chandler Crawford, Melanie Mitchell, Megan Murphy, Dorothy Carico Smith, Annie Tucker, and Pat Walsh.

Everyone I met at Spalding University, especially Kirby Gann, Roy Hoffman, Silas House, Robin Lippincott, and Mary Yukari Waters.

The English department of Brescia University: Craig Barrette, David Bartholomy, Ellen Dugan-Barrette, and Vicki Combs.

Everyone at Diogenes Verlag, especially Daniel Keel, Anna von Planta, and Ruth Geiger.

Susie Thurman, Sharon Burton, John Dillingham, Jason Sheeley, Helen Clayton, Elena Lappin, Audrey Walker, Scott Taylor, and Randy West.

All the writers and musicians who gave me the light by which I could see my way through this awful manuscript.

And if everyone is indeed assigned one guardian angel, I want to thank mine:

Adam Goebel, my father.